The Falcon Flies Alone

A FIVE DIRECTIONS PRESS BOOK

The Falcon Flies Alone

A NOVEL

Gabrielle Mathieu

FALCON TRILOGY 1

This is a work of fiction. All names, characters, places, and incidents are products of the author's imagination or are used fictitiously. Any resemblance to current situations or to living persons is purely coincidental.

ISBN-13 978-3952468005
ISBN-10 3952468002

Published in the United States of America.

© 2016 Gabrielle Mathieu. All rights reserved.
Except as permitted by the US Copyright Act of 1976, no part of this publication may be reproduced, transmitted, or distributed in any form or by any means, or stored in a database or retrieval system, without the prior written permission of the author.

A Five Directions Press book

Images: falcon contemplating sunset © outsiderzone/iStock; woman © Sergey Nazarov/iStock; Swiss village and Alps via Pixabay (no attribution required); lone falcon on a branch © Denis Krivoy/Shutterstock

Book and cover design by Five Directions Press

Five Directions Press logo designed by Colleen Kelley

FIVE DIRECTIONS PRESS

We all have a beast locked within us,
But in Peppa's case it's more than a figure of speech.

Contents

Switzerland, 1957

1. A Precarious Situation 1
2. The Day Before 12
3. Full Moon, Blood Moon 30
4. My Alias 41
5. The Survivors 52
6. One-Way Ticket 65
7. Transatlantic Communication 73
8. The Hierophant 85
9. Friendship 90
10. God of War and Vengeance 95
11. Breakdown 106
12. Spoken For 118
13. Insinuations of Insanity 128
14. Scientific Analysis 137
15. His Secret 150
16. The Peregrine 163
17. Reporting to the Devil 169
18. Personal Correspondence 179
19. The Kommissar 186
20. Greenhouse Escapades 194
21. Break-In 206

22. TEN RATS 211
23. FAREWELL 221

MUNICH, 1957

24. MISDIRECTION 229
25. LUDWIG...239
26. TAMARA 256
27. BESPOKE 269
28. THE LAND OF AVES................................... 279
29. ANIMAL TOTEM 285
30. HAPPY BIRTHDAY 296
31. THE SPARROW FALTERS...............................302
32. THE TRUTH SHALL SET YOU FREE 313
33. THE LAST SUPPER.....................................324
34. THE FALCON AND THE WOLF 333
35. REAP WHAT YOU SOW 341

BASEL, 1958

36. GIRLS ON THE WARD................................. 347
37. THE CAGED BIRD 360
38. BRACHIAL INNERVATION 370
39. BARGAINS..378
40. AN UNEXPECTED GUEST 385
41. GENTLEMAN CALLER..................................392
42. A LIST OF NAMES.....................................397
43. BLOOD SACRIFICE.....................................403
44. VIOLET STRUB 408
AUTHOR'S NOTE ON PSYCHEDELICS 420
ACKNOWLEDGMENTS 422
ABOUT THE AUTHOR......................................424

Switzerland, 1957

1. A Precarious Situation

I JERKED AWAKE, COLD AND HURTING. THE FLOOR WAS SO HARD. *And slanted?*

All around me, treetops waved in the wind.

This was no floor. This was a roof.

The roof of a three-story house.

Panic hit me, and vertigo flared. I squeezed my eyes shut. My head pounded.

Air riffled across my bare skin, raising goose bumps.

Bare skin?

My eyes popped open and my breath caught.

Where were my clothes? I was stark naked.

My hands scrambled to cover the essentials. What if someone saw me like this? Totally naked.

And now sliding toward the ledge.

I scrabbled frantically for a hold, grabbing the first thing I could: a small chimney.

Anchored. For now.

I had a more pressing problem than being nude. How would I get down?

I scanned the roof, hoping to find something within reach. A rope. A whistle. My clothes. Anything. The green tiles glistened like dragon scales. The morning sun was still low in the sky, a sky that seemed so near and blue, oppressively close. When I dared to look down, I could make out the rust spores of fern fronds that grew under the pines at the corner of the house.

I blinked, surprised at my acuity.

The glimpse of the garden at least confirmed my location. It was the De Penas' grand house at the edge of the village—I'd just arrived there yesterday. The air had a queer greenish tinge, though, and little particles glinted, moving.

Clinging to the cold chimney bricks, I closed my eyes to think better. Had I been up here all night?? Panicked questions screamed through my mind, and I panted from pain as the pounding in my temples intensified.

So high up. If I fell...

I was too young to die. I'd only been with a fellow once, and he'd run off on us the next day. I wasn't even twenty.

How did I get on a roof?

And how would I get down?

I wished Da was here to help me. He'd have the answers.

No. Da will never help you again. He is not an angel in heaven, looking down on you. He's worm food.

My eyes got wet. I swallowed my sadness. He might be dead, but he didn't raise me to be a sobbing baby.

My head pounded so much I wondered if I'd had a subarachnoid hemorrhage. I might die all alone in this tiny village in the middle of the Alps, and my dog would starve in the shed where I'd locked her up. I should have told someone where I was.

Like who?

My breath ripped through me, ragged gasps. All I could picture was poor Simone, a heap of crumpled dirty-white fur in the cold, dark shed.

I'd left her alone.

Calm down, Peppa! Nothing makes sense. Think this through. I was Ivy League material, right? I'd kept the acceptance letter from Radcliffe College with my small store of keepsakes.

I should be able to figure this out.

First, assess.

I was on the roof of my new employer's manor. I turned my head, wincing, searching for the small window of my dormer room. It was hidden below the sharply pitched eaves to my left.

There was just no way I could have gotten from that window to here.

An agonizing flash went off behind my eyes, as a fragment of memory jolted me. I was a great bird, flying...

I pressed my lips together to suppress a wail.

I had a horrible, sick feeling. Images skittered. Distant farms like matchboxes, scattered lights glimmering far below me.

I've gone mad. Barking mad.

It must be the pain that's confusing me.

Just a neurological process.

Da would gasp that after he screamed from agony. "Pain is just a neurological process."

Pain. Fear. They have explanations. My adrenals pumped out epinephrine and norepinephrine in waves. But explaining my fear didn't help enough.

I shut my eyes again. I needed to get my heart rate down. Breathe. In. Breathe out. There. I felt better with my lids jammed closed, my nakedness hidden.

But my peripheral circulation was shutting down. I hung from my right arm like a carcass from a meat hook. I needed to move while I still could.

My window was the only one on this side of the roof, but to reach it, I would have to dangle from the jutting eaves by my fingertips and kick the window open. Not an option for reentry. I had to find another way.

I stayed glued tight, afraid to change position.

Poor Simone. She needs you. My dog would be pacing and shivering in the dark shed, tongue hanging out from thirst.

I forced my eyes open. The sun hoisted itself up, rays spilling over the rugged mountains. My gaze was drawn toward the imposing peak of Säntis, still bathed in shadows. Where I had...

No. That's insane.

I studied my position. My right arm was locked onto the smaller chimney, probably the one for the master bedroom. Another wave of vertigo washed over me, and pain bored into my temples. I tried to picture Simone's soft fur, comforting like a down pillow. Disturbing images intruded: blood, feathers, and broken glass. Hoarse screaming.

What happened last night?

I looked down again. Only a few meters beneath my feet, a horizontal snow-guard railing marched across the roof.

The railing would break when I crashed into it, and I'd plummet down three stories.

~

I pushed my belly and thighs flat against the tiles, and turned my head to one side so my shoulders were even, pressed against the roof. Slowly, very slowly, I let go of the chimney. I slipped a bit, then used my splayed toes to brake. The railing was less than a meter away now.

I looked down again from my new vantage point. The green shimmer still danced in the air, now very faint. I could see the empty milk bottles set out by the driveway. The milkman would be coming soon.

I could rest against the railing until he drove up, then cry out for help.

A ragged edge of black fabric fluttering in the breeze caught my eye.

An umbrella leaned against the door, forgotten.

An image seared through me like fire. I knuckled a fist in my eyes, keening.

The woman's eyes were sane and blue. She was looking at me. Then something changed in her wrinkled face. She bowed her head, and her arm moved up. She fell.

She'd thrust the spiked metal top of her umbrella into her eye socket. Not even a scream to warn me.

I allowed one whimper out before I shut the door on the image. I reminded myself of who I was. A chemist. A rational young woman of good standing.

Now. To move down the remaining meter to the snow guard.

I forced my body to obey: one foot and then the other, like toddler steps, quivering, testing out, the limbo loose without tension, the belly pressed flat against my new best friend, the roof.

I reached the railing and hunched behind it, shivering, trying to distribute my weight. I looked left. I looked right. I looked everywhere except at my naked body, my meager breasts, my bony legs.

I didn't want to wait for the milkman exposed like a scrawny plucked chicken.

But there was no other way down.

Which meant no way up. How the hell did I get up here?

Didn't matter. I looked down again. No trees close enough to reach. Only beds of dahlias and day lilies.

Was there a chance the De Penas hadn't left for Paris yet? They'd said they were leaving at the crack of dawn, but perhaps they'd overslept. Even if I didn't like Mrs. De Pena, it would be less embarrassing than calling out to a strange man.

The place was quiet as a graveyard. I could hear the rattle of my teeth.

Simone. Why couldn't I hear her barking to be let out? She'd been shut up in the shed since yesterday. I swallowed. The family pet was all that was left of my family.

Panic gnawed at me again. I called out a few times, hating the high reedy tone in my voice. I craned my neck to look for Dr. Unruh's shiny black car, in the vain hope he hadn't left as well. Though the unpredictable anthropology professor frightened me, he might have some answers. But it looked like the mysterious houseguest from Munich had departed along with his hosts.

The floppy dahlias laughed at me, sunny upturned faces. Soft, but not soft enough. Not from three stories up. I should worm my way around the periphery of the roof, look for a way down.

And if I were brave and strong, like John Wayne or Humphrey Bogart, I would. But my arms and legs shook hard now, my vision blurred, and I could have killed for a glass of water.

Although that was an unfortunate figure of speech, considering my recent hallucination. In which I had not only witnessed violence but committed it.

The stress of the past year had been too much for me. I *was* losing my mind.

Soon I heard the roar of the milkman's jeep, then the sudden silence as he turned off the engine.

I cringed. What if he saw I was naked? He might even laugh at me. Clothed, I had dignity and a certain poise. Naked, I was just a homeless girl. My face got hot.

If I let him leave, I'd never get down. I forced myself to shout out to him.

"Please. Help me," I pleaded until he rounded the corner of the house and came into view.

I could make out his face now, mild puzzlement changing to alarm. Since I was new to the village, I hadn't met him. I didn't know what kind of a man he might be.

I tried to reassure myself. He was far below. There was a chance he might not be able to tell I was naked.

He stepped back, craned his head up, and got a good look. "My God."

"Get me off the roof!"

"Oh my. We need a special ladder. We'll have to get the carpenter."

No fire department. I reminded myself the hamlet of Gonten was a long way from Boston. Telephones weren't even standard household equipment. There hadn't been one in the house.

"Hurry." Spots floated in front of my eyes.

He looked up at me again, longer now, and then his gaze bolted away. "You just hold on, Miss."

The engine fired up, and the jeep jolted down the drive.

I slumped down to wait, drawing long, shuddering breaths, my heart jittery-dancing like my schoolmates at the sock hop, bouncing to "Rock Around the Clock." Not that I'd ever been invited to one. But I'd watched through the gym window.

Gravel crunching under tires announced a new arrival. I twisted my head around, but the vehicle was out of my line of sight. I was weak and dizzy; I'd wait and lie still.

When I heard a car door slam, I called out. "Up here."

An authoritative voice answered. "Yes, hold tight, we're setting up the ladder."

I scrambled over the snow guard to the gutter, precariously close to the edge. I hunched over, trying to make as little of myself visible as possible.

Scraping sounds, two men at least, and then a thud as the ladder swung up and hit the roof near me. I startled and screamed, almost losing my balance.

The second man hollered. "Just a little to your left now. You can move over maybe one or two steps. Your foot should hit it soon."

I gulped. "I can't come down ... like this."

The strong first voice again. "Mr. Manser here, from Gonten. I can take over on the ladder. Mr. Lutz can climb up to help you."

"No, absolutely not," I squeaked.

"You'll be safe, Miss. He's our carpenter."

"I need Mr. Lutz's coat if I'm to come down." Shame made my voice too soft, and I had to repeat myself.

I heard Lutz say, "The milkman mentioned she might be…"

The word trembled in the air, unspoken.

Manser took charge. "Give me your coat, Mr. Lutz." I took a chance, and peered over the edge. Lutz stood bracing the ladder, feet planted wide, now in his neatly ironed blue shirt. Manser tucked the coat under his arm and nimbly began climbing.

As he drew closer, I pleaded, "Don't look. Just hand it up."

"Please. I am a decent Christian man." He sounded incensed. His arm snaked up, proffering the coat. I uncovered myself long enough to grab it.

"Thank you. You can go down. I'll follow once you're on the ground," I sniffled, totally humiliated. Snot ran out of my nose with the effort of swallowing my tears. I shrugged the coat on, trembling from the effort of keeping my balance. It smelled of hair pomade and tobacco.

"I'm back down now. We'll turn away while you descend, so as not to offend your modesty," Manser called out.

It took a few moments before I felt brave enough to try the ladder. My foot swung out over the air. There was no sound from below. They couldn't see me struggling, gritting my teeth, forcing myself to continue.

My flailing foot found the first rung, and I pushed it down hard before I dared to try the other. Then both were balanced, but I was bent over, my torso still on the roof, my rump in the air.

I pushed off gently, holding my breath, and grabbed for the sides of the ladder. After I'd wobbled down a couple of rungs, I gripped the ladder tight, then looked down to make sure they weren't peeking up the borrowed coat.

The big one called Lutz still had his back turned, hands wedged in his pockets.

The other one had come close to the ladder again, hands ready should my weight destabilize it. He studied the ground, eyes averted. The tiny white lettering on the tag in the shade of his collar said "Hans Manser."

How could I read that from up here?

Manser's pants and shirt were smudged with charcoal and dirt. I spotted several flecks of blood on his trousers. And the bulge of a pistol under his unbuttoned jacket.

The village policeman. *He's been there. He saw.*

I froze as a shock of memory hit me: The gaping eye socket of the old woman. Screams and flames from a kitchen. Glints of broken glass. A man fallen at my feet.

It was real.

I was done for. Buggered. Chingado.

I started back down, dread making me clumsier.

Finally, my feet hit the ground, and I retied the belt tight around the coat. I took a couple of breaths. My vision was normal now.

"May I look up?" Manser asked.

"Yes. I'm covered."

The policeman lifted his head. His tie flopped like the tongue of a thirsty dog. He was a nice-looking man, probably a devoted wife and daughters with tidy braids at home. Right now he looked exhausted, though, and there were dark rings under his eyes. He must have been up for most of the night. Probably got called when the fire started, and found more than he bargained for.

His voice was tight. "What are you doing here, Miss? This house belongs to the De Penas."

I started to reach out and shake hands but stopped, uncertain. Did Swiss women shake hands? I'd been in Massachusetts too long.

I inclined my head instead, like my idol, Grace Kelly. "I'm their new caretaker, Patrizia Waldvogel. Just arrived yesterday."

"You look like you need to sit down." There were no chairs outside; the De Penas weren't the garden party type. He gestured. "The car's just around the corner. Let's go."

I've got to get away from him. Then find a way to get Simone out of the shed.

"Could I get some clothes and a hot drink from inside?"

Manser pulled back, a hint of amusement showing in his shrewd face. "I could do with a cup of coffee myself. Been up most of the night. I saw the De Penas at the train station this morning. You'll have to let us in."

I cursed under my breath, remembering. The keys were with my purse and my clothes.

If my memory served me correctly, those were still at the inn. I'd been at the local farm inn, a Bäsebeiz, last night when all hell broke loose.

Mr. Lutz joined us, squirming, looking at anything but my bare stick legs marooned in his enormous coat. Manser's eyes bored into me, waiting.

"I misplaced the key," I admitted.

"Accompany me to the car. I want to show you something."

I followed them, and Manser opened the door, reached into the back seat, and took out my scuffed brown handbag. "Perhaps this is yours? There are keys in here."

I was too eager. I stepped toward him, smiling fixedly. "That would be wonderful. I can't believe I lost my purse."

His eyes never left my face. "I found something interesting in there." He took out my Swiss passport, the only identification I had, and flipped it open. There was my photo, black and white, but an unmistakable likeness all the same: big eyes, long nose, wavy short hair. My real name was typed next to it: Peppa Mueller.

"How do you explain this, Miss *Waldvogel*?"

Now I was screwed for sure.

2. The Day Before

I'D BEEN SECRETLY LIVING IN THE LIBRARY OF THE HISTORIC town abbey. I stayed there eight long days, wandering the cobblestone streets while the visitors toured, then sneaking in after five, Simone snuggled close to me for warmth as I dozed on my winter coat.

In two weeks, when I turned twenty, I'd become almost as rich as a Rockefeller. Right now, because of Swiss inheritance laws, I was a runaway with less than fifty francs, and I owned a German Shepherd. She ate six bratwursts a day from the butcher's luncheon cart. Her company didn't come cheap.

Poor women in the nearby Alps made money by boiling and sweetening pinesap, or embroidering lace during the long winter months. I'd helped Da synthesize his new drug, Paxarbital, translated Ovid, and read Marvel comics in my spare time. Not skills in high demand here.

In summer, I briefly found work as a governess. The mother, impressed I could read Latin, didn't bother to ask me for identification papers. Then came the evening six-year old Theresa pushed away her plate of liver. Her mother suggested I read her *Strubelpeter*, the children's book with its dreadful tales about the consequences of disobedience. When I read little Theresa the story about the boy refusing to eat his soup, shriveling up, and being blown away, her eyes filled with tears.

I winked at her, the way I'd seen Bette Davis do in American movies. "That can't really happen. Even if you don't eat supper."

I couldn't stop there, though. "What kind of normal person wants to eat liver anyway? It stores toxins. Besides, it's slithery and purplish. What's really good is a hamburger with fries and a milkshake, the way they serve them at a drive-through."

When the mother heard what I'd said she fired me on the spot. She didn't even bother to find out what a hamburger was.

So what did that leave? Prostitution was out. I'd never even been on a real date. My night with Da's graduate student, Patrick, didn't count. He'd inexplicably vanished from Boston shortly before my father's illness forced us to return to Switzerland.

Da wanted to die back home. But surely he hadn't intended for me to be at the mercy of my aunt, without access to our fortune.

And yet I was.

So when I heard about the De Penas through my friend Lupe, the abbey's cleaning woman, I jumped at the chance to visit them and ask for a job. Word had spread among the local Spaniards that the wealthy couple needed a caretaker who spoke English or Spanish. People didn't seem to like them, but at the time, I figured it was just rural prejudice.

That was before I met the De Penas myself.

The village of Gonten, where the De Penas lived, lay up in the Alps, east of town. It was a sunny Sunday morning when I set off; the train was filled with families carrying rucksacks and wearing walking boots, the girls dressed in modest skirts, the boys in knickers. I sat across from an elderly woman who smiled at Simone and asked how old she was.

I'd had her eight years.

My father bought Simone when we arrived at Harvard, as a present to cheer me up. A German Shepherd for our American arrival. Things were always a bit confused except when they had to do with chemistry. But Da was a genius. It was only to be expected.

When we pulled into the station at Gonten, the old woman got off as well. I followed her up the short steps to the main street. The entire town lined the sides for two blocks before giving way to farmland. There was a pharmacy, two restaurants, The Bear and The Lion, the church of St. Verena, then grass and cows.

The old woman turned to me as I stood there, clutching Simone's leash. "Be welcome," she said, in the peculiar dialect of the region. "Are you looking for something?"

"There's a couple called the De Penas who live around here. They wanted a caretaker."

Her hand brushed her crucifix, before she answered. "Just follow the street to the right. As you leave the village you'll see a larger house on the ridge on the left. It's newly painted ... purple." Her mouth puckered.

The buildings of the village themselves were a pleasing palette of light lemon yellow, warm peach, cream, and olive. I started to see why the De Penas might be unwelcome.

"Thank you very much. I'm Miss Waldvogel." I liked my alias. It meant *wood bird*.

"Mrs. Wäspi." She hesitated, thinking over her words. "You might want some fresh air tonight after your first day of work. I have a suggestion. My son, Hans, asked the Eugster sisters to do him a favor and open the Bäsebeiz tonight so we could eat there."

I gave her a quizzical look. Had she just mentioned a broom bar?

"Round here the broom outside the farm door means you can get a simple meal and a drink. That's a Bäsebeiz. Ours is at the Eugster's farm, up on the ridge," she explained. "Young Stefan Sepp said he'd come too. He'd like a newcomer to talk to."

I thanked her and said I'd have to think about it, then went on my way. It was a warm day, and sweat trickled down the bodice of my dress. I let Simone off her leash and lugged my suitcase along, wishing I could have worn pants. But this was a country village in Switzerland, not Harvard University in Cambridge. My frock was creased and bunched by the time I arrived at the De Penas house. There was no mistaking its vile violet color. I knocked on the front door, tentatively at first. Then louder.

I scuffed the dirt and swore under my breath. No one came.

I knocked as hard as I could.

The man who eventually answered was slender and fashionably turned out in his vest, suit jacket, and tie. He was only a little taller than me but had an imposing presence that made me step back. A neatly trimmed beard and black hair set off fine regular features.

Altogether a very attractive, distinguished-looking man.

I tried English, since they'd requested an English speaker. "Good day. I'm Miss Waldvogel."

He answered in German. "Unruh. Dr. Ludwig Unruh. From Munich."

I waited to see if he'd click his heels. Nope. He was über-Teutonic, though. He sported an old-fashioned tidy mustache with waxed ends, though he couldn't have been more than thirty. His eyes were dark and luminous, his cheekbones high, and his cheeks hollowed. I had a feeling I could look forever into those eyes, and yet he unaccountably repulsed me at the same time. He was too neat, as if he were not a man at all, but someone's idea of what a man should look like. He was handsome, though, so I stood there like a dolt.

I answered him in his own language, which thanks to my former tutor, Miss Gladys, I still spoke fluently. "I was given to understand you were seeking a caretaker. One who spoke English or Spanish." Although I was disappointed, thinking there had been some misunderstanding, and they'd likely hired someone already, I was also relieved. Something wasn't quite right here.

Simone thought so too. She whined, the fur bristling on her back.

"Your name is Miss Waldvogel?" he asked, studying me intently.

"Yes," I stammered. I hoped he wouldn't ask for identification.

"Waldvogel. Hmm. What's your first name?"

I needed to steer the conversation back to the job. I shifted, uneasy. Simone wasn't giving me any backup. She'd retreated three steps and lain down, her ears flicking, her haunches bristling. "Are you the head of the household?"

"Hardly. I could be the butler."

I stared at him. His shoes were immaculate, from the premier Swiss shoemaker Bally, his suit jacket an exquisite light summer wool blend.

He must take me for a country bumpkin. "My father was a university professor, so I do know what butlers look like. You're not the butler," I said, my voice tight.

He grinned, all at once fully focused on me. "You're correct. I'm not the butler. Think of me as the wolf at your door."

What the hell. Were we playing Little Red Riding Hood now? A frisson moved down my spine. Despite his urbane air, there was something feral about him.

A wealthy, patrician man who wanted to play games. And my dog was frightened of him. I gave him my back, turning to pick up my suitcase. I'd get by for two more weeks.

"Just a moment. Where are you going?" His tone of voice was concerned now, almost warm. "My sense of humor is not universal. I apologize."

I hovered, indecisive. Was he prepared to behave properly now that he knew I came from a good background?

"Please. I'll get Silvia for you at once. She's prepared to pay you well."

Money. Food for me and Simone, and a train ticket back to Basel to claim my inheritance.

"Silvia? That would be Mrs. De Pena then?" I asked resolutely. I'd gotten over my scare. Christopher Lee paled in comparison to Unruh's initial sinister manner, but I did not believe in ghosts, the devil—or God.

"Yes. She's Mrs. De Pena. You'll wait?"

I forced myself to meet his eyes again. He was definitely a higher calculus equation. Those get strange. He was like a space in between things. I could feel spit starting in my mouth, as if I'd gotten a whiff of some aldehyde, acrid and odd.

"I'll be right here," I said.

⁓

He returned in a few minutes. A woman with a rambunctious mass of jet-black curls elbowed him aside. "Are you torturing someone again, darling?" she asked in heavily accented English.

I got a closer look at her. She made a dissolute and slatternly impression. She was wearing a crimson silk wrap that did little to cover her negligee. I could smell wine on her breath. It made me want to gag.

I took a step back and Simone, obviously relieved, got up and shook herself.

Dr. Unruh retrieved me by the elbow and pulled me inside, leaving Simone pacing a few steps from the open door. It was plain she was afraid but would not leave me.

He spoke English now, with a German accent. "Here's your English speaker, Silvia. Just in time."

"Just in time?"

"We are going to Paris tomorrow," she explained. "I'm very bored here."

"You're very bored everywhere," he pointed out.

She twirled some of her hair around her fingers. "*Si, mi amor, pero nunca contigo.*"

The skin behind my ears got hot. She never got bored with Unruh? She hadn't asked if I spoke Spanish, and she probably didn't care, but I felt sorry for her husband.

"Look, she understood. She speaks Spanish too," Unruh pointed out.

"How wonderful," Silvia said, without enthusiasm.

"You'll want to pay her even more then." He gave her a significant look.

"Of course." She turned to me, a small smile playing about her lips. "Room and board for you and that horrible animal, one afternoon off a week, and three hundred francs a month. We'll be back in a week or two, after I finish up business in Paris."

I glanced at Simone's wise, patient eyes. Horrible animal indeed. In two weeks, when I turned twenty, we'd be gone. In the meantime, we'd have a place to sleep.

"So do you want to stay?" she asked.

"That sounds acceptable." I couldn't honestly say "want" factored into it. I reminded myself I needed money. I had Mother's gold locket, as well as Father's watch, but I could never part with those things. The locket with its photograph was the only memory I had of the time before, when we'd all lived in Basel.

She went through a list of duties: tidying the garden and sorting their mail while they were away. Once they came back: cooking, cleaning, laundering, sweeping.

As soon as they came back, I'd be off to our house in Basel, to visit my lawyer and claim my fortune. Nevertheless, I gave her what I hoped was an agreeable smile. "Very well. Do you want me to keep ordering milk after you've gone?"

"When he comes tomorrow, tell him we don't need him. You'll have to find something to feed the cat, though. Maybe some baby mice."

A black cat, no doubt. In America, I'd been introduced to the concept of Halloween. These people must celebrate Halloween all the time.

Mrs. De Pena spoke again. "You can start now. The kitchen is a mess. I want you to mop the floor too."

Simone was still crouched outside, ears flat against her head. "May I bring my dog in with me?"

She shrugged. I noticed they both stepped to the side. Simone did none of her usual wagging and sniffing. Her tail was low, almost dragging the ground, and her ears were still back. When Unruh took a step toward me, she stiffened, ears flicking. He retreated. "A beautiful creature. Purebred?"

I nodded.

"She's devoted to you. Her eyes haven't left you the whole time."

"She's my best friend," I said, my voice tight.

His eyes were amused. "Do you have trouble relating to people?"

"Mrs. De Pena, will this ... gentleman ... be staying here while you're gone?"

"There's no reason for him to, is there, my little slippery eel?"

"No, my dear. After tonight, the way forward should be clear."

I changed in the little guest bathroom in the hallway, putting on the snazzy black cigarette pants I'd once worn to a faculty cookout at Harvard, where Da taught pharmacology. Now they were dirty and torn from my summer job as a field hand, harvesting strawberries. The things a girl had to do to get by.

Then my new mistress whisked me into the kitchen, where she watched me work as she ate smoked oysters out of a tin with a silver fork. Her eyes stayed fastened on me as I scrubbed the pile of dishes from last night's feast and emptied the goblets and glasses of their dregs of red wine, white wine, and plum liquor. I'd not had lunch, but the sight of the day-old sausages oozing fat, rabbit in wine sauce, and a few token slimy vegetables effectively ruined my appetite.

"If you want something to eat, go ahead. Ludwig said to make sure you're strong." Silvia waved at the serving platters.

"Thank you. Perhaps later." How odd she and Dr. Unruh were. As if I would eat her soggy leftovers.

I couldn't help myself. "Are those oysters your breakfast?"

"I like salty meat. I ate human flesh once, in the jungle."

It was a bizarre joke to make, but I hid my revulsion, conscious of her gaze on me. She yawned and lit a Milady's from a pack lying on the counter. She flicked the ashes on the floor. Fair enough. I hadn't started mopping yet.

I watched the dirty water drain down the sink, leaving a ring of grease and particles behind. I certainly didn't want to eat *here*. It didn't look like I had much choice, though. On a Sunday, there wouldn't even be a store open in the village where I could buy a piece of bread and cheese to tide me over. Dining out, even at the farm inn, would be an extravagance. I was torn.

"Mrs. De Pena?"

She rubbed her nose and took another drag, blowing smoke out her nostrils. "Yes."

"Could I have a small advance?"

"Ludwig," she yelled. "The caretaker already wants more money. What do you think of that?"

His laughter drifted from the other room. "She deserves some reward for putting up with you, my precious darling."

Silvia didn't offer any money, though. Instead, she ground out her cigarette stub into the empty tin of oysters and moved away from the counter. "I suppose you'd like a wash-up?"

"Perhaps I'd best mop the kitchen floor first."

She'd come close to Simone, and now the dog actually bared her fangs when she growled. I saw Mrs. De Pena's painted red lips stretch over her pointed teeth. Had she just snarled back?

Simone growled again. "No. No. Bad dog." I set down the brandy snifter I'd been drying and walked over to her, stroking down her ruffled hair. "I'm so sorry. She's never like this. She's never bitten anyone."

"And cats?"

"We had a cat. She likes cats." We'd had a cat, a pet iguana, and a Wistar rat I'd rescued from the lab. The cat ate the iguana and the rat escaped. I didn't share all this with her.

"Well, put her in the shed for now. I don't like the way she's acting."

What could I have done? I should have never locked her in the shed. I left her there with only a bowl of water and some biscuits, and my feeble reassurances that I'd look after her.

I couldn't even look after myself. When Da had been alive, I'd felt on top of the world. Our chauffeur picked me up at four sharp every day from Milton, a progressive school near Boston. As long as I helped Da in his lab and completed the German assignments Miss Gladys gave me, he didn't notice I spent the rest of my time reading trashy paperbacks and watching gangster movies. With some coaching from our friend Mitchell Aaron, I'd still managed to be accepted at Radcliffe, Harvard's sister school.

This would have been the beginning of my freshman year in college, walking around Harvard Yard on the crisp, glorious fall days New England was known for.

Now I was just a displaced orphan, too smart for her own good.

At quarter to five I was allowed to take a break. I went straight to the shed. Simone gulped down the leftover beef and bread from the kitchen.

I was tired, but Simone needed exercise. "Come on, let's go for a walk." I headed for the woods, smiling as I watched her bound through the trees, stopping to sniff at roots and rocks.

She found a new scent and galloped toward a rocky outcrop. When she reached the jumble of boulders, she pawed at some tall grass, huffing. She'd discovered a small cave.

I didn't dare to be gone too long my first evening. Feeling guilty, I whistled her back, returned to the shed, and locked her up again.

I returned the padlock key to the hallway table, and Mr. De Pena showed me to my room. He was indeed small and fat and licked his lips constantly. His high cheekbones indicated some Indian blood.

My room, snug under the eaves, had a sloping ceiling. A lone dormer window let in some sunlight. A washstand held a large chipped china bowl and a jug. A huge armoire loomed against the wall. There were no lamps, and the narrow bed had one thin blanket. Though I wouldn't be able to reread my Captain America comic book at night, it was heaven compared with sleeping on the creaking wooden floor of the abbey library, the fumes from Lupe's polishing still strong in the air.

"Take a wash and rest. Afterwards, we want the American cocktail drinks. A Martini for me. You know this drink?"

The concept of cocktails was familiar, due to my addiction to American detective movies. I nodded.

"Good. Tonight, we have a fiesta."

"Is it your anniversary?"

"No. Big moon. My wife comes to eat at Löwen, with me and the doctor."

I looked at him dubiously. I couldn't imagine what he and his wife had to mutually celebrate. It looked to me like Dr. Unruh and she had the same arrangement my father and my German tutor Gladys had.

When I discovered Gladys in his bedroom at eleven o'clock one night, he'd been embarrassed. She'd gotten dressed in a huff, but I'd confronted her at the front door.

"Gladys, how can you do this?"

"Look kid, your mother's been dead ten years now."

"That's not what I meant. You're a junior at Radcliffe. Won't you get caught and expelled?"

She gave me a wise look, and winked. "Radcliffe girls get their own dorm keys. We're a little ahead of the times."

The next morning over our Ovaltines, Da covered sheets of papers with the configurations of sterol hormones on them, to explain why testosterone impelled him to liaisons that might better be avoided. All I could think about was getting into Radcliffe and becoming like Gladys, with her dark felt pants and signed copy of Kerouac's *On the Road*. I was unaware that even then my father was dying.

Mr. De Pena was staring at me. "Why you stand here, *chica*?"

"I'm fine." Though I wasn't.

"Silvia. She wants a vampire."

"Yes. A Vampiro," I corrected him. "She explained. Tequila, tomato juice, and lemon. Since she can't find limes in Switzerland."

"You're smarter than the last one. We had to kill her." He laughed. What kind of a bloody joke was that? I closed the door on his face and went to the basin, then scrubbed myself. I stripped down to my underwear and hung up my few clothes in one corner of the monster closet. After that, I lay down on the smooth sheets, luxuriating in the feel of a bed, stretching out. My body grew heavy with the need for sleep.

I bolted up, heart pounding, sure that someone was close.

Unruh lurked over my bed, his dark eyes set off against his fine white skin. His hair was swept back from his neck in a loose mass. He'd removed his coat but wore a cravat of finest paisley silk. His starched shirt was blindingly white in the gloom.

I drew in a sharp breath, clutching the blanket, blood pounding in my ears. A strange man in my room. What was I supposed to do? Da never covered this in our talks.

I couldn't afford to be outraged. So. He'd reacted well when he'd found out I was a professor's daughter. "This abhorrent behavior ill behooves you," I said in Grace Kelly's cool, patrician voice. "Please leave at once."

He drew back, and then burst out laughing. "I take it you read a lot."

"Umm. Yes."

"I like to as well. I'm actually just here because I forgot my book. I come up here sometimes for some peace and quiet."

What was wrong with the library? But perhaps I'd misunderstood. It wasn't as if I was so beautiful that no man could resist my charms. Even Patrick had run.

"There's no book here."

"Are you sure?"

"I don't miss details." Then I realized something. My bed faced the door, and I'd been lying on my back. Even half-asleep, I would have noticed him coming in. It was bad enough he was here now. I didn't want a nocturnal visitation. "Where did you come from just now?"

He pointed a slender finger toward the wall that ran parallel to the bed. "I wanted to avoid meeting Silvia on the stairs. She can be so demanding."

"So you walked through the wall?"

A smile quirked the corners of his lips. "That would be nice, but no. What do old houses often have?"

It took me a minute. "Ah—a secret passage." It must be concealed in the armoire.

"I doubt I'm the first man who felt an itch to visit the maid's room. But you're no maid."

I blushed to the roots of my hair. Surely he couldn't know about Patrick. No one knew. Or could one tell just by looking at a girl? I was no housekeeper. That's what he meant. He was disconcerting me.

"As long as I'm here, you and I could chat."

"I don't think so." But underneath the fear, a pleasant tingling started. So he *was* up here because he was interested. I ignored my body's message. I'd led a sheltered life, but even I knew he was bad news.

Unruh stepped close again, opening his hand palm down as if he was offering benediction. He could whisk that blanket right off me.

I hesitated, just a second.

"You leave my room right now. Or else." My voice rang out loudly in the small space.

His eyes locked on to mine, and I felt that vertiginous feeling. Something about him reminded me of the diabolical Robert Mitchum in *The Night of the Hunter*. Except that of course Unruh didn't have Love and Hate tattooed on his knuckles.

"Get out now!"

He backed away. "We'll meet again."

He turned and sauntered off toward the door, hands in his pockets. I heard a clink. From where I sat, I could see the image on the coin: the Helvetic maiden bearing a shield, circumscribed by stars.

"You dropped a two-franc piece."

"Oh." He acted surprised. "Your eyes are sharp."

I pointed to the door. "Sharp as a hawk's. Goodbye."

"Keep the coin. I hope we'll have a mutually rewarding association."

Then he was gone, leaving me speechless.

I served Silvia her cocktail by the light of a cluster of black candles. She wore a soft, violet flapper-style cocktail dress with a fringe on the bottom, covered with a man's smoking jacket.

"Are you getting settled in? We do want you to stay." Her solicitousness seemed forced, but it gave me the opening I wanted.

"Yes, thank you. I was wondering ... your friend, Dr. Unruh. Have you known him long?"

"We met in Brazil years ago when he did field work on native botanical medicine. He's a doctor of anthropology at the University in Munich." She narrowed her eyes. "Has he been bothering you?"

As if I was going to trust her. "I was just curious." Unruh didn't strike me as the typical bohemian anthropologist. I tried to imagine him, perfectly attired in a crisp linen shirt and creased khakis, gaining the confidence of half-naked men with darts and blow tubes. He wasn't anything like dear Dr. Shultes. I'd snuck into his lectures at Harvard, sitting in the back.

As I picked up the silver drink tray, I became aware of a burning on the back of my thigh. I went in the kitchen, hiked up my dress, and twisted to see. There was a red puffy circle. I looked around for some ice cubes, but of course, I wasn't in Cambridge anymore. I settled for a splash of cold water.

I'd felt a sharp pain in the bed after Unruh left. I took off the sheets and shook out the blanket, but didn't see anything. Strange. The cold water didn't help much. There was nothing I could do about the bite now. I'd have to check out my room carefully.

I brought Silvia a refill and walked around the living room, flicking the heap of cigarette ash on the sideboard into a used napkin and scratching off some candle wax. I rescued a book set face down so the spine would be damaged, then looked more closely, curious to see what she might be reading.

One phrase caught my eye: "Now let it be first understood that I am a god of War and of Vengeance." In the margin, in a rounded feminine hand, someone had written, "The falcon strikes." Silvia?

I felt her hot breath on my shoulder and set it down. The fog of her spicy perfume enveloped me.

"*The Book of the Law*," she said softly. "The age of Horus, the falcon-headed God, is upon us." Her full breasts pushed into me as she leaned over to pick it up. "It's by Aleister Crowley," she added.

I only knew who he was because the last time we'd visited my Irish grandmother, there'd been a copy of *The Mirror* lying around. The article about him, "Devoted His Life to Evil and Sex," had caught my attention and I'd read it in one go, though at age eleven, I'd mistaken the word orgy for ogre.

Black candles. Aleister Crowley. How had I ended up here?

Our eyes met. Up close, hers were beautiful, fiery, flecked with amber. Whatever she saw in mine made her draw back.

I wasn't going to play damsel in distress.

I made my diction distinct, as if she was hard of hearing. "May I please go see to my dog now?" When she waved her cigarette in dismissal, I wandered to the kitchen and took a handful of the Spanish meatballs from the kitchen counter. She wouldn't miss a few. I wondered briefly where she'd found albondigas and tequila. She seemed resourceful.

I called to her from the kitchen. "I'll return after the dog walk to clear off the dishes." I touched the two-franc piece I'd picked up. "Then may I be permitted to get some dinner?"

"You're free this evening."

I breathed a sigh of relief. I couldn't wait to get away from her. From them.

Simone whined behind the shed door at my approach.

I ducked inside. "It's all right, my love. I've got a nice treat for you, and tomorrow those horrible people will be gone. I'll take you in the house and you can sleep on the bed."

Simone growled. I didn't know what to do. Tentatively I extended my hand with the meatballs. Surely she would sniff them and act happy.

She didn't. She kept growling and growling.

She was a sweet dog. I'd never had any trouble with her before. "Come on out. Time for a walk."

She backed away into the corner of the shed. I smelled urine.

Tears stung my eyes. Strange. I hadn't cried when Patrick vanished the day after the hooch incident, though I'd expected more after waking up naked in his room. I hadn't cried when Da was cremated and his ashes buried in a graveyard, against his wishes. I couldn't stand this, though.

"Fine." I set the meatballs down. She had enough water. "I'll have to lock you back up for now."

I trudged back to the house, passing a shiny black BMW parked nearby. Dr. Unruh doffed his hat to me from the front seat. I hoped he'd leave me alone for the rest of the evening.

I replaced the key in the drawer and went to start up the hi-fi. Mrs. De Pena wanted to listen to the newest American star. His name was Elvis Presley. Gladys had told me when he swiveled and crooned, it was enough to make your head spin and your heart skip.

3. Full Moon, Blood Moon

Mrs. De Pena had pushed the chairs back against the wall, and as Elvis howled lustily to the twanging guitar, she danced. I found myself strangely fascinated by the lascivious gyrations of her hips. She definitely wasn't Swiss.

When her husband came in, he noticed me standing stiffly, still holding the tray. He tried to dance with her. When she shoved him away, he turned to me, his face red.

"Go. We have no need for you."

I took a deep breath and ran into the hall. Now where was that shed key? I was sure I'd replaced it.

I searched for more than five minutes. I thought of asking Mrs. De Pena, but the strange groans from the other side of the door unnerved me. Perhaps her husband had gotten his way after all.

It would have been nice to take Simone out with me, but when my stomach growled for a third time, I gave up on the key. All I'd had to eat was a croissant that morning.

After ten minutes I reached the Lion and saw Dr. Unruh's shiny black BMW parked outside. When I heard voices around the back of the restaurant, I walked toward the source, hoping it was only staff. I needed directions.

I found a skinny cook and an even skinnier girl smoking outside. The delicious smell of braising meat drifted out the kitchen door.

"Excuse me. I'm looking for the Eugsters' farm?"

The man gave me a considering look before grinding out his cigarette. "Turn left at the butchers and head up the road and you'll find the Eugster place. It's just the two sisters now."

It was a short climb after the village. The curvy high green hills around Gonten looked like they'd been scooped out of soil and covered in green velvet. I turned and looked back at the village. On the other side, the stony ridges of the Voralpen range rose bleak. Farther south, the highest peak in eastern Switzerland, majestic Säntis, came into view, silhouetted against the azure sky.

The freshly risen reddish moon loomed to my left, the sun not yet set.

Dusk was my favorite time of the day, a bittersweet time.

At this time of the evening Da and I used to sit in our study, him with his sherry and me with my Ovaltine. We'd spent the last months before he got sick discussing Paxarbital, the new drug we were developing. The name, based on the Latin word for Peace, was my idea.

The girls at Milton called me little Dr. Mueller, thinking to insult me. They didn't know how proud it made me inside. My father had five books published in the field of pharmacology. Students like Patrick and Gupta traveled from other countries, just to study with him at Harvard.

Da is dead. You watched him die, and that night when it got really bad, you couldn't take it anymore. You forgot the morphine, because you and Patrick...

I kicked a rock hard with my sandaled foot as I walked. My toe would be bruised. I needed to stop thinking about the past. *What's done is done.*

Food would make me feel more settled. Maybe I would even talk to someone, though the thought made me uncomfortable. Most people didn't know how to talk to me.

I turned the corner and there it was: a farmhouse shingled in dark wood, a few pines sheltering the outdoor tables. It was quaint. I liked Basel's St. Andreas Square better, with its cobbled courtyard and little tables thronging with students and retirees, conversations in French, German, and Swiss mingling, ebbing and flowing.

The tables and benches in front of the farmhouse were made out of split logs. There were only three tables, two of which were occupied. Other than that, the place was deserted except for ravens. There did seem to be a great many of them around, squawking with their ugly voices, although I noticed they gave me a wide berth.

Don't like odd orphans?

The old woman who'd gotten off the bus with me, Mrs. Wäspi, waved. She sat at the first table, the largest one. Next to her was a middle-aged man and across from him, a woman, who I took to be his wife. The man looked a bit like Mrs. Wäspi; he must be her son. He had the same blue eyes, set deep in a broad, sunburned face, but while his mother's expression was kind, he had a brutal look. His chubby wife sat with eyes downcast, twisting the hem of her faded blouse.

A pale young man with a grave expression sat alone at the middle table. He wore the traditional light blue striped Appenzeller shirt with suspenders. He stared out at the sky as if he could read the clouds. The last table was next to him; I headed toward that. He ducked his head at me as I approached, giving me a polite smile.

Mrs. Wäspi spoke up in her rural accent. "Good evening, Miss Waldvogel. So the De Penas hired you?"

"Yes." I suppressed my unease. "I'll be staying, at least to take care of the house while they're gone."

She turned to the man at her side. "This is my son, Hans Wäspi." He grunted a greeting.

The plump, anxious woman whom I'd taken to be the man's wife turned out to be his sister: "My daughter, Ursula Wäspi."

Unmarried then. I wondered how she got by. Life probably wasn't easy for single women in Gonten.

She gestured at the pale young man. "Sitting over there, that's Stefan Sepp. Our priest's nephew." Her son glared at Stefan, who shrank back. So he hadn't joined them because of Hans.

I didn't want to sit with Hans either. I took my seat at the remaining table, and a woman a few years older than I came out right away, wiping her hands on her apron. This must be one of the Eugster sisters.

The night was lovely, the air balmy, the dark azure sky clear except for a few clouds.

It was 7:30 by my father's watch. My stomach grumbled.

"What can I bring you to drink, Miss?"

I really wanted to wolf down a basket of bread, but it might be rude to tell her that, and not to order a drink. She tried to help me with my decision. "We have some very special herbal schnapps, with additions. A friend of the family made it."

I was always drawn to novelty. "Please bring me some of that." Then, waving my hand to make it seem like an afterthought, "Some bread as well, please."

She bustled off. Stefan Sepp turned from his table and addressed me, his voice friendly. "The schnapps is quite delicious, though unusual. I just started on mine."

"What's she offering for dinner?" I was hoping it was Rösti, the Swiss version of hash browns. I loved Rösti. It must be my Irish genes, to be so drawn to potatoes.

"She has sausage and Alp cheese. You could ask her if you want something else."

I did, and she was gracious. "I can make you some. I've already grated the potatoes for tomorrow's breakfast. The only thing is, I'm having a touch of trouble with the stove."

I picked up a piece of bread and tried not to stuff it in my mouth while she was watching. "How long will it be?"

"As fast as I can make it."

"Mrs. Wäspi said you're new at the De Penas'?" the young man asked, after she'd left.

"Just got off the bus today. I'm from the big city originally. Basel."

He shook my hand. "Welcome. You can call me Stefan."

I inclined my head. "Patrizia."

He took a small sip of his drink. "I suppose Miss Tschantz left? We haven't seen her in the village for several weeks."

I remembered Mr. De Pena's odd joke. *You're smarter than the last one. We had to kill her.*

A chill went down my spine. "I don't know what happened to Miss Tschantz."

He leaned in closer. He certainly was chatty for a villager. "No one from the village will work there, you know. It's haunted."

A suspicion grew in my mind. "The De Penas bought the house?"

"Yes, they didn't have to pay so much. Everyone knows it's haunted."

He had just said that, but I refrained from pointing that out. "Perhaps they knew. Maybe that's why they bought it."

His eyes grew rounder. "Why would they do that?"

"Have you met them?"

"Well, yes. I went by to invite them to our church service, but I don't think they'll come."

Maybe they'd like a black church with a goat behind the altar.

I kept that to myself. I didn't want to get him started on religion.

But the next words out of his mouth were, "Our big service is at nine on Sunday. You'd be very welcome. I could even come pick you up."

Was this his idea of a date, or was he just the welcoming committee to the church? Either way, I wasn't interested.

At least Patrick had been handsome, even if he was a heel.

"I'll be very busy with the cleaning," I said, and took a sip of my liquor. I'd not had anything stronger than ginger ale since the night Patrick and I had drunk our homemade alcohol concoction and I'd passed out. I'd been quite sick the next day, though I'd tried to hide it from Da as I ran back and forth with cold compresses for his pain.

My glass held a reddish, viscous liquid. It tasted only slightly better than it looked—like toothpaste mixed with cotton candy and fennel bulbs. It had a bitter aftertaste.

"Quite delicious," I lied.

"I've never tasted anything like it. There's a special ingredient." He gulped down the rest of his glass like a man finding water in the desert.

The woman came then, wiping her hands on the apron. "I got some help with the stove. I can start cooking now. Just came out to see if you needed anything else before I start."

"You're all alone today?" Stefan asked her.

"My sister got sick last night. She had to go to the hospital. Dr. Unruh took a look at her and said she might have appendicitis."

I sat bolt upright in my seat, almost spitting out a mouthful of whatever I was drinking. "Dr. Unruh said that? Why would you ask him?"

"He's taken a kind interest in us. Our village doctor is often indisposed, and Dr. Unruh is a professor."

"Well, I'd be careful." I was a newcomer to the village, and it wouldn't do to share my suspicions about Dr. Unruh too soon. He wore expensive clothes, and most people could look no farther than that. I already knew that from Pierre Latour, my Aunt Madeleine's new husband, suave in his Savile Row suits.

"I'll buy you another glass," my new companion said. His proper demeanor had changed. He smiled broadly, his face slack. "I'd like to toast you over a new one."

Another sip. My cares were melting away. For the first time I was able to picture Da's urn being placed into the earth without feeling like I would faint.

Then the bad feeling came again. I'd failed him. He'd specifically said he did not want to be buried in a churchyard. But I'd learned how much the word of a nineteen-year-old counted against that of her well-heeled and well-connected aunt.

I took another sip. The glass was empty. *Da's dead. He won't know you failed him.*

"Let's have another one, then."

I drained my second glass and blinked hard. My vision was blurry, a green haze at the edge of things. An acrid smell filled my nostrils, and warmth pushed through me. I brushed my cheek with the back of my hand. Hot. I leaned in to say something to Stefan. His pupils were large black pools in his pale eyes.

A nearby dog started howling, long and hard, like she never meant to stop. Ice-cold shudders went down my back, and I sat rigid. The scene was frozen in moonlight, though it wasn't dark. A ripple. Then another. It felt like an earthquake in the sky—like everything was upside down and inside out. The air was quaking. I thought of insects trapped in amber, their wings stilled in the golden light. We were all still, and yet everything was moving inside, the moonlight changing us.

Stefan went white. "Your hair's standing on end."

Waves pulsed through me. It was like holding a badly wired lamp.

Mrs. Wäspi rose from her seat, using her umbrella as a support. Her wrinkles were frozen into fissures in the harsh moonlight, her eyes wide with fear.

I turned to Stefan, so terrified I could barely mouth the words. "We need to leave. Something's going to happen. Something very bad."

Too late.

A scream from Ursula. Her mother hadn't made a sound, but she'd jabbed the metal spike of her umbrella into her own eye. She was slumped over, blood gushing out of the empty socket.

I felt a breeze behind me. As if wings were folding and unfolding. There was a strange aching under my shoulder blades. I tried to get up, but I was bigger than I remembered, and something hit a tree branch behind me. Something connected to me.

I turned around to find out what that was and flinched as I saw Dr. Unruh, hovering nearby. What was he doing here?

His eyes were fixed on the scene, his teeth bared in a frightening smile.

He'd been expecting this, even anticipating it. I'd seen the same look on Da's face when he watched a meticulously constructed laboratory experiment unfold, confirming his hypothesis.

We were puppets, connected to Unruh by invisible strings. The next act was about to begin.

Piercing screams. Ursula had punched her brother in the face with her closed fist. My eyesight sharpened. A spray of spittle blurred through the air as her teeth started snapping. She struck. She spat. A gobbet of Hans's cheek thudded onto the ground.

My stomach heaved, and I screamed too.

Hans jumped up, staring wildly about him. Didn't he know half his face was gone?

Then he broke his glass on the table top, leaving a jagged edge.

Panic froze me into place. "Do something," I implored Stefan. He held his rosary in his hand, the crucifix bearing down into his palm. I caught snatches of the Lord's Prayer as he muttered.

I turned around to beg Dr. Unruh to stop this, to stop it now. He was gone. Had I imagined him?

No. The blades of grass were still bent under the weight of his heel.

My head snapped up, as Ursula Wäspi started babbling. Her voice was a caricature of a man's. "You lovely thing. Come on. Yes, come here."

Her brother thrust the glass into her abdomen, twisting viciously. "Whore," he croaked.

She slumped down, eyes far away. She wasn't dead yet. She was in hell somewhere.

Hans drank from his broken glass. Blood seeped from his lips.

Then he ran toward us.

He lurched to a stop. His eyes were crazed. Soon he would stab me with the glass, tear out my throat...

I reacted without thinking. My right hand sprang up, pincering the back of his head. The knuckle of my left index finger dug in hard between his vertebras. My right hand twisted. Something gave way under my knuckle, a crunchy sound, and he jerked.

I froze. *What had I just done?*

His body slumped forward slowly; his mutilated face thudded into my shoulder. I staggered and pulled away with a cry. His corpse toppled to the ground. The top of my dress was soaked in blood. The blood shone, the night seemed darker now, almost black, the grass luminescent, green. Numbly I unbuttoned the dress, blinking to clear my eyes. I'd be in my underclothes, but I couldn't bear the slop of the blood-soaked fabric.

An explosion inside the farmhouse wrenched my attention away. The woman cooking, Miss Eugster. Was she safe?

Smoke began to pour out of the building.

I made a 180-degree sweep with my eyes. I'd let the dress fall; it covered Hans's destroyed face. Next to me, Stefan whimpered, tears glistening on his eyelashes. A fern two meters away quivered when a mouse moved. The blood on Ursula gleamed, silvery in the strange light. Even from where I stood, I could see it was already starting to coagulate. Green motes spun in the air like strands of a spider web.

Dr. Unruh was like the spider.

My skin prickled all over. My fingers sprang to my sides, stroking my arms and legs, as if releasing something lurking under the surface. The buckles and straps of my undergarments were impedances.

What was happening to me?

The clothing felt *wrong*.

I clawed my way out of my underclothes.

I stood naked, glorious, heedless of Stefan, who ground his knuckles in his eyes, moaning.

He was earth-bound, a mewling man-boy.

I was free.

I felt my great wings beating and then I was lifted, speeding away, borne on the wind of my own power.

The village dwindled away. I was flying toward Säntis, no longer a girl at all. No tears for the slain, no memories of Da. No room for love, no time for shame.

I was magnificent. I ascended higher and higher, spiraling in my own power, exulting in the sky.

Unbound.

Until I woke up on the roof the next morning, with no clear memory of how I got there.

4. My Alias

I PULLED THE COAT CLOSER AROUND MY NAKED BODY, HIDING myself from the policeman and the curious gaze of the carpenter. Dizzy, I leaned onto the car hood for support. The lawn was cold against my bare feet. At least I wasn't on the roof anymore, but I had new problems.

For one: the passport Manser held. There was no use pretending I was Patrizia Waldvogel.

Manser's eyes turned hard. "You are Peppa Mueller, then? The girl reported missing from Zurich five months ago?"

"I'm over eighteen. Nearly twenty. Old enough to be on my own," I offered.

"That's not what your aunt says. She's concerned about your deficient upbringing. Only your father around—till he died." He looked at the passport again, frowning. "Very careless. Your name is misspelled. It should be Müller, not Mueller."

The umlaut in our name disappeared as soon as we reached Harvard. Da wanted to remove any obstacle to his tenure, no matter how minor.

"It's not a mistake. The Swiss never make mistakes," I said bitterly, memories of my aunt's endless corrections flickering by.

Mr. Manser's jaw tightened. If he clenched his teeth any harder, one might crack. "Don't play games with me. I saw things that turned my stomach last night."

He turned to Lutz. "Go get the ladder."

"But I want to know. We all heard..."

"This is a murder investigation. I've got to follow procedure."

He took a step closer to me. "I found your purse. Next to the deceased man. Hans Wäspi."

Memories smashed through my wall of composure. There were three bodies outside when I fled the farm inn yesterday—Ursula dying, the other two stone dead. But I still couldn't believe it, had hoped it was part of the hallucination. The vicious attacks. The self-mutilation. Seething hatred traveling through the air, pulling us together in its web.

The glimpse of Dr. Unruh, standing motionless in the shadows. Silvia said he'd been to Brazil to study native plants.

Had he poisoned us?

Spots passed in front of my eyes. My body shook with suppressed sobs.

It couldn't. It couldn't be. They tore into each other. I'd never seen anything like it.

"Miss Mueller. I'm talking to you."

I could see he was close to slapping me. He must be appalled by what he'd seen, overwhelmed. Likely the worst he'd had to do before was break up a bar fight.

The killings took place then. The part about becoming a wild, winged creature must have been a reaction formation. The casual nudity an ego defense against the humiliating incident with Patrick. I knew a little about the defense mechanisms people could create when faced with the unthinkable, from talking with our friend Mitchell, a staff psychologist at Harvard.

Manser's face floated above me. I'd collapsed into a heap, blanket still clutched in my hand like a shroud over a corpse. My teeth chattered.

Now I wished I had the compound Da and I were testing out. Paxarbital, a barbiturate derivative, was developed to treat nervous exhaustion, hysteria, maybe even schizophrenia.

What if Unruh had just come by to check if Miss Eugster's sister was feeling better? Maybe I'd gone crazy last night—killed all those people myself.

It was possible. One time when Mitchell and Da thought I'd fallen asleep, they discussed a schizophrenic patient. She'd drowned all three of her children. She'd claimed they were mud goblins.

I stopped reading fairy tales after that.

Mr. Manser pulled me up, spots of red burning on his cheeks. I realized the blanket didn't hide enough of me and pulled it tight again. Mr. Lutz leaned the ladder against the car. His eyes shone eagerly. "Was she there? Did she see it?"

"Be quiet. I need to interrogate the witness." Manser snapped, taking out his anger on Lutz. It was me he wanted to shake a confession out of.

I felt numb. "I'm a witness?"

Only a witness? I'd been afraid he would accuse me of a murder. Vivid in my mind was the image of Hans Wäspi running at me after he'd cut up the woman's belly with a broken glass. I definitely killed him.

Not just killed him. I snapped his neck. His head lolled at an angle before I'd covered it with my discarded dress.

That was right before the place caught on fire. The woman who'd served us was probably dead too.

I retched up bile, barely missing the blanket.

I wiped my mouth with the side of my hand. "You said the De Penas left? Where's Dr. Unruh?"

"We'll talk about it at the station," Manser said. "After I call your aunt."

"I'd rather you call my godfather." Godfathers had an important role in Swiss culture, almost like a surrogate parent.

He narrowed his eyes. "The information posted by the City of Zurich said you were the ward of your aunt and her husband, Pierre Latour. They've been looking for you for five months. Who is your godfather?"

"Alex Kaufmann." When Manser didn't react to the name-dropping, I realized he didn't know about the LSD discovery. After all, very few people outside the pharmaceutical industry had heard about the strange new drug. "Dr. Kaufmann works at Sandoz. Da would want him here."

"I don't care what your father would have wanted, Miss. Madeleine Latour is the one who reported you missing."

As he took me by the elbow, I leaned away. "My dog."

"Mr. Lutz can see to that. He's got to break down the ladder. I'm taking you in right away."

"Simone won't want him. She needs me."

"We'll get your dog later; your uncle can take him back to Zurich."

"That's not my uncle," I spat out. As if things weren't bad enough. Pierre was the last person I wanted to see.

"We'll sort that out when he comes. In meantime, you'll tell us what happened last night."

Mr. Lutz added, "Can't get a word of sense out of Stefan. That boy's always been soft in the head."

I thought Manser would strike him. "That's enough." Lutz busied himself with the ladder, and Manser opened the passenger car door for me.

I couldn't get in that car. No.

I played my only card. I let the blanket slip some, exposing my small breasts. "Please let me in the house to get clothes."

My face burned in shame.

They both averted their eyes. "You can't take her to the station like that," Mr. Lutz said.

Manser hesitated a minute, eyes glazed with fatigue. "Come on then. Let's take you inside." He sighed deeply, beckoning for Lutz to accompany us.

He took out my key and opened the door. Mr. Lutz was dispatched to the kitchen to fetch me a glass of water, and I tottered upstairs with the policeman carrying my purse. I paused on the second story landing to catch my breath and shake out my right hand, which was becoming numb again. My shoulder clicked, and pain shot through me.

"Are you all right?"

I was alive and the man who'd attacked me was dead. It could have been the other way around. From that perspective, I was all right. From any other perspective, I was not.

His voice turned harsh. "I asked you a question."

"I'm cold. I need to get dressed."

"Where to?"

My apology of a room was more the size of a closet. When we entered it, I walked over to the dormer window. Could I have sleepwalked over to it yesterday night, hoisted myself up without a stool, and then crawled over to the spot where I woke up this morning?

That made even less sense than turning into a falcon.

I thought about Unruh. He'd said he studied anthropology and botany. Could he have made that viscous red drink with "a special ingredient"? The two classes of Dr. Schultes I'd sat in on concerned his anthropological research into peyote ceremonies. Maybe this was something similar.

I walked over to the large armoire. My dress wasn't there. Had I walked all the way home naked from the Bäsebeiz under the influence of some hallucinogen? It hadn't been that late; someone would have stopped me.

There had been a fire. Manser must have been called to the scene after people noticed the smoke. "Did you find a dress and sandals by my purse at the Bäsebeiz?"

He nodded, studying me, his eyes squinting. He was trying to make up his mind, wondering if I was capable of murder. "The clothes are covered in blood. I've sent them to the forensics lab," he finally said. "But you could just tell me now. Whose blood is all over your clothes?"

His voice was menacing. Or was it my guilt that made it so?

"It could be Mr. Wäspi's blood. He was bleeding when he ran at me," I said, to appease him. Then I dared the next sentence. "If you want answers though, you might want to talk to Dr. Unruh."

"Are you telling me how to conduct my investigation?"

"I was just wondering if he's left the village yet."

"Get dressed," he bit out. "We're wasting time here."

I held out my hand for the purse, and he lifted an eyebrow.

"My handkerchief." I took the purse from him before he could reconsider and made a show of taking out the folded lace cloth and dabbing my puffy eyes and snotty nose. I slung the purse over my shoulder.

"You'll have to give that back."

"Of course. As soon as I've freshened up."

My battered suitcase was still where I left it, next to the bed. My boots were under the bed. My remaining skirt and the worn black cigarette pants hung in the closet like abandoned bodies.

"So what happened up there?"

I hesitated. Wasn't he supposed to be asking me that at the station? I had to tell him something, with him staring at me like that, his sunken eyes holes of hopelessness.

"They attacked each other. Hans and Ursula."

"Goddamnit. I've known them my whole life." A blue vein pulsed at his temple. "Ursula died this morning. Her little boy will be sent to the orphanage." He wiped at his eyes, but not before the light caught the glint of his tear.

I swallowed. What had Dr. Unruh done to us?

My hands hesitated, brushing past the black and torn cigarette pants, and then went back. For what I was planning, a skirt was not a good choice. I pulled out the hanger.

Manser noticed. "Those are not decent," he said, barely containing the loathing in his voice. "Do yourself a favor and at least make a good impression. I've tried to keep things quiet, but there are a few people waiting around to get a glimpse of you."

Great. A lynching.

I grabbed some underclothes and a shirt. Lutz thumped up the stairs. He came in and set the glass of water down by me. If I had three hands, I could drink it and still wear my blanket.

"May I please change in peace?"

The two men looked at each other.

"Where can I go? There's only the one window."

"We just got you off the roof," Manser said in a tone of voice that indicated he wasn't stupid, no matter what I thought. "Maybe you flew up there. If so, maybe you can fly down."

I tensed. He was clearly joking. But I did. I did fly up there, in my nightmare, after I left the massacre.

But even if I did, I didn't know how to fly anymore.

"Close your eyes."

He sent Lutz out, closed the door, and turned his back to me.

I got dressed, hurrying, my fingers shaking so hard I could barely button my blouse. It was tempting to just go along with

Manser. I'd be protected against whatever had happened, safe in a cot behind bars of iron.

But as one of two survivors, I was naturally a suspect. Perhaps he thought I killed them all. I was the stranger; the others were people he'd known his whole life.

There was still Stefan. The last time I'd seen him he'd been mutilating his hands with his crucifix.

No telling what he would remember.

I *had* to get away from the cops.

I stepped into the armoire. The sliding panel Unruh had used opened noiselessly, but a draft of stale air entered the room. Manser coughed, and I froze. "You're taking a long time there."

If I answered him, he'd hear my voice echo in the nearly empty wardrobe. I stepped back out in my socks, holding my sturdy walking boots in my shaking hands.

"I'm sorry. The hooks are fiddly."

"Hurry up. My colleagues are down at the station waiting." He'd likely called for backup.

"I'm trying." I darted back in, squeezed through the opening, and then closed the sliding panel. It was dark and I felt for a latch to lock it, but there was none.

Droppings crunched under my feet as I started walking. Mice. Or rats. The passage took a sharp right turn, and I banged my head hard on the wall. I had to pay attention. Be here right now. Never mind my other problems, the ones that had come last year. A new one had come up, the worse one, the dead bodies.

As soon as I got Simone, I was going to find out what happened to us last night.

A nail tore through my sock, puncturing my skin. I stopped to think for a minute. Would it be better to put on the boots? Manser might hear me.

Despite the darkness I was still able to see. In front of me a space opened up. It was my guess I'd emerge in the library. One of the bookcases had to swing out.

I hope those are stairs.

My room was on the left, toward the back corner of the house. I'd gone right, and right again. The library would be under me.

An excited voice echoed down the passage. They'd found my escape route.

I had to be quicker. My head still pounded, and I'd never gotten that glass of water. My throat ached for it.

I could bear it.

When I was ten, my once-best friend Emil Nussbaum had found the newspaper clippings that his father kept hidden in the bottom drawer. Together we read about the concentration camp prisoners, most of them Jewish, like Emil's family. Afterwards, I'd gone all day without food or water, driven by a perverse fascination with the horrors they'd experienced. My mother, Ainslie, preoccupied with packing her art supplies for Brazil, didn't notice I wasn't eating or drinking until the next morning. She'd sat me down and made a big bowl of Cream of Wheat. Then she kissed my head. She never asked me why I'd done it, though.

I heard a crash behind me, followed by cursing. I sped up, nearly running into the dead end in front of me. My fingertips probed, searching for a catch. No luck.

Footsteps came down the stairs now. *Hurry.*

Despite my headache I could make out thin lines around the panel of the hidden door. My vision was unnaturally sharp today. I breathed deep, reached up, and pushed where I thought the catch should be. There was a click, and I stepped out into the solemn splendor of the library.

The clock ticked loudly, making me wince. I ran past bad paintings of the Orient: lurid harem scenes and camels in the desert.

The closest window had an elegant walnut writing desk in front of it. Someone had been reading there, enjoying the garden view.

I scrambled over and pushed aside the books. Even in an emergency, I was unwilling to damage them. Nietzsche, a tome on alchemy, and an illustrated guide of birds of prey.

I climbed onto the desk and opened the window. On impulse, I snatched the bird guide up and stuffed it in my purse. I hated being without something to read, and pretend-science didn't interest me. Then I jumped, landing too close to a rosebush. Even with the headache and dizziness, the thorns still hurt. I hurtled across the lawn, toward the nearby woods. I wondered what animal Simone had scented by the little cave. Probably something dangerous lived in there, a badger.

Better than Mr. Manser.

Trees rushed past me, stripes of yellow sunlight alternating with dappled shade. There were puddles; when I found one on a rock, I lay on my belly and lapped like a dog, lapped it dry, the stone chalky and smooth against my tongue. I struggled on. Far behind me I could hear crashing. There were still only two of them. But not for long, I reckoned.

After I'd rested, I'd wait till dark. I'd have to try to break Simone out from the shed. The padlock was old and rusty. Maybe I could smash it with a stone.

And what would I do if they'd set a guard? Simone would attack to protect me. But I didn't want to risk her. She was all I had left of home.

I'd have to see. I'd have to see.

But first I had to hide and rest.

There it was. The opening of the cave, just big enough for me to wriggle into.

A long stick by my side served as a prod. I pushed it as far as I could, but it didn't hit anything. Whatever creature lived there, it wasn't there today. At least I hoped not.

I lay on my stomach and went in feet first. If there was something back there, I'd rather have it bite my shoes than my head. I was able to get all of my body in with some room to spare. Without the sunlight, my head felt a bit better. I was still hungry and thirsty, but I felt safe, as safe as I'd felt since yesterday morning, when I'd gotten on the train to the village of Gonten.

5. The Survivors

I COULD NOT REST. MY MIND WENT AROUND IN LITTLE CIRCLES, like an adrenalin-injected lab rat before the dose of the Paxarbital placated it.

I couldn't have killed someone. How would I have known how to snap someone's neck like that? But Manser saw dead bodies. If I hadn't killed Hans Wäspi, who had? No, I knew I'd done it. But how could I have...

And how was Simone doing, abandoned in the shed?

Maybe the desperation about my dog explained why I dared leave my hiding place when I heard Stefan Sepp's voice. He used the name I'd given him yesterday, Patrizia Waldvogel. Or maybe I came out because we were both survivors of the horror last night. I needed to know what he'd seen. He'd struck me as a gentle young man, at least before he had the drink and started mutilating his hands with the silver cross he wore. If I had to, I could knock him over and run away.

He was facing away from me, looking the wrong way, back to the house. "Miss Waldvogel. Patrizia. Where are you? I won't turn you in."

"Stop that racket. You'll get the police here." My tongue stuck to my dry mouth.

"Thanks be to God. You're all right. You're all right."

"I'm dehydrated. Need water." Too much to hope he had ergotamine for my migraine. I knew all about that since Uncle Alex had researched ergot.

"Mr. Manser has guards on the house now. He called the surrounding villages for help. We'll go to the stream."

I followed him unquestioningly. Puffs of clouds dotted the blue sky. Through the boughs of the evergreens I caught glimpses of the slate gray sides of the mountains. The sun was much lower in the sky. I must have slept after all.

I smelled the water before I saw it, and started running. My feet tangled up and I fell. So much for overpowering Stefan if I needed to. I'd overestimated my strength.

He helped me up. I tried to ask him if the Bäsebeiz had completely burned down. All that came out was a croak.

"There, there. Almost to the water."

I fell on it like a ravening animal, sticking my face in the pool between the rocks, lapping at it with my tongue. As the clean taste of it hit, I realized how bad my mouth had tasted before. I didn't even have a toothbrush. I hadn't eaten since yesterday morning.

I sputtered and stuck my face down into the water again. When I came up for air the second time, black spots swam before my eyes. I tried to sit up, but wobbled.

"What's wrong?" His pale eyes regarded me anxiously.

"I never did eat."

"I brought a sandwich, just in case. I hope you like our local Alp cheese."

The stuff smelled like Da's laundry after I'd forgotten to call for the faculty laundry service for two weeks. I held my breath each time I took a big bite.

"Better?"

I dusted off the crumbs. "Why are you helping me? You know the police are looking for me."

"They'd be looking for me too, but I went to them first thing this morning. I talked and talked. They sent me back to my uncle. I'm in his custody."

"I hope your uncle isn't like my so-called uncle." I thought of Pierre Latour, with his pomenaded hair and Cartier watch, reeking of aftershave. My aunt must have been besotted when she married him.

"My uncle is the priest here. I'll take over the parish after I finish my studies."

He'd mentioned something about being a theology student yesterday.

"You still didn't tell me why you're helping me."

He looked embarrassed. "You're an angel. I saw."

If he'd been watching, he'd seen me break a man's neck. Is that what angels did in his universe?

"I am definitely not an angel, if there are angels, which there aren't."

His grin was lopsided. "I saw your wings for a moment."

Did you see everything else, I wondered, flushing. I still had trouble accepting that I'd stripped naked in front of a stranger.

"They were feathered."

A shiver passed over me then. I'd been a falcon, soaring up into the air, circling while the village grew smaller beneath me.

No, I'd been poisoned with a hallucinogen. Something like that LSD Uncle Alex worked with, but way worse.

I twisted my mouth into a sarcastic smile. "So you think I'm a superior being? That's why you want to help me?"

"You survived. I survived. This is not something Mr. Manser and his colleagues can explain, believe me."

"I have a theory..."

He looked at me expectantly.

I couldn't stop thinking about Simone. She must be desperate. "First, could you help me with my dog? She's been locked up in the shed near the house for a day. The key should be inside the drawer of the hallway table."

He hesitated.

I tore at a loose fingernail. Was I going to have to beg him? "She hasn't had anything to eat or drink. Please."

"What kind of a dog is she?"

"She wouldn't hurt you." Though I wasn't sure, seeing how she'd acted around Mrs. De Pena.

"Is she a German Shepherd?"

I bit back my impatient words and sucked up some more cold water from the stream. I was going to have the stomachache from hell. Water dribbled down my chin, and I wiped at it with my sleeve. "Are you scared of big dogs?"

He spoke slowly now, anxiously watching my face. "Dr. Unruh stopped at the bakery this morning for some fresh bread. That dog was locked in his car. She was yowling."

I started crying. I had lost my mother Ainslie, my father, my trust in my aunt, my virginity, and my house. I couldn't take the grief anymore. It filled up my chest and poured out in tidal waves that made me rock, back and forth.

Simone was the last thing I'd had.

I hated Dr. Unruh. I wanted to snap his neck.

A flash of memory: Da. We'd arrived in Massachusetts that August. It was a freezing winter evening, and I'd forgotten to close the gate of our little yard. Simone, still a puppy, escaped. Da said, "Your dog trusts and loves you. It's a gift and a responsibility. Take care of her."

Da and I searched for three hours, but we found her, and celebrated with giant mugs of steaming-hot Ovaltine. And I'd get her back now. I sniffed a few times more and wiped my face on the back of my hand. Then I sat back against a tree trunk and took the apple that Stefan proffered.

I bit and chewed quickly, so I could speak. "Any idea where Unruh was headed when he stopped at the bakery?"

He shrugged. "Back to Munich, I guess. Why does he have your dog?"

I leaned in intently. "I think Dr. Unruh poisoned us. Maybe he took Simone as a way to control me, if I make trouble for him."

His eyes showed doubt, and he chewed on a piece of grass. "He was kind. Our doctor is drunk every evening, and if someone gets sick, Dr. Unruh helps them. He fixed up a burn on my Grannie's hand."

"He struck me as an odd one." I shuddered. "I saw him when Hans killed Ursula. He was right behind us."

"Oh dear. Tell me all of it," Stefan said.

I thought talking would be a relief, but it wasn't. When I finally stopped, exhausted by the effort of reliving that dreadful night, I had a knot in the pit of my stomach.

Da and I wanted to help troubled people with Paxarbital. Now I'd become one of them, a murderer suffering under hallucinations.

I raised my face to meet Stefan's clear blue eyes. I saw no condemnation. "I told you I killed Hans Wäspi. Isn't confession supposed to be good for the soul? I don't feel any better."

"Only God can forgive your sins. I can't."

Three dead. At least. "What about the woman who brought us our drinks?"

"Anita Eugster? No one's seen her. They're looking through the ruins of the kitchen for her bones."

Despair descended over me, and I had to fight an urge to scream. I splashed my face with cold water, biting my lip to fight the pain inside.

"They found me on the roof this morning." My voice sounded hollow. "Did you hear?"

Stefan moved away from me a bit, rubbing his hands as if he was cold. I understood. I'd like to get away from myself too, if I only could.

I dug my nails in my palm. I would not be weak. "We really were poisoned. I could prove it."

"I saw your wings, Patrizia."

"My name is Peppa."

"You turned into an angel."

I rubbed my eyes. What I needed was a lab. That meant getting in touch with my former best friend, Emil Nussbaum. His mother, Elena, attended Da's funeral. She'd told us Emil followed in his father's footsteps, working at one of the research labs at the University of Basel. Not that I'd heard anything from the little bastard himself, since he shoved me into the sideboard and chipped my tooth.

Ten years without a word of explanation. When we moved to Cambridge I'd been homesick and written him a total of fifteen letters. I'd never gotten a reply.

He'd shown me that I couldn't count on anyone but Da.

But ... I needed Emil now.

If I could identify the poison, I'd know for sure that the falcon had been a drug-induced hallucination. That meant I could still trust my basic decision-making processes, find a way to get Simone back and to clear my name of murder. It was self-defense.

But how much of my memory could I even trust?

"What did *you* see?" I asked Stefan.

"Ursula attacked Hans, and then he sliced her belly up with broken glass." He started shaking and his voice dropped to a whisper. "He ran over to us, but he was hairy all over. His face melted, and I heard a rushing and a howling. I thought devils were coming. Then I realized you were an angel and I thanked merciful Lord Jesus. When the kitchen exploded there was fire. I thought I was in hell. I ran home to our barn and hid in the hay. At dawn I woke up my uncle, begged him for confession, and then took three aspirin. My head still throbbed. We waited at the station until Mr. Manser came."

"What did Mr. Manser say to you?"

"Lots. He shouted. He asked me if I killed Hans. But I'm sure I didn't. He would have asked me more, but then Mr. Schmidt drove up in the milk truck. He went to get you."

"How come the police didn't put you in jail? You *could* have killed all those people yourself."

He looked down, embarrassed. A faint pink stained his cheeks. "Everyone knows about me."

"Knows what?"

"I had a nervous breakdown when I did my military service. Loud noises like guns make me nervous. Also, fighting."

I gave up. The villagers felt they knew their own, and suspicion would naturally fall on the outsider. Though in this case, I really had…

My heart pounded. *You killed someone, Peppa Mueller.* I stared at my hands, the long fingers and big knuckles. How had I known how to twist someone's neck? I must have read it somewhere. I had an eidetic memory.

I turned to Stefan. "How are your hands?"

He looked proud. "I received stigmata. A sign of favor from the Lord. He protected me by sending an angel."

"You made those wounds yourself. With the crucifix you held."

He looked confused. "No. I wouldn't have done that. It would have hurt."

"I bet it hurt when Mrs. Wäspi poked her own eye out with her umbrella."

He grabbed my hand hard, crying out in pain as soon as he did so. He didn't let go, though. The whites showed under his iris. "She was my Bible teacher. What happened? What happened?"

I made myself sound calm. "Trust me. There was something in that drink. I need you to get some more of it."

"But most of the Bäsebeiz burned down. There are police all over the place."

I tossed my apple core into the woods, wishing I could throw Stefan after it. What now? Maybe I could collect my urine, check for any metabolites once I reached a lab. It wasn't an appealing idea.

Stefan's face lit up. "I just remembered. I took my glass back home. It was the Holy Grail." He looked at me uncertainly.

"The drink was a psychotomimetic, some kind of hallucinogen. Maybe even mescaline."

"What's that?"

I flung up my hands, desperate to explain. "Red toadstools with white dots. It could have been something like that. Something to make you and me see things."

"I should take my cup to the police then. They can analyze it."

"But I'm your angel, remember?" His eyelids fluttered, and I felt a flash of loathing for myself.

"I'll bring it to you then. What will you do?"

"I'm going to Basel. Home."

Tears pricked my eyes and I closed them. Da was home again only three weeks before he died of liver failure, but the place was vivid in my memory. A narrow white three-story house, built 1762, tidy green shutters framing the windows, opened to let in the cool smell of water. Potted planters, overflowing with pink and blue petunias, framing the lacquered red front door. A brass nameplate: Dr. Johann Mueller and P. Mueller. The broad ribbon of the green lazy river, fifty meters from our front door, wending its merry way toward France.

"Patrizia, are you all right?"

"My name's Peppa Mueller. You'll find out soon enough. My father ... is ... was ... from Basel originally."

He wrinkled his brow. "Why didn't you tell me who you were?"

"I ran away from my aunt five months ago. I've used a false name since then."

"You should be with your family now. You would be safer. What happened to us, it's dreadful. If you're even a quarter as scared as I am, you'll want to be home with your aunt and uncle."

"Oh, but I won't."

"Why? Your aunt wants to take care of you, I'm sure."

My mouth twisted into a bitter smile at the recollection.

They must have thought I was still out that May afternoon when I overheard them. Madeleine had just returned from viewing her friend's new purchase—a device called a television, where you could see as well as hear people. Never mind that there was only an hour broadcast every night. I could hear Pierre moving around in the living room after his nap, probably still cross that I beat him at a game of chess.

They'd started out with their usual inane exchanges.

"Hello, *chouchou*. You look ravishing in that dress."

"I've missed you, darling."

I rolled my eyes. They'd been apart a whole three hours. When my father said goodbye to Gladys forever, she'd remained dry-eyed and tight-lipped while she shook his hand.

I went back to my reading.

Then his voice caught my attention, sharper and petulant. "Your niece talked about Radcliffe endlessly today. When are you going to tell her?"

Her voice, conciliatory. "I haven't mentioned it to Peppa yet. She'll be very upset."

I'd slammed closed my *Merck's Manual of Pharmacology* and sat bolt upright. I already had my dorm picked out—

Holmes Hall. I'd even written my new roommate, Mary from Vermont.

"For God's sake," Pierre huffed. "Lausanne is waiting for the deposit. It's one of the top finishing schools and still costs less than four years at Harvard."

"Radcliffe, dear. Harvard is for the boys."

I crashed into the living room. "What do you mean? I'm going to Radcliffe. It's all arranged." The thought of seeing the newest gangster films, attending more of Dr. Schultes's weird lectures, and buying several pairs of pants was all that had kept me going since the funeral.

Pierre stood up, glaring. "Not anymore. I wrote them a month ago and withdrew your application. You're in Switzerland now, and you'll obey your elders."

~

Stefan touched me gently on the shoulder, and I jumped. "I hate my uncle. As if my life wasn't ruined enough, he took away my chance at university."

"I'm very worried about you. I have my parents, my uncle, and Christ. But you don't have anyone."

"Well, I have you?" I tried to smile at him, though I was gritting my teeth.

"Yes." He nodded. "If you find something in that liquor, what then? What difference would that make?"

It would make a big difference. I would be armed with the tools of science before I approached Dr. Unruh. I tried to think of what would make sense to Stefan, though. "Mrs. Wäspi was your Bible teacher. Don't you want to know why she would take her own life?"

"The devil did it, the devil did it!" His voice regained the high-pitched wavering quality. Then he stopped. "Your eyes looked brown. Now they're greenish, hard as the stones of Säntis. I see no mercy."

We'd talked about our shared experience, but now he stared at the ground, doodling the shape of a cross with a pointed stick. While I, I felt like a statue. I knew at times like this my face stayed expressionless, my lips pressed hard together. I'd been told.

"Angels protect, and mete out justice. They can't be soft," I finally said. I needed food, liquids, and sleep. I needed Stefan.

"Will you stop this evil?"

"If you help me." Which was a lie. I had no idea of how to stop Dr. Unruh.

"What do you want from me?"

"I'm still sick." This part was true. If I moved my head too fast, bolts of lightning flickered across my vision. My whole body felt as if someone had pounded it with a nightstick. And where those wings had been—that ached. Though of course there hadn't been any wings.

"I feel bad too. My head feels like claws are digging into it. You should rest. When are you going to Basel? They'll be watching."

"How far is it to walk to the train station in St. Gallen?

"Maybe five hours. Longer if you're ill."

"I'll try it tomorrow. I need lots more food before I'll be strong enough."

"There's a barn close to here, a walk up. My father uses it for the cows in summer. You could sleep there. I'll try to bring you bread. Whatever's around that won't be missed."

"That would be much appreciated." I waited a beat. "Stefan, I also need money for the train. I would pay you back."

"I only have the church fund. But I guess it will go to a good purpose. You're on God's side."

I shook my head. "I don't want to lie to you. I haven't been to church in a long time."

"Do you lie or cheat or fornicate?"

Did fornication count if you were dead drunk and couldn't remember a thing? I settled on saying, "I have morals."

"Then you're on God's side. I'll take you to the barn now."

It was close to seven and the sun was going down. The shadows of the trees grew longer, the dark became substantial, lapping at our feet, closing in on us. The moon did not comfort me as it once would have.

A bird shrieked, and then the uhu owl began its plaintive cry. It sounded as lost as I felt. I'd been born and bred in a genteel city, and the dark forests and still meadows echoed the new wildness inside me. I'd felt the bleak power of instinct unleashed, as violence throbbed in my vein. I was a survivor. But did I like that?

Once you know you can easily kill to save yourself, it changes you.

"Patrizia, this way." I'd missed him turning up a small path.

"Sorry. I'm tired."

"I don't know if I can bring you more food tonight. But tomorrow morning, certainly. I'll bring you a map as well."

"And the cup of liquid. That's the most important."

"Watch your step here."

The cows and rain had made a muck of the path; one of my shoes got sucked down. I pulled free.

"We're almost there."

I stumbled on.

"Here." The barn still smelled warm, like manure, though I could see it had been raked out. The heap of dung and stall scrapings steamed outside, decomposing into rich fertilizer.

I threw myself down on a heap of straw. "Thanks for your help. Have a good evening, Stefan."

What a ridiculous thing to say. The Irish part of me wanted to scream and sob. I was stuck with a religious fanatic as a friend, and a Satan-worshipping professor had kidnapped my dog. But it wouldn't do to be impolite. I was half-Swiss, after all. I knew the rules.

He looked at me as if he really saw me. "You're a good person. Goodnight, Peppa."

6. One-Way Ticket

THE NIGHTMARE STARTED.

The full moon, the reddish drink, sickly sweet, then bitter on my tongue, Mrs. Wäspi with her umbrella and Hans rushing toward me with his bloody face. I'd twist Hans's neck, but his head would right itself and he'd keep coming, punching me with his fists. My talons scratched out his eyes, and he slammed my head into the ground. When his hands closed around my throat, I awoke, covered in sweat.

I groped for the comfort of mother's locket. It held a tiny version of the last photograph of us, before she died of malaria.

I remembered it well. Even in Cambridge, I'd kept the framed original on my dresser.

I'm standing between Da and my mother, Ainslie, under the linden tree in our yard. My little brother is tucked away in Ainslie's womb, a secret seed that will prevent her from taking quinine. Emil's mother carries a haphazard bouquet of lilac clutched to her chest. Emil is turned toward me holding our favorite toy, a hobbyhorse.

You can't see Emil's father. He took the photograph.

It was my father's birthday, April 4, 1949.

I went back to sleep, comforted. The dream came again. This time Ursula ran toward me, guts slithering out to the ground.

I woke up. My entire body ached. I wanted to cry.

Da's watch showed it was 4 AM. I was quite cold.

I snuggled into the straw. Simone would have kept me warm. What did Dr. Unruh want with her?

He wanted to hear from me. He'd watched me with Simone. She was his lure.

One thing at a time, Peppa. First thing, reach Basel and find Emil.

What if Unruh killed Simone? But he'd struck me as a calculating man. What would killing her accomplish?

Somehow I fell asleep again. This time I dreamt Ainslie was illustrating a vine Da had found in the jungle. It was growing up the side of a tree, and its leaves shimmered green. She had a jar of pencils by her side, and I was afraid she would put out her eye with one. I called to her, but her beautiful features were set in concentration, and she never even looked up.

Stefan woke me with a gentle nudge. I screamed, then stopped, embarrassed, when I realized it was only him. "Here's an old satchel. I got what I could. You need to leave soon. They've put together a hunt with men from the area and they're going to comb the countryside for you. I told them again that Ursula attacked Hans and he killed her, and that I didn't remember after that, except for the fire. Hans was found dead by your chair, though, and you ran away from them, so you're their suspect."

"They should be going after Dr. Unruh."

"He was at the restaurant. Everyone saw him there."

"Everyone?"

"Manser talked to the waitress, Susi. She's my friend from school. He was there, except when he smoked his pipe."

"See. He went outside."

"The Bäsebeiz is a ten-minute walk from the restaurant. He wasn't gone long."

"He has a car! He could have driven."

"He could have. Stop screaming at me, Peppa."

I bit my lip. If even Stefan didn't believe me, how would I ever convince the police?

I'd just have to make sure they didn't catch me.

Stefan continued, "I only asked my friend because of what you said. You're the only one who saw him, and you won't go talk to police, and your aunt and uncle are very upset. It's a big mess."

That was an understatement.

"I ought to go." I hoisted the satchel. It was heavier than I'd expected. I set it back down. I should make sure the poison was there.

He'd poured the viscous liquid into a thick glass jar with a screw-on lid. It couldn't have been more than a deciliter. I wrapped the precious cargo in an extra pair of socks he'd brought for me. I replaced the other items: a loaf of bread and some sliced sausage. Two apples. A big, black book.

A Bible.

"What's this for, Stefan?"

"Protection. And there's a letter of introduction in there."

To Jesus? I can't wait.

"Where do I take that?"

"My friend Christian. You can find him at the Evangelical Mission, in Basel. He's very smart. He can help you. He's seen a lot of things."

Wonderful. More religious fanatics.

"I don't think I'll be able to visit the Mission. Working up a new compound is very time-consuming."

He looked tired. He hadn't slept well either. "You should keep the letter. You never know when you need help."

I shouldn't pitch the Bible into the bushes in front of him. He meant well. I tore some bread off and started eating. He'd brought a canteen of coffee too. "You've helped me so much, but there's one more thing…"

His hands shook as he took out a heavy purse. "The money is here. Our church collection." He didn't hand it to me, though. "Mr. Manser came to my uncle and asked him if atheists were more likely to suffer from insanity. Were they talking about you?"

It would be so easy to say I believed. Otherwise, what would I do? I'd probably get caught.

I couldn't speak.

He shoved the purse at me. "Just take it. But swear to me you will find out who is responsible, and why they would do this. Mrs. Wäspi und Ursula were my friends."

I took the purse and stuck it on top of the satchel. "I want to know as much as you do."

"Swear. Swear you won't just save your own skin. You find out! I want to know why! Why."

"Yes."

"Promise on the Bible."

Our eyes met. "I see," he said, in a defeated tone.

"I will swear. On what I believe in."

"What's that then?"

"The periodic table of the elements. The division of a cell. The heart that pumps blood in my chest at the rate of seventy-five beats a minute."

"You should find something personal to believe in. But I accept your promise."

He said goodbye and then there was nothing for it but to walk to St. Gallen. Which I did, somehow.

~

Fatigue wrapped my brain in a fuzzy woolen blanket, which was good. It kept my fear at bay. Sometimes a wave of exhaustion rose and my heart hammered. I just concentrated on putting one foot in front of the other till it passed.

At first, I descended past well-kept farmhouses and barns. They were bordered by fenced gardens full of bright dahlias, orange calendulas, and tended blackberry canes.

Soon I was back in the forest. The steep grade challenged me to keep my balance. Once I slid down a hill, my tumble halted by a tree.

The woods were beautiful; September unseasonably warm, as if the sun was reluctant to abandon us to the winter howling of the wolves and the chilled darkness.

For then we would be alone, stripped of protection.

Somehow Stefan's last question had unsettled me. He believed God would protect him. I couldn't reach for that placebo.

No God. Therefore, no occult forces.

But there was something different about Dr. Unruh. I sensed something submerged in him, something mysterious and feral.

I sat down, leaned against a pine, and took off my shoes, rubbing my sore feet.

There was something wild in me too. I'd called it a raptor.

As I got up to go on, the words from Silvia's book came back. "Now let it be first understood that I am a god of War and of Vengeance."

I searched within myself for hatred and found desolation. There was only the wind stirring the branches of the evergreens, the dapple of the light on the path, and my boots, picking their way through stones and roots. Descending.

The shadows grew longer and the air chilly by the time I reached the steel bridge that crossed the river Sitter. I paused there, gazing at the green water far below, and felt an irrational urge to throw myself off the bridge and glide through the air.

It nagged at me. It felt so real. Why a bird of prey, why not a wolf or a dragon?

I remembered Patrick's brogue as I corrected a few of his equations. "You've got a hawk's eye for mistakes there, luv." I'd never gotten over his sudden disappearance, and likely, I'd created my delusion based on his remark.

Like most fanciful tales, there was a simple explanation.

~~~

It was near six when I stumbled toward the railway station. There were three Italian workers sitting on a bench nearby, smoking. The one on the edge, closest to me, was about my age, the other two in their forties or fifties. Perhaps they were waiting for someone; perhaps their apartment was just overcrowded.

I counted out some money from the purse Stefan had given me: enough for a bribe and third-class tickets to Zurich. Then I moved closer to the group.

The younger man glanced at me, and then his eyes slid away. Italian boys weren't supposed to talk to Swiss girls. Even I knew that. My Italian wasn't very good; we'd never had an exchange student from there. I tried Swiss-German.

I held out my big shiny coin. "How would you like to make five francs?"

His German was passable. "What do you want?"

"I need you to go buy a train ticket for me. One-way." The police might have alerted the ticket agents to be on the lookout for me—I couldn't take a chance.

He took a long drag on his cigarette. "Sorry, I cannot help you." He met his compatriot's eyes, and they exchanged cautious glances.

I moved away a little and concentrated on the ticket sellers. I could see their faces with exceptional clarity. As a woman about my age approached the seller, he looked down, as if checking something, and studied her face. After a moment's hesitation, he issued her a ticket.

They're looking for me.

The Italian men, still smoking idly, chatted, and one of the older men guffawed.

With the Latin and Spanish I knew, I could pick up a few words. They were discussing my looks. The boy I'd been talking to, Antonio, didn't like the teasing. He looked at me out of the corner of his eye and replied.

He'd said I wasn't pretty, like La Lolla, sexy Gina Lollobrigida. Why did boys have to think so much about the way girls looked? I couldn't help it that I towered over boys in my heels, and that my face was all planes and angles.

One of them said something, waggling his hips.

Whatever that was, they thought it was pretty funny.

Antonio glanced at me again. "*Lei mi da l' impressione di esser ferale.*"

The boy had said I looked lost. None of us belonged here.

I studied the crowd of prosperous burghers, compliant in their conservative dark hats and dark suits, the women outfitted in heels and gloves. I must look like a vagabond to them.

Taking a deep breath, I went back to them, addressing the young man and ignoring the old-timers. "I'm in big trouble. I ran away from my aunt."

"Why?"

"She and her new husband wanted to send me to a school I didn't like. But now the police are looking for me. I need to get a train pronto."

"Forget it," one of the older men rumbled. But Antonio pushed his curls out of his eyes and held out his palm. "I understand. Give me the money."

I had to hope he wouldn't just take it and disappear. I counted out the money for the ticket, plus the five francs, and nodded. "One-way to Zurich. Thank you." In Zurich I had to change trains to Basel, but I had something to do in the city first.

I kept at a discreet distance to make sure he went to the ticket window and didn't just disappear. I had enough for what I planned to do in Zurich, but not much extra.

Antonio came back. "I wish you luck. I do." He handed me the change together with my ticket.

"Aren't you going to take my money?"

"You gave a guy like me a chance. Trusted me to behave with honor."

He'd trusted me, not knowing I was only giving him a partial version of the truth. I shuffled my feet, considering. "I'd like to send you some money as a reward. Soon I'll have plenty. What's your address and last name?"

"I don't have a pencil, Miss."

"I'll remember. Tell me." I could remember most things by the simple trick of picturing them.

He recited his address.

"In two weeks, I'll send you a reward." I walked off rapidly, on the lookout for some place to hide until it was dark.

Only two weeks. I'll be twenty. I'll have our old house, access to our bank accounts. The world will recognize me as an adult.

Though I don't remember being a child.

7. Transatlantic Communication

I'D WAITED TILL LATE AFTERNOON TO CATCH A TRAIN, WHEN IT would be the most crowded. I covered myself with my coat and pretended to be asleep, leaving the ticket visible in my outstretched hand. It had worked—this time.

I disembarked in Zurich with women and toddlers, workers and men in suits, and walked over to the old town, on the left bank of the river. I'd spent my first night away from Aunt Madeleine there, in a hotel for women of ill repute. The proprietress, an old woman by the name of Graciela, originally from Barcelona, wasn't fond of the police. I thought she might let me pay to make a transatlantic telephone call without any fuss. There was someone I needed to talk to.

My father first met Mitchell Aaron at the covert meeting for atheists, in a corner of a little café at Harvard Square, squeezed in next to Harnett's Drugstore. Neither was a Boston Brahmin—Mitchell was Jewish, Da Swiss. They both treasured Old Fitzgerald's whisky, which Da liked to serve up in laboratory Pyrex beakers, along with Ritz crackers and slices of hard-boiled eggs. Soon Mitchell started showing up evenings at our house to wait while Da finished up in the lab. In the meantime, he flirted with Gladys and introduced me to Marvel Comics and John F. McDonald's hard-boiled detective novels, in the name of acclimatization. Mitchell was a psychologist, after all.

Which is why I was calling him. If I was insane, I wanted someone to alert me.

In Cambridge, Massachusetts, it was noon. Mitchell liked to eat lunch at his own apartment, which had double-cased windows that let summer breezes in. He'd hop onto his prized burgundy Lazy Boy recliner for a peanut butter sandwich and a short nap, before returning to his office to cope with Harvard's Cabots, Putnams, and Roosevelts.

I contacted the international operator and settled down on the stool in the stifling telephone booth. Twenty minutes later Mitchell came on the line. The connection was faint, and crackling ebbed and flowed. He sounded like he was on another planet.

Well, Cambridge was like another planet.

"Oh boy. Peppa. I've been thinking about you. I miss you. I'm sorry I couldn't come to the funeral."

Of course. I didn't know anyone except Da and me who'd been on a transatlantic flight. By the time the *RMS Queen Elizabeth* crossed the Atlantic and reached the French harbor, Da's burial would have been long over.

"It's okay," I said, falling naturally into American lingo.

"You're calling me from Switzerland. Is something wrong?"

I wanted to present this carefully. "Mitchell, I need a professional opinion."

"You're not my patient, Peppa, but I'll help you any way I can."

"I'm not an angry or violent person, am I?"

A snort that might have been stifled laughter. "I remember when the girls at Milford put the mouse into your locker."

"Right." I'd had a lot of trouble catching the creature, but I'd finally grabbed hold of its tail and taken it home in my Roy Rogers lunch box.

"They did that to be mean."

"I suppose so, but it turned out well." My mouse, Captain America, learned to sleep on my shoulder while I read.

He was definitely laughing. "Anyone else would have been teed off."

"So maybe—you think I'm weird?"

"You are the product of a unique upbringing. What else can I say? Your Dad was a dear friend."

"Did you worry about me? Even before Da got sick?"

"Maybe," he admitted. "You were almost too stoic. Preternaturally calm. I know you had a big crush on Patrick, but you just seemed to shrug it off when he disappeared."

"I was busy packing for the move," I said, defensive.

"So calm," Mitchell mused. "The only time I ever heard you shriek was when you got your acceptance letter from Radcliffe. Why didn't you come back to the States, sweetheart? I would have helped you settle in."

I bit my lip. Obviously, Mitchell didn't know about my aunt.

"I had this terrifying nightmare," I blurted out.

"Tell me."

I pictured him sitting among his treasured antiques, in his J. Press suit and white shirt, dressed like everyone at Harvard dressed. He was a big, easygoing man, good-looking despite the black-rimmed glasses he wore.

The international call would cost a small fortune. I forced myself to begin a concise account of the massacre. I left out the sticky drink. I described the full, red moon and the brutal mutilations. I said I'd killed a man by twisting his neck. Another man, a wizard, stood behind me, witnessing my transformation into a falcon, but then disappeared. Naked, I flew into the sky.

I paused. "That's about it. I killed someone." I thought it was justified, but didn't murderers always rationalize their deeds?

"*Yich*," he exclaimed. It was one of his favorite Yiddish expressions. "A very realistic dream."

"Yes. Now I can't sleep."

"I bet. I wish you were here. How can I help you?"

"Well, you like to study Jung. What's the meaning of the dream?"

"What does any dream mean but what you want it to mean?" he said. "Everything is a dream." Like many Harvard men, Mitchell had an abstruse bent.

I waited for him.

"No, I get it. Even though you love violent gangster movies, even though you read John F. McDonald detective paperbacks, you're troubled that you *killed* someone."

"In a dream," I reminded him.

"Let me think ... that falcon is pretty crazy, isn't it? Like a Beat reverie..."

"I don't like that part either."

"That's all about transcendence. Rising above it."

"Rising above a murder?" I asked, wondering how much longer I could afford to stay on the phone.

"Peppa, dear. The way I understand this dream—and I could be wrong—you're not my patient..."

"Go on."

"You would be dead if you didn't defend yourself. It was like some underworld. Your inner spirit rose to protect you from harm."

"Inner spirit? Mitchell, what are you talking about? You don't believe in God."

"But I believe in an internal guidance system. Something watching out for you. Some instinct, buried deep in your oversized brain, short-circuiting your thinking process when it gets in the way. Because sometimes that process gets in the way. For you, for me, for everyone."

"So the falcon is an internal guidance system?"

"If we are to believe Darwin, we descended from sharp-toothed creatures in the jungle. Some part of us remains primitive. But primitive, instinctual, does not mean inferior. That is where the church is wrong."

Crackling sounds crescendoed on the line. "We're breaking up. I can't call you back," I yelled. I couldn't afford another call.

"Send a telegram. Write me a letter. Any time." I could barely hear his last words. "We'll see each other again. Somewhere weird and unexpected."

The receiver was warm in my hands, but the rest of me was ice cold. I left the stifling phone booth and glanced at the clock. I'd missed the last train to Basel.

Graciela was smoking a Gauloise while reading about US Teamster Jimmy Hoffa in the evening edition of the paper. I noticed the fresh flecks of oil paint on her hand. While her girls plied their trade, Graciela liked to paint still lifes of fruit, featuring oversized bananas. Her art work decorated all the rooms.

I settled the telephone bill with her and held out a two-franc coin. "That's all I've got to spare, and I need a place to spend the night."

"As long as you don't expect me to change the sheets, *querida*. I'm too tired to move."

I handed her my coin. I'd sleep in my clothes, and try not to think about what went on there.

The next morning, I mopped the hallway for Graciela, while I waited for rush hour to end. I had an irrational fear I'd encounter Aunt Madeleine's husband, or one of their acquaintances, on their way to work on the tram. Manser would have already told her I was wanted for questioning about a murder.

This time I didn't dare buy a ticket or ask a passerby for help. I could take an express train to Basel; that took three hours. I'd have to stay out of sight for that time, using the bathroom as an escape whenever the conductor came to check tickets. It was risky, but I had little choice. I had to get that compound worked up. A telephone call to Dr. Unruh was another necessity. I was so worried about Simone.

While I waited for the Zurich-Basel train to pull in, I bought a toothbrush, tube of toothpaste, and a comb. I was muddy and scratched up, and would no doubt attract attention in my pants. I didn't have to smell on top of it, though.

Once I boarded the train, I cleaned myself up in the bathroom, then made myself at home, covering the toilet lid with my coat. My description might have been on the wireless news broadcast.

My plan worked. I left the door unlocked so the conductor wouldn't wonder who was in there. When someone came to use it, I acted embarrassed as if I'd forgotten to lock. A few people gave me strange looks, but they didn't turn me in.

I took out the illustrated book about birds of prey, wondering if Silvia had been researching hawks because of Horus, the hawk-headed god. I flipped idly past owls and vultures, until I came to the sections on falcons. A full-page illustration of a peregrine caught my eye.

She was buff-colored with gray barring along her legs and chest. The head was slate-colored, her eyes large and profound, the darkness of them more pronounced by the light rim around them. The artist had captured her in full flight, her wings outspread and the tail feathers fanned around her tucked claws.

A stab of yearning—where was she going?

Seconds passed, then minutes. I couldn't look away from her. A conviction seized me that if I looked into the mirror, I would see her curved beak and piercing eyes instead of my homely features.

I could not face my reflection. Instead, I forced my trembling hand to graze my nose, my cheeks, my eyelids. Familiar. Ordinary.

I slammed the book shut and pushed it to the bottom of the satchel.

I told myself I would read the Bible instead, as a courtesy to Stefan. Soon I started feeling queasy. Was it the ungrounded superstition of religion or the swaying of the train? I closed the book, rested, and considered the concept of the holy host, central to Catholicism.

I knew about nuclear transmutation, in which one element becomes another one through the process of nuclear decay. But transubstantiation was a more mysterious thing. Through the grace of the spirit, inert matter became flesh and blood.

Little tasteless wafers and sweet communion wine became something powerful, something that could save you

What a wonderful conceit. That some grace could save you, lift you up.

~

The door pushed open again, breaking my reverie. I stuck my hands under the faucet as if I was just finishing up. Then I looked up and saw it was the conductor.

The excuse about forgetting to lock the door wasn't going to work with him. I reacted fast, slamming the door in his face and locking it.

"Miss. You'd better open up in there."

I said nothing, while my thoughts scrabbled frantically.

"Do you have a ticket?" he called through the door.

I tried to sound confident. "I'm in the carriage to the left. When I'm done, I'll meet you outside."

"I've already passed through that car twice. You've been in here a long time."

My breathing turned ragged. "Just give me a minute more. I'm sick."

"I'll give you five minutes to come out and explain yourself. I'll be waiting."

I couldn't stay in the bathroom. But once I came out, he'd restrain me, give me over to the police. They'd lock me up. I'd never get Simone back.

I'm screwed.

I heard the footsteps move away. A passenger talked, her voice querulous. As near as I could make out, someone in her compartment refused to close the train window, and the train made an awful noise when it went through the tunnels.

I darted out and mouthed "soon" at the conductor, who'd turned around to glare.

The old woman drew herself up to her full height and tapped him on the shoulder. "Are you going to make them close the window or not?"

"In a moment." He tried to turn away, but she tugged his sleeve.

I sprinted down the car away from them. The idea of the tunnel tugged on my mind. We were approaching one. The train would have to slow down.

I threw myself onto the wooden slats of the seat, ignoring the pain from my knees, and yanked the window open.

Beyond the train was freedom. The opportunity to fix things.

But the train moved fast, the regular clackety-clack swallowing the kilometers. I pushed my head and chest out the window. The track pitched and yawed, the wind brought tears to my eyes. If I flung myself out, I'd get hurt, maybe die.

If you could turn into a peregrine, you could escape.

How could I think something stupid like that? It was as foolish as thinking the host turned into flesh.

The black eye of the tunnel rushed toward me. Footsteps approached in the carriage. In a moment I'd feel his hands on my ankles.

Despite the wind, I was sweating. I closed my eyes and went inside.

And opened them with a jolt. I'd felt something new: an intense, and wild energy, buried deep like the source of a spring.

Now my eyes noted even the tiniest detail. The blades of grass and veins of leaves almost glowed, they were so green. In contrast the metal of the tracks looked darker, almost black. My head whipped back and forth. It was easy to calculate the train's speed, to see when I'd need to jump, how I'd need to position myself.

The train slowed down. One black sheep grazed with a flock of white ones in the soft green field. Another minute and the tunnel would swallow my chance of escape.

Now, now!

I threw the purse out first, then wriggled all the way out, holding the satchel in front of my chest. I tried to push off the window frame but crashed down, narrowly missing the tracks. The train thundered past me, only centimeters away, the pungent odor of hot steel and fuel intense.

I floundered, gasping for air, and dragged myself away. Stars danced in front of my eyes. The last car pounded by, the train whistle reverberated in the tunnel, and died away. When the ground stopped vibrating. I got up on all fours and crawled a few paces to my purse. A ram wandered over to halt my progress. For a few moments, we were eye to eye. His golden eyes were flat and alien. What did he see when he looked at me?

There was no Super Soldier Serum outside of the comic books, just as there was no heavenly Savior looking out for me. I couldn't fly. I couldn't even glide.

I dove into the satchel with shaking hands and tossed out the Bible. There was room for my purse in there now. I unwrapped the jam jar. The lid was still on tight, the precious liquid safe.

I staggered to my feet when I heard another train coming. My train would pull into Basel soon, where the conductor would report me.

As I crossed the pasture, I kept stopping, overtaken by dizziness. At least my ribs weren't broken; my breathing had eased. Both my elbows were scraped and bleeding. I touched my face—it had escaped serious damage.

I waited till the lances of pain settled down to a dull, persistent throb before I hobbled out to the road, asked for directions, and found the nearest tram stop.

On the way into town, I ignored curious glances and considered my next course of action. My appearance was a disaster. Not to mention that I felt even worse than I looked. The authorities would guess I was heading to Basel.

I couldn't go to our house on Rheinweg. It would be watched too. Uncle Alex worked at Sandoz. He had lab assistants. It was too risky to go there. Not to mention the funeral incident.

Reluctantly, I withdrew the letter of introduction that Stefan had given me. On the envelope, neatly printed, was the name: Christian Engel.

Christian Angel? Was this Stefan's idea of a joke? Or some misguided attempt to overcome my atheism? I hoped Christian Engel really existed.

I'd find out soon enough.

I changed trams at the Barfüsserplatz, heading toward the Spalentor. My injuries had stiffened while I sat on the tram. I limped the three blocks to the Mission House.

The four-story enormous cream-colored building was set back from Mission Street, in its own lavish park. I took the path to the main entrance with its broad stone stairs, passing a group of earnest men heading toward the street. My eyes were drawn to the roof with its clock tower, crowned by a bell, and guarded by the Evangelical cross on each side. Two obsessions of the sober Swiss Protestant: God and clocks. All it needed was a bucket of scalding, soapy water to symbolize cleanliness, and the trinity would be complete.

The lobby was cold, the cloudy morning keeping the interior dim, despite the high arched windows facing the park. The murmur of voices drifted down the corridor from a nearby classroom. A dismal painting of a crucified Jesus threatened misery behind the reception desk. I approached the young woman seated there. She was wearing a starched mint-green blouse with a plaid Peter Pan collar.

"I have a letter for Mr. Christian Engel. Do you know him?"

"Everyone knows him."

"Please take it to him. It's urgent."

Her look was cool. "I would have supposed that," she said, and tapped off up the stairs, her heels echoing on the wooden floor.

After a few minutes, she returned. She looked friendlier. As I was to find out, meetings with Christian tended to produce that effect.

"He's coming down soon."

Nearby, a door slammed and there was the sound of shuffling as future missionaries left a lecture, heading toward the lobby. I moved closer to the desk, concentrating on the stairs, until I saw someone appear at the top.

"Is that him?" I asked, shocked.

She smiled in his direction and gave him a jaunty wave. "Down here."

He wasn't what I had expected. At all.

8. The Hierophant

WHAT STRUCK ME FIRST WAS THE UNFAIRNESS OF IT. THE BEST-looking man I'd seen since Patrick Doherty, and this one was a priest. That was just a waste, as far as I was concerned.

Then the color of his skin. It was honey-colored. His eyes were dark, slightly slanted, and his hair, black and shiny, was bound in a thick braid, fastened with a turquoise ring. He looked Asian, but his sensual mouth looked Western. Not necessarily Swiss.

Then his energy. He'd bounded down the stairs, as if excited to see me. As if he'd been waiting for me for hours. He looked like he'd never been sick a day in his life.

He wove his way through the throng of seminary students that had just filled the lobby. Among the pinched, suspicious faces, the high-bridged noses and pursed lips, his open face shone like the sun.

He smiled at the woman. I could see she had a weakness for him by the way she brushed at her collar as if she was hot. He spoke Swiss-German with only a slight accent. "Thank you so much for getting me."

Then he turned to me. "Miss Mueller. You look ill."

I nodded. My elbow throbbed. I felt faint and hot. I wondered if I had a concussion.

"Could we just this once, Miss Egger, look the other way and let me take this poor child to my room. You know nothing untoward will happen."

This poor child? I looked at him more closely. He couldn't be more than twenty-five himself, but he had the confidence of someone older.

He held out my scraped elbow for her inspection, and a drop of blood fell on the counter. She frowned.

"It would be best if I see to this personally."

Her voice wavered a bit. "I suppose."

"Our mission is to tend to the needy. I'll arrange proper quarters for her as soon as she's tended. I'll speak to the Father myself." He took my satchel and supported me as we walked up the broad stairs.

We entered his room. There was a sofa bed on the left side and on the right, a desk piled high with books. There was a strange smell in the air, like cooking food but not so good. I tottered over to the window, half-expecting to see police converging on the Mission House. Instead I saw neat rows of broccoli and cabbage and two men with hoes.

"A nice view, isn't it, Miss Mueller?" He was close behind me.

I turned. His face was only a hand's breadth away from me. Perhaps people stood closer in his country. His eyes were the color of new chestnuts, bright and amused.

"You mustn't call me Miss Mueller."

He stuck out his hand. "Wonderful. I'm not one for formalities myself. Christian."

Reflexively, I shook his hand. I never wanted to let go. It was warm and strong. The energy of a sunlit land was stored there. "I'm Peppa. But I meant, you shouldn't call me by my name where people can hear. I'm in lots of trouble."

He looked at me, waiting to see what more I would say. This was a patient man. A happy man, even.

"What did Stefan write?"

"The bearer of this letter is Peppa Mueller. She will need help."

"And?"

"That's all."

"He didn't write anything about me being an atheist?"

"No. Are you?"

Me and my stupid big mouth. I sat down on his bed and looked at the floor. What had made me bring that up? And why did I care what this Christian thought of me anyway?

"I see that you are. Wonderful. I get so few people to try out my arguments with. It's no fun preaching to the converted."

"You don't sound like a typical Christian."

"I'm not a typical anything. I grew up in India."

"Your father's a missionary," I guessed.

"Yes, in Dehra Dun, North India."

I said the only polite word in Hindi I knew. "*Namaste*."

He looked surprised for a second, then burst out laughing. "We're going to be wonderful friends, Peppa-la."

I felt the events of the past few days press down on me. "It's no joking matter."

"No? Demons don't like laughter, you know."

"I don't believe in demons. But I believe in the police."

"Have you done something bad?"

I was disconcerted by his direct question. "I did, yes. But I wasn't myself."

"Who were you?"

"I'm still wondering about that."

"You'll tell me when you're ready then. In meantime, your elbow is a mess, and your cheek is swelling up. You're covered in dirt. What did you do, roll around in a pasture?"

"I lost my balance and fell down."

"Mmm. Your ankle's blue. Do I have your permission to examine it?"

"Of course."

He crouched on the floor, balancing on the balls of his feet, while his cool hands probed my foot.

"It hurts too. Everything hurts." Much to my embarrassment, a tear trickled down my cheek.

He jumped up again and bent down to get something out from underneath his sofa bed. The fabric of his dark trousers smoothed and tightened against his backside. A wave of heat swept through me.

He retrieved a black doctor's bag. "Now you're quite red."

"It's nothing," I murmured.

He started in with gauze and alcohol on my elbow. I sucked in my breath at the sting.

"Sorry. But otherwise you'll get an infection. We have a sick ward at the Mission. My mother's the nurse; a doctor comes once a week."

There was a hard rap on the door. He jumped up, agile as a deer, and flung it open.

"Ah, Father Kneipp. So glad to see you."

The priest shouldered his way through the door. He was a thin balding man with glasses, and he sucked his teeth as he looked at me. "Girls aren't allowed in the rooms."

Christian smiled politely. "I understand. Not for socializing. But she's come to me for help."

"If she's got girl trouble, we could send her to the home."

Christian shook his head slightly. "At her low weight, she's not pregnant. But she's scraped up, and probably in shock."

"Urge her to visit a priest."

"The matter has been entrusted to me, and to me only," Christian said, bowing his head.

"Are you defying me?"

"I wouldn't want to, Father."

It looked like Christian was defying the priest to me. "Please. I don't want to cause any trouble." I got up, swayed, and sat back down on my rump.

"Is this your girlfriend, Christian?"

"I don't have a girlfriend, and if I did, it wouldn't be this young lady."

I was crestfallen, to hear it put so bluntly. I tried to console myself. *Radcliffe accepted me.* The thought just made me sadder. How would I ever get back there?

The priest gave up. "You're a sensible fellow and a hard worker. I'll look the other way. She needs to be gone by dusk."

"Excellent. Thank you. Let me see you out." Christian closed the door firmly behind him.

He cleaned my elbow and brought me a jug of water for my face. The ankle received a thick smear of reddish paste and a cloth bandage wrapped tight around it.

I sniffed appreciatively at the spicy smell. "What is that?"

"Sesame and Tibetan safflower. Someone I helped made it for me."

"Did you set their ankle too?"

He laughed, but there was something in his eyes. "No. I helped him reach Arunachal Pradesh."

Wherever that was. I had more important things on my mind. "Why are you helping me anyway?" I supposed it was the religion thing.

"I'm trying to make amends. You'll have to leave soon. What else can I do for you?"

I didn't think Christian had a mass-spectrophotometer tucked away under his bed. It was time to keep my promise to Stefan.

But I didn't like it. It meant I had to ask Emil Nussbaum for help.

9. Friendship

EMIL AND I WERE ONCE BEST FRIENDS, JUST LIKE OUR PARENTS were once best friends. We'd learned how to count on our abacuses, caught newts in the spring, and played doctor while our parents consumed large amounts of Beaujolais. That was, until the day he'd unexpectedly called my father a bastard. We'd scuffled, and he'd left our house, slamming the door. His family hadn't even come to my mother's funeral the next week, and after that, inert with grief, I hadn't contacted him for a while.

Then Da got his position at Harvard, thanks to Joe McCarthy and his hunt for Communists. Da's predecessor had once subscribed to the socialist journal *The Monthly Review*, which put him on the investigative list for the House Un-American Activities Committee and ended his Harvard career.

Though Da was a handy replacement, he didn't get a tenured position, of course. That could take more than a decade for a medical school appointment. The joke at Harvard was, ask where they keep the letterhead before you ask where your office is. That was so you could figure out what to do when tenure never materialized.

My new dog Simone made up for a lot, but I still wrote to Emil from Cambridge fifteen times before I accepted that he'd never answer.

At least his mother, Elena, attended Da's funeral, so I knew that Emil worked in a lab while he studied biochemistry. She'd also said he was very sorry for how he'd treated me. Now I'd see just how sorry he was.

༄

Christian was waiting for me to tell him what I needed.

I made myself say it. "Could you please telephone a man by the name of Emil Nussbaum? He works at Dr. Wyss's lab at the University."

"What do I tell him?"

"Don't mention my name. Say you're calling for the girl with the chip on her front tooth." That was from falling into the marble-topped sideboard when Emil shoved me back. "Ask him to suggest a meeting place this evening."

"You trust this Emil? You don't seem to like him."

I glanced at Christian, surprised. "Emil owes me."

"I could help you."

"You're a priest. I don't want your help."

He gave me a strange look. "Very well."

I'd been rude to him, and I didn't quite know why. It wasn't just that he was a priest. It was because he'd been so kind. I wasn't comfortable with that, especially from a man I found so attractive.

"I'll go to the study to use the telephone. Want something to eat?"

"That's nice of you. Please."

"I'll see what I can find." He stepped out of the room. I hobbled over to his desk to jot down some notes for Emil, and my eyes fell on the small photograph. It was taken in front of a long, low hut built on stilts. An earnest but handsome light-skinned man in baggy pants and a loose shirt stood next to a plump Asian woman with beautiful eyes and a broad smile. She wore a light-colored nurse's uniform and a hat. They must be in front of an infirmary.

Christian came back about half an hour later, a bundle in one hand and a full tray in the other. He carried both with no difficulty. "Leftover cheese and sausage salad, and a glass of fresh cider." He set the tray down by me, and I took a few gulps of juice.

He continued. "Emil said he'd meet you. He sounded cautious. I wouldn't tell him who I was. I hope you'll respect my privacy."

"Of course, Father Christian."

"I'm not a Father."

Oh, he was still studying then. I gestured toward the photo, hurrying to finish chewing. "Your parents?"

"Before they had me."

"Is your mother Tibetan?"

"From Bhutan. A village called Tshebar, in Dungsam." He looked sad. "You've never heard of it, have you?"

"I never even heard of Bhutan," I admitted. "Where was the photo taken?"

"Taken at the mission. India." The way he said it made me realize he didn't like the mission much. Maybe too many people got sick. Tropical diseases had to be a scourge in India. Like they were in Brazil.

"Are your parents still alive?" I asked.

"Yes. And yours?"

I couldn't answer. There was a sudden lump in my throat. He looked at me intently. "What was your mother like?"

I swallowed and dabbed at my eyes. "I don't think anyone's ever asked me."

"I'm asking, Peppa-la."

"What are you doing with my name?"

"Oh, that." He colored slightly. "It's like saying Miss Peppa."

"My mother was an artist. A botanical illustrator from Ireland. She met Da in the tropical greenhouse here at the university."

"I love illustrations."

"I do too. I wish I could draw."

He brightened. "I've got a tattoo. I paid a lot, but he was one of the best artists in Bangkok. You can see the top." He opened his shirt collar and pulled down the back slightly. I caught a glimpse of a green reptilian head.

"Your shirt's covering most of it," I complained.

"That's the point. Some people don't like tattoos."

"I do." I'd only seen them in films.

"It would be immodest to remove my shirt."

I tried to sound blasé. "My father was a doctor. I've seen a man without a shirt before." Of course, he'd been an obese stroke patient with carotid stenosis.

He flashed a smile. "Well, then. Since you asked me."

I tried not to stare. He had a lovely body, muscled broad shoulders, and a hairless chest tapering down to a slim waist. On his back, wrapped around his ribs and ascending his vertebrae, curled a fabulous green and red dragon.

"Oh. That's fantastic." A flush of heat smoked through me.

"My homeland. The dragon land." He put his shirt back on and became more formal. "I promised Father Kneipp I'd set up the room for Bible Study. Before I go, I can pull out the couch bed so you can sleep. The nightmares may not come during the day as much."

"Don't go to any trouble. I've only got a bit of time before I have to leave."

He ignored my protest, flinging the blankets and sheets to the side, and tugged out the bed. "I'll come wake you."

I stopped him as he got to the door. "How do you know I have nightmares?"

"Your eyes." Then he left.

I woke up on my own, peaceful and warm under Christian's blanket. If I'd dreamt, I couldn't remember it. The lamp was burning. I recognized the smell now. It was butter. Christian sat up straight in his chair, his eyes on me. Not a muscle in his face moved when he saw I was awake.

My voice sounded squeaky. "You've been watching me."

"I was watching *over* you. What happened to your father?"

"He died this year. Three days before his fiftieth birthday. Cancer with metastasis to the liver."

"He's a hungry ghost."

On the surface of it, that sounded ridiculous, but there was something about the way that Christian said it that made me shiver. "He watched over me. When he was alive. Da and me—we were best pals."

His eyes were grave. "You must miss him."

It wasn't just that I missed him. I didn't even know who I was without him. At Cambridge, we'd been a team: the eccentric Swiss professor and his gangly, precocious daughter.

I shook my head at myself. In half an hour, I'd have to meet Emil. We'd had great fun as kids: exploding homemade stink bombs and swimming in the Rhine River on hot lazy summer days.

I had really thought we'd be best friends forever. I was the only girl he knew who liked science as much as he did.

I remembered my toothbrush and comb, and tried to restore some order to my appearance. It wasn't just for Emil's sake. Much as I hated to admit it, I wanted Christian to like me.

A future priest. You are a wretched thing, aren't you, Peppa?

10. God of War and Vengeance

CHRISTIAN HAD PROCURED SOME CLEAN CLOTHES AND A SPARE purse from the donation bags kept for the needy. I hurried off to see Emil dressed in a wrinkled wool skirt and a baggy cream-colored sweater. The outfit looked strange with my walking boots and socks, but there hadn't been any shoes my size.

I knew this part of Basel like the back of my hand. I took a shortcut up the hill dividing the university district from Grossbasel. The whitewashed walls of townhouses from the thirteenth century lined the steep cobblestone alleys.

I was headed toward the Sperber Bar. A strange coincidence—Emil choosing that bar. A Sperber was a sparrowhawk.

I used the street door rather than entering through the main lobby. It wasn't that busy, but busy enough. The Sperber was part of the Hotel Basel, a convenient place to drink for tourists and conventioneers.

I looked around uneasily, wondering if I'd been seen. A man started toward me and I backed up, before realizing who it was.

Emil was a Jewish boy, who, ironically, had grown up to look like one of the Third Reich's Aryan heroes. He was blond-haired, blue-eyed, and looked like he did sports.

He moved toward me smoothly, taking my arm. "We can't stay here. There's the little park by the hospital trolley stop. At this hour it'll be deserted."

We took the narrow side streets up toward Nadelsberg in awkward silence. He loped in front of me, blocking out the streetlights. How had he gotten so tall? When we reached Petersgasse, down close to the river, he turned left, and we reached the triangle of parkland. An ambulance bleated down the street, delivering its quarry to the Emergency Room of the nearby University Hospital. I sat on the bench, closer to Emil than I wanted to, so the woman waiting for the trolley wouldn't hear us.

He finally broke the silence. "Hello, Peppa. It's been a long time. I'm sorry about your father."

"So he's not a bastard anymore?"

He didn't answer.

I changed the topic. "You took me to a quiet place. So you know."

"I know. The whole town knows. The other students talked about it all day, till Dr. Wyss reprimanded us for gossiping."

"What's being said? They don't know it's me, do they?"

"Inferences are being made. The wireless announces that you, Peppa Mueller, are a missing person. We all know that's a euphemism for fugitive, so they can legally use your name." He gave me a sly smile. "The morning edition of the newspaper comes out with the gruesome story about people attacking each other in a small village in the Alps. A survivor, a young woman, is wanted for questioning. Of course, they couldn't publish your name in the paper, but everyone in the department knows who 'the daughter of a reputable, recently deceased professor' is. Lovely photograph of the burned-down farmhouse, with the corpses in front. What happened?"

"I'm not sure. I think I was under the influence of a drug."

He sounded skeptical. "What drug would do something like that?"

"That's what I need help on."

"I did you wrong. I know. I'll try to help you now. But tell me how you're doing?"

"We've got no time for small talk. I need to know the composition of this liquid." I took out the little bit I had, less than 1 deciliter. "It's some kind of hallucinogen. Try some on the rats to be sure. Then start testing for known compounds. I've jotted down some thoughts."

I handed him the piece of paper with my scribbling: alkaloids, indoles, amine groups? I'd sketched in some variations on the only hallucinogenic compound whose chemical structure I knew.

Emil looked at my diagrams for a while, frowning. "Isn't that lysergic acid diethylamide?" He pointed at one structure.

"Yes, it's the LSD Alex discovered," I admitted.

"You sound surprised I know what it is. Father is still on a friendly basis with Alex."

My godfather had accidentally isolated the compound from ergotamine, but no one knew what to do with it. His wobbly trip home on his bicycle after accidental ingestion had caused some merriment in our social circle.

"Whatever this liquid is, I doubt it's LSD. There's no more of it, so be very careful. I also need some of Da's books from our library." I showed him the titles I'd noted.

Emil nodded. "I'll find time to fetch them. Do you still keep the extra key hidden behind the petunias?"

"The petunias must be dead, but the pot should still be there."

I heard the strike of a match as Emil lit up. "Heard you ran away from home."

I ignored his comment. "I also need you to contact Da's lawyer, Mr. Baer. You remember him, right?" I only had twelve days to go till my birthday, and then I'd get my money and hire a criminal lawyer. Mr. Baer would know the best.

Although that wouldn't help Simone. My stomach knotted up. Maybe it had just been a whim. Maybe I could convince Dr. Unruh to just return her. Maybe pigs could fly.

Emil puffed hard on his cigarette. "Yes. I know him. Your father suggested him for the divorce."

"What divorce is that?"

He blew a smoke ring. "I have the distinction of being the only child of divorced parents in my social circle. As if it isn't hard enough being Jewish."

"Oh, so that's why your father didn't come to the funeral." I'd never noticed any problems between Emil's parents, but I'd only been eleven. "What happened?"

He blew another smoke ring. "No small talk, you said." He looked down at the jar I'd handed him. "What's this called?"

"I don't know. That's the problem." I thought for a moment, and my eyes fell on the nearby street sign, Totentanz. "Call it Compound Totentanz."

"Compound Death Dance? That's rather gruesome."

"So was what happened," I said.

"I read there were several dead. Everyone drank that, then?"

I closed my eyes, remembering. "Yes. It must have been the cause. Once we identify this, we'll be further along."

"*We*? So we're a team again, just like when we were little." He sounded sarcastic.

"You said you wanted to help. Find the chemical structure of this liquid. At least identify the class. It's a botanical."

"That could take years."

"It can't. I need to understand what happened. Use the mass spectrophotometer."

He looked at me like I was crazy, but now I was distracted. Something on his body ... his pocket.

"My mother told you we had a mass spectrophotometer? She's a dunce. Wyss requisitioned one, but he didn't get it. And anyway..."

"Shut up." It was a mouse in his shirt pocket. A pet mouse. Normally I liked mice, but...

A sensation of dark wings stirring behind me. I blinked.

"What's happened to you, Peppa?"

Across the park, a moth settled on a late blooming flower. On a balcony a street away, a man flecked a piece of lint off his jacket as he stared out into the night.

Dark wings beating. The moonshine sluiced through the park. The wings had rhythm, strength.

"Why are you looking at me like that?" Emil sounded scared. He stood up, dropped the lit cigarette without noticing, and took a step back.

I had an overwhelming urge to grab the mouse out of his pocket. If I gave in, took it in my hands, it would be dead within seconds. I'd kill it.

What was wrong with me?

My hands stretched, then flexed.

"Button your overcoat," I told him.

"What?"

"Do it."

He gave me a sardonic smile. "My new manly body too much for you, perhaps?" But he buttoned it.

I felt disoriented. I'd barely stopped myself from snatching that mouse up. What would have happened afterwards? "Here's what you do, right. Take the liquid to the lab. Collect my books. Contact my lawyer."

Emil nodded, wary. "What just happened here? You looked like you were going to hit me."

I watched a snail retract its antenna a couple of meters away. "I need money. Got any?"

He peeled out thirty francs and laid it on the retaining wall, rather than moving close enough to hand it to me. "I think I'd like to leave now."

"I know." I took the money and walked away into the night, and the dark wings settled slowly, till I only felt them brush at the edge of my awareness.

I wandered the streets, trying to decide where to go. My right shoulder hurt from when I'd hung onto the chimney to avoid sliding off the roof. My bones ached, reminding me I'd jumped out of a moving train today. I seemed to be accumulating disasters.

I wobbled, and sat down on a bench. I'd thought about Emil for so many years, anticipated our meeting. It was anticlimactic. He'd turned into a distant, calculating young man. The wildest thing about him was his James Dean hair.

Maybe he never really liked me. Maybe it was just because our parents were friends. I supposed Elena and David Nussbaum had their own problems, problems that overshadowed any concern they might have felt for my mother's illness. One minute Da would be galloping up to her room with the hot water bottle as she froze, the next minute she'd be screaming for cold compresses.

Malaria, hiding in her red blood cells. It was what was hidden inside you that could kill you.

I absentmindedly played with my father's watch. At Harvard, the football games would be going on, and people would be cheering themselves hoarse on the stands, then huddling under blankets in the cheerful frenzy that seemed to grip Americans at sports events.

Father hated American football. In fact, I wasn't sure he even liked America. He hadn't noticed I was wearing cigarette pants and saddle shoes, saying "okay" a lot, and chewing gum when I was anxious. He certainly hadn't seen the Marvel*f* comic books I kept under my Latin homework.

But Aunt Madeleine and my godfather, Alex Kaufmann, noticed my new manners and appearance. And they hadn't been pleased. Though Alex corresponded about drug experimentation with dashing writers like Aldous Huxley, he was still a typical conservative scientist. His LSD discovery had been a fluke. And Madeleine? She was still getting used to the idea that women could vote in most of Europe.

It was getting cold. An elderly couple walking their dog stopped and stared at me, before moving on. I didn't have any place to go. I didn't have anyone to turn to. Except a stranger...

I walked up Hebel Street, past the familiar buildings of the university, back to the Mission.

It was quite dark when I arrived. Father Kneipp would not approve of a nocturnal visit. Maybe I could get Christian's attention, have him come outside to meet me.

And then what?

I needed help. It had nothing to do with the sight of his naked torso, with the beautiful undulating dragon or his shining dark eyes.

Pathetic fool.

I started flinging the pebbles I'd gathered at his window. It didn't take long. He opened it and peered outside. I waited for him to tell me to get lost.

Instead, he raised a finger to his lips. Then he held up five fingers.

I could wait that long. I could wait for him even longer. If only he wasn't studying to be a priest.

He came down and found me where I'd stepped into the shadows." I thought you might be back."

I capitulated. "The police are looking for me."

"Let's go, then." He started walking. I noticed for the first time he had a small overnight case.

I followed him. "Sure. I mean, I suppose. Where are we going?"

"To my grandparents' house."

As we walked down Mission Street, a group of students approached us and slowed. They gaped, and a girl raised her hand to her mouth and giggled. Christian took me by the arm and crossed the street, face like stone.

Once I caught my breath, I whispered, "How could they know what I did?"

He looked surprised. "It's me, Peppa. They've never seen someone like me before."

Neither had I actually, but it would never occur to me to stare and laugh. I sighed with relief to know no one would be ringing the police station. Soon we took a left on Pilger Street, and Christian slowed down as we reached a three-story brick house, set off from the street by an iron wrought fence and a garden. Hortensias still nodded their blue heads, and the bushes had recently received a vigorous trimming. A kitchen window was open on the bottom floor; pots and pans clanked as someone washed up. The second floor appeared dark and deserted. It was bordered by a generous curved balcony that ran along the entire right side of the house. On the third floor someone played Glen Gould's Gottlieb variations on their hi-fi.

"I'm not sure this is a good idea, Christian. Your grandparents will have all sorts of questions."

"They're at the Kurhaus Klosters. My grandmother has a nervous condition." He ushered me into the stairwell and pointed up the stairs. "They live in the middle flat. The one with the balcony. The ground and third floors are rented by students."

"Rich students, by the look of things." The house was very nice, almost as nice as our place on the Rheinweg.

Christian unlocked the door of the flat. "Grandfather Engel was a professor of theology before he retired. He wanted a place close to work."

He took our coats and hung them in the entry hall, gesturing toward the sitting room. It was comfortably if conventionally appointed. Oil paintings of pastoral scenes hung on the walls, the wireless had a place of pride on the drinks cabinet, and the sideboard held the usual assortment of long-stemmed wineglasses, tiny sugar-plum-colored espresso cups, and flowered candy dishes.

He leaned in close when he asked, "Would you like a glass of white wine?" I caught a whiff of a fresh, woody scent.

"Wine is good," I lied.

I felt very grown-up. A handsome stranger was offering me drinks.

I corrected myself. *A handsome soon-to-be priest.*

Outside church bells pealed, and he waited for them to end before he spoke. "I'll take the sofa, and you can use the spare bedroom. It used to be my father's."

"That's very kind of you. Are you sure it's no trouble?"

"I wouldn't offer if I was not prepared for you to accept."

The silence drew out between us. At length he asked, "How did your meeting with Emil go?"

"Satisfactory. He'll do as I asked."

"And when he's done. You'll be safe then? The nightmares will stop? The terrible loneliness?"

I flinched. *Am I lonely?* I tried to navigate my way to a safe answer. "A cruel man has my dog," I told him, knowing this made no sense.

He cocked his head.

I tried again. "When I get my dog back I won't be lonely. She's called Simone de Beauvoir."

He smiled at her name, waiting to hear more. After I explained to him about Dr. Unruh, he said, "I don't think you'll get your dog back until you find out what he wants."

I dug my nails in my palms. "I should call him then. Shouldn't I?"

"Tomorrow. You can use the telephone here."

I nodded, dreading what I had to do. "Can we talk about something else now? Anything else."

"Let start with Sartre and Simone de Beauvoir."

I looked at the floor. "I haven't actually read Simone de Beauvoir. But my mother was reading her book right before..." My voice trailed away. It had been on her bedside table when she died.

"We can talk about them anyway." His smile was warm.

We cooked and laughed and listened to Schubert on the hi-fi. The dark wings that had frightened Emil were far away.

We sat after dinner like old friends. Christian talked about his time as a mountain guide in the Himalayas. I wanted to see the places he'd visited on the map he took out, but instead my eyes closed.

I was warm and full. He helped me to the bed, where he'd set out a nightdress, starched and folded. "It belongs to Grandmother. That's all I have."

When he wished me good night and closed the door, I changed and lay down. I fell into slumber like a stone into a pond. Ripples traveled around me and turned into flying swallows and then I was truly asleep.

When the nightmare started, I couldn't remember it was a dream. Dr. Unruh looked at me with his terrible eyes, calling me to my doom. My screams woke me up.

Quiet footsteps, then the weight of a lithe body swinging onto the far side of the bed. I smelled the cedar fresh smell. Christian. All of a sudden, I was wide-awake.

He plumped a pillow against the wall, sat, and stretched out his pajamad legs. His hand found mine and squeezed, driving the terror back deep in a hole.

He did not say anything, and I did not ask. I was sure Father Kneipp would have been very angry to find him on a bed so close to a girl in her nightclothes. When I was nearly asleep, he pried my fingers off his hand and slid away. "I'm sorry. I need to get some rest," he whispered.

I was just so grateful I would have thanked his God for the loan of him, if I'd thought there was a God to hear me.

11. Breakdown

We took our coffee on the balcony, though the sky was a dirty gray this morning. I wanted to feel the cool autumn wind on my face.

Christian drank his black as he sorted through the mail. He hadn't done his hair up in a braid yet, and it fell in a shimmering wave over his shoulders. He studied one letter, a light blue airmail one, and pushed it to the side, shaking his head in exasperation.

"Who is Mr. R. Singh?" I asked. The recipient's name was printed in messy block letters, and the address was hard to make out.

"No idea. The postman brings me any mail with an unusual name, on the presumption that I might know who it is. It's tedious."

Christian wrote "Not at This Address" and put it at the bottom of the pile. He looked at the street below, studying the office workers in their puffy skirts, and the men with their hats and umbrellas. A svelte woman, perfectly coiffed, went by in a tight red dress and he raised his eyebrows appreciatively.

"Ooh la la. Chic. She must be French," I pointed out.

He chuckled. "Western women are a mystery to me."

I set down my coffee resolutely. "Yesterday was lovely. But I can't believe you're helping me. This is too much to ask of a stranger."

"It's a promise I made, Peppa-la. To help someone in need."

I narrowed my eyes, studying him. He was handsome, but not pretty like Rock Hudson. More like Gregory Peck, with slanted luminous eyes. Christian had done a lot of living. He looked honest, though.

It must be that religion thing.

His smile was tight as he turned his head away from my scrutiny. "Seen enough? If so, I suggest I get us some croissants and you take a bath."

I flushed as I realized I hadn't bathed in four days. Most people here only bathed weekly, but I'd picked up the habit of daily baths in Boston's warm summers.

"That would be good, yes."

A tense silence enveloped us. "What is it?" he asked.

I felt sick, the coffee gathering in my throat. But I had to know.

"You'd better get the morning paper while you're out," I said.

"I was planning to."

I lay in the tub and scrubbed and scrubbed till my skin hurt, washing away invisible blood. The contrast between our civilized evening last night and the horror in Gonten made me feel crazy. What kind of poison would make a sister maul her brother or a woman take out her eye? I doubted mescaline or ergot derivatives drove anyone to those extremes. Dr. Unruh had come up with something new.

I'd turn twenty the following Saturday, which meant I'd have control over all my bank accounts, no matter what my aunt said about me needing adult guidance. The Monday after, I planned to visit the criminal lawyer with the proof of the hallucinogen. It had driven Hans Wäspi mad, and I'd had to kill him to defend myself.

Sounded plausible.

A deep sigh escaped me. I pulled down the towel to dry myself and pulled on the tatty clothes from the Mission.

Nice women didn't defend themselves like that. They might scream and protest. Not break someone's neck. They'd wonder how I learned that. I wondered myself.

The other problem with that scenario was it only helped me. It didn't help Simone.

I smelled Christian's bakery-fresh croissants before I even saw him. He'd set them on the kitchen table, along with strawberry jam and butter.

"I think the person downstairs is home. She must have heard me draw the bath after you went out," I said.

"So?"

"What if she says something to your grandmother?" I was familiar with the habits of neighbors.

He thought it over. "I suppose Vreni might. Grandmother would be upset. Nothing new. I often make her nervous."

So he wasn't close to them. My maternal grandmother owned a grand estate near Cong, a small village in County Mayo. I hadn't heard from her since Da and I had visited in 1951.

"Grandmothers," I said, rolling my eyes. "I find you very calming." I hoped I wasn't flirting.

"When I went swimming with Stefan, Grandmother saw the tattoo. That alarmed her. When she had her friends over for dinner, I got up and left the table without saying goodbye. That offended her."

I creased my brow. "That *is* rude."

"It's not rude in Bhutan." He wiped the crumbs off the table with his hands. "Also, Grandmother doesn't like my mother." He stared at the ground while he said it, and a muscle twitched in his jaw.

No more questions about that then.

On the street underneath, a Rottweiler pulled on its leash. The older woman walking it cried out in exasperation, cuffing him. The dog hung its head. I winced.

"It's time for me to make that call to Germany."

⁓

The Munich operator informed me that Dr. Ludwig Unruh had a private number. I argued and pleaded with her but got nowhere. The secretary at the Munich University Department of Anthropology wasn't helpful either. Dr. Unruh had taken a sabbatical. No, she could not, under any circumstances, give out his home number. No, she did not know when he would be checking in with the office.

I slammed down the receiver, picturing Simone trussed up in a dark closet or bound to an exam table, howling while being injected with Compound T. My hands started sweating.

Christian had sat close by while I dialed. "You didn't want to talk about Unruh yesterday. Maybe it's time you did."

"Have you dedicated your life to helping people? Is that it?" I waited. If he said yes, I'd keep quiet. I didn't believe in that myth. Doctors became doctors so they could tinker with people. Priests, so they could control others.

Instead he said, "This is a unique situation. If I were going to call the police, I'd have done so yesterday. You need to trust me."

He wasn't asking for my trust. He commanded it with his composure.

I took a deep breath and started by describing the De Penas, with their occult books and unsettling habits. I ended with Dr. Unruh's abduction of my dog. He just sat afterwards. I didn't get the feeling he was frightened or confused. There was a settling stillness about him.

"Unruh's a demon," he finally said.

I made a diagram of intersecting lines on the pad by the phone table. "I still can't think of how to find Dr. Unruh's telephone number. Even demons have telephones, don't they?"

"Don't mock me. I mean he's a dangerous man, a prisoner of darkness, without perspective. He's looking for salvation. Through you."

Ashamed of my sarcastic remark, I tried to understand Christian. "Oh, right. Stefan thought I was an angel. So you think I can save the demon?"

He shook his head. "For some, death is the only salvation."

I thought of the phrase I'd seen in the occult book. *I am a god of War and of Vengeance.* "I don't want to be an angel of death."

"You're no angel. You've already killed someone. Haven't you?" I heard no threat in his soft voice.

A pain stabbed in my chest. "No. I didn't. It wasn't me." I sounded weak, apologetic.

"Who was it?"

I looked down, bewildered. "But it was me." I choked on the words.

His palm touched his chest. "Open your heart. Don't run from your feelings."

The pain was worse. I fell to the floor, dragging down the telephone, which hit with a loud crash.

"For the love of God, stop," I moaned.

"You need a drink," he muttered, and got a bottle of schnapps from the cabinet. He took a few swigs himself before he handed it to me.

I gulped it. It eased my chest, but only for a moment. "It hurts so much. I'm having a heart attack."

"No. That's what your conscience feels like."

I lay there for a moment, stunned. My eyes pricked with the first tears, then the flood came. I pulled a brocaded pillow from the sofa, rocking back and forth with it, and bit down on a corner. I wouldn't scream.

My sobs gave way to sniffling, and at last, thankfully, to silence. I looked up cautiously, expecting to be alone.

Christian hadn't moved. He sat like a rock on his chair, arms crossed, face impassive.

I broke for the bathroom and cold water. A stranger's face stared back at me from the mirror. Puffy eyes, red swollen skin. Grotesque.

I couldn't go back out and face him.

After a bit there was a cautious rapping on the door. "Are you all right?"

I cleared my throat. "Aren't you angry with me for making a scene?"

"Angry with you?"

"I acted like a hysterical female."

"Peppa-la, didn't you cry when your father died?"

"Of course not. He wouldn't have liked that."

"Oh." A pause. "I doubt I'm like him. Why don't you come out now? I'll fix you Tibetan-style butter tea."

I splashed more cold water on my face. By the time I reached the living room it was ready.

I sipped. The taste was milky, bland, but soothing.

"How'd you like it?"

"It's ... odd."

"You should taste it in Tibet. Made with rancid yak butter."

I didn't have the energy to answer him. Crying had drained me.

"It's about time for lunch."

"I'm not hungry." I pulled on my fingers, hating my big, ugly knuckles. The clock on the wall sounded like a hammer in the quiet of the living room. "I killed Mr. Wäspi. He was probably going to hurt me, but it wasn't his fault."

"Yesterday's article didn't explain much."

"They were a family, and they set on each other. I feel terrible for them. It's so sad." I closed my eyes, wanting to shut out the normalcy of the room with its African violets and crocheted lace doilies. "And the woman who brought me the drink was only a little older than me. Miss Eugster. She's probably dead too."

"I'm going to telephone Stefan. If they've found her, he would have heard." He looked meaningfully toward the balcony. "Want some fresh air?"

"I suppose." I trudged out and threw myself into the chair, staring at nothing. After a while, I heard the voice inside stop, and steps went into the kitchen. I smelled onions frying. The thought of food repulsed me.

The Wäspi family would never eat again. They were boxed up in some desolate graveyard, without any relatives left to mourn them.

The tears started up, soft but steady.

When Christian came outside, I realized hours had gone by. I'd been staring at the clouds as they turned from gray to charcoal. My cheeks were cold from the bitter wind.

He'd brought me a cup of hot linden tea. "Are you all right?"

I made an effort to talk. "You reached Stefan?"

"Yes. They haven't found Miss Eugster."

"She's dead."

"Odd the body would be missing. The police came to talk to Stefan's uncle. He overheard. It's hard to tell because of the fire, but there might be some clothes and shoes gone. Like she left."

"Did Stefan tell you Dr. Unruh poisoned everyone?"

"No. He thinks the devil came to punish the family."

"Why would he think that? What an awful thing ... how could any family deserve that? See, that's what I hate about religion!" I realized I'd raised my voice and stopped myself.

When I spoke again my voice was husky. "What's the devil punishing me for, then?"

"I don't know. Besides, you're alive, not dead like them."

It felt like Christian had struck me. I clenched my hands.

"I wish I wasn't. I can't stand feeling this way."

"What way?"

"So sad. And guilty."

"We can do something good. I've been making preparations, hoping you'll join me. It's the fifth day since the family died. Once five days have passed, the Bardo visions become less divine, and it will be too late to perform funeral rites."

I was stunned. "A funeral rite?"

"Come on. You'll feel better."

"I'd feel like a hypocrite, praying."

"Mourn their passing. No faith is required. Just join me."

Christian had made an altar on the coffee table. Cut geranium blossoms and candles surrounded his butter lamp. Behind that was a silver frame with a photo of a kind-looking, bald, man.

"Is that your grandfather?"
"That's the fourteenth Dalai Lama."
"Is he the king of Bhutan?"
Christian groaned.
"What? Is Bhutan Communist too?"
"No. It's not important." He arranged a book and a bell. The bell was the size of my hand, almost as big as a cow bell. The covers of the book were made of copper, engraved with figures and runes. I bent forward to see it more closely. The workmanship was exquisite.

"My grandfather got this in trade. He makes musical instruments for the monasteries."

The paper inside was handmade, a rough weave. He pointed to the beautiful cursive text. "Made with an inked wooden block."

"Quite a religious artifact."

"It's a treasure. Prayers. You spoke the Hindi greeting as if you enjoyed it. I thought you'd have more tolerance for another culture's religious artifacts." He pronounced the words "religious artifacts" very carefully.

I flushed. "I just didn't want to pretend."

"You'll feel better if you find some way to mourn. You can't draw a chemical formula for sadness and horror. You have to experience it."

"Norepinephrine and epinephrine, dopamine depletion." But I knew what he meant. I lit the butter lamp the way he showed me and repeated the words of the opening ritual after him, slowly and rhythmically. They did bring me peace. A placebo.

But still.

I was surprised by what Christian showed me next. He'd penciled a detailed portrait of the Wäspi family.

"How did you..." I whispered.

"Newspaper photograph."

The drawings were excellent. The faces leaped off the pages at me—round anxious Ursula, rough Hans, the wrinkled face of their mother.

He propped the portrait against the butter lamp. There was a photo on the table nearby, face down. I looked at it expectantly, but he made no move toward it.

"I'll ring the bell before we start the actual prayers for the dead. My conch shell broke, so I want you to make a conch sound like this." He demonstrated, cupping his hands in front of his mouth.

"I'll feel silly."

He gave me a look.

"Of course, Christian. Just tell me when."

⁓

We were at the chanting for so long I started worrying about missing my appointment with Emil. Not that I wanted to go. Our voices sent a soothing resonance through my chest. Christian had explained we were urging the souls on toward a better reincarnation.

Privately, I also sent thoughts Hans's way. *I'm really sorry. I hope it didn't hurt. I'm really sorry.*

Then Christian grabbed the portrait and thrust it into the flame of the butter lamp.

"No! Don't. That was good," I protested.

"I have to. We can't cremate the actual bodies. Stefan said they're being buried. But cremation or air burial prevents the bodies from being attacked by vampires."

I watched the flames obliterate the faces. Something in me eased a bit.

"When I get a chance I'll take the ashes and mix them with clay—make a stupa. A little sacred tower. I'll hike up to Aescher-Wildkirchli, build it there."

I knew that place. It was a religious site near the village of Gonten. A hermit had lived there in a cave, centuries ago.

He continued, "I'll visit Stefan too. He's shaken up by all this. Lots of nightmares."

Stefan reminded me of the church. I'd been so caught up in the rite I'd overlooked something strange. "You seem like you know so much about this—what is it—some eastern religion?"

Christian watched the flames. "Yes. Buddhism with Bon-Po mixed in. The animistic faith that preceded it."

"Won't that conflict with the church, when you become a priest?"

He rocked back on his heels. The Oriental cast to his eyes was pronounced, his cheekbones like scimitars in the shadows. "Did you really think I was a seminary student?"

"I called you Father."

"I told you I wasn't."

"I obviously made a mistake. You could have corrected me."

"That's not our way. Not until we know someone well."

"You already know me better than anyone alive."

His eyes shone. "I like what I know, *didi*. You're a *rara avis*."

A rare bird. He was more right than he knew. "Is a *didi* like a dodo?"

"Not quite." A hint of a smile. "A dodo is an extinct species of bird. *Didi* means little sister. I thought you spoke Hindi?"

"Not really. I was just showing off," I admitted. One of the Harvard microbiology professors was Indian. I hesitated, embarrassed. "Am I like a little sister because I ask dumb questions?"

"No." That quirk of the lips again. "I feel ... close to you. Is *didi* an acceptable form of address?"

"I like that better than Peppa-la."

He studied me intently. The silence stretched on, gathering tension. Entranced, I watched as his hand reached up to stroke my cheek. He leaned over. He was going to kiss me. Tears started in my eyes from the wonder of it.

His sleeve brushed the mysterious photograph from the altar, and it fell like an autumn leaf.

12. Spoken For

I CLOSED MY EYES, WAITING FOR THE KISS THAT NEVER CAME. When I opened them again, Christian held the photograph. It portrayed two Asians: a toddler and an attractive woman. They had the same round face, the same tilt to their head.

But the boy looked even more like Christian.

A weight settled on me. Christian wasn't meeting my eyes. We both knew what had almost happened.

I tried to keep my voice light. "Who's this then?"

"That's Sherub. He's two."

Too young to be Christian's brother.

"Do you like children?" he asked.

"I suppose." I didn't know any. "Why'd you have the photograph on the altar?"

"I prayed for them too. I always do."

I coughed. "Are you related ... I mean are those...?"

His eyes were wary. "Yes, that's my son." I wanted to ask how he could leave his son behind, because he obviously had. He'd deserted his wife and son, and they were sad and lonely, and I was too. How could I have trusted him?

Instead, I got up, a little dizzy. "I'm meeting Emil soon."

He stood up too. "Let's look through Grandmother's closet for a hat with a wide brim. And stay out of the light as much as you can."

I'd forgotten to look at the newspaper, caught up in my grief. I couldn't bear to look it now. It was enough to know I needed to be careful.

And not just of the people on the street.

Of everyone.

~

I'd reached the door of the flat before I called out, "Goodbye."

I was in my baggy secondhand sweater, coat in one hand, satchel with the purse in the other. It had warmed up outside; I didn't need a coat. Unless I didn't come back.

Christian was fast. He reached the door before I could get out and down the stairs. Though it's true I slowed down at the last moment.

"Come back in," he said, his voice level.

"I'll be late."

"I'm sure he'll wait. I would."

Our voices were carrying in the stairwell. I let myself be pulled back in and stared at the parquet floor, a sulky child.

"I called my grandmother today. Told her a pipe was broken, and the kitchen floor was flooded. She'll stay at the hot springs a few more days."

"Why did you do that?"

"So it would be safe for you to stay here." He looked at my satchel and coat. "What time will you be back from your meeting with Emil? I'm going out, but I'll be back then."

Right then, I knew what he meant about it being easier not to correct someone's misapprehension. "Oh, I don't know. Might be quite late."

I wasn't going to get away with evasion. He sat on the entryway chair and held my wrist with an iron grip. "You're angry at me now. I understand. I was close to doing something reckless."

"It's all right," I said listlessly. That minute, I didn't care if he was married or not. I'd never been properly kissed before, and I ached with loss. If I ended up in prison or the asylum, I might grow old before I got another chance.

"You're thinking about not coming back. Don't take the risk. You can't go to a hotel. The police will be watching your home."

I frowned at him. "Like I said, you know all about me. But I don't know much about you. That bothers me, Christian."

"Then let's start with my name. I prefer Tenzin. Christian's a joke between me and my mother, though it is the name on my passport."

"I don't understand." He hadn't let go of my hand, and I tried to pull it away. His fingers tightened.

"The holy missionary, Father Engel, was in her bed after a month in Dehra Dun. When he got her knocked up, of course he wanted to get married. She loves Father, but he doesn't understand our ways. She's not going to go traipsing down the aisle in a long white dress. Not even to save his face."

"Priests can get married?"

He looked at me for a moment, surprised. "Protestant priests can. Didn't you have religious instruction?"

"I went to school at Milford Academy in Boston. It wasn't part of the curriculum," I said. "Tell me about your parents."

"My father was angry and made her life difficult, so she called me Christian. A living rebuke to my father's hypocrisy."

"But you grew up at the mission," I asked, reflecting on his excellent Swiss-German.

"I tried hard to make it up to my father, and to make peace between them. He can't send her away. He'll never get another nurse as good as her. And she just laughs him off."

He looked at me intently. "People from different cultures should not fall in love with each other. It's just asking for trouble."

"Lucky for you then that you have an Indian wife," I shot back.

"Pema's from Bhutan," he said shortly. "Does that bother you too?"

"You left your little boy."

He smiled. "Of course he misses me, but he has his mother and his uncle, his grandparents, fresh air."

"Why are you here?"

His eyes glanced at the clock. "Short answer: I have a useless degree in German language and philosophy. I'm here to enroll in the University of Zurich's doctorate program in psychology. I want to turn my life around. Helping you is part of it. But if I want to help you, perform my dharma, I must maintain a clear mind."

"Perform your what?"

"Dharma is the work one does to accumulate spiritual benefit. I'm a guide, a path seeker. But I have to find a better way to do it."

I got up, pulling my hand free. "I'm going to be late. Emil might leave."

"I'm meeting my friend Jakob for drinks, but I'll be back after 9 PM. I'll be waiting for you."

I nodded once and ducked as he tried to kiss me on the cheek in the Swiss way. It was wrong coming from him. "Thanks for the prayers today," I said, meaning it, and I walked out into the night.

―――

Emil was on the bench in the park when I got there. He kept looking around.

"Seeing if I've been followed?"

"Just alert. You were odd yesterday."

I knew what he was talking about. He hadn't brought the pet mouse today, thankfully.

"I suppose I'm nervous. I don't like failure," Emil explained.

"What failure?"

"I didn't make any progress on the chemical isolation of your poison. I had to hide the rats' bodies at the bottom of the trash bin."

"What!"

"They chewed each other to bits. Then I was delayed trying to get in your house. The police let me in when I said I'd come to check the mail on behalf of your aunt. Which I did, by the way."

He plunked down my old schoolbag. It was full of books, as well an assortment of letters, many of them the blue envelope of overseas mail. I checked the books first: De Quincy's *Confessions of an English Opium Eater*. Baudelaire's *Artificial Paradises*. A book by Moreau, *Hashish and Mental Perception*. Of course Aldous Huxley's book, *The Doors of Perception*. Two pharmacology texts rounded out the offerings.

"You've got a lot of homework."

"I can handle it."

"You're going to figure out how to isolate that compound?" Emil scoffed.

"Sure," I said, trying to sound confident. "You're not making much progress."

"You're smart. But not all that smart."

I hated when people said things like that. I watched my hands shake and willed them to stop. "I did get into Radcliffe. That's Harvard's sister school." I'd noticed two envelopes with the school's letterhead in the stack of mail. Probably wondering what had happened. A deep sigh escaped me.

He asked the question I'd been dreading. "Why not talk to Alex Kaufmann? He's an obvious choice. He discovered LSD. He's got his own lab at Sandoz."

"I can't take the risk."

"He's your godfather. He would do anything for you. Which is more than I can say about myself."

Whatever grudge Emil nursed all these years, it wasn't completely gone.

The last time I'd seen Alex was at the funeral. I'd been wearing my black cigarette pants and thick white bobby socks with loafers. The pants were the only black article of clothing I had. I chewed my last remaining stick of Doublemint gum frantically to hold back my tears. He'd reprimanded me in front of everyone, asking me to go spit out my gum, and then offered me his wife's coat to cover my "unsuitable clothes."

"I won't be contacting Dr. Kaufmann," I said.

He nodded. "Still stubborn, like you always were. Got you something else besides the books."

"What?" I looked at the big Globus department store bag he held out toward me, making no move to take it.

"The clothes you're wearing make you look like a tramp. People look."

His tone made the comment a reprimand. "I didn't ask you to go shopping."

"Yes, but I'm associating with you, taking a big risk. It could affect my future career."

I couldn't bring myself to say thank you. The dress rustled as I took it out from the folded tissue paper. It was crushed brown velvet, cut on the bias. A pair of sensible but fashionable calf's leather shoes with low heels lay underneath. He'd even thought to buy nylons.

"Why, this is lovely," I said, surprised. He'd guessed my measurements, and the color suited me perfectly.

"I love to shop." He flushed. "Actually, that's because my fiancée is a top model. That's the only reason I even know about clothes."

"Your fiancée!" He was still the boy I'd caught newts with, in my mind.

"I hope you're not disappointed. We used to be inseparable, after all. Remember we got teased about getting married when we grew up."

"I hadn't remembered that. But I certainly don't aspire to be your girlfriend."

"You don't think I'm handsome?"

Emil needed to be taken down a peg or two. "The man that's helping me is much better-looking than you."

He looked offended. "Oh, I'm too Jewish for you? Is that it?"

"You're being ridiculous. Da's best friend at Harvard, Dr. Aaron, was Jewish."

"Your father's a different story. He likes Jewish women too."

"What the hell is that supposed to mean? Ainslie was Irish."

Emil lit a cigarette with his silver lighter, pausing to draw in deeply, before he spoke again. "Why do you call your mother Ainslie?"

"She's been dead a long time. I presume your family *did* know she died, right?"

"I would have come to the funeral, but my father wouldn't let me."

Something was tugging at the edge of my mind. "What did you mean with that remark about Jewish women?"

He sat down, narrowing his pretty blue eyes at me. He had long lashes, almost girlish. "I guess it's wrong to hold you accountable."

I wished I had a stick of gum. "What? Just tell me. Why did you abandon me? You were the only friend I had," I wailed.

There. It was out before I could stop it. I liked Milford Academy and got good grades, but it wasn't as if I'd made a lot of new friends in Boston. For years, I'd appeared at our picnics and beach parties with a braid and long skirts, while the other girls wore flip hairdos with headbands and clamdiggers with matching blouses.

Emil was quiet.

"Tell me," I said, calm now.

"Look, your father and my mother had an affair."

It felt like he'd sucker-punched me. All the air went out of me, and I felt a piercing pain. "Are you sure?"

"My father was sure. That's why he divorced Mother. And your father ran."

The endless job applications: Cornell, Berkeley, Stanford, till finally Harvard took him, and he danced through our living room in joy. He was so sure he'd make full professor and get tenure. Or was he?

"We left because he couldn't stand to stay in our house after Ainslie died."

Emil gave his cigarette two firm taps and dislodged the ash on one of the ever-present slugs wending its way around a clump of fall anemones. "Maybe. But I think everyone saw it as an admission of guilt."

Embarrassment made me bury my head in my hands. I didn't mind that Da slept with Gladys. She was a daring Radcliffe debutante, and he was a widower. But for Da to have done this to David Nussbaum, his closest Swiss friend besides Alex. And to my mother…

Emil's voice interrupted my thoughts. "I need to go soon. What do you want me to do about your compound?"

"Umm. I haven't had a chance to look through everything. Why don't you do some screens? Marquis reagent. That would be good." I tried to look wise.

"Peppa?"

"Yes?"

"Please take my advice. We need Alex."

I knew where this was going. "Alex might turn me in," I whispered.

"Just let me telephone him. I can't betray you. I don't even know the name of your new, mysterious friend. The one who's so handsome."

I thought it over, looking at the daunting pile of books I intended to study. I was a fast reader but no genius. "Fine. Talk to Alex. I'll meet you tomorrow morning at ten. Where we threw the water balloons that one time and got into loads of trouble." I smiled at the ghost of the memory. "You can tell me what he said then."

Emil stubbed out his cigarette carefully before putting it in an empty cigar box, which he placed in his trouser pocket, presumably for later disposal. "It's not really any of my business, but are you safe with this foreign man? He's not—I don't know—molesting you?" He shuddered, as if repulsed.

"He's studying to be a priest. I'm absolutely safe." The truth was I missed Christian, or rather Tenzin, already. "He's waiting for me. You'll come tomorrow?"

"I'll drive my car. Look for a spanking new Chevrolet Bel Air. Red as danger."

I used the park lavatory to change into the dress and shoes. The grandmother's hat was a broad-brimmed brown felt with a few feathers stuck in it; it actually didn't look too bad with the outfit. I blew out my lips, making a fish face at myself in the mirror. I felt silly in my finery, but Emil was right. I'd attract less attention if I didn't dress like a tramp.

Still, I felt conspicuous on the street and stayed in the shadows. I was glad when I reached the safety of Pilger Street. The ubiquitous Vreni seemed to be home again, so I unlocked the front door as quietly as I could and stole up the stairs.

Tenzin opened the door in response to my knock, still holding a book in his hand. I glanced down; he'd been reading Jung's *Modern Man in Search of a Soul*.

"Father knew someone who works with Carl Jung," I said, setting down my bag of books. "Maybe you could meet Jung someday."

He hung up my coat. "You know someone who likes to shop as well. You look wonderful. How'd you pull this off?"

"That boy Emil bought them for me. He said I was too noticeable in the other clothes." When I twirled for Tenzin in the dress, he laughed. "Let me get you a drink."

"Actually, I'd prefer hot Ovaltine. But let me tell you the good news first. Our family lawyer's looking for a defense attorney right now; as soon as I turn twenty I'll hire him. It's only a week away! You can come visit me at my real house."

I stopped at his expression. "What is it?"

"I turned on the radio to get the evening news. First there was a missing person's bulletin. The radio announcer stated your name, age, description. Asked people to call the police station."

I jumped up and ran to the window, as if I'd see a crowd gathered there, pointing. I whirled around. "I'm safe here though, right?"

"I hope so. But there's worse. You haven't read tonight's edition of the paper. You'd better take a look."

The *Basel Nachrichten* had a headline under the Basler City Mirror section. The bold headline shouted: **With Her Own Two Hands She Broke His Neck.**

13. Insinuations of Insanity

I READ THE ARTICLE ONCE. THEN I READ IT AGAIN, MY NAILS digging into my palm.

The first paragraph described the crime and the deaths of the Wäspi family members. I was referred to as "the suspicious party who fled the scene of the crime."

The second paragraph began with the bolded promise: **A look into an unbalanced mind.**

I was never mentioned by name, of course, because of Swiss privacy laws. The article identified me as a witness to the Gonten massacre. I was described as an orphan whose concerned relatives had taken her in.

A Dr. Ganz from the University of Basel Psychiatric Clinic had spoken to a reporter regarding the case. "Based on the reports of her relatives, the young woman may be suffering from sexual identity disorder and asocial inclinations. She insists on dressing and acting as a man."

Was this because I'd told Aunt Madeleine I preferred playing chess to having huge wire rollers jammed into my hair in a beauty salon? And once, before I was angry with them, I'd done my James Cagney imitation. What provincial stupidity.

I looked up to see Tenzin's eyes on me. "Still want an Ovaltine?"

"Let me have whatever you're having."

I knocked down the schnapps he brought and gagged. "I'm going to be sick."

I raced to the bathroom, stubbing my toe on the lintel. Afterwards, I rinsed my mouth out.

My head spun. This was so unfair. I'd even had sex with a man, which proved how wrong everyone was. It wasn't my fault Patrick Doherty, my father's graduate student, had disappeared from our house two days later without an explanation.

Tenzin came to the bathroom door and knocked. "Is everything all right?"

I ducked out, my cheeks hot. That was the second time he'd had to retrieve me from his grandmother's bathroom.

"I'm not a homosexual," I said, once I'd recovered my composure.

"I know you're not." Tenzin took me gently by the hand. "You shouldn't gulp schnapps on an empty stomach. Come to the kitchen table and I'll fix you something. The bread's a little old, but the cheese is fresh."

I plunked myself on the kitchen stool as Tenzin set to work. So much for turning twenty, hiring a lawyer, and moving back into my house on the Rheinweg. If I were declared insane I would lose all rights. I'd get insulin therapy. Some patients even got lobotomies.

I supposed I could offer up my lack of virginity as proof that I liked men, but that brought its own set of problems. If I could just contact Patrick...

Tenzin slipped the plate right in front of me. "Eat."

"Not hungry. Why are you so set on feeding me?"

"I told you. I was a mountain guide. Hungry people don't do well in rugged terrain."

I took one bite of the sandwich and chewed. The bread stuck in my throat.

My aunt and uncle had twisted my harmless remarks. Even if I did crave the freedom men enjoyed, how did that make me mentally ill?

"I can't trust anyone," I muttered.

"I know what it's like to be singled out for being different. That's why you can trust me."

"And for some reason you've decided to take me on as your project. Is it because you're studying psychology? You wanted to investigate the crazy girl?"

"Be sensible. This newspaper article hadn't even come out when I met you."

He stalked over to the kitchen drawer and returned with a pair of sharp scissors. "Speaking of being different..." He laid them on the table between us, his shoulders tense and rigid.

I looked at the scissors, puzzled.

"Each time you appear on the street with me, you become noticeable because I am noticeable. Everyone is looking for you now. We can't afford to take chances." He touched his braid self-consciously, and I understood.

"No," I snapped, before I'd even thought about it.

"I can't do anything about the color of my skin. But I can change my hair," Tenzin said stubbornly.

"I like your hair."

"Western men have short hair."

"Dr. Schultes showed us photographs of American Indians at a peyote ceremony, and one man's hair reached the small of his back."

"Peyote-ingesting Indians. That proves my point."

"I'm not cutting your hair. I've had enough of people trying to change me. I won't do it to someone else."

His face darkened, and he laughed. "Then help me while I try on grandfather's hats."

As Tenzin looked for a hat large enough to hide his pinned braid, I ruminated. The newspaper article made my decisions easier in a way. If I couldn't hire my own lawyer, I'd keep hiding and find a way to get Simone back. I'd concentrate on that.

Tenzin adjusted a homburg in front of the mirror, pushed the last wisps of stray braid under it, and then turned to me. "This ought to work."

I nodded my head in approval. "One problem solved. But I have to find a way to telephone Dr. Unruh." I drummed my fingers on the table, my mind a blank.

Tenzin shrugged. "You should get some sleep. Think about it right before you drift off. You might get an answer."

My eyes must have shown doubt.

"Once you get in touch with what's inside you, you'll find there's a whole other world." Tenzin's smile was sudden and radiant.

In my dream, Ludwig Unruh and I danced a courtly minuet. We were both dressed in rich brocades. My ruffly dress had cascades of fine lace. The music though, was odd, tribal drums and a reedy flute.

"Enjoying our dance?" he asked.

"I don't want to be partners." I realized what spoke lay behind my girl face. It was a falcon head, and I saw through *her* eyes.

"But we are." Dr. Unruh's face turned into a finely made portrait on translucent paper. Behind it lurked a hairy snout, jagged teeth. His eyes, profound, studied me from behind the holes in his mask.

"You know me," he said. "I want you to find me."

We kept dancing, our steps small and delicate, and the jungle grew as we moved, lapped at us with snakelike vines and big brilliant blossoms, dropping dew like teardrops.

Gradually the dream merged with images from the night of the massacre. A red full moon peeped through the lianas. I glimpsed a patterned snake as thick as a tree trunk hidden in the leaves. She regarded us with amusement before slithering away.

Then Ursula slumped on the bench, holding her ripped and torn belly. Her mother ran toward me, socket gaping; on the spike of the umbrella she carried, her impaled eye, still intact, looked at me.

Can you see now, can you see now, the wind through the lianas whispered.

I wanted to scream, but I had lost my voice. All that came out were the croaks of a wounded bird.

But Tenzin had heard. Half-asleep, I felt his body settle on the bed, and reached out for the comfort of his hand. After a while he tried to pull away. "Stay," I said. "Sleep here."

There was an awkward pause, and I heard him shift. A pillow edged its way between us. "Just in case, *didi*." Tenzin said. "I wouldn't want to…" His voice trailed off, and our hands met again over the pillow. He might just as well be a priest.

I woke up right after dawn and heard his even breathing close beside me. The pillow in-between us had magically disappeared. The woody smell rose from him, mingled with soap.

I was half-dizzy with sleep, faint from some nameless feeling stirring in me. I reached out with my hand, skimmed the side of his pajama-clad thigh. He felt so solid. So real.

He stirred in his sleep and murmured Pema's name. My hand jumped as if it had touched a hot stove.

Or did he say my name?

I lay stiffly, flushed and itchy. I couldn't get back to sleep now.

It was too early to call. I got dressed and skimmed Aldous Huxley's accounts of mescaline, looking for anything that resembled my experience. I'd set it aside and was studying the pharmacology textbook by the time Tenzin ambled in, still wearing his striped pajamas.

His long hair was tangled, and he flicked it out of his face. "I hope I didn't bother you when I slept."

I fidgeted, remembering how I'd reached out to him, like a greedy child stealing candy. What would he think if he knew about the drunken episode with Patrick?

"It's not me that would mind. It's Pema."

His smile vanished. He opened the balcony door. As the cool breeze came in, he began doing a series of slow stretching movements, his arms flowing up and out.

I put down my book, fascinated. "What's that?"

"One of our quaint customs. Qi Gong," he said. "It requires concentration to perform correctly."

I took the hint and went to rummage in the kitchen for some Ovaltine.

Finally, it was nine. I was trembling.

"May I call Germany again?"

He was leafing through Baudelaire's book, absorbed. "Give it a try."

When the international operator put me through to the University of Munich, I made my voice sound like that of an American person speaking German. "This is Miss Camp, calling on behalf of the *Journal of Ethnobotany*. Our issue is almost at press time, and I still haven't received the corrections from Dr. Unruh."

The secretary sighed. She didn't know when Dr. Unruh would be available.

"I'm afraid without the corrections we cannot go to print. I know he'll be very disappointed."

"What's the article about?"

Dr. Unruh had met Mrs. De Pena in Brazil, which was also where my mother had died from malaria. I knew something about Brazil from the times I'd sat in on Dr. Schultes's classes at Harvard.

"That tribe by the Orinoco delta and the witch doctor's use of the flowering vine."

"Let me find you his phone number."

I jotted it down, noting it had a Munich exchange, then said goodbye. Outside the day had started off sunny, but now clouds were building. A red leaf spiraled down from a tree outside.

I made a mental list of what I wanted to know: Why had he taken Simone? Why had he performed the experiment? What was the action of the drug he'd administered?

After taking a deep breath, I dialed.

I hadn't expected him to answer right away. His voice was distracted. "Unruh. Yes?"

I was overcome by longing for Simone's soft fur, her familiar smell, her trusting brown eyes. "Give me my dog," I blurted out.

"Ah, the lovely Miss *Waldvogel*. I was hoping you'd call."

His accent wasn't Bavarian. He must not be from Munich originally. "It's not as if you left a calling card."

"If you hadn't been ingenious enough to find my telephone number, you'd hardly be worth the trouble."

"What trouble?"

"The trouble of cultivating your acquaintance."

My face got hot. Did he think we were at a tea dance? "You stole my dog. If you hurt her..." I let the rest of the statement hang, as I realized how ridiculous I sounded. What would I do, exactly?

But he took me seriously. "I like dogs. I'm concerned about yours. She's languishing."

"Can I have her back?" Hope made my voice a thin reed.

"You could be reunited. If you play the game, my dear. Let's start off with the report I need."

I remembered Da: *I need that report, Peppa*. It had been lying next to the dissected rat. I'd been afraid to fetch it.

"The murders, or afterwards?" I asked.

"Everything. I want every detail."

"I can tell you about how those people killed each other because of what you did." My voice rose.

"I am capable of reading between the lines in a newspaper report, Miss Mueller. Of particular interest is the interval between your flight from the Bäsebeiz and the time Mr. Manser found you."

I froze. He'd addressed me by name. That hadn't been in the newspaper. At least not in the Swiss newspapers. Perhaps I'd made the news in Munich. Or was it even worse than that? Did they have posters of me all over Germany? No...

His even breathing pulsed through the receiver.

"The roof?" he finally prompted.

"I can't remember," I admitted.

"But you have some idea."

"Do you understand what happened?"

"You're being evasive. I saw you on the roof that morning. How did you get there?"

One question he didn't know the answer to. If the falcon had protected me, now I wanted to protect her. I couldn't speak.

His voice turned cold. "I find I don't have much patience for your rectitude. It would be a shame if your creature were to be locked up without food or water."

"I thought you liked dogs."

"I do. But I like getting my way even more."

My jaw clenched. "I'll try to remember."

"I expect a full report tomorrow morning. Keep out of the way of the police."

"Why did you..."

Click. He'd hung up.

I sipped my second Ovaltine of the day, more for the warmth than because I was hungry.

I felt chilled. I'd taken his bait, and the trap was closing.

As far as I knew, I was the only one who'd hallucinated becoming a wild creature that night, although I couldn't ask the Wäspi family. Stefan had been caught up in religious fervor. I had no idea what happened to Miss Eugster.

My experience had been different from the other five people there. But why?

I was different from other people anyway. My upbringing should have inured me against the magic of the drug, but my thin veneer of civilization proved to be a lie.

Dr. Unruh had seen that too. He'd known I'd be drawn into the dark currents he'd released that night.

Now he wanted a full report.

I was a scientist's daughter. I knew how experiments worked.

I was the rat.

And when the experiment runs its course, the rat is sacrificed.

14. Scientific Analysis

THE SUNLIGHT WAS BRIGHT OUTSIDE WHEN I LEFT TO MEET Emil, and I longed for yesterday's clouds. I hurried down Mission and across the broad intersection, loud with the clatter of a trolley and the rumble of cars, passing under the arch of the Spalentor. I'd now entered the welcoming shade cast by the multistoried buildings of the Spalenvorstadt, shops on the ground floor and three floors of families above. One of my grandfather's apothecaries had been here, and Da was born above it. The road and trolley tracks arched right past the Tor, forcing oncoming traffic to maintain constant speed to avoid creating a bottleneck. I'd chosen the pickup spot for that reason, hoping to escape scrutiny.

I stayed huddled in the gap between the Spalentor left-hand turret and the bookstore at Schützengraben 1. It was a good place to hide, whether you'd just thrown water balloons during the riotous Basler Carnival or were evading the police for more serious reasons. I stepped out every few minutes to check the progress of the tower clock. Emil was late.

Since it was warmer today, I'd taken a man's straw boater from the apartment wardrobe. I pulled it down further over my face, before realizing that looked conspicuous as well. I fidgeted. If Emil didn't get here soon, I was going to bolt back to the flat.

My hand still tingled from Tenzin's grasp. He'd said, "Have Emil drive you to St. Peters tonight at seven. I'll be waiting for you." Then he'd squeezed my hand. "If you need me, I'll be at the Mission all day."

Emil pulled up in the Chevrolet. He honked, and I ran into the street and tumbled in. He looked as if he'd been awake for hours. His James Dean do was carefully combed into an alluring tumble.

"You were late."

He shrugged. "My mother needed me." His tone was carefully neutral.

"Did you call Alex?"

"Yes. I'm driving you to Sandoz."

"No. I can't take the chance. He doesn't like my American ways."

The light turned red, and we stopped. I ducked my head, aware of cars around us.

"I've already made the decision." He stepped on the gas, and we roared off down the quiet street.

I shook my head. "I'm a fugitive."

"That's what I mean. If I'm to help you, there must be some benefit for myself. That would be working with Alex, possibly making a new discovery."

I blinked. "Is that what this is all about?"

"Maybe I could be co-author if we publish."

"That's a long way in the future. I have other problems right now."

"I'm just telling you what I expect," he said, setting his jaw.

We parked on the side of the one-story plain brick building, at the far end of the parked cars and bikes.

After Emil took a quick look around the lot, I ran to the back door, which led right into Alex's private lab.

The familiar penetrating scent of organic solvents greeted me, along with the fruity aroma of some aldehyde. Alex waited, his round frame perched uncomfortably on a stool. His prominent widow's peak and dark eyes made him look fierce, but I knew better. He got up and kissed me on the cheeks. He smelled like cough drops. "I guess you're too old for me to offer you a honey Zältli? Nearly twenty."

"I had breakfast, thanks." This was our private joke. Before Ainslie died, Da and she had what they called get-away weekends, when they would go somewhere romantic and leave me with friends. One weekend I'd gone to stay with Uncle Alex. His wife Clara was visiting her parents with their three children. Alex was softhearted, no match for a persistent little girl. I'd eaten mostly honey drops and chocolate, eschewing the more sensible options that he tried to tempt me with. The incident earned me my first biochemistry lecture from Da, as he explained the actions of the pancreas and insulin to a seven-year-old.

Alex still studied me. His words made me nostalgic and sad. We'd been so close once.

"Why didn't you come to me at once?"

"I didn't think…" I didn't want to talk about the incident at the funeral, especially not in front of Emil, who was already checking the Bunsen burner connections and setting up ring stands.

"I'm not crazy," I blurted out.

"You're safe with me. I want to help you."

"What you read in the paper It's not true. I even had a boyfriend, in Boston." Patrick Doherty hadn't technically been my boyfriend, but since he boarded at our house, we'd certainly spent enough time together.

Alex rubbed his eyes. "That was odd anyway, for your aunt to involve herself in a public discussion of your behavior." He shot a quick look at Emil, who discreetly lounged against the far counter, and lowered his voice. "What's Pierre La Tour like?"

"I can't stand him. I had a place at Radcliffe, you know? They didn't let me go."

"Radcliffe is expensive and America is far away."

"I'm well off—more than well-off. Or I would be, if I could access my fortune. Now, with doubts being cast on my sanity…"

Alex and I stared at each other. Clearly the same thought had just occurred to both of us.

He coughed delicately. "Please don't say it."

"Madeleine and Pierre are conspiring to get father's fortune by having me declared insane?"

Alex groaned. "Let's not jump to conclusions. I've met Madeleine a few times. I can't believe this of her."

"Pierre *is* heartless." I looked at Alex more closely. Now that I wasn't wracked by grief, I saw a clear-eyed, warmhearted man in front of me. At that moment, I was glad Emil had forced me to come.

"Alex, what about your job? What if someone discovers you're helping me?"

"You don't sound like a crazy person."

I looked at him, questioning.

"You're showing concern for others and are aware of your predicament."

"Yes, I am." I cleared my throat, wishing I had a glass of water.

Alex patted the stool next to him. "Tell me what happened?"

I felt dread gathering in the pit of my stomach. Of course he'd want to know about the night of the attacks. I could barely bring myself to talk about it, but he was risking his good name to help me.

I remained standing. Emil pretended he wasn't listening, but moved closer. "The man…" I started, then cleared my throat.

I tried again. "He ran at me. After he attacked his sister, and she lay dying. She'd just mauled him."

"You must have been very frightened."

"Yes." I buried my head in my hands. "I won't lie. I did kill someone. His name was Hans Wäspi."

"You really broke his neck?" Alex rubbed his temples. "How?"

"I don't know. Something happened to me."

"Tell me the whole story."

I told Alex almost all of it, the savage killings I'd witnessed, Simone's kidnapping, and my flight to Basel. I left out anything with supernatural implications and omitted any details about Tenzin.

Alex's eyes were troubled. "What is your goal now?"

"I want to know what Unruh did to me. How he did it." I got up and paced. "I want to be prepared."

"For what?"

"Facing him."

"You can't go anywhere near the man. If what you allege is true, he's very dangerous."

I bit my lip. "Please help me."

"Did you bring the compound?"

I waved Emil over. "Show him, please."

Emil carefully took the jar out of his satchel and set it on the counter. In the artificial light, the reddish fluid glistened.

Alex stiffened, like a hunting dog on the trail of a fox. "This is it? All you have?"

"Most of it was consumed."

He stared at it a while, and took off the lid. He tentatively moved a finger toward it.

"Don't. Er, don't touch it."

He arched his eyebrow.

Emil explained. "I administered some to rats via oral gavage. They chewed each other to bits."

Alex swirled the jar gently, assessing the color and viscosity. "You think this Dr. Unruh made it? From what?"

I discussed Dr. Unruh's friendship, if that was the term, with the De Penas. "It could be a botanical compound from Brazil."

"That's an awfully big place. Schultes just spent seven years there. He's got listing after listing of potentially psychotropic plants."

I nodded. "The drink was bitter. I'm guessing we're dealing with an alkaloid."

Alex scratched his head. Emil said what was on everyone's mind. "A basic compound containing nitrogen. That really narrows it down. There are only ten thousand or so."

I was burning to share my plans. "If we do those spot tests that give us instant results, that's like a screening, isn't it? I could do a Van Urk's and see if it's an indole." The lysergic acid that Alex had accidentally discovered was an indole.

Alex shook his head.

I felt humiliated. "I'm sorry. I read as much as I could before I fell asleep. What's the correct answer? Should we do the Marquis screen for amphetamines?"

Alex corrected me gently. "No screening tests for now. We've got very little. Let's start with an extraction so we can do the paper ascending chromatography afterwards. Peppa, could you get the dilute hydrochloric acid and hexane. In the cabinet by the sink."

I took down the two labeled brown glass bottles, noticing that the sink was littered with Burette glass, Erlenmeyer flasks, and condensers flecked with particulate matter. Emil fetched the other reagents.

Soon the lab was filled with the penetrating sweetish smell of chloroform. The clank of the glass stirring rod, the rustle of our starched lab coats, and the whoosh of the extraction hood created soothing background noise. Once in a while Alex would hum, usually the bars of Beethoven's Fifth.

By eleven we'd made a slurry of the extract. We still had several hours before it would be dry enough to filter.

"I ought to clean the sink," Emil said. "You got rid of your assistant because of us, didn't you?"

Alex said, "Don't worry about that. How about organizing us some lunch and some coffee? I'd prefer not to go into our break room."

"I'll go to the bakery; get us sandwiches. I'll park down the street this time. Someone might notice the car."

We placed our orders and sat back.

~

Alex normally took his lunch on the stoop, but we settled for opening the back door to let in some fresh air. We overturned one of the big wooden packing crates, now empty, and dragged it over to the backdoor to make a bench. The smell of acetone still lingered on the wood, making me think of Madeleine's bottles of nail polish.

Emil rubbed at a blue splatter on his cuff before taking the last bite of his cheese sandwich. "Your investigation here could take months."

"Or years," I said. The impossibility of the task I'd set myself was becoming evident. But I knew why I'd become obsessed with this.

It was better than thinking about facing Dr. Unruh in person. But how else would I get Simone back and keep my promise to Stefan?

I pulled at a piece of unraveling yarn on my old sweater. "I'm hoping for a miracle. But I can't stay in Basel for too long. The police suspect I'm here." It made my stomach hurt to even say it.

Emil lit a cigarette. I noticed he smoked Lucky Strikes. "Dr. Unruh knows what's in it. Perhaps he's waiting for you. Why else would he take your dog?"

I wrapped the strand of loose yarn around the tip of my finger, watching it turn pink. "Even assuming he wants his lab rat under his direct control, how am I supposed to get there?"

"You'll be twenty next week, is it?" Emil stated.

Alex and I both looked at him. "If I get caught, I'll be packed off to an asylum for a nice rest with insulin therapy, even if I'm rich. Maybe especially if I'm rich."

"We could just go to the police with the remaining liquid. That might be the safest course of action."

Alex said, "That wouldn't necessarily clear Peppa. There's always the chance she could have made it herself."

"Why would the police think that? Sure, I helped Da in the lab. But we didn't make any poison." Da had a good salary and his teaching duties. Our main additional income derived from the organ extracts we made for endocrinology, and Da had turned a profit as well running a few lab tests for cardiology. Piddling stuff. Alex knew all that. Da had hoped that Paxarbital would bring us the kind of fame and money Alex had achieved with his migraine medication.

"The Paxarbital research looked promising," I said. "Da wrote to you about it, right?" Surely he would trust his oldest friend.

Alex turned red and started playing with his tie.

"What is it?"

"Your Da kept some things from you."

My voice quavered a bit. "He always told me everything."

He shook his head.

Emil rubbed at his blue spot again. "I don't think your father told you much at all."

"I mean, he told me all about his research. We loved talking about work."

Alex balled up the paper bag and brushed crumbs off his lap. "There were some things he didn't share with you."

"Experiments he didn't tell me about?"

Since Alex didn't answer, Emil spoke. "Was there any time in the lab unaccounted for? Outside of regular hours?"

"He used to leave after dinner and go back to the lab. He was running the spectrophotometer, working with that Sigma kit for the determination of SGOT. Cardiology asked him to look into it."

"What's that?" Emil asked.

"The enzyme, glutamic oxaloacetic transaminase," I explained, using the biochemical term that he might be familiar with. "SGOT is elevated right after a heart attack." I turned back to Alex. "Was Da trying out other compounds on the rats?"

"No. I wish he had been."

I buried my head in my hands.

"You should tell her, whatever it is," Emil urged.

"Johann was my best friend. I promised I'd keep his secrets."

"You always did," Emil said. There was an uncomfortable silence.

I finally spoke. "Da wouldn't have made anything to make people crazy. In fact, Paxarbital stops people from getting like that."

"It's nothing to do with a psychotomimetic compound. It's more about his approach to scientific inquiry." Alex got up, leaving me to glare at the cheerful blue sky. One withered leaf fell, skittered toward us in the wind, and hit my shoe. The chloroform fumes had made me dizzy, and I stayed outside a few more minutes, enjoying the fresh air.

When I finally returned to the lab there were a stack of black notebooks, the same ones Da recorded his experiments in. I snatched up the first one. It was Da's writing.

Alex came and put a hand on my shoulder. "I never promised Johann that I'd keep his journals hidden."

⁓

While we waited, I put the five black notebooks in order and started the one from 1954. Nothing very exciting. He reported a meeting he'd had with the administration about getting more funding. His usual complaints about the Harvard stodginess and antipathy to foreigners.

I took note of his idea to take in exchange students. "Peppa needs socialization." *Right, Da. I needed much older, foreign boys who were interested in chemistry to socialize me. What a great idea.*

Although I had learned how to make a mean chicken vindaloo.

Alex interrupted my thoughts. "I've finished the vacuum concentration. Come see."

We had a nice amount, at least a tablespoon full. I carefully scraped the dark brown gum into a bowl.

Emil smirked. "Got some hashish, Peppa?"

"How would you even know?"

"I've been around. Even if I haven't made it to America."

Alex shook his head. Hashish wasn't a joking matter to him. "Would you make the final preparations for the solvent system please, Mr. Nussbaum?"

In the meantime, I took the tiny glass tubes, dipped them in our extraction, and dotted samples on the paper. The liquid solvent would carry the spots along as it migrated across the paper strip. At the end of several hours we'd remove the paper and examine the new spots. The distance they'd migrated would give us further information. I'd learned the entire procedure from Da just last year: it was called paper chromatography, after the colored spots that formed in new places after the strip was soaked.

I passed the time by reading Feigl's *Qualitative Analysis by Spot Tests*. Da had never even mentioned me in his journals, except to note that I'd done some assay particularly well. There was no clue as to any secret experiments.

When the paper was finally dry, I sprayed it with Dragendorff's reagent. The three faintly fluorescent spots dutifully turned rusty red, confirming we had an alkaloid. But we'd already suspected that.

"That would be a nice color on you," Emil offered. I frowned at him.

"Tomorrow we can do column chromatography and go from there," Alex said. That meant placing our leftover gummy sample on the top of a long glass column and washing it. The column had a stopcock on the bottom, which would allow liquid to drain out. After a series of complicated steps, we'd find the pure alkaloids in the stuff that came out the bottom.

The pure alkaloids—whatever they were.

It would take months to properly identify them, but only a few days to use up my sample. This wasn't going to work, much as I wanted it to.

I idly blew out a pipette, thinking of my favorite actress, Grace Kelly. I'd recently seen her in the cinema in *Rear Window*. She'd climbed into the murderer's apartment to get the proof. Nothing frightened her.

I might never be beautiful like her. But I could be brave. "I'll get Unruh to let me come. Then maybe I can winkle it out of him."

"Not a good idea. He'll play you," Alex warned.

"If you can even get there," Emil added.

"I'm not accomplishing much here. We have no idea what we're looking for."

"At least I can keep you safe," Alex said. So that's why he was letting me spend my time on this hopeless quest.

Emil reached for a Lucky Strike, and then put it back, remembering the ether. "Either go to the police or flee to Mexico."

"You've been reading too many novels." I stretched and twisted. My shoulders were sore from hunching over test tubes. "I wish I understood Unruh better. Do you suppose he's an occultist?"

Alex polished one last test tube on his shirtsleeve. "I can ask some colleagues what they know. Frederick went to a conference in Munich last year."

"What's he expecting? Why is he doing this?" I persisted. I knew what Tenzin thought, but his way of thinking was alien to me. I wanted to know what two scientists would think.

"No doubt he's an ex-Nazi looking for a comeback," Emil said.

Alex edged toward the door. "Clara will be wondering where I am. But I'll come tomorrow at noon to unlock the lab, and we can see. I promised my son I'd go ride bikes with him in the morning."

I'd forgotten tomorrow was Saturday. Nearly a week had gone by.

I waited till I heard the secretary leave, then went to the bathroom to wash up and put on my new dress.

When I met Emil at the car door, he looked at me appreciatively. "It's an improvement, but you have a ways to go. I should have bought you lipstick."

I shook my head at him. "Are you my fashion adviser now?"

"My girlfriend Monica never goes out without lipstick."

I looked out the car window, willing him stop talking. He was just helping me so he could get closer to Alex, maybe get a job at Sandoz.

I did look forward to seeing Tenzin. His broad smile and warm brown eyes made the boys I'd known seem like pallid ghosts.

15. His Secret

EMIL DROVE DOWN PETERSGRABEN. I TOLD HIM TO STOP BY ST. Peter's Church. Tenzin was waiting in the paved churchyard to the side, looking intently around. He smiled when he saw me get out.

I paused, holding the car door handle, and turned to Emil. "I'll meet you at the Spalentor again at 11:30 tomorrow. Thanks for helping today."

Tenzin moved quickly beside me, blocking me from any view of oncoming passersby. Emil gave him an appraising glance, starting from the topknot and going down to his worn boots. "You're Peppa's new protector? Are you Indian?"

"Leave off, Emil," I snapped. Tenzin had cautioned me against sharing any information that might lead to our discovery.

"My nationality needn't concern you. She's safe with me." Tenzin said in impeccable High German, masking his Swiss dialect.

"You ought to be aware what you're getting into," Emil said cryptically.

"I can take care of myself."

The two men studied each other. If they'd been canine, the fur on their necks would have bristled.

"*Tschüss*, Emil," I said, as sweetly as I could.

Emil didn't start the car, though. He squinted at us, a crease forming on his brow. Tenzin said gruffly. "You're better off not knowing my name if the police pick you up. You have my word I'll treat Peppa like my own family. I've got to get her off the street now." We left Emil sitting quite still in the Chevy, looking pensive.

The Café Hebel was half a block down Petersgraben, deserted, dark, and smoky. I'd passed by it before, but the students usually headed to nearby Harmonie, with its giant servings of Rösti smothered in cheese.

Tenzin entered first and took us to the table right behind the short wall that separated the entrance from the room. The room itself was only big enough for eight battle-scarred tables. Light from the small paned windows showed off the old beamed ceiling, its wood painted with swirling charcoaled motifs, but our table was hidden in gloom.

The swarthy bartender had the newspaper spread out behind the counter. He barely glanced up when we came in.

"The usual," Tenzin said.

The bartender tapped the ash off his cigarette onto the counter. "I'm in the middle of reading about the Negroes in Little Rock. They're forced to go to school with the white children now. It's a goddamn tinderbox." His voice was guttural, his accent harsh.

Tenzin smiled at me reassuringly. "What do you want to drink?"

"Anything but schnapps," The bartender didn't seem hospitable. "Who is that man?" I whispered.

Tenzin shrugged, not bothering to keep his voice down. "His nickname is the Angry Anatolian, but he's not Turkish. One night he drank with Jakob and me and told us he inherited this bar from a distant uncle. Wherever he's from, he hates Switzerland. Says it snows too much."

"Oh?"

"Likely it's the people staring at him. I'll get your drink." Tenzin went behind the bar himself and poured a glass of white wine. When he returned he touched my sleeve, then dropped his hand. "I've been worried about you."

"I was with Alex all day, working."

"Did you find out anything?"

"No, not yet." The Angry Anatolian threw down the paper with a disgusted grunt and started polishing a glass with the corner of his baggy sweater. "What are we doing at this bar?"

"I've asked a friend for help. He can hide us till we decide on the next step."

"I thought we weren't going to talk to anyone?"

"Vreni asked me today who's been staying with me. I put her off, but we need to find some place safer. Jakob is our best chance."

"Where's he going to hide us?" I pictured some small dank place in the cellar or behind a wall, like Anne Frank's hiding place during the war.

"You sound worried. No need. It's a nice place. A greenhouse on an estate."

"But..."

"Let's wait till you meet him. He'll want to answer your questions himself." He pointed to the notebooks. "What are those?"

"A couple of my Da's diaries. Though I don't know what I'm looking for. There are still three at Sandoz Labs."

Tenzin watched the door as I spoke about Da's experiments. When I finished, he nodded, and then looked around the room restlessly. His eyes fell on the wooden figurehead of the *Lolle König* on the facing wall, with its popping blue eyes and long, lolling tongue.

"That head reminds me of a Tibetan demon."

"That's the Lolling Tongue King."

He looked at me bemusedly.

"You know. Our mascot here in Grossbasel. Because Kleinbasel, across the river, has the Lion, the Wildman, and the Griffin as their mascots. The statues are on the bridge, facing Kleinbasel and showing us their behinds." The wine made me chatty.

"I grew up in Dehra Dun," he reminded me.

"My grandfather and yours, the professor and the pharmacist, they're Grossbasel folk. Little Basel was the working-class neighborhood. And our Lolling Tongue King sticks out his tongue at them."

Tenzin rubbed his eyes. "The longer I'm here, the more I realize what a strange place it is."

The door opened, and a slender older man came in. He was wearing baggy trousers, knees stained with dirt, and an old shirt, a cap, and a gentleman's coat that harkened from a different era.

"This is Mr...." Tenzin started, but the man interrupted him. "First names only. This is safer." He spoke German, not Swiss. He extended his hand. "Jakob."

I shook it. "Hello, I'm..." I hesitated. My name was unique.

He smiled coolly. "I can guess who you are, Peppa. I visited the university botany office the other day, and all the gossip was of Dr. Mueller's daughter, who'd gone mad."

I looked down, considering what to say next, but Tenzin spoke sharply. "What's said of her. It's not true. I've been with her three days now..."

"Are you thinking with your brain or your heart?"

"My heart. I always think with my heart."

"If you're implying that Tenzin and I have been canoodling..." I started indignantly, but Jakob laughed.

He got up abruptly and went to the bar. The bartender quit polishing and poured him a schnapps, which Jakob slammed down our table. Then he spoke again. "I don't care what you've been doing with him. How long am I supposed to hide you for?"

"Until we can find a way for me to cross the border into Germany." I said firmly. I'd fiddled around long enough. Simone would give her life to defend me; I should at least be willing to assume some risk to help her.

Jakob cocked an eyebrow at me. "Oh, so now it's over the border, is it?"

Tenzin started to say something, but I interrupted him. "We both know I need to do it."

He turned to Tenzin. "You didn't tell me this. You presume too much."

"She doesn't know," Tenzin said.

Now I was confused. "Know what?"

"I wasn't always just a gardener," Jakob said. "But before I help you, let's get clear on something. Did you kill someone?"

Tenzin looked at me gravely, and the familiar cold dread began in my stomach. I pleaded, "Why do I have to talk about it?"

"Because Jakob is the only person I know who can help you get to Munich."

I took a deep breath and tried to talk. Inside, I saw Mr. Wäspi's head lolling at an odd angle, the drops of blood from his cut hands. Nothing came out of my mouth.

"She needs an Ovaltine," Tenzin said, looking at my glass of untouched wine.

"The hell she does. This is not a child. She killed at least one person, maybe more. Those I helped before were refugees. I don't help criminals." He pushed his glass of schnapps in front of me. "Drink this and talk. I want to hear it from you, not Tenzin."

It made me cough, but something in me loosened. I described what happened at the Bäsebeiz and my subsequent telephone call with Dr. Unruh.

Jakob snorted. "Probably a Nazi *Schweinehund*." He stomped over to the bar, ordered three more schnapps, and put them down on table. Tenzin wordlessly gave Jakob five francs and moved one over to him.

Jakob finished his in one gulp and took the second from Tenzin. He looked me in the eye. "This is a pretty crazy story. Are you lying?"

"I left out some personal things, but I'm not lying. I had to defend myself."

Jakob drank down his third schnapps more slowly, as Tenzin watched him warily. "Now I'll talk, Peppa Mueller. I'm a German Jew. Made it over here just before all hell broke loose. I helped smuggle 133 men, women, and children into Switzerland when the border closed to non-Aryans in 1938. My current employer's husband turned the greenhouse and garden properties over to me, with the plea not to implicate his family."

"So you'll help me?"

"I've never smuggled anyone *out* of Switzerland and into Germany, but yes, I guess the same procedure and route could be used."

"Then let's get started." Now that I'd made up my mind to go, I was consumed with anxiety. What if I'd misread the situation, and Dr. Unruh didn't want more information from me? What if I had nothing to offer him? Would he kill Simone?

"Passports are expensive. You got money?"

"How much?"

"Five hundred francs for an express job and transport over."

I had a hundred times that in the bank, not to mention that the house on Rheinweg was paid for. Alex knew we were rich. He'd loan me the money.

"I'll get it for you."

"Can you swim?"

"I grew up on the banks of the Rhine."

"Good, because the boatman will expect you to jump in if it looks like he'll be discovered. The passport is for later, just in case. It wouldn't fool the crossing guards."

"So when do we…"

"The sooner the better. We're having a big party at the estate next Saturday, and we'll have workmen setting up tents for the fete. You definitely need to be gone by then. I'll see what I can set up."

"Thank you. Thank you."

"Meet me here tomorrow, same time. With the money."

༄

We walked back to the flat, avoiding the pools of light that spilled from the street lanterns. I'd left the grandmother's hat at Sandoz. I tucked my head down, hoping I just looked cold. As we approached the house on Pilger Street, I craned my neck, checking to see if Vreni's lights were on. Though it was dark, my heart still beat fast. What if she rode up on her bicycle just as we were unlocking the door?

Once we reached the safety of the living room, I flung myself on the horsehair sofa and blew out my breath. "So you're sure about this Jakob?"

"Jakob's had a hard life. He was interrogated by the Nazis at one point. Most of his family died at Auschwitz. But I think we can trust him. We have to trust him."

"He sure does drink a lot."

Tenzin shrugged. "Yeah. That he does. He still plays poker well though, even drunk."

He went to the small refrigerator and took out some cauliflower and onions. "Rice and curried vegetables. Can you eat spicy foods?" He still looked handsome, even with his grandmother's apron on over his gray flannel trousers.

"Sounds wonderful." I couldn't keep my eyes off him tonight. I told myself it was the novelty of seeing a man cook.

I went to the secretary desk in the living room and took out the fountain pen and some paper. I jotted down notes about the Bäsebeiz, including Dr. Unruh's presence. He knew that I knew. There wasn't any point in pretending.

He'd been explicit in wanting details of my experience as a falcon. That would be harder since I remembered nothing. I started leafing through the books that Emil had brought me, taking a note here and there. I'd always lacked imagination, but notes might help me invent something.

The phone rang and we both jumped. Tenzin left his cooking and spoke for a few minutes. Yes, the plumbing leak was fixed. Yes, he would mop the floor just to make sure it didn't get moldy. There were a few more exchanges and he hung up, after conveying greetings to his grandfather.

"Were you worried your grandmother would be upset? You jumped when the phone rang."

"I'm expecting another call. It could take several days. Maybe more."

―❦―

After we'd washed up the supper dishes and talked about my conversation with Unruh, Tenzin wandered over to my stack. "What are you doing with all those books?"

"I'm looking for inspiration."

"He'll know. Didn't he say that? He'll know you're lying."

"If I don't have something to tell him tomorrow, he'll lose interest."

Tenzin sighed. "You realize what danger you'll be in if you go to Munich?"

I wavered. "I can find out more, help Simone."

"And then what? Then you'll go to the police?"

"Yes. At some point." I could hear the doubt in my own voice.

"Peppa. You're a nineteen-year-old girl. You think you can handle a monster like Unruh?"

Something savage stirred in me. "I *will* protect myself and Simone if forced to."

"You want to have two deaths to explain?"

I set my head on my arms, blinking back tears. Underneath, anger stirred. *I am Horus, the god of war and vengeance.*

I felt Tenzin nudge me. "Look up." His face was grim. "I'll go."

"He won't see you. He wants me."

"No, I mean, I'll go to Munich to be near you. I'll assemble gear in case we need to get away. A high-altitude tent, supplies, sleeping bags. Can you rough it?"

"I guess."

"How much can you carry, do you think?" He seemed to be ticking off items in his mind.

"Maybe 15 kilos. Why are you talking about escape?"

"If you go, one of you will die. I pray it's him."

"You think he'll try to murder me?" I wrapped my arms around myself, cold despite my sweater.

"No, no. Not that. I couldn't stand for you to go if I thought that."

"Then what?"

"I can't explain. It's correct that you go. You must finish with him. But only one of you can win."

I had to go. I had to help Simone. Tears blurred my eyes again. I couldn't talk.

Tenzin closed his eyes, like he was concentrating on an inner image. "Afterwards, we'll head for the mountains by Zugspitze to hide out. Before winter comes, we'll cross the border into Austria. There's sure to be a safe house there, for people fleeing the Iron Curtain. I'll just need money—for bribes, supplies. Lots of it."

"I'm not leaving my dog."

"Less work than the baby was, at any rate. Simone can hunt for food."

I wiped my eyes and sat back up. Tenzin was trying to tell me something. "What baby?"

He didn't blink. "I've done this before. I was a smuggler in Asia."

———

When we looked up from our conversation, it was an hour later. Tenzin had taken forty-three people out of Tibet last summer and fall, after an uprising in Tibet's eastern province. He'd been a mountain guide before, taking rich British mountain climbers up into the Himalayas. He'd met Pema during one of those trips, never really lived with her.

The smuggling work was hard and dangerous, but it gave him satisfaction to cheat the Chinese of their victims. Then the Chinese crushed the uprising, and things settled down. Tenzin decided to start a new life in Europe. His Swiss grandparents offered to pay for his studies; he earned a little extra helping the Mission plan garden projects in tropical countries.

Tenzin took a final swig of schnapps. The bottle was empty.

He forced a smile. "So now you know the Dalai Lama is not the king of Bhutan."

"Now I understand why you can hold your liquor." I studied his strong hands. I thought inebriated men were supposed to get flirtatious. His were folded primly in his lap, though his eyes kept returning to mine, studying my expression. "Why are you willing to give up so much for me? You wanted to start a new life."

"I like you."

I looked at him, questioning. I wasn't pretty. I was too smart for a girl, interested in the wrong things.

He regarded me steadily. "I've met enough women over the years to know you're different. The British women in India treated me like I was some exotic novelty. Asian women, except the Bhutanese, are convention-bound, waiting for their arranged marriage to take place. But me, I like to think for myself. And so do you." He got up, restless, and watered an African violet from the miniature watering can. "I like you a lot."

My head swam, though I'd had nothing stronger than raspberry syrup with water. I wanted to know what it was like to be with a man—with this man. I didn't remember anything about my night with Patrick.

He shifted toward me, his hand rose and hovered by my cheek. Did he feel it too?

He pulled back and folded his hands in his lap again. His voice became matter-of-fact. "Once my grandmother finds out there was no broken faucet, I won't be going to the university in the spring anyway. And we're about done at the Mission with our gardening project. Might just as well help you."

"She doesn't have to find out."

"I won't lie. And besides, I can't be who she wants."

"So you'll help me? It's that easy?"

"It is."

~

It was midnight, and I still had no convincing narrative about my experience as a falcon. I threw the book on the floor and got up from the armchair, stretching.

Tenzin stirred from his place on the couch, where he'd been reading a psychology textbook, despite what he'd just said about abandoning his studies. "I have an idea. How much do you trust me?"

"Why? What are you planning?"

"You don't trust me. Otherwise you wouldn't ask like that."

I massaged my temples. The sense memory came, of his arms wrapped around me on the bed. I'd trusted him then. But that had been at night, when I was vulnerable.

Trust? Next we'll be talking of love.

I wrote down one of Baudelaire's sentences. "There was the hashish, glimmering like emerald fire in my chest." Could I claim something similar? *There was the compound, burning like a crimson tarantula in my gut.*

I couldn't concentrate anymore. Dr. Unruh would see through my fiction.

"I could use some help," I admitted. "What do you have in mind?"

~

Half an hour later I was bathed, wrapped up in Tenzin's robe, and lying on the bed, only candles lit around us. The situation could have been romantic, in another context. Instead, Tenzin sat on a chair he'd pulled up, a notebook ready at his side.

"Let the experiment begin," I said.

"Let's start with the body. Your head is very heavy. Your body is very heavy. Your heartbeat. Listen only to that. You are getting sleepy ... very heavy."

He spoke some more, his voice soothing, then started counting backwards, an elevator going down one floor, then another, deep down, deep down...

I smiled to myself. Tenzin was trying, but I didn't believe in hypnosis. Though this was calming. He had a beautiful voice. I got to lie near to him, wearing his robe.

Someone analytical like me was a poor subject...

Then I felt the beat of the wings in the room, stirring the air. I know Tenzin felt it too, though his face didn't move a muscle. Then it was like a huge push.

As if the storm seized a child on a swing, pushing, pushing...

And I was gone.

16. The Peregrine

Awake.

A woman screams. Full moon, blood moon time, when baleful spirits hum through air, and death stalks.

Old woman with a purple bleeding hole in her face, falling on her knees.

Danger comes and I must protect the girl whose body I wear.

Only scrawny limbs? My wings are felt, but wavering, not quite. No talons, no curved beak?

But I will defend us.

Who to fight first? The fancy man who poisons is standing near. His inside animal sniffs.

Scent of sweat, tears, blood.

He turns and runs, trailing a thick fear smell.

A second man, bigger, comes. Fingers oozing blood from glass shards. His animal is awake as well, and it has gone wrong. It hurt his kinswoman. She draws grunting breaths. Waste leaks from her belly. Soon she will die.

A cry comes from the room of cooking food, then bright fire in a ball. A woman slams through the door, hurtling into the woods.

The kin slayer scrabbles nearer. His animal is lumpy, a snout, a snaggle tooth, fetid breath.

The girl and I will not be your prey.
You will be ours.
I have no notched beak. But now I have hands that can grasp, twist—knuckles that dig like tiny pointy daggers between the crunchy neck bones.

His head separates from the back long bone. His current broken.

Dead. But not fit for a meal.
Who else?
The pale boy man bores into his hands with a metal cross. No animal there. He reads the big black book, and his animal cannot come. So easy to kill him.

But no need. Killing takes energy.
The girl wears elastic cloth, it pinches her ribs and binds her legs. I do not like that. It is my body for now.

Tear off.
Now we are better, closer, more one.
Come home with me, girl. Come to the Jade World. It is up past the highest mountain, where air turns to starshine, where you turn into me.

I saved you.
And I rule you. You were us, and now you are me.

The old woman's soul twists and turns, a speck in the dark dim sky. I feel her question for white winged creatures of sweet smiles, her hope for the old god-man with a beard.

Not where I go.

Naked rocks. The mountain peak called Säntis is the first step, then the fog wraith coiling above, the leap to the Jade World.

Day becomes night. Seconds turn back and eat themselves, and old women become babies, and everything lives a second life, a before, an after, behind the clock.

The sky is the color of curdled moss. It would be twilight, if the days were green and the nights were black. But there are no days and no nights. There is no sun but only eight moons, eight other worlds, hanging in the sky, shrouded. Each world with its own Guardian of Time.

I glide over the chambers of Absalom's palace, ceilings crumbled away, walls lichen-crusted, leaning. The sky-open courtyard where he sits has rusty red high columns marching, roof beams hidden in a net of gray fog. The smell of swords laces the air. He sits among litter.

Many bird spirits live here for the count of year hundreds. They rise from their graves, bringing their tarnished and chipped drinking vessels, broken spears, and shattered daggers.

Nothing whole from the former world enters this one. Except I have the girl in me, and she still lives down *there*, her body entire.

Lord Absalom must be told.

He smiles in welcome. He has filed teeth, his head is bald, his lashless eyes glint like emeralds in the gloom.

He writes in a book, writes pages and pages and pages of what has been and what will be. The ink is soot and powdered bones. The words belong to the swarms of cawing inky ravens, the goshawks that nest in the turrets, fighting and snapping, the buzzards trawling through the mist until feeding time comes.

In the woods are flocks of timid sparrows, a swamp of ibis, sometimes a trilling nightingale or a sole cardinal, jouncy in scarlet.

Raptors reign in the castle. We do not need meat, but still we crave it, and Absalom, our lord, gives it to us. It is our due.

I swoop to him, settle, fluff and preen. He feels the girl's presence and shakes his head. It is not allowed for her to be here.

I must go back. While her heart beats and her breath flows, I must protect the flesh house. It is law.

I spread my wings and rise. I will go to the place where the fur-kin is kept. Her heart smiles when fur-kin is near. But I do not like the rooms of the purple house. The roof is the best place to roost.

Someone was tapping my head. Over and over. I brushed at the fingers. A squawking sound came out of my mouth.

Tenzin's face was close to mine. "Do you remember?"

"I do now. Somewhat." I blinked. The images I'd seen were still clear in my head. At the time I'd understood everything, but now the knowledge had been swept away. This is what it must be like to be crazy. It wasn't as unappealing as I'd thought.

"This is totally insane." A suspicion formed. "Did you put ideas in my head?"

He smiled. "That might be difficult. It's already packed full of information."

"It's crazy. Wait till you hear…"

"You talked to me."

"I did?"

"It sounds like you were in some alternate world."

I snorted. "The alternate world of psychotomimetics."

He half-closed his eyes. "No. You didn't sound confused or drugged. Just … different."

I tensed, remembering I'd shifted into another being. If he'd noticed too, that made it more real. "How *did* I sound?"

"Your voice was hoarse and low. Your words simple, like a child's."

Children were defenseless and useless. "I was a falcon," I snapped.

He looked intrigued. "How do you know?"

I leaned down and hoisted up the satchel. The book on birds of prey was still at the bottom. I took it out and flipped the pages until I saw the peregrine.

"That's her," I explained.

"That's you?"

I shrugged. "I saw with her eyes. I felt what she felt. The Jade World—it's like home to her."

"Then we've succeeded. You know what happened."

"No. I can't explain how I shifted to become her. I don't understand where she goes."

"Why does that matter?"

I looked at the glowing candles, thinking about the ceremony. "I'm glad we prayed for those dead people. But it's not enough. I need to understand what Ludwig did. So I can stop him from doing it again."

"You're courageous."

Embarrassment made me brusque. "I'm going to be cold unless I get under the covers. I should give you back your robe."

"I've never known a woman who was part falcon before." His smile was tender, his eyes warm and curious. My breath caught, and my attraction for him made me feel faint. By then he'd already turned away and was walking out the door. "You're welcome to keep my robe while you're here, *didi*. I hope you don't have bad dreams tonight."

I bit my nail. Why, oh why, was he married?

Grow up, Peppa.

I had the nightmare, but this time, after I killed Mr. Wäspi, I retained a part of myself.

I asked the peregrine where we were going.

"Far, far away."

"What kind of a place is it?"

"A place no living man can see."

"But you can?"

There was no answer.

"Where am I, when I am you?"

"In the deep, and I am in the light. In your world, you are in the light—I'm like a seed buried in the dark."

"Are we the same?"

"We are one, but not the same."

And then I grew dizzy and forgot it was a dream. As the great lifting off came, and with it, the shift into the Jade World, I screamed.

That woke me up. I curled in a ball, shaken. Emerald motes danced at the edge of my vision. My body felt foreign, heavy and lumpy. There was another being in me now. I recognized her the way you'd know your twin, even if you'd never met her before. Familiar.

But a twin raised in the depths of the jungle, by beasts. Different: savage and dangerous.

Sleepily, I thought, "I'll have to give her a name."

Even in the dark, I saw Tenzin walk quietly in, his face and hands glowing with eerie light. He hadn't changed. My eyes had. I closed them, unsettled.

I felt his body settle in behind the customary pillow, and he took my hand. His touch was a balm.

We slept till seven, when I'd programmed myself to wake up. I stretched and looked around, noting with relief everything appeared normal. I slipped away, though I felt his eyes on my back. I had to prepare myself for my telephone call to Germany.

17. Reporting to the Devil

I'D SAVED THE LAST SIP OF OVALTINE FOR EIGHT O'CLOCK, THE time I'd decided to call him. I didn't want to appear too eager, so I'd made myself wait. But if I waited too long, he might go out.

I dialed the operator to be connected to Dr. Ludwig Unruh.

He answered on the third ring. Tears sprang to my eyes as I heard Simone bark in the background. She was alive.

"Unruh. Hallo?"

I was so relieved I couldn't think clearly. "I guess you don't have her locked up somewhere."

"Miss Mueller?"

"Yes. It's me."

There was a pause. "The report?"

"I want some information in return."

"Bargaining, are you? I'll consider your questions. After the report."

I spoke about the Jade World, feeling foolish, as if I was telling a fairy tale. He didn't seem surprised by anything, though. He let me talk on, asking a question now and then.

I leaned back against the sofa afterwards, spent, still puzzled. "Is this what you wanted?"

Unruh's voice was dry and deep. "Not a bad start."

"Simone's in the house?"

"This is your big question? I have her leashed to the banister right now. Jochen will take her outside for a walk soon. My chauffeur."

I took a deep breath. Miss Eugster hadn't been accounted for. Tenzin had checked his notes from our hypnosis session, and she might have run away when the house burned down. Had Unruh strangled her and left her in a ditch? Was she tied up, awaiting administration of the compound?

"My question is about Miss Eugster."

"That's none of your business." He paused. "Obviously the police haven't caught you. How is that?"

"I'm at my wits' end. Hungry. Sleeping outside. I'm surprised I'm not ill." I waited a beat. "I just don't know who to turn to."

"Maybe I could help you. You could come to Munich."

I pounced. "What did you do to Miss Eugster?"

"You think I garroted her? Fed her to wolves? What?"

"No one's seen her. Did you kill her?"

There was no sound for a while. I swallowed, my throat dry. Of course he'd killed her. He'd given the Wäspi family, Stefan, and me, a toxic psychedelic. He wasn't going to let her go after that. I must be mad to think of going to Germany.

I was astonished when there was a catch in his voice. "You're upsetting me, Miss Mueller."

"I'm fairly upset as well."

"I'm not some unconscionable brute. Do you have me confused with a Nazi?"

"So where is she?"

"On a beach in Brazil, catching some sunshine. Drinking fancy drinks with little umbrellas. Screwing her brains out without worrying about the locals gossiping."

His vulgarity took me by surprise. "How'd she end up there?"

"I paid her. Now then, will you consider coming here, or are you going to end up in a straitjacket instead, where you won't be of any use to anyone?"

"What do you want from me?"

"The results of my further experiments were disappointing. Maybe I could use someone like you."

"I've already told you everything I remember." I gave voice to my fear. "I hope you're not thinking of using me as a subject." My skin pimpled as I said it, my scalp grew tight.

Once again he surprised me. "Your father was Johann Mueller."

"Yes. You've heard of him?"

"You could say that."

"I helped him with his experiments."

"Yes. You're co-author on two of his papers. Quite an achievement for a young girl."

I couldn't help but feel pleased. "I earned that credit."

"Come help me."

"Will you give Simone back to me?"

"I won't do to her what I could do. Which would be to give her some of the compound. I wouldn't even have to mix it into schnapps."

Now it was my turn to be silent. I'd heard from Emil what the rats did.

"Don't think I'm a fool. Come with vengeance in your heart, and you both shall suffer. But come willing to be my pupil, and there may be rewards. You may find you like me more than you suppose."

"It's not easy, getting to you."

"I read the Tarot cards. The Ten of Swords. You will be embarking on a journey. But I don't like the Hierophant. What shall we do about him?"

I swallowed. Dr. Unruh was a delusional occultist, but he still frightened me. "Who is the Hierophant? Maybe it's you."

"Oh no. The Hierophant card crosses us both. You are the subject of the reading. I drew the Queen of Swords for you. My card covers you. You can guess what card that is, right?"

I remembered seeing a Tarot deck once, when Aunt Madeleine had a friend who dabbled in the supernatural. If he wanted to play at being an occultist, I'd humor him. "You're the Devil?"

"You flatter me. My card, a representative symbol, is the Devil. I am not the devil. Nor am I hairy with cloven hooves. In fact, I despise body hair. A sign of primitive ancestry. But the hypocrite churchmen like to call those who search for hidden knowledge devils. As if we should all prostrate ourselves in front of the pope and his lackeys, or the Hitlers and Stalins of this world." He laughed then, bitter. "You assumed I was an ex-Nazi. I serve no warlord. Adolf Hitler was a stunted man with a loud voice."

"My father didn't like the pope or Hitler either," I said.

"Then you should feel right at home here, Miss Mueller. You can devise and measure and notate. And when your turn comes, I'll tie you to a chair, drop the scorpion on your soft white thigh, and place a teaspoon of elixir into your sweet mouth."

"How dare you," I hissed and then clapped my hand over my mouth. If he did something to Simone, I'd never forgive myself.

His voice was dispassionate. "Good girl. I have no use for weaklings. You'll be a suitable assistant. "

Relived that he wasn't going to hurt Simone, I forced myself to concentrate. He'd mentioned a scorpion. Surely the drink had been an intoxicant of some kind. But did the venom have a synergistic effect? Maybe it served as a catalyst.

I remembered the red weal on my thigh the night of the massacre. "I had a scorpion sting, didn't I? How'd you arrange that?"

"Don't you remember how I stood over your bed? Your eyes got so big."

"You dropped one in my bed?"

"All part of the process. I hope you won't let it dissuade you."

Right then, I thought of another one of our childhood games, the "Cattle Car"—Emil Nussbaum locking me into the closet under the stairwell. I'd borne it, even instigated it a time or two. Maybe I wanted to know the limits of my endurance. "Are you asking me to be your assistant or your subject?"

"I wouldn't force an experiment on you."

"You did last time."

"No. You chose to drink. You were curious." I heard a doorbell ringing in the background. "I have a visitor to attend to. I'll have to go."

"Wait!"

"We can't wait too long. You'll be caught, and poor Simone will have to live with me forever. However long that would be. Can a dog die of a broken heart?"

I gritted my teeth. "I'll come on one condition."

"Do tell."

"You're a gentleman?"

"I should hope that would be evident."

"Will you give me my dog?"

"I will give you your dog. You have my word. Just make it across the border to Freiburg without getting caught. I have an address for you. Report there. You'll be given assistance."

"I'll come as soon as I can."

When he gave me the street name and told me the area of town it was in, I asked, "What should I expect?"

"He's my scorpion dealer. I might just as well get you used to those creatures." He laughed softly. "I hope you arrive soon. Your dog's barely eating."

"Aren't you going to tell me where you live?"

"That can be dealt with later. Goodbye, Miss Mueller." I stared at the receiver, emitting its beeping sound. He'd just disconnected.

Tenzin strode over, his look challenging. "Are you still going to go? You look like you've seen a ghost."

I pressed my lips together. "I don't believe in ghosts."

"Did you have the nightmare last night?" Tenzin asked, dipping the end of his croissant into his coffee.

"It began as one. Then I felt her."

"The spirit I talked with?"

I started to point out that spirit was a ridiculous description. What was she, though? Instead, I said, "I'll give her a name."

"Good idea. Like a pet."

I choked on my coffee.

Pet? He understood nothing of the murderous intent that she embodied.

Tenzin handed me a napkin, his face impassive. "What will you call her?"

I thought for a minute. "I'll name her Chlora. For the green in chlorophyll. And for chlorine. Chlorine is volatile, a reactive gas. It only needs one electron for its outer shell to be complete."

"So that's why chlorine is dangerous?"

Clearly. Was he laughing at me, or did he just not know the first thing about chemistry? I reached for the stack of journals. "I've got reading to do."

I picked up another notebook and started to skim. It disconcerted me that Dr. Unruh seemed familiar with Da's name. Could they have known each other?

The journal was from five years ago, and after the first thirty pages I became bored. He'd detailed a lot of correspondence with the University of Hamburg and letters back and forth with Arvid Carlsson about dopamine. I shifted on the sofa and reached for the pharmacology textbook.

Tenzin held up a journal. "You should see this one."

I startled. "I didn't say you could read them." The secret I'd learned from Emil was bad enough. I didn't want Tenzin stumbling across more delicate information.

He ignored my comment, though a flicker in his eyes told me he'd heard. "Everything's always about your Da. Finally, I found something your mother made." He handed the notebook to me. "Her drawings are quite good. There are some water colors as well."

"Let me see." As I leaned over, the locket dangled from my top. I rubbed it out of habit, thinking about the photo inside, a moment of happiness preserved.

I caught my breath when I saw an ink sketch of the jungle, filled out with washes of green and black. It must be the Brazil journal. The trip they made right before she died.

This would tell me nothing about Father's secret experiments, but at that moment I missed Ainslie so. My mother.

She'd been an active participant in this journal. The very first page had a hand-drawn map with fanciful watercolor insets of red parrots and vivid emerald vines. I read over Da's notes quickly, more entranced by the drawings and occasional photo. One showed Da standing on the prow of a dinghy, binoculars in hand, scanning the jungle. There was another photo of an Indian with a monkey perching on his outstretched arm.

Then I saw it.

It couldn't be.

The journal dropped from my nerveless hands, clattering on the parquet. I tasted bile.

"What is it?" He picked it up, studying the chiaroscuro drawing. The darkened charcoal page had lines picked out with a white pastel pencil. An eraser had been used to highlight the areas illuminated by the unseen campfire. My father was depicted deep in conversation, a bottle on the table, a tent behind him in the gloom.

But it was the young man sitting across from him, shown in the act of offering a toast, which had caught my attention.

I'd know that face anywhere. It haunted my nightmares.

"Read her caption to me," I whispered.

"Johann and colleague, in deep conversation about witch doctors."

"What did Da write?"

"Let me turn the page." He studied my father's angular, tiny scribbling for a moment. "Today, deep in the jungle, we were astounded to meet a fellow scientist. Ludwig Unruh from the University of Munich is here working on his doctorate."

I restrained myself from snatching the journal from him. "Let me see the rest of that."

Dr. Unruh had accompanied them till the next village, where he went on his way to follow up on a report from Dr. Richard Evan Schultes. He sought a particular species of Brugmansia, one that the witch doctor of the neighboring tribes used. Apparently he'd found it. Ainslie's watercolor of the flower and characteristic thorny apple seedpods graced the next page. She'd even noted the blossom length of twenty centimeters and the scent, unusual in that it was fetid rather than sweet. The Brugmansia flower was milky pale green, shaped like the angel's trumpet of the Datura, which it was related to.

"A nightshade," I breathed. "Do you think this could be Unruh's poison?"

"I know about potatoes and tomatoes. What do they have to do with this?"

"I just read about them. Nightshades are a large family of plants that include belladonna and henbane in Europe, and Datura and Brugmansia in South America. They contain scopolamine and other poisons that induce terrible hallucinations."

"Can you test for that?"

I couldn't contain my excitement. I got up and paced on the Oriental rug. "With Uncle Alex helping I can. Scopolamine and atropine. Those are the key chemicals. If we identify that in our mixture, we know it's probably Brugmansia-based. "

Tenzin nodded approvingly. "Sounds like you'll be busy. Good. I'm going to start cleaning. Grandmother's coming back this afternoon. Jakob will take you to the new hiding place."

Tenzin hadn't said anything about coming along tonight. Maybe he wanted a few days alone before he went to Germany to help me. I'd never spent this much time with a man before. We'd been oddly intimate, but our relationship was also restrained and awkward. Part of that was because I had to work hard to remember he was married.

There was one thing I really wanted to know but was nervous about asking. "Why do you put the pillow ... wedge it, I mean."

"On the bed?"

My cheeks felt warm. I nodded.

He looked at his feet. "I haven't been with a woman for a while. I just didn't want to ... well, forget my manners," he concluded in a rush. Then he announced, "I'm going to launder now."

I felt my breathing quicken as he retreated to fetch the sheets. Did that mean he'd been tempted by me?

I shook my head at myself. *Married.* I settled back down to skim the rest of the notebook, before starting *The Historical Uses of Hallucinogens.*

Da had only written two terse sentences. "Unruh's gone his way. Hoping that's the last we see of him."

As usual, I understood Da's feelings perfectly.

18. Personal Correspondence

WHEN EMIL AND I ARRIVED AT SANDOZ A FEW MINUTES PAST noon, Alex was just finishing up the vacuum distillation.

I was confused. "You did the column chromatography already? I thought you were going to spend the morning with Andreas."

"Clara noticed I was worried. I had to tell her."

"No!"

"She's sensible. You know that."

I couldn't very well expect Alex to keep secrets from his wife. Clara was a friendly, capable woman who never raised her voice. "How did she react?"

"She took the children to the zoo so I could start working. I got here early."

"I found something that might help us," I took out the notebook with Ainslee's illustration of the flowering plant and laid it out on the gray Formica counter.

Alex's face creased. "Is that a Datura?"

"Almost. A Brugmansia. Dr. Unruh actually met my parents." I leafed through until I found the portrait of my father and Unruh talking. "Here he is."

Alex pondered. "Johann said there was a chap he met there he didn't like much. This is an odd coincidence. It troubles me."

Unruh was familiar with my father's work. I wondered at what point he'd realized I was Dr. Mueller's daughter. After all, I'd introduced myself to him as Patrizia Waldvogel.

Emil interrupted my thoughts. "Are you sure this is the plant Dr. Unruh used?"

"No," I admitted. "The nightshades have a bad reputation, but what happened at Gonten is worse than anything I've read about." According to my morning's research, alleged witches had been smearing their brooms with henbane and related scopolamine-containing compounds for centuries. The poison was absorbed through the vaginal tissues while they sat on their broomsticks. Vivid hallucinations, including delusion of flight, resulted. But as far as I knew, the witches had been simple villager healers, not murderers.

"Maybe Dr. Unruh performed some supernatural rite in conjunction with the poisoning," Alex said.

I decided not to mention the scorpion venom, the likely adjunct to the Brugmansia. Alex would react with alarm to Unruh's revelation, perhaps even try to forbid me to go to him. Instead, I said, "You're a scientist. You don't believe that."

Alex scratched his head. "I suppose not. An admixture is more likely. But now that we have an idea of what the main compound is, we can use what I just isolated and test it against known standards. All we need is some scopolamine and atropine from the pharmacy."

I glanced at the clock, horrified. It was now past twelve thirty. Only the emergency pharmacies in the hospital or at the railway station would be open. "Look at the time."

"We've got to get this settled. I know Mr. Hollenstein. He'll still be straightening up and counting the till. He'll open the door for me." Alex snatched his hat off the counter and took off running, his white coat flapping around his knees.

"Your lab coat," I called after him.

He made a click of exasperation and tossed it on the floor.

~~~

Emil reached into his coat pocket, and I tensed, expecting the pet mouse. It was only a blue envelope from overseas. "This letter fell into one of my books when I picked up your mail. Who do you know in India?"

I frowned. "I don't know anyone there." My heart beat faster as I recognized the writing. Patrick Doherty. My first. And my last for a while, considering how things had gone.

"Just another man I believed was my friend," I said, outraged dignity fighting with the desire to rip open the envelope right away. I hoped it was an apology.

"Like me, you mean?"

My emotions were too close to the surface, and tears trembled in my eyes. "Like you, in some ways. You can't trust anyone. You just can't."

"Jesus, what happened?"

He already knew my father was a lecher, so why not just tell him I was a strumpet? "I got drunk with a boy and woke up naked the next day. Patrick was my father's boarder, a PhD candidate at Harvard. The next day he just left. Could it really have been that bad for him?"

Emil stifled a smile. "No matter how bad it is, most guys are hanging round, waiting for more." He became serious. "Maybe he was a homosexual?"

"He didn't seem like one."

"You can't always tell. Just read the letter. I'll leave you in peace."

He got up, playing with his pack of Lucky Strikes. "Peppa?"

I looked up.

"I'm sorry. I've been a shit. My mother drinks and cries all day. She's never really gotten over the war. I'm an only child like you. I'm stuck with her, and we're short of money till I make some."

My hand flew up to cover my mouth. "I'm really sorry. I liked her."

He shrugged. "Everyone likes her, but she's weak. Anyway, I shouldn't blame you. You're in a pickle, and you can trust me." He gave a wave and sauntered off to the back door. Bolstered by his apology, I tore open the letter.

June 1, 1957

Dear Peppa,

So sorry I split on you and your Da, especially seeing as he was so sick. I hope he's recovered, and you weren't left on your own. Switzerland must be quite a change for you after Cambridge.

I'll get to the heart of things. I never even said goodbye, and I'm very sorry for that, and all your troubles. We never talked politics, you and I, but your mother was Irish, after all. I hope you'll understand. The overall situation there is still touchy, though Ireland's been made an independent republic. That doesn't help you when you grow up like I did, a Catholic in Northern Ireland. Northern Ireland is still under British and Protestant rule. I did some things as a hotheaded lad that I'm not proud off, and they followed me across the Atlantic to Harvard. So much for the sedate life of a doctoral student. When I got the tipoff that the police were coming, I had to leave fast.

I didn't get a chance to tell you that you woke up naked because you heaved all over your clothes. You should never drink homemade booze with an Irishman. Your Da might have heard me if I'd gone rummaging around in your room, so I undressed you and put you in my bed. You were, and are, dear to me, and I did not take advantage of you in your sorry state. It was a lovely kiss we shared though, before the drink had its way with us.

The train is pulling in, and I must be off. Perhaps we'll see each other again some day, though I doubt it, unless they come up with an amnesty program.

For the sake of our friendship, please keep my correspondence to yourself.

Yours sincerely,
Patrick Eamon Doherty

My first reaction was relief. So I hadn't driven Patrick away. His flight had nothing to do with our ill-considered laboratory experimentation in distillation. Then I realized that Patrick hadn't been my first. That experience was still ahead of me, to be enjoyed with a clear head and a glad heart.

Twenty minutes later, as I was tapping the last of the powder out from the funnel, still smiling about my letter, Alex returned. He was sweaty but triumphant.

Emil had the double beam balance ready and took the envelopes from Alex, weighing out a gram of each. I daubed our unknown purified extracts onto the chromatography paper, and Emil made two neat rows next to mine, using the pharmaceutical grade atropine and scopolamine. Those would be our standards. Alex inserted the strip into the solvent tank.

"Now what?" I said.

Alex smiled, "Emil can help me put away the reagents and you can get some coffee going in our break room."

In the break room, I loaded up the fancy espresso machine and took out the three neatly wrapped ham sandwiches. While I waited for the water to heat, I flipped through Friday's morning newspaper. More news about Oman and the Suez Canal. A listing under the church news caught my eye, because it mentioned Christian Engel. He and Father Kneipp would be presenting a short slide show about the infirmary in Dehra Dun, followed by drinks, dinner, and donations. The event would take place at Violet Strub's mansion, in Riehen, just outside of Basel.

Violet Strub. I wondered what she was like. Tenzin no doubt knew her personally, but he hadn't mentioned her. My imagination conjured up a luscious, buxom blonde.

The water was boiling, and so was I.

I took a deep breath, opened the window, and stuck my head out. It was none of my business who Tenzin knew, and what he did with them.

After lunch, we still had more than an hour to wait while the solutions migrated in the solvent tank. Emil and I sat on the upturned crate by the open back door, while Alex paced.

"It makes sense. Munich does." I said again. The mention of my imminent trip had provoked his restlessness.

"I still think you ought to go to the police. You're so close to having proof." Emil argued. I fancied there were thoughts of an official research project with a salary motivating him.

Even as I considered mentioning that the proof would be incomplete without the scorpion venom, Alex shook his head. "Too risky right now. She has no proof this came from Gonten, except for her word."

I had Stefan's word to back me up, but hadn't he made me promise I would find out what happened and why? "I've already made the arrangements to go to Germany." I tried to keep my voice steady.

Alex spread his hands. "I can find a place to hide you, given time. We'll get this all settled."

"I've *been* hiding. I want Simone. I want to find out what Dr. Unruh did to me."

"How will you defend yourself if you do see Unruh? He sounds dangerous."

My hand groped for my golden locket, looking for security. "I didn't think that far ahead." I had actually fantasized about snapping Dr. Unruh's neck, but that wasn't something I wanted to discuss with my supporters.

"Peppa's got a mean streak in her," Emil offered up, smiling to gentle his words.

Alex frowned at Emil. "I doubt Dr. Unruh will frighten easily. I was able to reach Frederick last night. Said he remembers him from last year's conference. The man gave him the chills. Unruh hates the Nazis, but apparently he defended the idea of human experimentation. Claimed experiments should be done on prisoners."

Just then we heard a car pull into the parking lot.

19. The Kommissar

EMIL DARTED OUTSIDE, AND ALEX SLAMMED THE DOOR SHUT, locking it. We breathed heavily, waiting for Emil, who knocked minutes later.

"Two men. They tried the front door of the building, and now they're coming to the back. They saw my parked car."

Alex, moving quickly for such a deliberate man, pushed me to the floor by the heavy wooden crate we'd been using as a bench.

"Can you get under this?"

I was 1 meter 70, tall for a woman, but I knew I could. It was like the cattle-car game. Locked up in the closet under the stairwell by Emil, I'd practiced taking up as little space as possible, hatching plans to kill the imaginary "Nazi guards." In the meantime, the adults drank Bordeaux, and my father presumably began his subtle seduction of an unstable woman.

I wondered what games Tenzin had played when he was eleven. Probably something normal. I remembered a mention of archery tournaments.

Alex lowered the crate over my head as I squeezed myself into a tiny ball. His heavy tread echoed as he walked to the door. The crate creaked as Emil sat down on top of me.

I could hear even through the wooden crate, so I assumed the visitors would hear me as well. I bit my lip hard to stifle a sneeze as the smell of acetic acid tickled my nose.

"Hello. I'm Kommissar Karrer of the Basel Police Department, Dr. Kaufmann. I hope I'm not disturbing you and Mr. Nussbaum."

"No, no."

"Actually, we hadn't been expecting Mr. Nussbaum to be with you. Quite a stroke of luck."

There was a long silence. No doubt they'd been to Dr. Wyss's lab and heard that Emil was absent yesterday.

"You gentlemen are very industrious. This being a Saturday and all."

"I could say the same of you." Alex sounded testy.

"Ah, well, you see, I dropped my card off around the neighborhood. This is about Miss Mueller. We thought she might come here."

"Peppa? I haven't seen her."

"That will reassure your friend at the pharmacy. He was quite concerned when you banged on his door and asked for some atropine and scopolamine."

I recognized the second man's distinctive rural accent. "We warned him Miss Mueller is dangerous."

Karrer introduced him. "I'm working with Officer Manser of Gonten."

Emil spoke up. "We've got a bit of a secret project going, see. So we'd appreciate you not mentioning it around."

Karrer spoke. "A secret project. So secret you couldn't even tell Dr. Wyss?"

"Our families were all close friends, as I'm sure you've found out. Dr. Mueller left his latest pharmaceutical research to Alex Kaufmann, in the form of documentation. When he returned to Basel, he shared his concern that drug testing would halt on the very promising antipsychotic he'd developed. It has fewer side effects than Thorazine. But it can cause dizziness and nausea. I've been helping Dr. Kaufmann, testing it out on myself. I asked him to buy the scopolamine in case I get dizzy again."

"A secret?" Karrer repeated. "Is this true?"

Alex said, "Yes."

"Why wouldn't he have left that research to his daughter?"

"Ah well, she's a woman. It's too complex for her," Emil said smoothly. The men made grunts of assent while I boiled in my crate.

Manser asked, "Has Miss Mueller been in contact with you? A telephone? A letter?"

Alex answered. "She's just disappeared."

Karrer took over again. "Miss Mueller is your godchild?"

"Yes, she is. Known her ever since she was a baby. Haven't seen much of her in the past decade, though."

"Then we can understand this might be hard for you to accept. We must warn you, she's mentally unstable. According to Dr. Ganz, she might be schizophrenic."

"Well, I sure hope you find her, so she can get some help." Alex sounded sincere.

"May we look around?"

"I'll have to go with you. The other offices are locked."

Alex left with one of the policeman. Emil stayed sitting on the crate.

"It's imperative we find Miss Mueller." Manser's voice went up a notch. "She's devious. She appears to be so calm and stoic. But if you'd seen what I saw…"

There was a small silence.

Manser spoke again. "Reports are that your father and Dr. Mueller had a falling out. Why would you be involved in his pet project now?"

"My mother and Mueller still corresponded occasionally. It was a small kindness he did for her."

Emil paused, then asked, "Why are you so sure Miss Mueller is mentally ill?"

"She lacks the comfort of Christ. She's antisocial. Dresses like a boy." He lowered his voice. "And then there's what she did to Ursula Wäspi. Gutted her."

I shook under my crate. I didn't care about Mr. Manser, but it was terrible to hear myself talked about like that. And I'd never even touched Ursula Wäspi or her poor mother.

"I thought she was just wanted for Hans Wäspi's murder."

"I've been pondering that. Our witness is a little ... well, let's put it this way. The boy never liked Hans Wäspi. Hans teased him, maybe a little more than he should have. But Hans was devoted to his sister. Spent all his time with her. I don't believe he attacked her."

I wanted to scream. *She mauled his face.* Didn't he see that? Or poor Mrs. Wäspi, impaled on her own umbrella. Or did he think I'd done that as well?

"Ah, it must be a vexing case."

Manser's voice turned sharp. "Yes, it is. Now where's that Paxarbital you're working on?"

Emil's shoes clacked across the floor. "Right here. Pills are the final product, and this is just preliminary testing."

Someone exclaimed, as glassware shattered, followed by cursing from Manser. "*Scheisse*! What was in that flask! It ate a hole through my shirt."

"Sulfuric acid," Emil explained, hiccuping out the words. Manser started coughing. The fumes were caustic.

"Laboratory work is not always pleasant," Alex remarked mildly. I hadn't heard him return.

"Let's get out of here and leave these two to it," Manser snarled.

"Call me if anything turns up. Here's my card," Karrer snapped. I heard the sound of the running water, as if he was washing his hands.

"Those burns can be nasty. Maybe you'd better get the pharmacist back to his shop. Get some salve," Alex advised. I knew Alex would have a first aid kit. Likely, he was enjoying the thought of the pharmacist being woken from an after-lunch nap.

The door slammed in answer.

They waited a few minutes before they released me. Emil helped me to my feet, dusting me off. "Just like old times. Into the cattle car with you," he barked, mimicking our imaginary cruel guard.

So he remembered as well. "And then I burst out and kill the Nazis," I smiled.

'We were stupid children," he muttered. "No one killed the Nazis."

There didn't seem to be an answer to that. I took a look around. Shattered glass everywhere. A fresh dusting of sodium bicarbonate covered the splattered sulfuric acid, but the fumes still stung my eyes and made breathing hard. Alex had the dustpan out, sweeping.

I crossed my arms, trying to quiet the tremors in my hands. "Quick thinking, Emil."

"She lacks the comfort of Christ," he said, mimicking the detective's phrase. "I suppose that means all the Jews are mentally ill too."

"They suspect us," Alex said. "They'll be back. You can't stay in Basel. Maybe we could find a quiet place in the country. My cousin's best friend has a farm outside of Solothurn."

"I'm not going to hide."

Alex sighed. "Peppa, you're extremely intelligent. But you know so little of life. Of men."

Tenzin had cautioned me to keep his involvement quiet, but it was time to tell Alex. "I won't be alone. A man by the name of Tenzin Engel has been hiding me. He's coming to Munich as well."

"The missionary's son? I don't know anything about him either. How do you know he is who he claims?"

I explained how I'd met Tenzin and what he'd done to help me. "He could come to meet you. Maybe tomorrow."

"I've seen him," Emil said. "He looks like a decent fellow. Could use a better hairstyle."

Alex emptied the dustpan. "I'll need to talk to you both about this plan. I want to know how you're getting across the border."

I pasted a bright smile on my face. "We'll talk. Everything will be fine. I can handle Unruh. Let's get back to work."

"We have to wait for everything," Emil pointed out.

I eyed the dirty sink. "I can tackle that glassware."

~~~

After I got done, Emil checked inventory and Alex showed me the catalogues and let me fill out order slips.

"Sorry about my comment regarding women," Emil said, unexpectedly. "I know you're capable. I'd be proud to work with someone like you."

Maybe Emil and I would turn out to be friends after all. First an apology, and now this.

Alex put away the beakers I'd just cleaned. "I suggested to Johann he send Peppa over some time. I could use a pair of steady hands."

I noted down the number of vials of pH strips as Emil called it out. "Really? He never said."

"Doesn't surprise me."

"I would have liked to apprentice at Sandoz."

"I certainly wouldn't waste you on doing inventory. I'd train you on the chromatography equipment."

For a minute I forgot I was going to Munich. A simple joy filled me. I liked working with Alex. With him, I didn't need to apologize when I was ignorant of a procedure.

I pecked him on the cheek. "Thanks."

Our final step was to dry the paper strips and spray them, like we'd done before. The substances we'd extracted in the column had migrated the same distance as the known atropine and scopolamine Alex had bought at the pharmacy. That meant our unknowns were identical to the two standards. When the spots turned brick red with Dragendorff's, it confirmed that they were all alkaloids.

We looked at each other, stunned, and then Emil whooped with joy. Alex pursed his lips and gave a low whistle. "Hello, Brugmansia."

Alex found an unopened bottle of champagne in the refrigerator, and we sipped from espresso cups as the shadows lengthened outside, and night stole in.

We'd done it. The impossible.

Thanks to help from my mother.

Ainslie's drawing of the vine was fresh in my memory, fresher than her voice or her physical presence. It occurred to me now that Simone was gone, the locket and the illustrations were all I had left of her. Da had given away her billowing white linen shirts and her fragrant boxes of Darjeeling tea. Her art books, with valuable color plates of Gustav Klimt and Odilon Redon's work, disappeared overnight. Her orchids languished, untended, until my aunt threw them away during a visit. I was sure he'd loved Ainslie, like he'd loved me. But it was a pity he'd needed to expunge every trace of her. Why hadn't I ever seen that before?

I narrowed my eyes at Alex. "Are you going to tell me about Da's experiments before I go to Germany? You might never see me again."

His cheeks sagged. As an old man, he'd be jowly. "I wish I could tell you. But Johann made me promise. He wasn't an easy man, Peppa. But I loved him like a brother. And I love you like a daughter."

Emil coughed to remind us he was there.

It was a kind thing Alex had said. I didn't know how to respond, so I didn't. Instead I said, "We should go soon. Someone might see the lights and call the police again."

Alex finished his champagne and hung up his lab coat. "I hope Tenzin can come tomorrow. I'm not convinced about this trip to Germany."

Emil laughed. "Have you ever tried to talk Peppa out of anything?"

"Not successfully."

We agreed to meet the next day at ten o' clock.

20. Greenhouse Escapades

I MET TENZIN AT CAFÉ HEBEL. HE'D PACKED MY BELONGINGS and, I saw with relief, a bag for himself. Wherever I was going to be hidden, he'd be coming along.

While we waited for Jakob, I told him about our successful day but also about Alex's fears for my safety. I concluded, "We're all going to meet at the lab tomorrow morning. I hope you'll agree to come with me."

Tenzin's eyes shone, dark, unreadable. "Of course I'll meet with Alex. I suppose I'll have to talk to Emil as well?"

"You don't like him?"

He covered my hand with his. He didn't wear a ring. Not that I'd been in the habit of checking until now. "Your eyes were hooded when you talked about him. But I see that's changed. You're not angry with him any longer?"

"No. He had his own difficulties. Let's talk about our plans."

He looked at me so long that my cheeks grew hot. I'd only meant our escape plans. I said something to break the intense silence. "What are you seeing now?"

"Trust. Affection. Friendship."

I blushed. I doubted that was all he saw. I was glad Patrick and I had gone no further than a kiss. What I felt for Tenzin was new and intense, putting my first innocent crush into perspective.

While we passed time waiting for Jakob, Tenzin sat drinking a glass of red wine, his foot tapping restlessly, eyes far away. He worked on a list sporadically, his questions to me growing increasingly disquieting.

"What size winter boots would you need?"

"How much do you think you can carry in a pack? Is 20 kilograms too much?"

"If we have no food for Simone, will she hunt?"

"Can you use a gun?"

At that point, I said, "Let's not get carried away, Tenzin. It's enough for me to know you'll be in Munich."

"Peppa," he sighed, in a way I took to be condescending. My nerves were on edge.

"I liked you better as a priest," I snapped.

He scowled. "You can be naïve sometimes. And I very much doubt you liked me better as a priest."

Did he know how attracted I was to him?

I dropped my gaze and started leafing through an early journal. Maybe I could find some more drawings from my mother.

My heart beat faster as an idea came to me. "Tenzin?"

"Yes."

"Do you know how to pick locks?"

His face became tight, like when I'd looked at him on the balcony that morning. "Why?"

"My mother met my father at the University of Basel's greenhouse, where she was making sketches. The greenhouse has a huge collection of exotics. Maybe they have one of the Brugmansias that Unruh used."

"You're asking me to break into the greenhouse?"

"Yes. I'd go with you, of course."

He tensed, considering. "That's even riskier. But then you'd know for sure about the poison?"

"Except that there's probably a pretreatment step involved, a venom that transmutes the plant compound. It could be a synergist, bringing out certain qualities of the Brugmansia, or it could be a catalyst of some kind, making the hallucinogen stronger."

"What haven't you told me?"

Reluctantly, I recounted my conversation with Dr. Unruh, including his disclosure about the scorpion. Tenzin's occasional questions were penetrating, and he winkled out Unruh's threats.

Afterwards, he stared at me, then gulped down the rest of his wine. "You've barely touched yours? Shall I drink it?"

"If you want to. You've kept me talking."

He pulled my glass over to him and helped himself. His eyes were far away. "I did have some good news I wanted to share with you. But now…"

"Tell me."

"All I can think about is Ludwig Unruh dropping a scorpion on your exposed thigh. He'll get to you. You know that. He'll exploit your youth and vulnerability. He'll alternately charm you and frighten you till your head is spinning."

"I'm not a little girl. I'm almost twenty."

His expression was bleak. "So you want to be exploited?"

Perhaps it was a good thing I hadn't had more than a sip of my wine. I was blurting out things. Now I said, "Unruh tried to frighten me, but that just made me angrier. I won't let him near me. But don't treat me like I'm a porcelain doll. I wouldn't shatter if someone touched me."

"Are you saying what I think you're saying?"

"If you're going to drink my wine, then I want an Ovaltine."

"Or are you telling me you're still a child, Peppa? Which is it?"

"What do you care? First I think you're a priest, then I find out you're married," I burst out.

We both sat breathing heavily.

"My first consideration should be to protect you. Since you have no instinct for survival." Our eyes locked, electricity passed between us. "Anything else is just a distraction," he added.

How could he say I had no instinct for survival? I'd killed the last man who'd come for me. I got up, approached the Angry Anatolian, who was engrossed behind the bar with a game of Solitaire, and asked for the Ovaltine myself.

He didn't even meet my eyes. "Don't have that. Cup of tea?"

"Do you have some milk for it?"

"No."

"Fine. I'll take it anyway." I shrugged and waited. Back at the table, I took a cautious sip. It was tepid. Tenzin folded his hands. He looked out the window at the gathering night without seeing it. "What are you thinking about?"

He sighed, as if deciding something. "I'm not a priest. And I'm not married either. Pema and I love Sherub. It will have to be enough."

I slammed down my cup in exasperation. "So now you're not married?"

"I'm not the type of man who's looking for a Sata-Savitri. A dutiful wife."

"But she's like your wife. You have a son with her," I persisted.

"Her brother Jamyang and I took the Khampa refugees out of eastern Tibet. We'd stop at Jamyang's village for a day or two, take care of the sick, tend frostbite, eat. Pema always brought us food. We started spending the night together when

I came through. I've never even lived with her. If it wasn't for that one photo, I might forget what she looks like."

I was relieved, but at the same time I was furious. Every time I thought I knew where I stood with Tenzin, the ground shifted. I wanted him so badly, it made my teeth hurt. "So how do matters stand?"

He smiled. "Her brother's in India right now settling in some of the people we brought over. I finally reached him by telephone. He says she would understand."

Understand what? I felt my heart soar, even as I cautioned myself not to jump to conclusions. Before I could ask anything though, Jakob walked in. He stopped at our table on the way to the bar. "Father Kneipp's hanging around the estate, discussing the place cards for the tables. Big Donor A is sleeping with Big Donor B's wife. They have to be kept apart. Let's have a drink here while we wait for him to bugger off."

Father Kneipp. The paper had said he would be showing a film before the fundraiser at Violet Strub's estate. Could Violet Strub be Jakob's employer? He'd warned me about keeping her identity secret, so I kept quiet.

Tenzin finished my wine. "Another drink sounds good. By the way, Jamyang says he'll mail the spruce seeds you asked for."

Jakob nodded. "I still want my Meconopsis. The blue poppy."

He limped off and came back with three schnapps, plunking one in front of me. "Boatman will do it. Passport's underway. I need the money, though."

I spread my hands, palm up and empty. "It's Saturday. I could get it for you Monday."

"Too late. You might be leaving Monday. Storms are forecast starting Tuesday."

I took off my watch. "This was my father's. Just till you get the money. I'll need it back. Please."

Jakob picked it up, balanced it on his palm, testing the weight. He squinted, looking for something, and seemed satisfied. "The stamp's there. Real gold."

Tenzin's jaw clenched. "The forger can wait for his money. So can the boatman. Just tell them to relax."

Jakob tossed down his first drink. "The watch is good. I'll take that."

Tenzin's mouth turned down in disgust. "I never knew you were like this."

"Like what? We don't know this girl. Only what we read in the paper, and that we do not like."

Tenzin's voice sank to a growl. "I know her. I like her."

Jakob drank down the next schnapps, savoring it this time. "I'm taking the risk, not you. What would you do for her?"

"I'm doing it."

"Would you do ... the same ... you know ... as you did for the others. Up in the mountains that autumn evening." Jakob gave us a broad wink.

"You're drunk." Tenzin's voice was hard. He looked fierce—like a bandit.

"My fucking leg hurts from my old bullet wound. Nazi *Schweinehund*. But at least I only got shot. I didn't shoot someone in the chest—at close range."

Stony silence. I grabbed the third drink. I didn't want it, but at least it was out of Jakob's reach.

"Ask your boyfriend what he did," Jakob said.

Tenzin's fist slammed down, making the glasses jump. "That's enough."

He stared at both of us defiantly, his eyes black stones. "Yes. I'd kill someone again if I had to. Just to keep Peppa safe."

I'd wanted to ask Jakob to take me to the University Conservatory to check for the Brugmansia, but now it seemed wiser not to say anything. I was blindfolded, lying down in the backseat of his car, so I wouldn't see where we were going. Tenzin knew, but Jakob didn't trust me.

The silence was like cement.

I could feel from the way the car was weaving that Jakob was tipsy. When the car crunched over gravel and then slid into something softer, he turned the motor off. I breathed a sigh of relief.

I felt hands on the blindfold, then an arm pushing me up. Jakob smelled different from Tenzin, earthy and pungent, more like schnapps.

"Your new home," he said, as I stepped out.

We were out in the country; the sky was dark and clear. Stars pricked their silver light, and a pared sliver of the moon punctuated the sky. It was past most Basel burghers' bedtimes.

He'd parked parallel to two greenhouses, situated at the bottom of the garden, against the fence. Ahead of me the two-story mansion rose, ghostly white. A large balcony with French doors gave view over the rose garden, the gazebo, and the fountain. A yew hedge, though low, obscured part of the greenhouses from view.

"If you have to do your business, go over there." Jakob jerked with his thumb. "I don't want to step into something tomorrow."

Tenzin's jaw was still clenched tight. "Thank you," I said, for both of us.

Jakob sounded thoughtful. "Peppa, I will need that money Monday, though."

"My godfather will get it."

Tenzin spoke. "I've got some money left. I'll give it all to you. Just shut up before I hit you."

Jakob nodded. "Easy there. We're friends, right."

Tenzin shrugged.

"I'll have my day off tomorrow. It would be better if you left the estate. My lady's having some friends over for tea and cucumber sandwiches. She makes them herself from the greenhouse cukes."

"Can I please talk to you tomorrow?" I'd try to bring up the University of Basel Conservatory when he was sober.

"I suppose. Sure." He walked off, favoring his left leg.

⁂

The greenhouse was heated, at least in the orangerie where two sleeping mats had been placed on the floor. The oranges were still green and hard. I brushed against a twiggy plant that released a strong lemon fragrance. Basil flowered in the pots, nearly at end, and a cucumber vine twined up a trellis. I tried a cherry tomato, letting the flavor burst in my mouth.

"I'm hungry," I said to the man I'd thought was a priest, who turned out to be a smuggler, and now a murderer. I didn't know what else to say.

"Mountain guides are always prepared." Tenzin pulled out a loaf of crusty white bread, some beef tongue, a hunk of Roquefort, two pears, and a bottle of wine.

"Is there any water?" I asked, once I'd smeared my bread with Roquefort.

He looked abashed.

"You know, water. For those of us who don't drink wine all the time."

He shrugged, looked over to the watering can.

"Fine. I suppose I can..." I tried to pour the water out the spout down my throat. It spilled all over me. Suddenly we were both laughing, great heaving bellows. The more we tried to be quiet, the louder we got. Tears came to my eyes, and then wouldn't stop.

"Peppa."

I blinked, sniffed, and tried to take a bite of the pear.

"I'm glad you know."

"All I know is you shot someone. I don't know when or why." In the dark corner of the greenhouse I saw a lacewing fly from the basket of petunias. Each individual vein shone. My shoulder blades itched and I scratched. Stretched. Flexed.

Tenzin. He killed someone. I'm all alone with him.

He sensed it. "Oh God, Peppa. I would never, ever, hurt you. It was a Chinese. Comrade Chan. That's what his badge said. I had five children and two women with me. They would have been sent to labor camps if we'd gotten caught."

I heard the appeal in his voice, and it made me soften. I forced my voice to be stern. "Tell me more."

"It was a cold, snowy night. We were close to the border of Bhutan, maybe half a day's walk. I didn't expect a patrol, but I always carried a gun. Chan must have wandered off from the camp, maybe to take a piss. I don't know what he was doing. The gunshot brought the others running, but they'd been drinking. It was a hard snow. They didn't see our footprints—ran right past us. I had to stuff my hat in the little girl's mouth—she wouldn't stop crying." His hand trembled a little bit as he picked up the wine and drank it straight from the bottle.

"People will sacrifice everything for the freedom to live as they see fit," he said at last. "They left their homes and families, gave me all their money. I had to keep them safe."

"And yet—you wonder."

"Who doesn't wonder? Only a monster. Chan. He was someone's son, maybe someone's husband, someone's father."

"Did you perform the ritual for him?"

"Not right away. I got all my people over the border, sick and frostbitten, but alive. I went back to Pema and my friends, got drunk. Ignored the next request to smuggle refugees, decided to see my grandparents instead, and went off to

Tshebar. It was like a worm turning into a dragon inside me. It got worse and worse. I saw Chan following me sometimes—but then it would be no one—a stranger."

Tenzin wasn't eating now. I took the untouched bread from him. "Go on."

"So I talked to a lama my grandfather knew. Very wise old man. He showed me the ritual. We talked about my future, about what I'd do now. He encouraged me to go to Europe. I wanted to give him lots of money for his help. He took only a little and said I should help someone in turn. He said I'd know when that time came. It was a year ago. And now I met you."

"So you're helping me so you can feel better about the man you killed."

"I wouldn't put it like that, but I suppose so."

I picked a leaf of basil and rolled it between my fingers, enjoying the fresh scent. "You haven't been very honest so far."

"How could I tell you I killed a Communist guard?" He couldn't meet my eyes then. "But I know what you mean. I'll try to be honest. Ask me anything."

"What did you and Pema's brother talk about?"

"Oh, that." He turned away, showing me his profile.

"You're going to be completely honest." I didn't try to keep the sarcasm out of my voice.

"If I met someone else. I mean, we'd talked about that before. I think she had someone when I was away. You know, it's not like here, in Europe, where you have to make a vow as soon as you're intimate."

"I've gathered that."

"So I asked Jamyang, what if, what if I had ... I mean, if I would..."

"And what did he say?"

"Pema is not waiting for me. There are two brothers who like her. Likely she'll marry into that family. They will accept Sherub."

Then it was very quiet for a long time. There was just the sound of his breathing, and the scent of jasmine. A moth fluttered up against the glass wall, beating his wings ecstatically.

His voice was low and intimate. "I would like very much to kiss you. But I won't be performing my dharma if I allow that to happen. And you're not even twenty. Besides…"

"I had a friend who told me 'stop running from your feelings.' It was good advice."

A sharp intake of breath. Then his mouth met mine, and after a while his hands slipped against my bare skin. We could have stopped any time, but we didn't.

We could have doubted, we could have been afraid, but we were hopeful and ardent, and in that moment, the dark future was forgotten. The present was a velvet robe enfolding us, the scent of sweet flowers made us dizzy, and I finally understood what making love should feel like. Like a spiral staircase to the moon made of whispers and sighs.

I woke the next morning, the heat from Tenzin's body keeping me warm. I now understood why this act guided so much of adult behavior. It combined the excitement of discovery with addictive pleasure. I stretched, for once not hating my thin legs and flat chest. He'd said I was beautiful. I knew he meant it.

I touched his hair and skin. My father and I had never embraced, and I had avoided Aunt Madeleine's pecks on the cheek. It was a new luxury to run my fingers across his broad chest.

He awoke with that. "Are you happy?"

"Yes."

"Did I please you?"

"Oh yes, especially that thing with the…" I became quiet, lost in the sense memory.

"Peppa?"

He sounded guilty. I hoped there wasn't a further revelation that would upset me. But all he said was "I'm not ready to get married."

I laughed but stopped when I saw the stricken expression on his face.

"Don't European girls expect to get married after this happens?"

I looked away from Tenzin then, trying to puzzle things out. I'd been preoccupied with outwitting Unruh and staying ahead of the police. Tenzin's desire and affection came as a wonderful revelation. But women didn't just sleep with men unless there was a future in it—unless the men were older and rich, and the girls were needy or reckless.

I had never given weddings much thought. There were no wedding photographs in our house, and Da never spoke about that day. Coming to think of it, I didn't even know where my parents were married, or who attended. Had there been a celebration?

Tenzin was still looking at me, frowning.

I patted my hair down with my fingers before answering. "Maybe we could have a long engagement. Get to know each other properly."

"As long as you're not expecting…"

"I might be understanding this love thing better." I frowned, realizing perhaps the man was supposed to bring that up first.

His cheeks became pink, and he smiled. "I also feel better acquainted with this love thing." He was gently mocking me.

I didn't care. I gave him another kiss, which turned into a longer one, until we both heard footsteps.

21. Break-In

JAKOB APPEARED AT THE DOOR, GRUNTING A GREETING.

"Just a minute." I dove into my sweater, abandoning my brassiere, which was crumpled under a bench. Tenzin began tidying up.

Jakob squinted his eyes at the mats pushed together. "Ah ha."

I ought to feel ashamed. Girls weren't supposed to like this. But I couldn't keep the big smile off my face. "Good morning, Jakob."

He set down two mugs of coffee. "I'm off for a long hike today. Where do you want me to drop you off?"

I looked at my watch. "It's only eight. I can't get in at Sandoz till ten."

Tenzin slurped his coffee. "You were an asshole yesterday," he informed Jakob.

Surprisingly, Jakob grinned. He didn't even seem hungover. "So what else is new, schlemiel?"

"Peppa wants to ask you a favor."

I explained about the botanical drawing that my mother made and the accompanying notes. "This Brugmansia's leaves are about 8 cm in the wild state, bluish green, evenly serrated. The flower is quite striking, not just from the trumpet shape but the color. It's milky-green outside and yellow inside. Seed pods about 4 cm, usual thornapple shape, the prongs a bit more pronounced than is typical of the genus."

Jakob pruned the budding spike off a basil plant. "So? Why are you telling me?"

"I'm wondering if you've seen a plant like that at the university greenhouse?"

"Range?"

"Brazilian highlands."

"There might be one. I was there recently to check the bromeliads, and I noticed they had some angel trumpets."

I clasped my hands together. "I need it."

"I might be able to get you a cutting in a couple of weeks. I know Dr. Bamberger slightly."

"No, no. I need the whole plant. As much material as possible."

"Well, you can't have it. It's in the greenhouse at the University."

Tenzin gave him a sideways look. "It's not as if it's guarded."

Jakob stopped his pruning. "I don't like where this is going. Are you suggesting I drop you off there?"

"No. I wondered if you could wait while we get it," I explained.

He looked dumbfounded. "Why would I do something like that? This is my employer's car. She trusts me to be discreet."

"Please. I can't take a tram holding a large potted plant."

He still stared at me. "My job was just to get you over the border and away from the Swiss police."

"I'm trying to stop Dr. Unruh from hurting more people. We've identified his poison as a scopolamine. But now it's all used up. If I made some more, my friends can go to the police if I don't return. They can explain what he did."

"You think it will be that easy? Anyway, I don't have time to take you and wait around while you commit another crime. My friend is expecting me at nine."

"Please. We really need your help."

"She made me braided egg bread, and she has homemade raspberry jam to go with it. And she's Swiss, so she hates it when someone's late. I was late the first time I asked her out, and there almost wasn't a second time."

Tenzin held up his hand when I tried to talk.

"Unruh's threatening to experiment on Peppa. The more she knows about the plant, the better for her."

Jakob cocked an eyebrow at me. "Poor girl."

Tenzin's voice deepened, became curt. "You know you're going to do it, so stop arguing."

"My friend's always wanted a mulberry tree. An Indian one, not a Persian one," Jakob said.

"I'll see what I can do."

As Tenzin and I neared the greenhouse, we heard the easy laughter of a few students leaving the nearby building. We tried to look nonchalant as we approached the door. Jakob's car was parked down the street, waiting.

Tenzin took out his Swiss army knife while I scanned the street, alert for anyone coming our way. I hoped most of the students were still sleeping off Saturday evening's festivities. Minutes later I heard the click as the lock gave way.

We stole in, turning left under a row of palms and elephant ears, then passing a tinkling fountain. The beams of sunlight highlighted things at random; a striking purple flowering succulent, a strand of delicate vining Clerodendrum, the red heart-shaped flowers small but vibrant. The smell was atavistic, moist and earthy.

We turned down another aisle, large plantings of Euphorbias clustered along the edge. And there they were, behind the tall lanky plants with their dots of flat yellow flowers. Three pots of Brugmansias, clustered next to a jacaranda. And not just any Brugmansias. One still sported the telltale bloom, milky green, like Pastis liquor on ice. The inside looked like summer, buttery yellow.

Tenzin pulled out his knife again, leaning in through the Euphorbias. "What do you need?"

"They're in pots. Let's just take an entire pot. I want to try different extracts: the branches separate from the leaves, and another batch from the roots."

"A whole pot?"

I planted my feet and tried to pull the pot toward me, nearly losing my footing.

"That's the one you want?"

I nodded, and Tenzin dove through the Euphorbias, encircling it in his strong arms. "Keep the top stabilized then, and let me carry it," he directed.

We'd just reached the glass door when we heard voices. Some people had stopped, speaking in French. Were they planning to come in? I couldn't understand their rapid, rolling vowels. Tenzin and I glanced at each other, and he drew back in the shadows of a palm with his burden.

If we moved, they'd hear us. I barely dared to breathe. He stood stock still, the muscles on his arms bulging as he held the Brugmansia to his chest. When the voices receded, I let out a sigh of relief.

We walked as quickly as we dared and reached the Packard, where Jakob rolled his eyes at the plant but loaded it onto the floor in the back.

"I'll be glad to see the last of you," he grumbled. "Now where to?"

I gave him the address of Sandoz Labs.

"Rahel will not ever talk to me again."
"I'm really sorry. This is very nice of you."
He waved me off. "Manners don't suit you."

22. Ten Rats

As Jakob pulled away, tires squealing, I bounded across the parking lot of Sandoz Laboratories, eager to start. Tenzin lagged behind, struggling with the swaying Brugmansia. The lone flower held on valiantly. Alex poked his head out in alarm at the noise, and his eyes widened when he saw the plant. "Is that what I think it is?"

"We have all day long to find out."

"We ought to do toxicology; see if it elicits aggressive behavior. I'll send Emil for rats."

I hesitated, as Tenzin lugged the plant past me.

"I could ingest our extraction," I finally said. "The last rats attacked each other."

Alex cut me off, his voice loud. "Never try something out on a human until all the animal studies are done. Never. What is wrong with you?!"

I'd never seen him angry before. "Fine. We'll use rats. Low doses, though, and watched carefully. I'll not have them tearing each other to bits. It's cruel. Is Emil here?"

"I'm here and ready." Emil's hair was shiny with hair pomenade today, falling over his comely face in a soft wave. He waved at Tenzin. "Hello, Peppa's friend."

"Sorry, I should introduce you. This is Tenzin Engel."

They shook hands like two proper young men, and then Alex told Emil to get us some rats from Wyss's lab.

"That's a pity," Emil said, thinking perhaps of his pet.

"We need to have a defense prepared for Peppa if she gets caught. I brought a camera to take shots of their behavior."

"I'll pick up some sandwiches while I'm out. The railway station will have an open kiosk," Emil said, reaching for his car keys. "Hope I don't miss too much."

I reassured him. "I'll leave the actual alcohol extraction for you. We have to dry the leaves first anyway."

Emil left and Alex looked at Tenzin, waiting.

When Tenzin said, "I'd like to speak with you about our plans," Alex nodded approvingly.

"Let's get the leaves drying first."

They cut off leaves and I laid them on the oven tray. Then we made ourselves comfortable in the break room. Clara had baked us braided egg bread, and Alex unpacked butter and jam for it. He even remembered some Ovaltine for me.

"So." Alex stirred some sugar into his coffee. "Peppa tells me you want to go to Munich as well."

"We're going to meet there," I explained.

Alex said, pleasantly enough, "I'm speaking to the young man now. Why don't the two of you just go together?"

"Peppa will be brought over to the German side of the Rhine on a small skiff. She'll find a bicycle hidden in the bushes for her. She'll have to ride to Freiburg to get further instructions from an associate of Dr. Unruh, and catch a train from there."

"Brought over? You mean smuggled, don't you?"

"It's better the border police don't see the forged passport. It's a good job, but the best forger lives in Paris now. Not enough time to use him."

Alex raised an eyebrow at that. He had more questions about the trip arrangements, but finally he was satisfied. "So what are you planning for Munich?"

Tenzin played with the end of his plait. "The thing is ... may I be frank?"

"I'm hoping you will be."

"They'll get in a confrontation. I can sense it. The push between them."

"Could you be more specific? I'm a chemist. I don't *sense* things."

"I think you might, though, Dr. Kaufmann."

Alex snorted. "Go on."

"This confrontation. Peppa's spirit is powerful, but he's determined to harness her. One of them will win. One of them lose—probably die."

"We can't let it come to that. I'll only agree to let Peppa go on the condition she gather concrete evidence about his experimentation. Then he'll be arrested."

"Yes, in an ideal world. But one can't always depend on the law."

"Justice should be served."

"Where was justice when the Chinese invaded the western province of Tibet, turned the monks out, burned the temples?"

Alex's brow wrinkled, but his face had its usual expression of patient forbearance. "This is Europe."

"A continent recently ravaged by war," I pointed out. "Were the Nazis examples of civilized behavior?"

Alex reacted like a patriot. "We're in Switzerland, not Germany."

When no one answered, he said, "How is Peppa going to find you?"

"I'll stay at a hotel nearby. If she's in a tight spot, she can contact me. I'll help her and Simone get out, flee if they need to."

"You sound like you know your way around a tight spot. Is that right?"

"I don't like to talk about myself."

"Is your father really a missionary?"

Tenzin frowned. He brushed at his arms and started scratching.

"Something wrong?"

"No, no. My skin just feels warm and prickly. I'll be all right." His voice soft, emotionless, Tenzin spoke about his upbringing in Dehra Dun and his work at the Mission House, up to the time he received Stefan Sepp's letter.

Alex nodded, got up and checked the baking leaves, and sat back down. "How did you and this fellow from the Appenzell get to be friends?"

"The same fellows that teased me about the braid were making fun of him. Any violence upsets Stefan, makes him cry and shake."

"And then what happened?"

"Well." Tenzin looked at the ground. "I picked the biggest one and head-butted him. They didn't bother us again. They're seminary students. They shouldn't be ugly like that anyway."

"Are you going to fight Dr. Unruh too?"

"I'd rather not. But I'll do the needful."

I knew Tenzin would kill him if he had to. If I didn't kill him myself. But that would alarm Alex. His eyes were already full of doubt.

I took Alex's hand in my own. "No one will get hurt. I'll just go for a few days, until Unruh drops his guard and I can get evidence. Then Tenzin can help me get to the police."

Alex was silent, his expression somber.

"I've got to go, don't you see?"

He brushed at the corner of his eye, water leaking out. "I just lost my dear friend last spring. I don't want to lose you too."

"You won't."

Tenzin had left to pick up the passport, and it was time for us to start working. I added ammonia to the dried leaves in the mortar, then ground them with the pestle. The place smelled like someone getting a perm. My eyes smarted.

Alex poured alcohol onto the mix. Emil filled five full Erlenmeyer flasks with the resulting slurry, while I set up the ring stands and Bunsen burners. I started stirring the first one, eying the green juice with a mixture of trepidation and curiosity. "Why'd you get so angry when we talked about experimenting on people?"

"It's a bad idea."

"But I was just going to try out a tiny bit myself. It's my responsibility, after all."

His voice was sharp. "It's *my* responsibility to prevent you from doing stupid things." My jaw clenched at his harsh words.

We had an hour till the extraction process was finished. I decided to make a mash with the roots and stems while I was waiting. Alex helped me tip the heavy potted plant over into the large crate I'd used to hide in the day before. As I crouched down and started brushing off the loamy soil, I considered Alex's angry reaction. Da had often been away in the evenings, doing research. Had my father been experimenting on patients without telling them? I would have noticed. Wouldn't I?

Like I noticed that his health was declining? I hadn't. Da had sat me down one evening and given it to me straight. "I've got liver cancer and maybe two months to live. We're going home."

My hand slipped, and a thin line of blood welled up from the knife I'd been cutting the roots with. I popped the finger in my mouth.

"You'd better concentrate," Alex said.

I looked at my pale knobby fingers, the same ones that had brought pleasure to Tenzin the night before. I went over to the lab sink, splashed my face with cold water, and recited the capitals of Europe in reverse alphabetical order. Then I started the maceration.

By one o' clock we'd filtered the leaves, stirred the liquid with activated carbon, and removed the chlorophyll with a little bit of silica gel. We ate our sandwiches on the backdoor stoop, alert to any sounds of intruders. I swept up the crumbs and handed them to Emil.

"Give them a little treat. No reason they can't have some fun before the execution." My words took on an ominous tone as I considered my upcoming trip. I was going to see Dr. Unruh. I'd had my fun, and now I was on my way to the spider. The food stuck in my throat, and I took a hasty swallow of the closest thing nearby, Alex's beer.

I am the god of war and vengeance. Unruh wasn't going to find me an easy prey.

I followed Emil inside and watched from a safe distance, alert to any alterations in my heartbeat or breathing that might indicate the rats triggering the falcon's kill instinct. When nothing happened, I moved a bit closer, until I noticed the rats becoming more agitated, squeaking and moving around.

If the falcon was a figment of my imagination, why were they reacting to it?

Emil gave me a swift glance. "Move away, would you? They must not like your perfume. I'll do the testing."

We would try the extract on the rats in various dosages, but it was hard to tell when a rat hallucinated. I still wouldn't know if the scorpion venom or the Brugmansia was responsible for that.

If only I could observe the action of Brugmansia alone in a human.

Which gave me an idea. An idea of how to kill Dr. Unruh, if I had to. Make him take it.

But how? He'd know right away if I offered him a drink.

Not to mention he'd be more dangerous. But the justice of punishing him with the same weapon he'd used on me was pleasing. Very.

Emil had just idly mentioned perfume, casting about for a logical reason the rats were frightened of me. Perfume...

I watched him measure out 0.1 milliliters with a dropper and grab the rat. Alex took the syringe with the flexible catheter and inserted the rubber tube in the animal's mouth with one quick motion. We'd sweetened the solution, and the rat swallowed willingly.

They placed it back in the cage. Emil pulled up a stool in front of it, poised with notebook at hand. I went back to my root maceration.

Emil called over. His rat ran around in circles, looking confused. Alex tapped on the glass, but it didn't rise to the bait.

Alex pulled on gloves and grabbed a second rat, dropping it in by the first one. Emil leaned over intently, ready to separate them as soon as things got bloody. The first rat ignored its new companion. The second one flicked its tail, rose on its hind legs, and tried to climb out.

"I don't blame you, *Mäuschen*," I said from my place in the corner.

Alex measured out a larger dose for the next rat. He'd laid down his lab notebook, and it was opened to the page with glued-on paper chromatography strips. The neat circles of the potion extracts still shone brick red from the Dragendorff's reagent. Shone like lipstick.

I fidgeted impatiently, waiting for Alex to finish his work before I asked him my question. "Could you get me some lipstick, face cream, and perfume today?"

Alex kept his eyes on his rodent. "I could tomorrow, when the stores are open."

"I've got to go when Jakob says. It could be any time. Doesn't Clara have anything like that?" Alex's wife was always properly attired in a hat and gloves unless she was picnicking or riding bikes.

Emil raised one fine eyebrow. "This is a change of direction for you. What happened to the androgynous look?"

"I'm going to take some extract, cook it down, and then pour it into a perfume atomizer. It'll be my secret weapon, hidden in with the makeup."

Emil grinned. "Brilliant. Give him his own poison."

Alex looked interested and horrified in equal measures. "If you give it to Dr. Unruh, it could make him sick. Kill him. Isn't Tenzin coming to protect you?"

"I wouldn't use the poison unless I had to."

Emil took my side. "Don't send Peppa without any weapons. I'll give you the keys to the Chevy, and you can go home and fetch the items. We'll be right here."

"A bottle of perfume?" Alex shook his head, but he took the proffered car keys with a deep sigh.

At five o clock that evening, rat number 9 rose on its hind legs and tried to bite Emil through the glass after oral administration of 1.5 milliliters of the leaf decoction. Unable to reach its target, it battered itself against the wire mesh of the top, while Alex snapped several portraits with his Leica camera. It was dead within five minutes.

The autopsy would have to wait. I had one more thing to try before we packed up for the night.

I bit my lip, hating what might come. But I had to know. "Emil, please bring subject 10." I poured in 5 milliliters of my concentrate, diluted it to 5% with 100 milliliters of water, and asked him to immerse the squeaking, terrified rat.

Ten minutes later it lunged against the side of the cage, shaking with blind rage. This time I was ready with Alex's ether-soaked handkerchief, and it crumpled, anesthetized. At least it would not destroy itself.

We'd made a variation of Compound Totentanz, even without the scorpion venom. Both topical and oral administration was highly toxic.

I funneled 150 milliliters into one of the two bottle of Eau Du Temps perfume Alex had brought. Fifty milliliters went into a bottle of Estee Lauder facial toner. I zipped them up in the cosmetic case, next to the red lipstick and eyeliner.

I smelled like rat urine. Curious, I sprayed myself with the second Eau Du Temps bottle that Alex had taken from his daughter's vanity table. I'd never used perfume before. Maybe Tenzin would like it.

We had three full flasks of Compound T left.

"What do we do with that?" I asked.

"Store it. It's our proof. It's not too late to go to the police," Alex said. He went to a drawer and took out large glass vials.

I shook my head. Tomorrow I'd be crossing the Rhine. "If I don't come back..."

"Don't say that."

"There's a professor Da used to write to. Maybe you know him. Dr. Cegny in Geneva. You can send it to him with an anonymous note. I don't want either of you to get in trouble."

"You're coming back." Alex took out a wax-sealing block. "I'll make sure these are air tight, and put them in the back of my freezer. We don't know what the compound's stability is." He rotated the block so the heat from the Bunsen burner softened the wax on all sides. Emil helped me seal the thirty vials while Alex labeled each one with the date, his initials, and the designation "Compound T."

I'd never really appreciated Alex's calm and foresight properly till now. I wished he could safely bottle up my essence in a jar too, while the rest of me went to meet Dr. Unruh.

23. Farewell

I SAID MY GOODBYES TO ALEX, HOPING HE WOULDN'T GET INTO too much trouble because of me.

Alex looked anxious until I promised Tenzin would call Monday night, when he arrived in Munich. Then he gave a deep sigh and embraced me. "Be safe."

Emil took me to our regular meeting place, the bar, where Tenzin would be waiting. He parked the car, leaving the engine idling.

"Tenzin can wait in the bar. Let's talk," I told Emil.

"I'd like to. This might be the last time I see you." His voice shook.

"You sounded confident in front of Alex."

"It's what you wanted. You've always been fierce. I wouldn't hold you back."

"Thanks for your help. I've got something for you." I handed over the key to a safe deposit box at Basel Kantonal Bank.

"What's that for?"

"Da closed down his lab at Harvard when we left. But the safe deposit box contains all the documented methodology for Paxarbital, our new drug. He changed out a couple of carbon bonds on the basic barbiturate structure ... well, you'll see. Everything's ready to go. Another round of animal testing and then clinical trails with humans."

"This should be your masterpiece, Peppa."

"Yes. But if I get back, we can do it together. I'm depending on you to synthesize some, so we can get to work."

"Wyss won't let me..."

"You don't need him. There are five thousand francs stacked alongside the paperwork. Rent a lab, work at night. You're resourceful."

"But the bank won't just let me access the box."

"Father wrote your name on the list along with mine and Alex's. I never understood why. We fought about it."

"Oh. What did he say?"

"Don't judge him. His life hasn't been easy."

Emil met my gaze, his blue eyes intense. "I won't let you down. I'll go straight to the bank from here."

"Good. I have to go, Emil."

"Be safe."

We shook hands formally, but something in my heart eased. My friend was back.

I passed the time waiting for Tenzin by looking through the most recent journal Da had kept. There was one odd entry.

Took Carmen out and bought her martinis. She finally told me what I suspected. It will be on the market soon. I actually remembered that day. Carmen was some old acquaintance from Basel, who'd come to a pharmaceutical firm convention in Boston. Da returned reeking of booze and in a foul mood. He even slapped at Simone when she jumped up to greet him.

The other unusual thing was the handwritten chart with ascending SGOT levels. It looked like he'd only recorded one subject's test values. The dates were from the previous year. Of course, he'd kept records of the cardiac patients that were referred to him for testing. Those data were entered and tabulated in a notebook kept by the Sigma spectrophotometer.

The cardiologists from Massachusetts General could drop by any time and correlate the SGOT levels with the clinical evidence of a myocardial event, even add notes of their own. SGOT rose after a heart attack and eventually fell back to normal level. These SGOT levels, recorded weekly in the diary, had kept rising for six months.

Did he have a secret patient in our basement who suffered from a never-ending heart attack? I smiled to myself at the ridiculous idea.

Tenzin walked through the door. The sight of him made my heart do flips.

He sat down, signaled for a drink, and put down the large suitcase. "I've got a *choba*—a sheepskin coat, for tonight. It's supposed to get cold. I brought some other things too. How did it go today?"

I was just telling him about the perfume bottle full of Brugmansia when Jakob hobbled in to collect us. On the way to the estate I kept quiet. Jakob had put the blanket on me again so I couldn't see where we were going, though of course I'd already guessed that we were at Mrs. Strub's estate.

When we pulled up in front of the greenhouse, Jakob opened the door for me. He avoided looking at me while Tenzin passed him a sheaf of crumpled notes. "It's all I had."

"I can try to get the rest of the money from Alex at lunchtime tomorrow," I offered.

Jakob shook his head. "Tenzin will pick it up from Dr. Kaufmann. You're leaving before dawn tomorrow morning. Passport's ready. I'll take you to the meeting point on the Rhine."

"So soon?" My voice sounded childish.

"Every day you stay here is a risk for her."

I bowed my head. "Of course. Thank you."

Our lovemaking was urgent and passionate. I rose and fell against Tenzin's bronze body until I was sated; then a stirring reignited us. An ocean pounded through my heart, the waves slamming me back onto him, every time I emerged.

Finally, we lay next to each other, fingers entwined. I drifted in a tide of pleasure. The moon rose, a cold wind blew in, an uhu gave its lost cry.

Tenzin stretched languorously. "We ought to make plans."

"Yes," I said. His hair was tangled. "Let me braid it."

I struggled to weave the shining dark strands in a plait. It was harder than it looked. "Your ears are red and hot."

"All of me is hot," he murmured.

"No, really. Your ears are swollen."

He scratched one absentmindedly. "I found out where Dr. Unruh lives. I got the operator to tell me. The phone number is unlisted, but since I knew it, she gave me the address."

I imagined Tenzin's voice, friendly but puzzled, the hapless foreigner trying to find a resident.

"She even knows the neighborhood. Schwabing, by the university."

"Did you make a new friend?" I teased, picturing him winning her trust.

He smiled. "I'll be at the Pensione Kaiserhof. It's not far." He told me the phone number and address. "I'll arrive Monday night and buy supplies the next day in case we need to run. If I can, I'll try to make a sign on Unruh's mailbox, or the corner of the building. That way you'll know I've arrived."

"What sign?"

"A blue swastika." He noted my expression of loathing. "The Nazis stole that from us. It means 'eternity.' The ability of the soul to continue on, though the form changes."

I thought of the falcon who was part of me. I used to be sure of who I was. Now I was splintered, part of me softened by love, part of me hardened into talons and claws. I wondered what would survive, and what would be burned away.

Tenzin looked me in the eye. "You put Compound T in that perfume bottle. Do you mean to kill him?"

"No." I waited. No reaction. "Maybe. I don't know what I should do. I couldn't just poison him. That would be cruel. Wouldn't it?"

"But you're curious to see what it would do?"

I shifted uneasily, dropping my eyes. "Am I a monster? Is there something wrong with Da and me? The hungry ghost, you called him."

"That's a very good question."

"Well, is there?"

"I am not the judge of your life, nor your father's. But you made yourself over into a copy of him to win his love. Know what that entailed."

I stood up in disbelief, taking a step back. "I had to win his love? Is that what you just said?"

"Perhaps I should have said it differently."

"Did I ask your damn opinion of my family? My father loved me."

"Yes, he did. Yesterday I read, 'I'm enjoying talking to little Peppa. She's getting more interesting since she's been able to grasp elementary principles of chemistry.'"

I sat down again, cradling my head in my palms. I felt defeated. "I'm the wrong person to go see Dr. Unruh. I'm very confused. I know all the wrong things."

"You're exactly the right person to deal with him."

"You mean I'm no better than him. I'm thinking about running experiments on him, just like he wants to experiment on me."

Tenzin took my hand. "I've struggled with the idea of you harming him, but I'm clear on matters now. If you find fate presents you with an opportunity, you should end his life. And end his pain."

I pulled back, shocked. "You're encouraging me to kill him! Dr. Unruh isn't suffering."

"Any being so out of harmony is suffering. Return him to his source and pray he can be reborn."

"Why don't you do that?"

"I'm not opposed to it. I can't take a gun over the border, but I have a knife in a holster around my ankle. It could be a merciful death. More so than poison. If he's at peace when he dies, his next life will be better."

I must have gone pale, because he asked, "What is it, Peppa? You got quiet."

"I can't justify killing him."

He kissed me. "If you could, I couldn't care for you like I do. But you'll do what you need to. Now, I want to give you a gift."

"You already have." I smiled, feeling warm inside, my skin tingling where he'd touched me.

He looked at me seriously and took out a tiny bronze vessel wrapped in a white silk scarf. "It's in here. My grandfather's most prized possession. A long time ago, he made some kanglings, trumpets made from femur bones. He brought them and some drums to the monastery in Yongla. It's a beautiful place—you can see the Himalayas to the north and the great plains of Assam to the south. The musical instruments were first used during the making of a sacred sand painting."

I looked at him, questioning.

"The sand paintings are mandalas, sacred interlocking designs meant to focus the mind. They're formed out of millions of grains of colored sand, only to be destroyed once they're completed."

"Like your beautiful portraits."

He shifted, trying to find words. "Over here everyone aspires to create something eternal. But that's an illusion. Generals, popes, kings—they too die and are reborn onto another stage. Trying to hold onto something just creates pain. We're not masters of our fate. I hoped to absolve myself of the guilt from Chan's death. But instead I'm in a similar situation."

He stared at the ground. "I may have fallen in love with you."

Tears filled my eyes. To hear this now, something I'd never even let myself want. To hear it from a man who admired my strength, who wasn't afraid of my intellect.

To hear it now, when I had to leave.

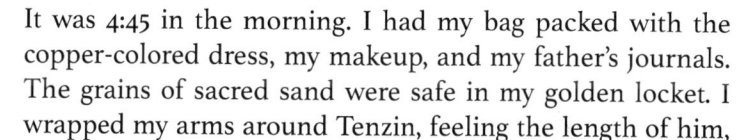

It was 4:45 in the morning. I had my bag packed with the copper-colored dress, my makeup, and my father's journals. The grains of sacred sand were safe in my golden locket. I wrapped my arms around Tenzin, feeling the length of him, the reassuring warm solidity, the vibrant energy.

I was practically engaged to a wonderful man who could look past my plain features into my spirit. At least the terrible events of the last few months had led me to love.

Tenzin cradled my head against his shoulder, stroking my hair. "Promise you'll think of me. Don't let him manipulate you. Be careful."

"I can handle him. I'm just going there to get my dog, and then..." When no words came, he kissed me long and deep.

He kissed me goodbye.

"My very writing became a different adventure ... a lucid building ... the work of a chemist who weighs and divides, measures and judges on the basis of assured proofs, and strives to answer questions ... I now felt ... a complex, intense, and new pleasure."
—*Primo Levi*

Munich, 1957

24. Misdirection

GERMANY. IT WAS FULL OF GERMANS. WE SWISS-GERMANS, united by similar language and cleaning habits, separated into two countries through natural borders of mountains and lakes, had long distrusted them. Since the Blitzkrieg tactics of 1939, we also hated and feared them. Germany was the bully older brother whom we looked and sounded like. But we weren't like that; Switzerland was a tiny and modest land, known only for financial acumen and pharmaceutical expertise. And of course, nonaggression and neutrality. Even our dialect, singsong and sprinkled with diminutives, was a twittering echo of their menacing guttural speech. We were taught proper German in school, but they couldn't have understood our dialects if they wanted to.

Caught up in my dark thoughts, which mingled with my hatred of Dr. Unruh, I hadn't realized a policeman was standing close by. I had just gotten off the train in Munich, a small suitcase in one hand and the carrying case for the ten scuttling African scorpions in the other. They were hairy little monsters, just like the man who'd prepared them for delivery.

The policeman held a clipboard in his big hand. He turned toward me. He looked like he could have been Hermann Goering's twin brother.

I started toward the first exit I saw, trying to move nonchalantly. He was next to me in no time. "Miss. Stop."

My legs felt like water. He was built like a bull, his shoulders massive. Goering had killed himself, hadn't he? I couldn't remember.

His voice was like a bullet. "Are you listening? I asked you where you were from."

"I'm Swiss." My new passport identified me as Kristina Moser, from Kandersteg, a small town in the Bernese mountains.

"Let's see your passport."

I handed it over. There had been no time to doctor a photograph of me; they'd used another young woman who had the same short hair and long face.

As he studied it, I thought about making a run for the street. Then I saw another policeman approaching from my left, cutting me off from the exit.

Germany was a democracy now, wasn't it? So they couldn't interrogate prisoners brutally. Or could they? I felt frozen to the floor. In a minute the other policeman would be here.

He spoke to the Goering look-alike. "Let's try the place outside for lunch. They sell that new stuff—the pizza. It's only fifty pfennig."

"I'm ready. My stomach's been grumbling for the last hour." When he handed me back my passport, I walked toward the exit as fast as I dared. It might be irrational prejudice, but

I was terrified of the German police. I hadn't been to another country since we'd last visited my grandmother in '51, and at that moment I felt very young and alone.

I stood on the steps, taking deep gulps of air.

A woman approached me. She wore a sober and dark suit, and had a pale and delicate face. "Dear, are you all right?"

"I need to get to Turk Road." The address the scorpion dealer had given me matched the one Tenzin coaxed out of the telephone operator.

"The tram's right that way," she pointed to where I saw the tail end of a blue trolley swishing down the street. "Next one should come in less than ten minutes."

The day was warm and clear, leaves shivered in the breeze, and birds sang. In my shabby, secondhand clothes, I'd expected to fit right in with the humbled citizens of the Third Reich, but I was ten years behind times. Munich had a purposeful and busy air. Next to the scattered rubble, lots razed clean of memories invited new apartments and stores. A group of workmen shoveled dirt and stacked bricks, giving me cursory glances as I walked by, head bent. Across the street, a row of green VW Bugs stood guard in front of a crane.

A woman swayed her hips in a sleek black dress, her hair gathered back in a ponytail. On the corner a group of American GIs smoked in a huddle, watching her appreciatively. I'd heard that right after the war German women slept with them for a bar of chocolate or a pack of cigarettes. These days, the soldiers might have to try a bit of gallantry.

I passed a double amputee and fumbled in my purse for some change. The scorpion dealer had given me a train ticket and some German coins.

Once I was on the trolley, I asked the old man next to me when to get off and received a polite answer. Where had he been and what had he been doing fifteen years ago? I probably didn't want to know.

I got out on the corner of Turk Street. On the wall next to me, a poster of a man with his arms swung out wide invited me to the 1957 Oktoberfest. He wore a big red heart around his neck and held a rose and a fish in one hand, a giant beer in the other. I looked away, only to have my eye drawn to a political poster, a bearded man in silhouette, extorting people to choose the SPD party and do away with the shadow.

I pursed my lips. I hadn't followed politics much. It looked like Munich was rushing into the future full-force. The city made the measured pace of Basel look slow. Thin, bespectacled students rushed past, heavy book bags slung over their shoulders. An ice-cream shop squeezed between two fancy clothing boutiques tempted a woman with a perambulator. Ladies with high heels navigated the crowds, and men with hats whizzed by on bicycles. I came to a stop in front of an enormous modern monstrosity, white with small metal balconies. While it was new, it certainly wasn't luxurious. It reminded me of a steel beehive. I checked the address on the paper against the building in disbelief. Did Dr. Unruh scrimp on the rent so he could buy elegant clothes and a BMW? Where was his shiny black car anyway?

After some searching, I found the doorbell that said Dr. L. Unruh. When there was no answer, I pressed again. A woman appeared at the small balcony on the fourth floor, just big enough for one chair. "I heard you the first time," she said, irritably. "Wait."

A few minutes later she waltzed out the door. Her support socks had rolled down, revealing pale, swollen legs. She had a scarf knotted around her head and wore a faded blue dress, fastened by a man's belt.

"Do you have something for Dr. Unruh?"

"I was told to bring his exotic pets." The scorpion dealer had coached me not to call them scorpions.

"You must be the girl he was expecting then. I'll telephone his chauffeur, get you picked up."

My mouth fell open. "Doesn't he live here?"

Her laughter was shrill. "Dr. Unruh live here? I should think not. He's my landlord. Though I'd invite him to spend the night fast enough. He's a real gentleman; there are few enough of them left. All the real men are dead."

You've got no one to blame but yourselves. The concentration camp of Dachau had only been half an hour from Munich by car. I pressed my lips together. The bigger problem was that Tenzin would be expecting me to be here.

She was closing the door when I said, "Where does he live then?"

"I haven't a clue, and if I did, I wouldn't tell you. He sends the chauffeur to collect the rent every month." She slammed the door.

Scheisse.

The purring BMW glided like a black swan through an intersection manned by a policeman in a white suit, hat, and gloves. We crossed broad boulevards named after Bavarian kings and headed toward a green leafy strip and a broad bridge. Were we leaving town? How would Tenzin ever find me?

"Where are we going?"

All I could see of the chauffeur from the back seat was his jaunty dark cap and solid neck. I repeated my question.

He answered reluctantly. "We've passed Schwabing. Going to Bogenhausen."

"When did we leave Munich?"

His laugh rattled me. "We're in the middle of Munich, country mouse. Driving through the English Park."

My nervousness mounted. I couldn't keep my eyes off his broad, red nape, with its bulges of vertebra. It would take some power to snap a neck like that. Power that Chlora, my falcon totem, had.

We crossed a broad river and he turned to me as he braked to take a right. His eyes were pale, a washed-out blue. "I can feel your breath on my neck, Miss. What are you doing?"

"Sorry." I folded my hands on my lap and tried to look normal.

"The doctor warned me you might be dangerous. But I could crush your skinny arm in my hand without even breaking a sweat."

I wondered how he'd like one of those scorpions dropped down the neck of his uniform. But it was too early for a declaration of hostilities.

We drove down a short dead end street of regal mansions behind high fences. The chauffeur pulled into the last driveway on the right. The resplendent two-story mansion shone a lemon custard color in the fall light. Level with the broad windows on the second story, stone relief cupids flanked by fruit-filled baskets smiled down at us. A brass nameplate on the stone column by the iron gate said, "Treasures of the Amazon GmbH, Bad Brunnthal 4." From the GmbH, I surmised Dr. Unruh had a business registered at this address.

The chauffeur got out and unlocked the iron gate, before getting back in and driving through. My guess was he'd be locking the gate again after he brought me inside.

I stared at the lion-head knocker on the door while he got out another key and let me in. "Wait there," he ordered, indicating the foyer.

The lamp on the hallway table cast its light on pale marble and a coat stand. To my left, wooden stairs gleamed; the banister was ornate brass. Copper lithographs of a city I didn't recognize decorated the walls. To my right a partially opened door suggested the kitchen; the smell of baking bread still lingered.

Dr. Unruh made his entrance from a broad door at the end of the hall. Behind him, I glimpsed a spacious room, decorated in rusts and dark greens. The colors were at odds with the light and airy impression the lemon-colored mansion created from the outside.

Today he wore a navy blue waistcoat and a fitted blue jacket. Not a hair was out of place. He held out his manicured hand. "Welcome, Miss Mueller. I trust your journey wasn't too difficult."

Chlora shot to full attention, and I imprisoned my hands behind my back.

"You won't even shake my hand?"

"Where's my dog?"

"We can hardly begin in such an acrimonious fashion. Come into the living room, and you can see her outside." He swiped the carrying case from my hand in one smooth motion and put it next to his ear, smiling as he heard them move.

"This will go to the basement later. Come along now."

I followed him, the skin on my neck prickling.

The living room was wallpapered with a motif of dark green oak leaves and brown acorns against a gold background. Rust-colored drapes framed large windows that overlooked the grounds at the back of the house. I rushed to the first one.

Simone dozed underneath a tree, her nose buried between her paws, her white ruff blazing where the sunlight hit it. I saw no scars, no evidence of mistreatment.

"Jochen will bring her inside for you when it gets chilly."

"I want to see her now. Right now."

A cold smile played around his lips. "I haven't adequately prepared you."

I ignored him, running to the glass-paned garden door and fumbling with the handle, my hands slick with sweat.

Open. Yes.

I didn't even have to call her. Her head whipped around, and she ran, long graceful bounds, crossing the trimmed lawn.

And stopped, uncertain. Her tail wagged twice, then lowered. She backed up a step. Unruh came close to watch us.

"Simone?" I patted my thighs with my hands, the "come here" signal.

Her ears flicked, and she laid them back.

"Simone. Please." My voice broke. I swiped at my wet eyes. I couldn't bear to look at her anymore. Instead I turned on Unruh.

"What have you done to her? She's changed."

"You've changed. Not her."

I remembered the panicked rats, the hissing tomcat. But this was my own dog. Cold—no, freezing—I staggered to the closest chair.

Unruh whistled her in, gloating, and she came to lie at his feet, lowering her head submissively.

"It's teatime, Miss Mueller."

I'd only eaten a slice of bread that morning, but my appetite was gone. I slumped, breathing heavily.

"Where's all your luggage?"

I pointed to the valise. "Here."

"Were you expecting a short stay?"

I loathed this man. "It was difficult to get here."

"I imagine. Since the Swiss police are looking for you very hard. And no one helped you at all." He crossed his legs, resplendent in sharply creased hound's-tooth trousers. "Perhaps you flew across the border?"

My voice came out listless. "I had some money hidden. I hired a smuggler."

"You must love that dog." His voice was insinuating.

I raised my head to glare at him. "You've ruined her."

"If I accept you, she'll follow my lead."

My arms ached to touch Simone's soft fur, feel her tongue on my hands. I reached out to her, and she regarded me suspiciously.

"Miss Mueller." He had my attention. "It will just take some physical contact between us. Once she smells my scent on you, she'll approach. She'll recognize you once she's close enough."

I stood up quickly, my hands twisting. "Physical contact? What do you mean?"

"I suggest a friendly embrace." He took off his coat, draping it carefully across the chair.

"But why? Why does she like you?" *When you've harmed us so.*

"It's more a matter of respect. You might learn from her, you know."

He advanced toward me slowly, placing both hands formally on my shoulders. "With your permission?"

I blinked, to check my vision. Chlora had faded. "I suppose."

He held me, then pulled me closer. Even through his clothes, I could feel his body, hard and lean. The sweat smell, though faint, was sharp and lemony.

Chlora startled. My knees buckled. He let me go, and I fell back on the chair.

"Simone, here," he commanded. She stalked over slowly, sniffing. I stretched out my hand, weeping now at the strangeness of it all.

When I felt the wetness of her tongue, I threw myself on the floor next to her and buried my head in her fur. Finally, she let me hold her. Finally, I felt like I had what I'd come for.

Half an hour later, I was sipping a cup of strong Freesian tea, Simone acting as my personal foot warmer.

"Would you like a biscuit, my dear?"

I nodded, still not quite in control of my voice.

He rang the bell.

The maid must have been my age. She wore a dark dress, freshly ironed, and a white apron. Her shiny brown hair was tied back with a red ribbon; her hands were pink and smelled like silver polish. She'd kept her gaze on the floor, but now she looked at me curiously. Her eyes were her best feature, large and gray.

"Do you think you and Tamara are the same size?" Dr. Unruh asked, after she'd left.

She was slender but bosomy, and shorter. "No." I wondered what he had in mind.

"Your clothes," he said, shaking his head. "Such elegant bone structure, marooned in a cheap, ill-fitting dress. You must visit my tailor and have your measurements taken."

"I have a nice dress." I'd brought the copper-colored one that Emil had given me.

"I'd prefer to choose some items for you myself."

"I can't possibly let you do that, Dr. Unruh."

When he smiled, his teeth were small and pearly. "Please, call me Ludwig."

25. Ludwig

It was the next morning before I was able to leave Unruh's mansion. I'd acceded to his request to have two sheath dresses and matching jackets made at his expense. I hoped to find a phone booth so I could reach Tenzin at the Pensione Kaiserhof and tell him the correct address.

Jochen stood at the side of the BMW sedan, holding the door open. The weather had turned overnight. Leaves scudded along. The bitter wind tried to dive down the collar of my coat. My legs felt exposed in stockings; Ludwig had told me to wear the nice dress I'd brought, so I wouldn't "embarrass him."

Winter was coming.

"Good morning," I said, as cheerily as I could. Though Simone had slept on my bed, I'd tossed and turned all night. My mind had devised a multitude of unpleasant scenarios, until I'd finally gotten up and paced the room like a tiger I'd once seen in the zoo. The broiled beef filet I'd eaten for dinner lay in my stomach like a brick, and my shoulders were so tight it felt like someone was squeezing me in an iron grip.

"Morning, Miss." Jochen continued waiting, shoulders rigid.

"I could just walk to the tailor. I love a brisk walk."

"You could." He waited for a moment, to give me false hope, before adding, "If I wanted to lose my job."

I gritted my teeth and settled into the back seat of the sedan. "You like your job then?" If he was dissatisfied, I could turn him into an ally.

He turned on the ignition, before answering me. "It's a job. Where else am I supposed to get a job?"

"Lots of jobs about with Reconstruction."

"Not for me. Now if you don't mind, I'd like to concentrate on driving." His voice was flat.

―――

The tailor informed me of Ludwig's favorite colors, jewel tones of amethyst, forest green, and garnet. "Those will go lovely with your coloring, Miss. What did you say your name was?"

Jochen answered for me. "This is Miss Schmidt, Dr. Unruh's fiancée."

I spun around, denial springing to my lips, then decided it wasn't worth the fight.

The tailor took out his measuring tape and started with my chest, averting his eyes politely. "I'm so glad Dr. Unruh's engaged. A lovely man."

I literally bit my tongue.

"He's asked me to make his evening suits before. He loves symphonies and the opera. But I suppose you know that."

"Are we done? Can I go?"

The tailor looked taken aback. "Well, yes. Let me just record your height." He scribbled on the pad. "You're built like a model. Most clothes will look good on you. But don't you want to choose the fabrics?"

I pointed to a bolt of worsted wool, emerald-colored. "This reminds me of Ireland. Use this." I scanned the shelves, and a brandy silk caught my eye. "And this one." If Dr. Unruh wanted to play benefactor, I'd make sure he paid for the privilege.

The tailor clicked his tongue, calculating. "They'll be ready in two days. Shall I mail the bill to the Turk address, as always?"

Jochen steered me out the door by my elbow. "That would be fine. I'll be by to pick them up."

⁓

When we returned close to noon, I stood shivering in the expanse of gravel in front of the house while Jochen locked the gate. The palisade of iron marched around the property as far as I could see, unbroken by another opening. The nearest house faced us at a 45-degree angle, separated from Unruh's property by a dirt path that led down a strip of woods bordering the River Isar. The vast park called the English Garden stretched alongside the far bank of the river.

My bedroom window was boarded up, so I couldn't actually see any of this, but Tamara had told me that last night. Our rooms were the two on the left of the hallway, separated by a bathroom. Across from me was a locked room where Dr. Unruh stored some of his business inventory. Jochen's bedroom faced Tamara's; we had to share the bathroom with him.

Jochen returned from locking the gate to stand by my side. He lit a cigarette and inhaled deeply, watching me. His face twisted into an ugly smile. "Yes, the property's secure."

My stomach gave a lurch. "How long has Dr. Unruh been planning to hold someone captive here?"

He looked at me as if I was insane. "I meant you didn't have to worry about your dog," he drawled. "We let her out of the pantry during the day so she can get fresh air. It's not good to keep a dog locked in."

Same goes for me. I wondered if he knew who I was, and if Dr. Unruh had him under his power too. Or maybe he enjoyed helping him.

Unruh was dangerous in an elegant, subdued fashion. Jochen just seemed like an Aryan thug with some elementary smarts.

Tenzin must have reached Munich by now. He'd promised to come get me if I couldn't bear it anymore. The thought gave me comfort. He could take me up in the mountains, hide me from everyone. I could breathe fresh air, get my thoughts in order. I could hold him, feel his lips on mine.

I didn't know how much longer I could take this.

Jochen thrust his big head toward me. "I've got to go do some grounds work. Knock and Miss Tamara will let you in."

Tamara opened the door, her expression deferential but eager. "Did you have a nice time choosing clothes, Miss Mueller?"

"I don't like shopping," I said, and noticed her eyes widen. Perhaps poor girls dreamed of a morning spent with a tailor dedicated to bringing out their beauty, like waifish Audrey Hepburn in the film *Sabrina*. As the butler's daughter, she gets transformed into the epitome of elegance and grace, winning the heart of the master of the house. But perky Tamara would never be an Audrey Hepburn, any more than I'd turn into Lauren Bacall.

If she wanted to look nice, whom would it be for? Surely not for that thug Jochen.

"Master is in his study. He hoped you could join him."

I walked down the hall and through the living room, heels clicking loudly on the oak wood parquet. I couldn't get used to the sound of my new shoes.

His study was long and narrow, dark with paneled wood. Like Da's it was packed with books, but unlike Da's there were books on eastern religion: Zoroastrianism, Islam, the *Tibetan Book of the Dead*. There were also darker texts, those on witchcraft and Satanism.

He studied me as my eyes swept over the tomes. "As you can see, I approach the study of psychotomimetics from a different angle than your father."

"My father was a proponent of the scientific method."

"Oh, but I am too. This is what earned you the invitation. I saw you listed as a co-author on two of his publications."

"I tried to be helpful." I paused, but when he said nothing further, I added, "You mentioned on the telephone your experiments weren't going well."

"I said a lot of things. I need a brave and intelligent helpmate, not a hothouse flower."

"You tried to frighten me?"

"You will see many frightening things, but the world of discovery *is* frightening—and exhilarating." He waited a moment longer. "Now I will allow you to ask questions."

I didn't even know what questions to start with. Was his interest world domination? He seemed rich, but maybe he wanted to make even more money? Did he just enjoy torture?

I looked at his hooded expression, the almost translucent lids, and the dark brooding eyes.

He must be on the hunt for some secret. But what?

He'd said he needed an intelligent helpmate. "What will I be doing here, exactly?"

"That depends on your skill. I need someone who will not scruple to do what must be done. But I saw your eyes that night at the farmhouse Inn. How neatly you disposed of that uncouth murderer."

The hairs on my neck prickled. "It was part of the plan for me to kill him?"

"No. That particular experiment was a disaster. I had the mix wrong."

The mix. Was a certain ratio of scorpion venom and Brugmansia required? Or maybe a certain time interval between the two doses?

"One should strive to use flawless laboratory technique," I said, and squirmed as I realized I sounded just like Da.

He corrected me. "It was a bad mix of people. Mr. Wäspi was dangerous. He needed to be put down."

I bowed my head, feeling the familiar knot in my stomach. Maybe someone could have helped Hans Wäspi. Now he was beyond help. I'd killed him.

"Put down like a rabid dog," I murmured.

Dr. Unruh missed the irony, or chose not to understand it. "I appreciate your lack of sentimentality. Excepting your dog, of course. But Ainslie told me you'd always wanted one."

Of course I knew he'd met Ainslie, but I acted properly surprised. I wanted to keep the existence of Da's journals to myself. "Ainslie? How on earth would you know my mother?"

"I met her in Brazil. A fine specimen of womanhood, she was." He smiled, showing his teeth. "You look quite a bit like her."

"I look like Da,"

"Dressed properly, you will look like a lovely young woman."

I straightened my spine self-consciously and stared at my hands.

"Do you consider yourself a woman yet?"

I considered. "I'll be twenty this Saturday. The law will allow me to inherit."

"That's not what I meant."

"I thought I was supposed to ask the questions." I felt prickly and unsettled under his gaze.

"Yes. You see, I will tolerate such insolence, coming from you. I seek to tame you, little falcon, not to break your spirit."

Her name is Chlora, I thought to myself. I was happy Simone had accepted her presence.

"Could I start keeping my dog in my room? I can hear her whimpering. It would put me in a better frame of mind."

"That would make you happy?" He played the part of the well-bred host, concerned about his guest's needs.

I nodded, trying to continue meeting his eyes. The mix of solicitousness and cruelty was disconcerting. I should leave, run away. Let the police figure it out.

But then he would have won.

"I came for my dog," I reminded him.

"Very well. You can keep Simone in your room if you'll agree to be locked in."

"It's bad enough it's only got one window, and you've nailed the shutters closed. It's upstairs. As if I could get out."

"You don't believe it, do you? How do you think you got on the roof in Gonten?"

"I could have crawled from my bedroom window."

He shook his head. "Yes, you could have. The pertinent question then would be why. You have a fine mind, but you must expand your boundaries. Perhaps it would be best if we started you off just watching the test subject after injection of venom and ingestion of the extract."

"You won't try it out on Simone?" I whispered, horrified.

"Can she report her findings? Last time I checked, she couldn't talk." His voice was acerbic. "The moon is waxing, almost full. We'll have an early dinner, then try it on Tamara. I don't cook. You will be responsible for taking over her duties tomorrow."

A chill seized me, and I felt sick. I hadn't expected to see someone else undergo the torture. I didn't know Tamara, but I had a responsibility to stop him.

Tenzin had said I should end Dr. Unruh's life if I needed to. Was this what he'd meant? The poison was in my room, but I couldn't just take it downstairs and spray him. It might not even work.

And though I hated Dr. Unruh, I recoiled at the idea of killing him.

Take a life. Save a life.

I couldn't let him guess what I was thinking. I fought to make my voice neutral. "Won't we need a way to dispose of the body?"

"Your imagination's running wild. She'll be restrained, so she won't hurt herself. But she won't be well enough to assume her duties tomorrow." His eyes gleamed. "The bloodbath at Gonten wasn't my idea, you know."

"You seemed pleased. I got a glimpse of you, lurking in the bushes."

His voice was vehement. "I'm insulted. Whatever would make you say that?"

"You smiled."

"That was likely a grimace. I was as frightened as I've ever been. I should have never listened to Silvia."

"How was she involved?"

"It was the payment she demanded. I owed her a demonstration, in return for the financial backing she's provided. She's interested in marketing our compound for weapons development. All we need is a good name."

"Compound Totentanz," I said instantly, remembering the name I'd come up with in the park with Emil.

"Compound Deathdance? Grisly, but it has flair. I've already developed a Compound S, so this can be Compound T."

"What kind of a government would buy that?" I didn't add the rest of my sentence—now that the Nazis are gone.

"Do you follow politics much? You ought to. There are many rebel groups desperate for any advantage—the Viet Cong, the Basque freedom fighters. In your mother's country, there's the Irish Republican Army."

"Where are the De Penas now?"

"I said you might ask questions, but I'm certainly not inclined to answer that one. I just wanted to differentiate myself from them."

"You worked with them, and you let them do that. How different are you?"

"I didn't want you to be frightened, but I must say, I hadn't expected you to be quite so bold." He crossed his legs, the creases on his trousers perfect. "Very well. I'm scrying. Looking into the dark, teasing out the answer to a secret. "

I gave him a skeptical look. He was being evasive. "You must be planning something bad." I was hoping he'd be like a villain in the James Bond movie, mockingly share his plans for mass murder, so I would know what to do next.

"It's not bad. But you're not ready."

I prickled. "I'm a quick learner."

"Book learning. You wouldn't believe it if I told you."

I wanted to get up and leave. And yet I wanted to be his confidante, learn the secret he kept close.

I switched tactics. "What do you keep in the locked storeroom?"

"I'm not Bluebeard, don't worry. I always treat my lady friends gently."

I drummed my fingers on the table.

He shrugged, his voice casual. "I suppose I can tell you. It's my inventory room. I don't stock Compound T, but I do have another plant elixir, Compound S. There's also a medicinal salve. I have a very selective list of clients I sell to."

My grandfather had owned five pharmacies. "Wouldn't it just be easier to find a store to sell it for you?"

"I'm an impatient man. I prefer to enjoy my wealth now, rather than wait a decade for some bureaucrat's stamp of approval for my products. Now then," he inclined his head toward his well-stocked shelves. "I take it you like to read?"

"Yes, very much."

"When I am working, I must confine you to your room, until I decide how to best use you. I'll allow you to choose a few books for your education. An idle mind is the devil's workshop."

"Are you a Satanist?" I blurted out.

"Hmmm. Silvia found it to be very exciting, this idea. She's theatrically inclined. But why would I seek to exchange one master for another? The government, the society, the pope, the devil?" He stroked his neat beard. "I'm sure you agree with me. A governess who tells her young charge the fairy tales are wrong, just instruments of submission?"

How did he know about the incident with the little girl? It had never been in the paper. I looked at the floor. "Yet you wish to be my master."

"I wish to use you for the design you've been built for. When you experience the exhilaration of your true nature, you won't fight me anymore." He studied his nails. His next sentence was barely audible. "At least, that is my hope. I have been lonely at times and missed the company of a woman."

My shoulders stiffened and my cheeks flamed. I'd expected him to torment me right away; I'd been ready for that. But he wanted me to like him.

And heaven help me, a part of me did. Being with him felt so familiar.

"Take your books now and we'll go upstairs."

I walked around his library, feeling intoxicated by the wealth of knowledge. A locked glass case held tattered leather volumes. I peered in.

"Antiques?"

"Yes. I am the proud owner of *Lonicerus*, the herbal volume by the city doctor of Frankfurt. It was written in 1582."

When I didn't answer, he added, "I bought it after I earned my first thousand marks."

Odd that a man from a good family would show so much pride in his earnings. I looked around at the tasteful evidence of his wealth.

"You didn't inherit this book from your great-grandfather then?" I joked, trying to draw him out.

His lips pressed together. "Hurry. I have work to do."

I chose three, including *Phantastica* by Louis Lewin, the famous Berlin toxicologist, before going upstairs. I settled on my bed and tried to read. It was close and dark with the shutters nailed shut, and I couldn't concentrate. I kept seeing the twisted grimace of Hans Wäspi as he staggered toward me, covered in his sister's blood. Did Tamara know what was going to happen to her? And how could she have agreed if she did?

Dinner started off pleasantly enough, the long table covered with a white starched tablecloth, the glasses filled with a Mueller-Thurgau to go with the parsnip soup. Dr. Unruh wore an evening jacket, and I changed back into my copper-colored dress. I put on lipstick as well, and sprayed on some Eau du Temps from the second bottle, the one that held the real perfume.

Tamara trotted in with the main dish and a Zweigelt red after we finished the first course. She removed the silver cover, revealing thin slices of grilled meat, which she served both of us. Dr. Unruh tasted his and nodded approval. "Tamara, you may serve yourself 200 grams in the kitchen. Please put the rest away for your meal during the recuperation phase. It should last about eight hours."

She nodded. "Like last time, then."

A deep sigh escaped me. *So he's done this before. At least I won't see her die tonight.*

She was in peril, though. Maybe I could get her to help me. We were close to the same age.

Dr. Unruh's eyes followed the swish of her hips as she left the dining room. She and I might have more in common than I'd thought. Dr. Unruh had been lonely, but perhaps not too lonely.

There he sat, posture perfect, dark hair gleaming as if he'd put shoe polish on it, his lustrous eyes fixed on me. His skin was so fine; it would line quickly once he reached middle age. I judged him to be just past thirty now.

I bowed my head and started eating. *A lunatic. That's all he is.*

My fork hit something stringy and blue. I pushed it around the plate. It looked just like a blood vessel. "What are we having for dinner?"

"Calf's heart."

I put down my fork and took a gulp of the wine, which I'd barely tasted. I hadn't planned on getting drunk with my enemy.

"Peppa, eat. You liked it until you knew what it was."

Yes, that was true.

"You must not get attached to labels," he added.

Like right and wrong? I picked up the fork and took another mouthful, forcing myself to chew. "I've never eaten calf's heart before."

"My first cook was from Oberbayern. Viscera are a specialty there. She's the one who taught Tamara how to cook." He paused, and chewed with relish. "Once Tamara was ready to work, that is. It was a difficult year for us both. I had just left home myself, and then I had to take care of her."

I wasn't in the mood for a story. I pushed my food around some more. I'd heard they ate spleen, calf's feet, all kinds of things, there. Was I in for more treats?

"You will shop for food tomorrow, with the guidance of my chauffeur, and you may cook whatever you want. Within reason." Dr. Unruh's lips curved. "Making a poison mushroom dish would not be tolerated."

So he expected treachery. And he was right. He was taking a gamble, leaving me alive. But then, he needed me. I looked over at Tamara. She didn't look sturdy, mentally or physically. How many forays could she take?

The laboratory was in the cellar. Electric cables snaked down along the gravel-strewn, packed-earth floor. There were standing lamps, two on either end of the long laboratory bench and counter, and a canister of gas for the two Bunsen Burners. Other canisters were stocked on a shelf next to the coal chute.

The counter itself had the usual lab paraphernalia, pipettes, wooden racks of test tubes, and a jumble of condensers and connectors. A two-liter volumetric flask held something viscous and dark blue.

Other than that, it looked more like a witch doctor's hut. He had a grocer's scale, rather than a proper analytical balance. A large wooden cutting board paired with a sharp butcher's knife held an assortment of gray twisted roots. He did have the periodic chart of the elements, but hanging right next to it there was a lurid painting of a goddess wearing a scanty outfit and a necklace of skulls.

"This is really where you make your compound?" No telling how much it varied from one batch to another.

"As I said, I could use an assistant. In the midst of studying medicine, learning various Amazon Indian dialects, and receiving a doctorate in anthropology, I didn't have time to achieve a mastery of clinical chemistry as well."

Tamara walked over to something that looked like a dentist's chair. I raised my eyebrows at him.

"Belonged to my friend Dr. Schadl. He worked for the Nazis at Dachau. Shot himself when the war ended."

"What did you do during the war?" I ventured.

"Well, I didn't work in the camps, if that's what you're getting at. It would suit you to think that, wouldn't it?"

"He was at the university studying. So he wouldn't be conscripted," Tamara explained.

"Oh please," he waved his hand at Tamara. "You know I am fond of you, but I'll decide what to tell Miss Mueller."

"You didn't join the Nazi party?" I asked.

"Hitler was an *arriviste*."

"Dr. Unruh's father came from an established house. He was the mayor of Gotha. The Nazis wanted to take things away from the nobility," Tamara persisted, glancing at Unruh.

"That's enough. Let's get you strapped in."

She nodded and climbed on the chair. "Peppa, come closer. I want to show you how these buckles work. I've adapted them from straitjackets. Tamara made them for me. A clever girl."

"Thank you, Dr. Unruh." She sighed, a great luxurious letting out of air, as he closed them about her. Did I imagine it or did his fingers brush her clavicle tenderly before he snapped the last bolt?

He took out a beautiful antique pocket watch. "You do know how to take a pulse?"

I could do that. I nodded.

"You'll be recording every ten minutes. Be careful with this; this actually did belong to my grandfather. If the pulse is higher than 120, you must tell me immediately."

He gave me a folded flannel cloth. "Please tuck this in under Tamara's dress. Urinary incontinence has been noted with some of the test subjects."

She hitched up a bit to let me place it between her legs. I pushed my hand up, quickly withdrawing it after I'd thrust the cloth in. I wondered that he didn't do it.

The ten scorpions I'd brought had joined their brethren in the cage and rustled around. Dr. Unruh reached in with the hemostat and grasped one delicately. "You think you can do this next time?"

"I suppose. What chemical do you get from the scorpion?"

"All in good time. You'll be promoted to a proper research assistant when I can trust you."

When would that be? There was a boulder crushing my chest. I breathed in sharply. I didn't know how much of this I could stand. I should just try to escape. Or kill him. Maybe I should try to kill him. Then Tenzin would come...

"Your mind is wandering. Tamara is making this sacrifice for science. Please honor her with your full attention."

He pushed up the dress himself, exposing the inside of her thigh. She didn't flinch when he touched her.

They were definitely lovers. Master and servant. Lovers. I shuddered.

She looked at him, her eyes pleading. "Must we? The sting?"

His voice was stern. "We discussed it, my dear." The scorpion scrabbled restlessly, then started for the warmth under her dress. Dr. Unruh poked it with the hemostat, and reflexively it arced its tail up. Another slight prod and it swung down.

Tamara screamed, a short and shrill cry. Then she lay still.

"You will be quiet now?"

"Yes."

Walking over to the shelf, he waved me over. "Compound T has to be fresh for the best effect. A new batch."

Oh no. Would my compound still do the trick if I had to use it? "How fresh?"

"A week, maximum. Deteriorates quickly, and the results become unpredictable. Why?"

"I'm just trying to learn."

He handed me the flask of murky liquid. "Now I want you to measure out 100 milliliters into the beaker. Compound T induces insulin instability; therefore it's important the subject has adequate rest and a high protein diet before administration."

I filled the beaker. It looked exactly like what we had made at Sandoz. But we had made a simple plant extract, not a compound mixture.

"Bring it over."

I did so, and stared down at Tamara's pale lips. Surely she wouldn't do this. But Dr. Unruh inserted a straw into the beaker and she gulped it down, her eyes huge in her face.

He was tender with her then. "It will be all right. I'll look after you. I always have. I'm right here."

I felt nauseated and unsettled to be part of their intimacy and got up, intending to leave, but his hand shot out and took me by the wrist. "I need you. Here."

I sat back down, watching her begin to writhe, seized by a horrid fascination. This was no laboratory rat. It was a girl my age, her chest heaving, her skin flushing red and hot.

Feeling guilty, as if I'd caught her in a private act, I took her first pulse reading. Already 95. *Scheisse.*

Soon she started screaming, lips drawn back, her teeth showing. Her words were incoherent, guttural. She tried to bite me when I leaned near. In her eyes, clouded now, I could see hell crowding in, demons leaning close.

"Can we stop it? Please?"

"I have the option for administering a sedative. But I'll decide when that's necessary."

The bonds held the girl, but her body was rigid, arching in tetany. "She's suffering."

"She's suffered before. This is nothing."

"Please."

"You disappoint me."

"I can't convince you to stop? It's horrible."

When he merely glared at me, I asked. "Are we at least getting useful data?"

"Afterwards. She can report. Afterwards." Somewhere upstairs Simone howled, as if aware of our activities in the basement.

After an hour of her babbling, he took out the syringe, measured, and handed it to me. "I need an IM in her deltoid. Your father was a doctor. Can you give an injection?"

"What's in the syringe?"

"I asked if you knew how to give an injection?"

The nausea from eating the calf's heart balled up with the horror of witnessing this. "And I asked you what's in that!"

I had raised my voice, and for a moment we stared at each other. His pupils dilated slightly.

"It's an extract of Rauwolfia. It will sedate her and lower her blood pressure. This has gone on long enough."

I couldn't agree more. I took the syringe and plunged it into her shoulder. Fifteen minutes later I called Jochen, who helped Dr. Unruh carry her to her bed. I ran along, the guilty accomplice. I'd helped do this to her. And it was only my first day here.

26. Tamara

I SERVED DR. UNRUH BREAKFAST IN HIS STUDY THE NEXT DAY, a soft-boiled egg, toast, and coffee. Jochen had woken me at seven, taken Simone, and told me what I had to do.

Dr. Unruh smacked his lips, daubing them with his linen napkin, before carefully folding it and placing it on the tray. "Can you make jam? I'm almost out of my homemade cherry."

"I've never made jam," I said, my tone of voice final.

"You could learn. Breakfast was acceptable."

"Anyone who works in a laboratory should be able to cook an egg. After all, I'm just denaturing protein."

"In case that was a subtle aspersion on me, I do know how to cook an egg. But as long as I have two female dependents, I expect them to earn their keep. You're lucky I haven't ordered you to perform a sexual service for me."

Anger overcame my embarrassment, clawed its way up my throat. My fists balled. "Just you try it!"

"Save your defiance for when it matters. I'm well provided for in that area."

"Tamara?"

"Why do you care?" He cocked his head. "You do care, don't you?"

Because she lets you do horrible things to her. And then she looks at you as if you're God. Sickening.

I picked up his plate, with the glossy leak of yellow, and gingerly retrieved the used serviette. "You're done with breakfast?"

"Yes. Make something for yourself, and then fetch me when Tamara's breakfast is ready. Two eggs and a canister of coffee with hot milk. Notify me and we'll go up together."

Half an hour later we stood on the landing. The splintered worn floorboards groaned as he stepped smartly up to her door. No oak parquet here. He did her the courtesy of knocking.

"Please come in." Her voice was soft and thin.

I pulled the small table up to the bedside and set down the food. Today I was the servant and she was the rat. Only Unruh was always the same; the de facto king of our twisted court.

She cut the toast carefully into small squares before she spoke. "I only got to the mountain and the cloud cover. Couldn't get through. The dew hung on my wings and made them wet. Before that, I saw the soldiers again. I got to kill them. Thank you."

He patted her. "Some of them are really dead, no doubt. Such is the way of war."

"I'd like to know for sure."

"I don't know their names, dear. We've been over that."

"The clouds were sparkling green. The time before the sky was olive. Maybe the time of the day was wrong. Maybe we should try when it's morning here." She was anxious now, focused on her failure.

"You're a little sparrow. You can't help it. We need a stronger bird for the voyage to the Kingdom of Aves." He moved a strand of hair off her forehead.

That would be me. Chlora.

The knowledge tingled. I was sure none of the Wäspi family had been birds, whatever they'd turned into. But Tamara was another one. Like me, but fragile and weak.

Class Aves. The Latin name for birds. Could they be talking about the place I called the Jade World? I had hurtled into it like a comet.

Looking at her soft face against the pillow, I felt Chlora's strength in me gathering. I was fierce, indomitable.

A movement at my side checked me. Unruh. His dark eyes bored into me.

I quailed. Perhaps I was strong compared to someone like Tamara. But I wasn't sure I could get the best of Unruh.

He turned back to her, patting her cheek. "I'll check the mixture. I could double-boil it."

Was he insane? He'd had to give Rauwolfia yesterday. The mixture couldn't be stronger without endangering her.

As he got up and turned to leave, her hand fluttered. "Please don't leave yet, Ludwig."

"I must. I have some correspondence to see to. More orders coming in."

⁂

I wiped the egg from her lip after she ate, moved not so much by tenderness as by disgust. Seen this way, she was like a broken doll.

"Are you going to make him dinner?" she asked. "He doesn't like creamed spinach or turnips. And he has an allergy to fish."

"I suppose a platter of organ meat would do?" I said.

The sarcasm was lost on her. "Yes, he likes that. He works so hard."

"What's he want anyway?"

Her eyes got round. "I don't ask Master that."

No doubt she'd report everything to him. I tried another tactic. "What's that about the soldiers you said?"

"When he gives me Compound T, I get to kill them."

I tilted my head, not sure I'd understood. "You imagine killing them?"

"We have some of their things. Dr. Unruh helped me make straw dolls, so I could concentrate on the attack. In the afterlife. That's where I go when I take the drink."

Poor deluded girl. "So these were actual soldiers?"

"They were. Maybe some are dead now. But they can't hide from me." Her eyes filled with tears and her hands trembled. I'd been in safe in Switzerland during World War II. She hadn't.

"Nazis?"

"Russians," she said. "The Americans gave them Thuringia."

"Your family?"

"Well, my Mama's dead now. She tried to stop them when they started in on my sister." Her face had become cold and rigid, her voice without inflection.

"Your father?"

"Died on the Russian front."

"So Dr. Unruh's been taking care of you?"

She nodded. "He found an apartment for us. Let me stay with him while he went to school. He wasn't even twenty himself."

I wondered when he'd turned from her protector into her lover and tormentor. Did he experiment on her first, or were they intimate first? Either way, I wasn't going to find an ally in her.

259

But I should try. I didn't have much of a plan, except for Tenzin helping me escape. "I'm an orphan too. Ainslie died when I was eleven."

"Who's Ainslie?"

"I call my mother that." I supposed that was odd. Ainslie just didn't seem like a flesh and blood mother. She was more like a mirage—something that you thirsted for, that you could never reach.

"Oh, *your* mother. She died because your father didn't love her. Ludwig knows all about her."

I recoiled. "Not at all. She was traveling with Da. Wanted to go. She caught malaria. That's all. You're stupid to believe everything you hear."

"And you don't know about my life. I've eaten all I can. Please take the tray and leave."

Perhaps she was Dr. Unruh's servant, but she had no natural deference to me.

But then, why should she? I was near her age. I was the type of woman Radcliffe wanted, and if I ever had a chance to claim my inheritance, I would be very wealthy besides. But here none of these things mattered. Only the Master's opinion mattered.

We ate lunch together at his request, thin-sliced sandwiches of white bread filled with rare roast beef. Most German bread was thick and hearty, but the bakery made this especially for Dr. Unruh.

After I served us coffee from the lovely Meissen china set, he pointed to the chair next to him. "Sit. I won't bite."

Once I was settled, he looked at me over the rim of his cup. "What do you think of my household so far?"

"It's ... uh ... unconventional."

"As was yours. That's hardly something worthy of comment."

"How long are you expecting to keep Simone and me here?"

"You're not my prisoner. But I can't protect you against the authorities if you leave."

"Is Hermann Goering dead?" I knew it was a stupid question, but the image of the towering policeman haunted me.

"Ever heard of the Nurnberg Trials? Or is Switzerland like one of those glass globes, totally insulated by falling snow?"

I raised my chin and glared at him, remembering Hans and his sister, tearing into each other, and the woman on fire. "I shouldn't have to be afraid of the police. You're the one who's responsible for those people's deaths."

He shook his head musingly. "Silvia wanted to try it out in uncontrolled surroundings. I only did it as one last favor, before I dissolved our partnership. There are jars of Compound T hidden in the cellar of her house in Gonten, behind the preserved green beans. If she pesters me further, I'll be forced to report her to the authorities."

I narrowed my eyes at him. He'd been planning to shift the blame to her for a while.

"So you understand?" He gave me a charming smile.

"You are the one who made it."

"I was hired by her. I followed her directives. The authorities will find a letter to that effect in her study, covered in her fingerprints. The letter pleads with her to discontinue research."

He had it all set up, in case he and Silvia were discovered. I doubted she'd ever seen that letter. Not that I felt sorry for her. I stared at him defiantly. "But you *haven't* stopped."

"Only my household and you know that."

"And your scorpion vendor."

"The scorpions are the least of it. I wish I could trust you. I do. But you must think me cruel. Ainslie said you had a good heart, underneath your stiff manner."

I stared at him, appalled by the idea of my mother conversing with this man. "You sound like you were on good terms with her."

"She had my sympathies, dealing with your father."

My face got hot. If he was trying to get me angry, he was succeeding. "Why did you tell Tamara my father was responsible for her death? It's none of her business, and it's not true either."

"Why would a pregnant woman go to Brazil with her husband?"

My hands pushed into fists. "She wanted to go. She was an artist. It was her chance to sketch all the plants she'd heard about."

He was implacable. "A pregnant woman. A woman who cannot take quinine travels to an area where malaria is endemic."

"You tell me then."

"Your parents were friends with a Jew and his pretty wife."

Now I was frightened, as well as angry. "The Jew had a name," I spat.

He shrugged. "You started this, Peppa. Had your father kept his marriage vows, Ainslie wouldn't have gone. She didn't trust him in Brazil alone."

I wanted to say it wasn't so, that it couldn't be like that, but instead I remembered Da showing me the drawings of the sterol hormones after Gladys stormed out the door. "We are human, but our bodies are those of animals. And animals have instincts."

I wanted to smack Dr. Unruh right in his smug face. Instead, I whispered, "May I go upstairs?"

"Yes, but I'll need you in the lab in an hour."

Thankfully the next experiment involved cooking down mountains of fresh leaves and decocting a pile of dried roots. He showed me how to combine the two liquids with beeswax.

The result was a green oily paste for burn wounds.

I stirred harder when he told me. Another horrible experiment. "Who are you going to burn?"

"Scared at last?"

"I'd rather it be me than Simone."

"That's the first sign of altruism I've seen. What if I were to tell you I'll use it on Tamara?"

I should tell him not to. But it's not as if he would listen. "She's very devoted to you."

"Yes. And I am certainly not going to reward her loyalty by burning her. What a sick girl you are. My neighbor scalded herself. Another customer for my chickweed and Amazonian rush potion. You're making replacements for the three jars I'm going to sell her."

"Your Treasures of the Amazon business?"

He didn't answer me. Instead, he pointed to the stairs. "I'm going to go next door. Wait for my return in the salon."

I sat on the dark green sofa, playing with a salmon-pink silk pillow. Jochen had lit a fire in the grate. I studied the portraits of Unruh's illustrious ancestors, wondering if they'd been anything like him.

Unruh came in, whistling a little tune. He presented me with a heavy buff envelope. My name was written on it in a controlled, even hand; only the M of Mueller was allowed an extra flourish.

"Here is the contract with my expectations. This should clarify things."

I read it through quickly, and then once more, studying it more closely.

> *Welcome to my home and a world of new experiences. Now that you've had a chance to appreciate my work, I'd like to outline how we proceed.*
>
> *Step 1: You will serve as the subject. You will report everything for my benefit, keeping subjective interpretation out of the tale to the best of your ability. Your reward for consistently rendering service will be the removal of the boards on your window.*
>
> *Step 2: You will continue to perform your duties as outlined in Step 1, but in order to preserve your mental and physical health, you will have periods of rest during which you participate in experimentation as a research assistant, rather than as a subject. Your duties will be to correctly titrate and measure botanical philters, as well as to take notes and participate in medical care of other subjects. Your reward, should you perform these duties to my satisfaction, demonstrating both loyalty and intelligence, will be extended periods of freedom. However, your dog will remain here to demonstrate surety.*
>
> *Step 3: You join me.*

I shook my head in disbelief. "Is this like an employment contract?"

"I suppose, yes. You will be the next test subject. I'm concerned about Tamara."

"And she can't do it anyway!" I burst out. My hands were shaking.

He continued, as if he hadn't heard. "I outline the expectations and rewards. By the way, your room does have a beautiful view. I'll have Jochen take care of the boards tonight."

I didn't say anything. He was up to something.

"Tomorrow evening will be your turn. I'll administer a light sedative tonight, so you can sleep well. Tamara will be sure to give you optimal nutritious meals tomorrow."

"You're a lunatic. I don't want to do this," I protested, wondering if he'd have Jochen tie me up anyway.

He looked out the window at the garden, pensive. "Well then, we're wasting time. I thought I could depend on you."

"Why would I want to take your poison?" I did experience a brief frisson of curiosity. Could I become Chlora again? Could I visit the Jade World?

"You ought to help me, since you're in a pickle," he pointed out.

"There's a difference between helping you and becoming a part of a dangerous experiment."

"But that's exactly what I need help with. I can tell Jochen to cook me a soft-boiled egg, but I can't ask him to take your place." He kept his voice patient, though he'd picked up the envelope and was folding it into smaller squares.

"Because I'm the falcon."

"Yes, because you're the falcon." He looked at me, pondering. I felt like someone was scratching me with wool, itchy and agitated.

"I'm guessing your father treated you with respect and gave you a good deal of freedom," he said at last. "But you always looked forward to being an adult, yes?"

I nodded, wondering where this was going.

"What did you hope to do?"

"Get a chemistry degree from Radcliffe," I said, wondering why I was confiding in this psychopath. "And then study pharmacology like Da."

"You think a scrap of paper from Radcliffe would earn you respect? You've been out in the world now. You've seen a woman's place. You can expect at best, a life of refined confinement, treated as a mix between a domestic servant and a concubine. And at worst, imprisonment, perhaps a spell in a mental institution, till they've broken you."

My hands became sweaty. "That's not true," I said, too loudly.

"Name me the exception."

"Marie Curie, Florence Nightingale."

"Do you personally know anyone?"

"What does this have to do with the experiment?"

"You will be a falcon. There are no bounds on her. She can fly; she is free. She's magnificent."

"Will she fly to a particular place?"

"We'll have to see, won't we?"

I wavered. "If I do it. What do you want me to find?"

"Not what. Who."

"You're looking for someone?"

"If you participate, I'll tell you."

I felt coiled up and penned in. "May I please go take a walk? Think about it?" I couldn't stay locked in my room and just read.

"Jochen will take you. No letter to your boyfriend, I trust."

I'd been hoping to get to a phone booth and talk to Tenzin. I didn't even know where the neighborhood of Bogenhausen was, but at least I'd seen the address on the gate. I craved the sound of his calm voice almost as much as I missed the feel of his arms around me. I lowered my eyes. "I don't have a boyfriend," I lied. I got up to leave the drawing room. But at the door, I couldn't resist. "What did you mean when you wrote, 'I will join you.'"

He smiled. "As I said, it's been a lonely time for me. I'm very selective about my lady friends. You might make a good match."

I could feel my heart rate shoot up, and a hand seemed to close about my throat. I had to stop myself from bolting out the front door. Instead I went and fetched Simone's leash, trying to control my shaking hands.

Jochen waited for me outside, two umbrellas leaning against the doorway. I noticed the lit cigarette in his hand, and the pack lying face up on the window sill, out of the rain. His face was placid with enjoyment.

Lasso cigarettes. The pack showed a man seated on a prancing horse, lasso whizzing through the air.

I forced myself to smile at Jochen. "I used to live in America, the land of the cowboys." Cambridge didn't have any cowboys, but I was desperate for a way to reach him.

He grunted.

"You seem to like this brand."

"They're good dark cigarettes, from the Saarland. Cheaper than American brands. Besides, I hate Yanks."

I struggled for some way to connect. "My friend Emil smokes Lucky Strikes."

"I like Lassos." His smile chilled me. "We have a saying—he who smokes Lassos, eats little kids."

I grabbed an umbrella, walking quickly away from him into the misty rain, splattering water from the puddles to either side. I'd chosen a street that led away from the river into the neighborhood, hoping to at least make note of a mailbox or a phone booth. Jochen trailed behind me, trying to shield his cigarette from the rain. The sky was the color of pewter, so wet-looking it glistened.

If I agreed to Unruh's proposal, it would be my turn tomorrow. What would Chlora see? What would she feel? No matter what happened, I'd have to deal with Dr. Unruh afterwards.

Killing him would be a last resort.

I could try to appeal to whatever sense of ethics lay buried behind his cold manner. I'd have to talk with him as much as I could, earn his trust, make him appreciate my company.

He was lonely. He'd said as much.

I hoped I knew what I was doing.

27. Bespoke

AFTER I TOLD LUDWIG I'D TAKE COMPOUND T, HE BECAME expansive and friendly, encouraging me to roam around his house. I devoted the following hours to a study of my host. A glimpse of his bedroom suggested he felt soothed by green; I wore the emerald green dress he'd gifted me with. That night I cooked liver and onions with Calvados brandy, poured him wine whenever his glass was empty, and asked for his views in a less confrontational manner.

"What do you think of the supernatural then, Ludwig?"

He told me about a visit with a witch doctor who'd taken him up the vine that circled the world. When I asked him what type of plant that was, he played with his fork. "Sometime I'll tell you."

Who were his favorite philosophers? Nietzsche, of course. He liked a new book, *Atlas Shrugged* by an American woman called Ayn Rand. So I asked to borrow it.

How did he stay so trim?

Ah, that was the fencing. Normally, he practiced twice a week. He'd excused himself, telling his fencing partners his fiancée was visiting for a while.

Why had my dog accepted him?

He smirked. She was allied to his totem.

So he had one too, and he knew what his was. I assumed it wasn't a bird, or else he'd have no need of us. I waited till the next morning to ask him, when I served him perfectly browned toast and a pot of Freesian tea. He was quiet for a long time. Then he sent me for a walk. "You'll be done in after tonight. Better get some exercise while you can. Look out for your health."

I forced my lips into a smile. *Right. So you can subject me to a scorpion bite and a psychotomimetic poison, you murdering psychopath.*

Tamara served us dinner, this time a brothy, sour-smelling dish with bits of chewy material and something that popped in my mouth when I ate. I choked and set down my soup.

Tamara said, "I told you she wouldn't eat it, Dr. Unruh," as if she'd just remembered to address him as such. I was fairly sure they'd spent last night together after I'd been sent to bed. I wondered what she called him in private.

He gave me a look of remonstration. "You must have proper nourishment. Otherwise, I cannot be responsible for the consequences."

I forgot I was supposed to be the perfect companion. "What am I eating now?" I said, my voice thick with disgust.

"Protein," said Dr. Unruh.

"Lüngerl," Tamara explained, standing by his chair.

A wave of nausea passed through me. No wonder. This was some animal's lungs.

"I do feel you've contributed to the conversation enough, Tamara. Perhaps you could retire to the kitchen and begin your meal."

Tamara's lips set tight, and she swished out, banging the door.

Dr. Unruh shook his head. "They call them teenagers in the United States," he said conspiratorially. "Moody."

Perhaps he'd mistaken me for my mother, whom he'd mentioned once or twice more, always fondly. I was just shy of twenty myself. I thought about pointing this out, but instead I complimented him on his cravat, one I'd not seen before, a pale green one.

"You're being quite unlike yourself. Feeling more amicable now that you have a view?"

I'd spent at least an hour staring into the woods, straining for a glimpse of the footpath, hoping to see Tenzin striding toward our house. "The view is captivating," I said. "I'm still nervous about the experiment though."

"This will be an epic voyage," Dr. Unruh breathed. "In controlled, safe conditions. Not like last time."

I couldn't help myself, though I knew I should act agreeable. "When the old woman enucleated herself. And poor Miss Eugster fled her burning kitchen." My heart was beating much too fast. My hand groped for the locket with its grains of sacred sand. I didn't quite believe in the power of the monks, but it reminded me of Tenzin. He'd given me his most precious possession.

Unruh's voice was sharp. "I told you before. Miss Eugster was not hurt. I don't hurt women."

"Ursula Wäspi was a woman."

"She had a three-year old son," he snapped. "I didn't expect her along. She should have been with the brat. I made sure he had a tummy ache."

"I guess Ursula's husband stayed with the child."

"You're naïve. There was no husband. Her own brother bred her. That's why I chose Hans. And the old woman. What kind of mother is she to have let that happen? Even my mother could have done better, and she was easily deceived." His voice had risen, and he took a deep breath, then paused a moment, swirling the dark wine back and forth in the goblet. "I thought I'd help Ursula. Once her brother was locked up or dead, she could raise the abomination in peace without fear of Hans's fists."

I stared at him incredulously, remembering Ursula's attack on Hans. Had she been reliving her abuse when she attacked him? A kiss on the cheek gone wrong? It made a kind of horrible sense.

Stefan mentioned Unruh always went to church with the villagers. Had he been selecting his subjects, closing the noose about them? In a way, it was even worse to know that he planned this, that it hadn't been quite the accident he claimed.

I cleared my throat. "Are you suggesting there were ethics to your experiment?"

"I am not a monster," he said gruffly. "Sometimes my needs force me into exigencies I would prefer to avoid."

I struggled to find something reassuring to say. My plan was to win his trust, after all. Instead, I sat rooted to my chair, my face frozen. I was saved by Tamara, who glided to his side to refill his wine. Her smile shone with tenderness and admiration. It would have to do for both of us.

An hour later, we were down in the basement. My skin prickled and my stomach was in knots. At the edge of my thoughts I felt Chlora rouse. Shadowy wings beat.

"I'm not sure this is such a good idea," I croaked as I lay down. Tamara snapped the ties tight around my chest. I wasn't going to get any comfort from her.

"What did you do to those people in that little Swiss village?" Tamara asked him. "I read the paper after you put it in the garbage."

I tensed even more, waiting to see how he would tolerate her impudence. But he remained calm. "I've told you not to pry into these things. It's not acceptable in one of your status."

Perhaps it was the scorpion he was now holding with the forceps that made me blurt out the next thing. Or maybe it was the memories of Gladys after Da dismissed her. I saw her as I walked to the subway later that week. She was leaving Filene's Basement, clutching her bags, her lips set tight and her eyes red.

"Perhaps you shouldn't be sleeping with her then," I said.

The room went quiet. He considered, setting the scorpion down nearby, out of my sight. "You two seem to have a deleterious influence on each other. Peppa, I did not ask you for advice on my private life. Tamara, you tied these straps much too tight. Peppa is not going to lunge up and grab me by the throat. She weighs only a little more than you."

What could we say? We were squabbling children under his watch.

"I will take my own notes. Tamara, you may leave us."

Still she stood there.

"I told you to leave," he scolded.

After the door slammed, he drew up my dress himself, apologizing. His hand pushed between my legs with the cloth, and then he smoothed the dress over. "Just in case you wet yourself."

My flesh crawled as the scorpion scrabbled up my thigh. I cried, "Stop," but it was too late. The sting burned all the way up my groin and tears came to my eyes. "I don't want to do this."

"If you didn't want to do this, you would have never come."

"I thought I did, but I don't want to." My eyes watered, and a tear spilled out.

He soothed me, his hands caressing my brow and neck. "It won't be too bad. I'll look after you. Just a short trip. Then it will be over for another few days."

Feathers filled my mouth, and I couldn't talk. The falcon wanted to go. I could feel her straining in me, longing to be let loose.

What the hell is this? In me?

"Do it for me," he whispered, as he held out the beaker with the 100 milliliters of Compound T. "Please. Please."

Maddened by the conflicting feelings in me, I gulped it down.

And it began.

I roused. Fledgling seed in the dark shot to full power, as green magic shimmered through my/her veins.

I checked for threats. The fancy man hovered over the girl body. His arms held soft at his sides, his eyes greedy *for her*. His treasure. There was something unknown in his smile. What was it?

A puzzling word came from the girl's memory. *Tenderness.*

I saw only that he was rangy, tricky, strong. He could defend her.

I homed.

Jade air bathes my feathers in welcome coolness. Walls loom in the thick fog, stones shimmering with beads of rain.

I pull my wings closer, softening into a glide, arriving gently on Lord Absalom's arm.

I gulp down the proffered morsel of meat, fluff my wings, take note of his companions.

Maintaining respectful distance.

The huge snowy gyrfalcon is always on his left side. He faces north, waiting for the army of men he once commanded. They will nevermore march together, scattered across the Eight Kingdoms of the dead.

The merlin, charcoal wings tucked, the barred markings on his chest like the badges of metal that his man host once wore, to show his high rank.

Further back, skulking in shadow, another female, like me. The redheaded vulture, once a beautiful and cruel lady, skilled with poison. Now, grotesque red folds of leathery skin cover cheeks that were like silken rose petals.

Ravens wheel through the rooms without roofs, caw, circle once, and scatter toward the woods.

I let my eyes veil. No need to look further. Content. I settle in my own place.

Short rest, then comes his will, tugging, a soft mouth with steely teeth. The fancy man, the magic man wants something. He whispers in the girl's ear, far away, hoping I will hear.

I cock my head, straining.

But then. Distraction from above, quick turn into danger. A soundless blur of feathers, dropping, sharp talons outstretched.

I cry out.

The pain.

My/her heart shrivels.

It cannot be. Him.

I floated in and out of a delirium, vines snaking their way through my eyeballs and flushes racing through my body. Grinning skulls danced at the edge of my vision. Ainslie floated through, translucent and ethereal. "I love you," she said. "I'm sorry I talked too much. I gave away the secrets of our heritage." Then a wolf loped across an endless plain.

I watched as each stride left a glittering green tracer, arcing through the air. The grass bled tears where his paws touched the ground, and I heard the sound of bitter crying, like that of an abandoned child.

I awoke to a cool towel bathing my brow. Dr. Unruh bent over, his face a white luminescence, green energy filming over him, wisping this way and that. I must be in his bedroom. At least I was dressed and covered.

Sunlight peeped in through the drawn heavy drapes, but it was all wrong—a bronze color. My sweaty clothes stuck to me, and I threw off the soft eiderdown. I lay on a Himmelbett with a dark green canopy—presumably his. Each thread on the luxury sheets stood out in great detail. I tried looking across the room and glimpsed a spin of dust, each mote shining like a fallen star.

Why did everything look so weird? I closed my eyes and concentrated on what I felt.

Rage. Potent like liquor. Chlora didn't like being at his mercy.

His hateful face came nearer, peering, examining.

We spat at him.

He wiped the froth off his cheek with his sleeve. My mouth was dry, and my skin burning. The symptoms of scopolamine poisoning.

"What the hell am I doing in your bed?" My voice, normally clipped and cool, sounded like Humphrey Bogart's.

"You had a rough night. I wanted you in the safest place I could think of."

It certainly wasn't the safest place *I* could think of. "I don't want to be here," I declared.

"I'm inclined not to take it personally. The hostility," he explained, staring at me. "And you can be assured your sleep was unmolested. I am not a necrophiliac."

"You're a sick bastard!"

I'd been loud, and he glanced at the closed door. This time when he spoke, his voice had an edge. "Do control yourself. I'm trying to be understanding, but you keep insulting me."

"You made her come out." My strategy had been to try to please him and earn his trust. Chlora's strategy was to leap on him and kill him. Right now, I was stuck in the middle of those opposing forces.

"I did. That's true." My eyes met his, those dark tunnels into a foreign mind. I could feel his thoughts slipping this way and that, looking for the means to win me over.

As I'd tried to do to him.

He dropped his gaze, looking unsettled.

Neither of us really wanted to wound the other. I breathed in slowly, pushing at Chlora, bunching her into a little harmless knot. My sternum hurt with the effort of it. My anger slowly drained away, leaving behind an odd feeling of depression and futility. It was not that I doubted my strength—or rather, Chlora's. But I did not think Unruh and I could avoid hurting each other.

Our eyes met again.

"You had a difficult night. What can I do for you?"

"I'm thirsty."

"I bought some fresh-pressed apple cider at the market. Or there's Ovaltine. Would you like both?"

The scorpion bite itched, and I scratched absentmindedly. "Both. Did you give me Rauwolfia?"

"A little. Your blood pressure was stable, but your pulse was pounding. Did something frighten you?"

"Yes. I remember."

"Tell me."

"I want Simone."

He went to his door and called. Jochen must have been lurking about. He came right away.

"Ask Tamara to start heating the milk for the Ovaltine. In meantime, bring me apple cider and the dog."

Jochen hustled out to fetch, abandoning his usual languid pace.

"Please talk to me. I want to know what happened. You were almost there and…"

"I need a pain pill for the migraine. Then I'll start."

"Of course, my dear. I'll fetch something right away." Dr. Unruh was being more solicitous than my own father.

28. The Land of Aves

ONCE I'D DOWNED THE TREAT OF FRESH JUICE, I SIPPED THE Ovaltine, a heap of cushions behind my back. A cool breeze came in through the open window, carrying the smell of wood smoke. Simone lay at my side, occasionally rumbling deep in her throat at Unruh. He rubbed my icy feet, an intimacy I tried not to take notice of. I was exhausted, shaken, too weak to fight over small things.

This is what I saw.

Misty cold air over a mountain covered in snow. Not Säntis this time. It was the peak called Zugspitze. I recognized it from photographs. The falcon must gravitate toward the highest mountain in the vicinity.

Then the slip into the mossy, moist air and the sense of strangeness, the duality of watching and being. I was still me, but buried deep inside something else, something merciless, cool as marble, swift as a storm.

The falcon arrowed toward the castle as if she was heading home. Absalom sat in the courtyard, short and grinning. The inkstand with its paste of soot and powdered bones stood guard over his book. He laid down his plumed pen, and threw her gobbets of flesh she gulped down.

Here in the story I had to pause and drink some Ovaltine. The vile taste of the meat was still fresh, on top of the Lüngerl I'd eaten.

Dr. Unruh dabbed away a drop of Ovaltine from my lip with a corner of the sheet, causing Simone to growl softly.

"Simone, no. It's all right." *I have Chlora to protect me too.*

"So you were close to Absalom's book?" Dr. Unruh asked, his voice tight.

"Yes. You want something in there?"

"It's a list of names?"

"Who are you looking for?"

"I can't trust you." His voice was musing, slightly sad. "You don't even like me."

It would be disingenuous to deny it, so I said the truth. "There are things that I hate about you, but things that draw me closer as well. We have to find a way for me to defend myself in court. I can't hide at your house forever. Maybe we can strike a bargain."

"You're a sensible woman, Peppa. And I'm a reasonable man, one who does not wish you harm, much less imprisonment, for a crime you were forced to commit." He tried to stroke my knee, and I flinched away.

He sighed. "I'm sorry. I presumed."

I tucked my feet under me, pulled my wrinkled skirt down, and tried to sit up straight. "What is this place I go to? With all the birds?"

"I call it the Land of Aves. The birds are spirits of the dead. When people feel terror, their totem spirits fight for their life. If the person dies violently, the totem spirit persists. Absalom is a Guardian of Time, a ruler there."

Dead. The Jade World was full of ghosts. I didn't want to believe it, but I felt the truth of it as a deep chill in the marrow of my bones. I took another sip of Ovaltine to moisten my dry mouth and stroked Simone's soft fur.

There was concern in his eyes. "So, you saw the book. But then something happened? You started screaming."

"Absalom held out his arm for me to roost, and then..." The fear came up again and threatened to choke me. "Something horrible happened. A feathered white thing swooped down. Attacked me."

"That must be when I gave you the sedative and ended your journey. I told you I'd look after you."

"Till I get you what you want. Then you'll kill me," I said bitterly, tired of pretending we were companions on a great adventure.

"I've told you. I would never hurt a woman. I was falsely accused once. It ruined my life."

I narrowed my eyes, studying him. Why should I believe him?

My shoulder blades tingled, and my head filled with fire as wings stirred inner flames. My voice was shrill. "I'm not going there again!"

The logical part of my brain informed me that the potion destabilized me emotionally. The knowledge didn't help.

I'd lost control.

Unruh looked stricken. "Calm down."

Simone's growl was a steady rumble now, and he retreated off the bed, backing up to the dresser.

"Go yourself if you're so curious! Damn you. Damn you!" I threw the Ovaltine on the floor, where the china cup shattered.

"I would. But I can't. I need you to go."

"Why can't you go? Go to hell then. You play at being the devil!" The dark wings fanned my anger. Simone tensed, ready to spring at him. He bent down quickly and then came the glint of metal in his hand. He was going to shoot me, and it would finally be over.

But he wasn't pointing it at me. The pistol was leveled at Simone. "Quiet down. You're agitating your dog, and the neighbors will hear you." Simone's black lips drew back, exposing her yellow fangs. His voice cracked. "I'll have to shoot her if you can't control her."

It was as if ice dripped down my spine. "Simone, heel," I croaked. I patted the pillow next to me and made soothing noises until she jumped up on the bed and lay down.

He pulled up a chair to the bedside, holding the pistol loosely. My enhanced eyesight noted a bead of sweat gleaming on his temple. He waited.

I breathed.

In the quality of silence and concentration that surrounded him, he reminded me of Tenzin. But his was the concentration of a predator, and Tenzin's quiet came from a peaceful heart.

My hand went up to the locket he'd filled with the sacred sand and came away empty. It was gone.

My heart sank. "What did you do with my locket?"

He averted his eyes. "Removed it. I wanted your breathing unrestricted," he added quickly.

"Why did you really take it?"

"I wanted to see who my competition was." Pink stained his pale cheeks.

He hadn't opened the locket then. Otherwise, as the sacred grains of sand spilled out, they would have revealed the tiny photograph of my parents and me.

He must not have it anymore.

I pressed my lips together, wishing I wasn't lying in his bed. "I told you. I don't have a boyfriend."

His mouth turned down. "You lie. Do you really expect me to believe you evaded the police by yourself for two weeks?"

"I'll tell you how and you find my locket."

He nodded.

"Dr. Alex Kaufmann sheltered me in a storeroom where he works. He's my godfather. If I don't return, he's going to make sure you get caught."

"Sweet Jesus. I've heard of Kaufmann, of course. So he knows." He rested the pistol on his lap, muzzle turned away. "Just help me a little while longer. Then you and I will work something out. We'll make Silvia the focus of the police investigation." He passed a hand over his brow. "Though I hope you'll decide not to leave, even after the threat from the police is handled."

"You almost shot my dog just now."

"Only to quiet you down. I would share everything if I could trust you. I'm a wealthy man. Compound S is much in demand." He looked at me, something stirring in his eyes.

I drew back. "You promised me my locket." I ached for that reminder of Tenzin, his sudden, open smile, the clean smell of incense that scented his clothes.

"I'll see to it. I need a glass of wine." He replaced the pistol in his dresser drawer, locked it, and dropped the key in his pocket.

I staggered over as soon as he closed the door, looking for something to pry it open with. A manicure file lay gleaming on the table, and I stuck it in the keyhole, but succeeded only in scratching the beautiful walnut wood.

Upstairs, I heard the sound of raised voices, Tamara's, indignant, and his, reassuring. I'd have a bit of time. Maybe I could find something in his other drawers, some proof of his experiments.

Spots danced in front of my eyes and my head felt like someone had buried an ice pick in my temple. I gritted my teeth and pulled open another drawer, drawing back in disgust. A pile of black silk boxers. That was the last thing I wanted to see.

The argument stopped, and I heard him come back down the stairs. He'd get his glass of wine. I had a minute more. I frantically searched through the last two drawers.

The only noteworthy thing I found was a photograph of a lovely young woman, perhaps my age. The style of her elegant clothes and hairdo showed the picture was at least a decade old, if not older. Her dark eyes looked straight at the camera but there was something held in reserve. I shoved the last drawer closed and threw myself back on the bed just in time.

Unruh strode through the door. "I'm afraid I can't find your locket."

"Make her tell you where it is."

"What? Beat it out of her? Tamara said she doesn't have it. She wouldn't lie to me." He stretched out his hand. "Here. Pain medicine."

I took it from him but didn't swallow. "We made a bargain, Unruh."

"I'm sorry your locket disappeared. But I promise to make it up to you. I'll tell you my story when you wake up."

I swallowed his pill. I craved the relief of sleep. The memory of that threatening white blur in the Jade World haunted me. It was as if a loved one held a knife to my heart. Sorrow, horror, betrayal, all together in a tumult.

29. Animal Totem

I WOKE UP IN THE LATE AFTERNOON, STILL WEARING THE rumpled skirt and sweaty pullover from last night. My headache had settled down to a dull throb. I dragged myself upstairs to the bathroom Tamara, Jochen, and I shared, unwilling to use Unruh's. She saw me walk past and our eyes met.

I started to ask her about my locket, but she turned and ran down the stairs, ignoring me. When I shuffled back out of the bathroom, my teeth freshly brushed and face damp, I nearly ran into Jochen.

"Dr. Unruh wants you put on something nice and have an Apero with him. He'd like to explain a few things."

I rushed through dressing, throwing on my emerald wool and snagging my new silk stockings with a fingernail. I put on some lipstick to finish, checking the flacon of the disguised poison on my dresser. Compound Totentanz was still there, ready to do its deadly duty. I wondered what other mixes Unruh had up his sleeve.

As I started to leave, I remembered the missing locket. It occurred to me that other things could go missing as well. Wouldn't it be convenient for Unruh if my forged passport disappeared? I took a moment to find a good hiding place for it under my mattress, shoved way in the corner of the frame.

When I joined him in the living room, he looked shaken but determined. "Please sit." He sipped a small crystal glass of amber liquid while Jochen went to the kitchen to bring me an Ovaltine. "I didn't like that scene in the bedroom. It could have gotten out of control. You, me, a pistol."

I stared at him, visualizing drenching him in the poisonous perfume. I wonder what horror he would see before he went insane and died.

"I don't blame you for hating me. But I hope if I tell you more, you might hate me a bit less."

"Try me." My head throbbed, and my eyes felt gritty. What had that horrible white thing been, shrieking at me, pushing me away? I could tell even Unruh didn't have the answer to that.

He dabbed a spot of liquor from his impeccable beard and began talking.

It started with the witch doctor in the Orinoco. That had been the trip where he'd met my parents and extracted confidences from my mother, whom he described as a beautiful, gentle woman.

"Gentle as a dove."

I reminded him he was explaining about totems. I didn't see what his story had to do with my mother.

"You were nicer yesterday."

I forced down a sip of Ovo, despite my nausea. "Yesterday I didn't have a throbbing scorpion bite on my leg. I wasn't trying to digest Lüngerl and mystery meat from another realm. If you cut open my stomach, would it show what I ate there?"

He peered at me. "Don't be grotesque. I don't have the answer to questions like that."

He'd been sent to Brazil to look for a reliable source of rubber. Once there, he felt free to send a short informational letter every month to the post-Nazi government while he pursued his real interest: tribal witchdoctors. Shortly before meeting my parents, he'd charted a boat downriver to a reclusive tribe. He was the first white man to make contact with them for thirty years. At first he was treated with suspicion, but after he'd killed a large python that was strangling a child they accepted him.

I looked at him suspiciously. "You just happened along and killed the python?"

He made a click of irritation. "A few of the children liked to follow me when I went foraging for plants. The python wasn't that big, but the child was small. I had a machete on hand I was using to clear my path. It served to behead the snake."

After a nice meal of cooked python, washed down by a brew of Choca root that had been masticated into a fermented drink by the women, Dr. Unruh was invited to participate in a ritual by the witch doctor. He drank of the "vine of heaven." During his hallucination he envisioned a large gray wolf loping at his side, while the other participants spoke of snakes and jaguars. As the vision grew more intense, he felt the wolf weaving in and out of him. He jumped to his feet and ran into the jungle, where he found a cave. The tribe located him the next day by his howling.

I petted Simone. "Are you claiming you're a werewolf?"

He shook his head. "Let's not be absurd, Peppa. This was ten years ago, and since then it's been my primary preoccupation. We all have our animal spirits, which native cultures call totems. This is a part of us, perhaps located deep in the hindbrain, that ties us to the natural world. Under the right combination, the totem is activated."

"How's that?"

"My compound works by reactivating traumas and expanding consciousness. The totem spirit, which one could think of as the instinctual part of the human, springs into being to ensure the survival of the human body it's joined with."

"Where does that totem come from?"

"The affinity may be passed down genetically. I'm not sure; I've been working primarily on two families of animal spirits, those to do with the Canidae family, including foxes and wolves, and the Aves."

I rubbed my eyes. I would have never guessed the strange turn this conversation was taking. "You can't go to the Land of Aves, can you?" If he could, he wouldn't call it by a made-up, stupid, scientific name. It was the Jade World. I felt sure that it existed as a distinct place, accessible only to those with a bird totem.

"No, I can't. I have a wolf totem."

"Have you become a wolf?"

"When I took Compound T, yes. I run faster and faster till I emerge in the Land of Luporum."

"What's that like?"

"Beautiful. Like Thuringia. Old forest, snow, but I feel no cold. Only hunger that never leaves me, that crouches in my belly, springs in my limbs, pushing me on. It's the hunger that makes me feel alive."

"So if you like it, why not let me run the experiment, and I'll send you there?"

He laughed, a short bark. "Oh, you'd like that. Seeing me helpless in the chair. I doubt I'd ever wake up."

I settled myself in more comfortably on the sofa. I still felt shaken by last night's events, but I was heartened that Unruh confided in me, "But you *have* been there?"

He nodded. "For a while, Silvia and her husband would watch me while I traveled. Though I wouldn't have put it past Gordito to piss on me while I was in a trance. He was jealous." He stopped, and his eyes were far away. He longed for something. "That land is not important right now. The woman I seek has gone to the Land of Aves."

"I wish I could help you, but all I've seen so far is Absalom and the white thing that attacked me."

"Absalom has that book. It lists the names of the spirit inhabitants. He can call the one I seek. If we approach him correctly."

"How do you know that?"

"In Brazil, I had the luck to find a subject that had a condor totem. He was incredibly strong. He brought me so close."

"What happened?"

For answer he pulled up his crisp, striped linen shirt. His belly was hard and firm. A long scar ran across it. "I tell people it was a dueling scar."

"But it isn't?"

He pulled his shirt back down. "Are you sure you won't have some wine?"

"Perhaps I will."

"I'll get it myself. It seems Tamara's taken the afternoon off." He jumped up with a fencer's grace.

When he came back, Simone followed him at a safe distance, trotting over to my feet. "I let her out of the pantry. I assume you're not going to make a mad dash out the door."

Not when it was getting so interesting. I was drawn in, despite myself.

"Sometimes if the totem is very strong, it can actually merge with the human form. He raked me with his fingernail, but I have the mark of a claw wound."

"Did I fly up to the roof? Can I really fly?"

"Let's become partners and investigate."

I wondered briefly if the falcon and the wolf could work together, but the thought sent a chill through me. The two totems were both predators.

"You're being evasive. You don't really believe I sprouted a full set of feathers."

"No, no, I don't," he admitted. "But your falcon is strong, more dominant than I've seen in other cases. You felt safe climbing out of the window, looking for a place to roost. I wonder what it is about you..." He looked at me speculatively.

I didn't like that look. Time to change the subject. My Ovo was cooling off, and the sweet malty taste lost its appeal. I was part falcon, after all. "I want what you're drinking."

"It's bitter."

"Even better. I'm tired of sweet. Can I see the bottle?" I wanted to make sure I wasn't drinking another Unruh special.

He turned to the little silver and glass drink trolley and held the bottle up for me to see. "Amaro, from Italy. The brand is Cora. A good house. They've been making it since 1835." Cora was written in big, fat red letters on the bottle.

He poured me a taste, and I nodded appreciatively. This was more like it. Chlora approved too. Chlora. It was an ugly name, a name I associated with poison gas. But the peregrine helped me. She had earned Unruh's respect.

I would call her Cora instead. She would be my alter ego, bitter and bracing but smooth and golden.

"What are you thinking about?"

I didn't want to share my feelings about Cora with him. I cast about for a topic. "So he didn't want to work with you? The condor man."

He grimaced. "You could say that."

"Did you just try out people at random?"

"At first. Till I learned what to look for. When I saw the poster at the police station, I thought you'd be one."

"Wait a minute. That had to be before I came to Gonten."

His eyes bored into me. "It was no accident you came. I asked around for an English-speaking caretaker, hoping the job would lure you to us."

"I could have been anywhere. How did you know? How could you know?" Agitation pulsed through me.

"Miss Eugster was close to Manser. Lots of pillow talk." He winked. "The woman you worked for as a governess went to the police after she fired you. They alerted nearby police that you were likely in eastern Switzerland. What a gift for me."

I gripped the sofa arm. I couldn't believe it. "You lured me up there. Arranged the whole thing. Had Hans finally paid on Saturday, and put Miss Eugster up to offering the Bäsebeiz for a celebration party."

I massaged my temples. "How did you know I would have a bird totem?"

He corrected me. "A raptor totem. Your father had the same air about him."

"What air would that be?"

"Thin, ungainly arms, flapping around while you talk. High-bridged nose. Large beautiful eyes, set close together. Fast reflexes."

"That doesn't sound like much to go on."

"It's not. That's just the beginning," he gloated. "Raptors have excellent eyesight. Unlike other mammals, they have two fovea, where the cone cells are concentrated."

I remembered my anatomy lessons with Da's colleague at the medical school. "The cone cells—the cells that respond to bright lights and colors?"

"Correct. If raptors look at something nearby, they look straight on, using the shallow fovea to get a three-dimensional picture. But at a distance of six feet or more, raptors turn their head and utilize the lateral fovea to obtain a more acute picture."

I shook my head, trying to clear it.

He made a moue of disappointment. "You didn't read the book I left for you?"

I remembered the illustrated birds of prey book I'd stolen from the De Penas' house. "You *left* that for me?"

"I thought you might encounter it on your escape route. I've found it helpful to provide my subjects with a conceptual framework for their totem. It's disconcerting when the feral beast awakens."

I shuddered. He was fiendishly clever. "Get back to the explanation of the fovea. What does that have to do with me?" I said, forcing my face to remain expressionless.

"The first evening I entered your room so I could show you how to flee if necessary. I also tested you then. You identified the coin I dropped on the floor from a distance of several meters, turning your head sideways to do it. Raptors have poor ocular muscles. They have to turn their head, since they can't adjust their eyes."

I felt sick, knowing how he'd had the upper hand all along. "You dropped the money to see how I'd react."

"Not only that. I presumed you were tight for funds. You wouldn't have allowed yourself to go out to the Bäsebeiz without the extra coins. It had to be just the right amount. Too much, and you would have been suspicious."

I dug my nails in my palm and willed my voice to be even. "Is there anything I've done that you haven't anticipated?"

"Not so far. But I'm hoping you'll surprise me. I quite like clever women."

I got up and slapped him hard across the face. "Have I surprised you now?" I said through gritted teeth. I'd certainly astonished myself.

He rubbed his cheek. "Yes. But that wasn't clever."

I waited for him to grab me by the throat, or at least slap me back. Instead, he said, "I have to put ice on that," and turning on his heel, strode out. His steps were light, despite the anger that stiffened his shoulders.

My heart pounded with the impact of what I'd done. My head was whirling. Usually I could think my way out of any situation, but this ... this...

The phone sat on the table, such a simple thing really. One only had to enter numbers in, and a voice came out the other side.

If I could only hear Tenzin's voice, just for a few moments. Just to know there was someone there. I jumped up, jammed a chair under the door, and flew back to the phone. My hand was shaking so hard I could barely dial the operator. She connected me to the Pensione Kaiserhof.

I interrupted the woman's greeting. "Tenzin Engel? Is he there?"

"We don't have a Tenzin Engel."

"What!" I collected myself. "I meant Christian. Get him right away. It's an emergency."

"Calm down, Miss. I don't have someone by that name."

I gripped the phone so hard my fingers turned white. "No, that can't be. He's handsome, half-Asian, long black hair."

"I'm sure I'd remember someone like that."

"What about an Alex Kaufmann?"

"No, I'm really sorry. What's your emergency?" she asked, as a gulping sob escaped my throat.

"I'm Peppa."

The door began rattling back and forth. The chair wouldn't hold him off for long. His voice came from the other side, calm and courteous. "I'm rather fond of my furniture. Would you please remove the chair so I don't have to break it?"

"I'm at 4 Bad Brunnthal in the big yellow house," I whispered into the phone. I slammed it down, wondering what I'd just done.

"Peppa?"

I walked over, feeling as if the floor would open up underneath me any minute. My hands were numb and cold as I tried to pull the chair away. It clattered on the floor, and he pushed his way through.

"I suppose you took the opportunity to use the telephone. I thought about it as soon as I reached the kitchen. Perhaps it was clever to hit me after all."

My tongue stuck to the roof of my mouth.

"Did you speak to Alex?"

"I couldn't reach him."

He stood directly in front of me, one finger tracing the rim of his glass. He wasn't as big as Tenzin, but I could feel the intense emotions fighting in him. I sat up straight. I wasn't going to crumple in front of him.

The handprint showed red on his face, and his nose was slightly swollen. A bead of water slid down it.

The moment extended. Still he said nothing, and tension made the air electric.

My voice was stony. "Just punish me. Get it over with."

He threw himself on the sofa next to me, ignoring Simone's soft growl. "No."

I put some space between us and clutched one of the silk pillows, still wary.

"No," he repeated again. "That won't get us what we want."

"What do we want?"

"We want you to get Absalom to call Luci's soul. Then I must talk to her."

I thought of the photograph I'd found in his drawer. "What do you want from her?"

"I have to find out how she died. It's time my life went on."

"You can't go. You told me earlier."

"There might be a way we can join up. I can protect you from that thing, and you can speak my words." His hooded eyes tugged at me.

"I don't think I'd like joining up."

"Then we're at a stalemate. I'm going to my study to get some work done." He walked off, reconsidered, and came back. He yanked the cord out of the wall with such force that the phone slid off its table, crashing onto the floor.

He'd warned me.

30. Happy Birthday

I WOKE UP THE NEXT MORNING TWENTY, AND FEELING EMPTY. I was now legally an adult in every way. So what. I was far from Basel and my friends. I was even farther from Cambridge and the education I deserved.

Although I was getting a once in a lifetime education right here.

I stared at the white ceiling, Simone nudging my side with her soft nose. The morning shone with pearly wet whiteness through the window, now freed of boards. Idly, I wondered if I'd die if I jumped out, or just break my legs.

Yesterday evening had been anticlimactic. Tamara hadn't returned by sunset, and Unruh paced the sitting room as dinnertime came and went. His movements unnerved me, and finally I jumped up and said, "Let's see what's in the refrigerator."

I'd been scrambling up a skillet of eggs, ham, and mushrooms when I heard the front door open. I pulled the pan to the side and opened the kitchen door. I saw Tamara's back as she faced Unruh, who'd come to the stairs. Her hair was freshly styled and curled; the smell of the perming solution lingered. She carried a large shopping bag from Kaufhof's department store.

"I'm a little late," she said, her voice tense.

"I trust you ate already. Peppa's making dinner for the two of us now."

"No." Her voice rose in agitation. "That's my job."

"Not tonight." He'd turned his back on her and gone back to the sitting room, leaving her standing there.

I didn't know what mood I'd find the household in today.

But I certainly hadn't expected Unruh to plan a birthday celebration.

Our situation was absurd on the face of it. As long as I was a murder suspect, I remained the hostage of a lonely, deranged man who fancied himself a gentleman. I still considered killing him on a daily basis.

My birthday celebration began in the early evening. We sat in the living room, drinking icy martini cocktails with thin slices of lemon peel. Light slanted down through the trees in the spacious yard. Frank Sinatra played on the hi-fi. The broken phone had vanished, to be replaced by a vase of crimson roses. Jochen served us a light meal of steak tartare with brioche and oysters on the half shell, in preparation for the outing Unruh promised.

"Don't you want to know where I'm taking you tonight?"

"Someplace with no policeman, I hope."

"The police won't be looking for you at *Swan Lake*."

"Are you searching for more experimental subjects?"

He chuckled. "I do enjoy your sense of humor."

I didn't smile back. "I thought maybe the people who came to the lake might have water-bird totems."

"No. I meant ... surely you know the ballet?"

My cheeks turned red. "Is it a famous one?"

He scrutinized me. "Your father didn't take you out much."

"He didn't need to. We were happy at home."

"I've got tickets to the premiere tonight. You'll love it."

When I didn't reply Unruh pushed a small decorative box toward me. "Happy twentieth."

"Why are you doing all this?"

"My twentieth birthday was terrible. I want yours to be better."

"Weren't you with your family?"

"Open the box, Peppa."

I drew in my breath as I saw the necklace of dark green stones with matching earrings. Jewelry. A romantic gift. If only Tenzin was giving me this.

"Tourmalines from Minas Gerais, in Brazil. I've been waiting a while to find the right girl to wear them."

I studied them. If there were goblins, this is what their blood would look like. Finally, I said, "Thank you."

He rose. "We should go. The performance starts at eight. Where's your hat?"

I reached for the hatbox. My black lace concoction, complete with concealing veil, came from Adalbert Breiter, which had been in business since 1863, according to Unruh.

The pins went in the wrong way, and I tried again. The hat lurched drunkenly to the left. I attempted to fasten it, while Unruh checked his pocket watch.

I thought I had it by the time Jochen came in, smelling of tobacco, but as I rose, it slid off.

"Get Tamara," Unruh told Jochen.

She arrived a few moments later and stared at me, in my tourmaline necklace and fancy silk dress, with its tight waist and tiny pleats. Her ringlets bobbed up and down as she picked up the hatpin. The thought of a pointy metal object in her hand made my eyes sharpen. There was definitely a teardrop, trembling on her eyelashes.

She jabbed the hatpin in, and I flinched.

Unruh kept his voice measured. "Thank you. You may return to your room."

"Are you sure she's a sparrow and not a butcherbird?" I asked, after she slammed the door on her way out. My scalp still burned.

"Jochen, I think I've changed my mind about not wearing a scarf. Would you be so kind and get my silk foulard from my bedroom?"

He shook his head regretfully once Jochen left. "Perhaps I should have made things clearer to Tamara. She ought to find someone her own age."

I didn't say anything. I was thinking about Gladys.

"It would have either been me or Jochen. Can you understand? She knows no one outside this house. And Jochen? You can imagine." He shuddered delicately.

"So you became her lover out of altruism?" I offered.

"I don't know why I bother explaining myself. You're just like my mother and sister. Always judging." He forced a smile. "It's your birthday. Do let's have a nice time."

I put on my brand-new Eduard Meier pumps. Though I'd had to miss out on my personalized measurement from the pedoscope, a tracing of my foot had stood stead. When I rose, I frowned at my feet in their shiny black prisons. Was this what being a grownup was all about?

"Tamara can't be much younger than me."

"I found her in 1945, when she was ten. So she must be twenty two, yes? Older than you, even." He leaned close. "But you're a sophisticated, beautiful woman from a good house, with a superior education. And if I were your lover, I wouldn't be your first one, correct?" His voice was like warm caramel.

I hopped away, nearly falling over the nearby chair. "Don't say things like that, Dr. Unruh."

"Ludwig," he corrected me. "We both know it's heading there. Why try to fight the inevitable?"

"It is *not* heading there." I tried to make my voice forceful.

"If I'm closer to you, the experiment will work much better. You can feel that too."

I shook my head, a bitter taste filling my mouth. I didn't want to sleep with him. At least, the person who loved Tenzin didn't want to. But I was changing here. Becoming something strange and savage.

We sat in our private box at the ballet, where Ludwig helped me lift and pin the veil up. I'd never been to a ballet before. To me, some of the moves looked grotesque, the limbs twisted around in strange permutations. The leaps and bounds across the stage were beautiful, though, evoking the lightness of flight. For a time I forgot that I was there with my captor, an experimental subject given the illusion of freedom. I sipped the champagne Ludwig ordered, the tickle of it pleasurable against my palate. During intermission we stayed in our box and argued about the merits of the American author, Ayn Rand, who I didn't like.

Jochen picked us up and we had one last nightcap in the study, a smooth cognac for him, and a Cora Amaro for me and the peregrine.

My head spun from the alcohol. I hadn't had that much to drink since the night Patrick and I slurped down our homemade brew while my father dry-heaved in his cot next to the bathroom.

When Ludwig leaned toward me, I flinched, sure he would try to kiss me, but he only reached for my snifter. "I shouldn't allow you anymore. I just remembered the experiment is scheduled for tomorrow."

"Oh." I shivered under the caress of my expensive dress. "Maybe we should postpone it one more night."

He was slightly tipsy himself. "Work must continue," he said, exaggerating his intonations. "Until we meet with success."

"Or until the thing that was flapping around there kills me," I pointed out, trying to control the flutter of terror that stirred.

"We'll take care of it together." His voice was smoothly assured.

I met his concern with sarcasm. "Yep. That's us. A team."

"You assumed I would kiss you just now, didn't you?"

I fiddled with my hat, trying to think of something clever to say. I felt drunk and stupid.

"I'm waiting for you to ask me," he said softly. "I may be ruthless in my pursuits, but I'm not a sadistic brute."

When I said nothing, he continued, "I think you understand me more than you want to. Sympathize with my position, even."

"That family in Switzerland. They died."

"I didn't enjoy their suffering. But out of the choice of subjects I had, I took those most deserving of a harsh fate."

I stared at him. Did he honestly expect me to condone what he had done? How could I have been close to seeing him in a romantic light?

"The Russian commander probably had some rationalization too, when he let his soldiers attack Tamara's mother and sister."

His lips became a thin line. "Leave Tamara out of it." He got up, taking my hand and pulling me harder than he needed to. "I'm taking you to the kitchen to make you a soft-boiled egg. You didn't eat enough tonight. It will throw off the metabolism of the dosage tomorrow. And I'll need you at your best."

31. The Sparrow Falters

BUT SUNDAY BROUGHT A CHANGE OF PLANS. TAMARA IMPLORED Ludwig to let her fly once more, and convinced him to increase the dosage. According to his astrological calculations, Mercury, Neptune, and Pluto would be trined for the next three days, making our chances especially strong. Whatever that meant. For an intelligent man, Ludwig could be so superstitious.

I rubbed my eyes in disbelief when he told me. I was in my own room, late afternoon sunlight drifting through my open window. I'd been rereading Da's journals. My mind had been wandering though, remembering Tenzin's warm kisses, the feel of his muscular back as he made love to me. Where the hell was he?

"Dr. Unruh. I don't think that's a good idea."

His lips curved upwards slightly. "It's Ludwig, remember."

"It's still not a good idea." I paused for emphasis. "Ludwig." I was still a little scared of him, but that just made me want to defy him more.

"We'll try it with Tamara one last time. If we're not successful, you can go tomorrow."

"I can hardly wait."

"You really are a saucy wench."

I smiled despite myself. "You're in my room. May I have some privacy, please?"

He made a small bow. "You ought to go to the garden and join Simone. It's a lovely day. I can have Jochen pull the outdoor table over to a sunny spot for you."

"I can manage." It would give me another chance to check the fence for gaps. Though Ludwig had told me often enough I could leave whenever I felt like facing the police, I took those words with a grain of salt.

～

The fence was intact, and there was no way over. I sighed and decided to enjoy the warmth.

I had my chair pulled up under a linden tree, the leaves sheltering my fair skin. Simone dozed by my feet, then her ears pricked at the sound of the bell at the main gate. I heard raised voices. A commotion outside. One voice was Jochen's; the other, lower, was indistinct.

"My master isn't interested in your wares, young man. Now leave before I set my dog on you," Jochen said.

It was Sunday. Real peddlers didn't come around on Sundays.

I raced around the side of the house, ducking under the thick hedges that grew between the study and the fence. I skidded to a stop by the BMW, nearly knocking over Jochen's pail of soapy water onto the rag pile.

"Did you want some shoelaces?" Jochen asked. "So you can tie them together and escape out your window?"

My voice was icy polite. "I'm not following you. Who were you talking with at the gate?"

"One of those itinerant peddlers. Shoelaces. Combs. Spoons. Doesn't even have the decency to come during the week."

My chest rose and fell, as I considered racing to the gate and trying to hurdle it.

Jochen's eyes were like a winter lake. "I'll tell Unruh I've seen his competition. He's very pretty, with his smart suit and blue eyes. But I still think you're better off letting the doctor take a poke at you."

I almost slapped him, but thought better of it. "*Schweinehund*," I bit out. "Shall I tell Ludwig how you talk to me?"

A small crease formed between his eyebrows. "I'm sorry. I'd appreciate you forgetting that," he finally said. "But I will need to tell the doctor about the the pretend peddler. He's been expecting something like that."

It was hard breathing. I *had* used the telephone. I'd hoped to reach Tenzin. But Tenzin didn't have blue eyes. Didn't Tenzin care about me? I remembered now, warnings I'd heard about wanton girls. Maybe I'd ruined my chance with him, lost his respect. My heart sank.

We'd talked of an engagement. Tenzin had no ulterior motive to agree; we'd already been intimate. But then, why wasn't he here?

What a mopey cow I was. The better question was, who *was* here?

It sure sounded like Emil.

I heard Simone barking and wandered back to my place under the tree. At least she was with me.

I'd just sat back down when she dropped a rolled-up newspaper at my feet. Simone loved to retrieve things. I'd often thrown the ball for her. My hands were shaking as I unwrapped it.

A lone syringe of unknown material.

I spent a furious hour reasoning things out. My first letter to Emil, sent shortly after we'd moved to Cambridge, described how I'd trained Simone to fetch. Emil must have read my letters after all, even if he'd never answered.

He wrapped his private signal to me in a newspaper, hoping it wouldn't mean anything definite if it fell in the wrong hands. Knowing Emil's ambitious and exacting nature, this syringe contained the Paxarbital he'd promised to synthesize. I'd trusted him with a potentially lucrative drug recipe, and in turn he was reminding me I could depend on him. We were partners.

I just didn't see how he could help me further.

That night the moon was a thin wafer, hardly there at all. Like my courage.

Jochen grilled sausages for us outdoors, and Ludwig actually made some warm potato salad. He'd learned the recipe from his mother. When I asked him where she lived, he reached for his wine without answering me. Jochen grinned before he slammed the plate down in front of me.

Another misstep.

Then it was time. Jochen took Simone to the pantry. I went to my room to change into my work pants, and then Ludwig led the way down to the basement. I followed, holding an old-fashioned lantern with an actual candle inside. The capped syringe of Paxarbital poked into my hip through my pocket. I'd been afraid to leave it in my room.

Ludwig had been puttering downstairs most of the day, leaving Jochen to keep an eye on me since I wasn't locked up. A bitter smell filled the air, and a heap of leaves still lay on his cutting board.

The hairs on my neck stirred. "Maybe you should think about this some more." I paused, and then said "Ludwig." This time I made my voice friendly.

"The stars say now is the time."

I glanced over at Tamara, who looked pale and determined.

"I could go?" I offered.

I really didn't want to, and when she cried, "No," I said nothing further.

First came the scorpion; he stroked her thigh after and I looked away, embarrassed. Then he brought her the drink. My neck prickled again. The liquid was so dark this time.

As she gulped it down, I had the urge to flee up the stairs, but Ludwig had confessed he'd only finished two years of medical school. Who would look after her if I went?

Moaning, screaming, thrashing. I felt the currents in the air, as if wings fluttered madly.

She cried out, "*Lass sein, lass sein,*" protecting people now long dead. If it had been someone else, I would have taken her hand then.

Her hands made chopping motions, and her grunts of rage rang out. Then gradually, that passed and a sense of expansion filled the room, as if the outside had come in.

Ludwig pressed in close. "Are you there? In the castle?"

"Yes."

He looked at me, and then back. "Is anything ... else there?" I knew by his tone he meant the dreadful white thing that had attacked me.

"Absalom says..."

"What! What!" Eagerly he seized her hand.

"You must promise him a blood sacrifice. Flesh." She lay on the lounge in front of us, yet her voice came from a great distance.

Sweat popped out on his forehead. "It can be arranged. I have a suitable subject."

Not Simone. Let him not mean Simone.

Her voice grew fainter. "Absalom accepts. He asks the name of the one who you seek."

"I need Luci. Luci."

But now there was no answer. Tamara's eyelids fluttered. I took her pulse.

"It's 125."

"It's been higher," he murmured.

"Come on." My voice was sharp.

"We're so close."

I grabbed the stethoscope off the table, took her blood pressure. "It's 170 over 100. Her heart's pounding like a hammer." Mine was too.

He didn't respond. I palpated her abdomen, looking for any other signs of damage.

"Her abdomen's distended. I think she needs to urinate."

"I'll make her some dodder decoction afterwards. It'll help her kidneys."

Her breathing was stentorian now, her face flushed and ominously red. "Pulse up to 130."

He sighed. "Get the Rauwolfia."

I gave her the injection. I waited a few minutes and took the blood pressure again.

It was a bit better, 140 over 85, but her pulse was still racing. Her head had started whipping back and forth, and her hands struggled in their bindings. "*Nein. Nein. Nein,*" she begged, her voice high like a child's.

I pulled at Ludwig's lab coat, desperate. "Why isn't she calming down? What's happening?"

"One soldier was attacking her when I ... interfered. She never talked about it. I think she suppressed the incident. Till now."

"She was ten!" I said, outraged.

"Maybe that's why the other Russians just left after I shot him. We were lucky."

"She's unstable. You should have never subjected her to this." His hands were shaking. "You're frightened too, aren't you?"

"I don't want her to have to go through this. I daren't give her any more Rauwolfia." Her cries of terror rang through the house. Simone started howling upstairs. It sounded like an insane asylum.

If only I could give her the Paxarbital. We'd developed it for situations like this. It would be great to see it work.

But he was standing right there. "Ludwig, go make that dodder decoction."

"She needs me right here." He tried to stroke her brow, but her head moved back and forth too fast.

"If she can urinate, she'll excrete some of the compound."

He looked at me, stricken. "Should I?"

"Right now. Do it."

As soon as he'd left, I uncapped the syringe and injected the contents into the brachial vein. By the time he returned with his offering of dodder, her pulse was only 110. He dribbled the tea into her mouth, his lips pursed, watching her every move.

When her screaming became hoarse and stopped, the ticking of seconds was unbearable. Finally, her eyes fluttered open. "I tried. I really tried."

"I know you did, poppet. I'm so sorry."

"I wanted so to please you," she whimpered.

Unnoticed, I crept up the stairs.

That night I struggled with my thoughts, wondering what I should do. I'd heard the click when Jochen locked me in. But during the day perhaps, I could scramble out a downstairs window and run around the side. Sometimes people passed down the street, though it was a dead end. Surely Jochen wouldn't drag me inside while they were watching.

If I even managed to get away, I'd have to go to the police. Emil was reliable and cunning. I hoped he was staying at the Pensione Kaiserhof, where I could contact him. Would we be able to persuade the cops to break into Unruh's house before he hid all the evidence or hurt Simone? Tamara would lie to protect him. Jochen likely would as well.

Alex and Tenzin knew the truth too, but Alex was in Switzerland, and I didn't know where Tenzin was. I was afraid of the German police, afraid I'd be held in Munich.

Basically, I was just afraid.

Ludwig had promised Absalom a sacrifice. What if he didn't mean Simone? What if it had to be a person?

Would he kill me as soon as I got him his answer?

I was Professor Mueller's daughter. I would think of something.

The next day dragged on, and yet the hours marched too fast toward the inexorable end: the next experiment. Ludwig hadn't said anything to me all day; in fact, I'd barely seen him. He was close to his goal now. Perhaps he was looking at old photographs of Luci. She must have been very important to him.

I wondered glumly what would happen if I died. Would Tenzin be thinking about me in fifteen years? Was he even thinking about me now?

Jochen knocked. I was to join Ludwig in the study.

I painted my lips, studying the bottle of disguised Compound T. It didn't look any different from the day we'd decanted it. Ludwig had remarked that it wasn't stable, but at this point, I wasn't sure when to believe him.

He was drinking wine, looking out the window when I came in. His face was dappled in shade from the tree outside; the wind blew the branch aside, and light illumined him. He was a handsome man, there was no denying that.

"Are you going to feed me some more protein?" I asked. I'd already endured a bowl of Lüngerl for lunch.

"Would you mind cooking tonight? Unless you want more potato salad?"

"I'll make something."

"Tamara's sick." I noted the heaviness in his face.

"Something serious?"

"I'm going to take her to my doctor friend in a few minutes. She's had nausea and vomiting all day. I just examined her again. Her liver's enlarged."

"What can your doctor friend do?"

"He can at least measure liver enzymes. He'll draw blood for a SGOT level, and we can do a follow-up a few days later."

I saw Da's chart of SGOT levels in my head. Dizziness swept through me, like looking through the wrong end of a telescope.

"SGOT. That's for cardiac patients." My voice seemed to come from far away.

"Yes. Sure. But it's elevated in liver damage too."

"Ludwig, can I have some wine?"

He poured me a healthy serving. "You're nervous about tonight's experiment?"

I didn't answer him, my mind whirling. Da had told me a few months before his death that he had a cancer of unknown origin with metastases to the liver. Had he been recording his own SGOT levels? It would be like him to write down his personal data somewhere where no one would see it. He always wore long-sleeved shirts; he could have been getting one of the assistants to draw his blood. The first recorded SGOT level was in the spring of 1956; how long had he known he had cancer before he told me?

But the first level had been normal. Why would he even have measured it?

"Peppa, I'm serious."

I blinked. What had Ludwig been saying? His smile was tender.

"I've enjoyed being with you. Maybe it's time for me to let go of the past and move on. Things can't always be resolved."

"What?"

He spoke slowly, as if explaining things to a child. "I can't account for what happened to Tamara. I'm afraid you'll get sick too. We'll cancel further experiments for now, decide how to handle the police investigation."

But all at once I understood why Tamara was sick. I put the wine down, ran out of the room, and took the stairs two at a time. I yanked out the notebook with its table of SGOT levels and looked at the date of the first recording again: February 11, 1956.

Da and I injected a monkey with Paxarbital that afternoon. It had bared its teeth and screamed, and I protested. Da grinned. "I know. What we really need are humans to test this on. We could get much better data."

He sure hadn't tested it out on me, and the only other person around that day was him. It made sense that he'd take a baseline reading on his liver before he started.

But the SGOT levels became higher after the first month. Why hadn't he stopped?

I threw myself face down on the bed.

Paxarbital caused liver damage.

Da experimented on himself. That was the secret Alex alluded to. Da knew Paxarbital was dangerous, and yet he'd kept using it on himself. Why? Why would he do that? And why would he lie and tell me he had cancer?"

My hands clenched into fists of impotent rage. I skimmed the journal, flipping through the pages. The odd entry I'd noticed earlier was in the summer of 1956. *Took Carmen out and bought her martinis. She finally told me what I suspected. It will be on the market soon.*

When I heard Ludwig come in, I sat up on the bed quickly, pulling the blanket across my lap to hide the journal.

"What's wrong? I thought you'd be happy. We can take a break from the Compound T experiments. I have other things you can help us with. Demand for Compound S is increasing. Dr. Schnitzler is spreading the word for me."

"I want to go to the Land of Aves," I said, between clenched teeth. Da had a bird totem, like me. Tenzin had said he was a hungry ghost. I knew I'd find him there.

Ludwig frowned. "You're exhibiting erratic behavior."

"You got me into this. Let's finish it."

"Why are you so angry, Peppa?" He folded his hands. "I admit it; I tried to scare you, manipulate you. But I've come to care for you. Genuinely. You have spirit. Is it possible?" He arched an eyebrow at me, and then looked down, abashed. "That your hate for me would evolve into a neutral kind of interest?"

For a moment there, I truly liked him, saw a kindred spirit in him. Then a wash of rage against my father obliterated it. They were all the same, with their fucking secrets and selfish pursuits. Even Tenzin had doled out the truth, bit by bit, then broken my heart by abandoning me.

I was going to get some answers, even if it killed me. Starting with Da.

32. The Truth Shall Set You Free

Ludwig had burned something pine-scented in the basement and replaced the blanket over the chaise. When I commented, he said, "I gave Tamara too much dodder. But I've got most of the smell and stain out."

He hummed as he chose the scorpion. Now that I'd convinced him to go forward with the experimentation, he was like a little boy on Christmas Day. He swabbed Lidocaine on my thigh before, to lessen the sting. He apologized for the diaper as he handed it to me. "I'll let you put it on. I just don't want to have to clean up again."

"I'm not going to lose control of my bladder. I'm very healthy." I'd even gone to see his old friend from medical school, Paul Schnitzler. He'd given me a complete physical, with Ludwig peering over his shoulder.

"It's standard procedure."

I shrugged and slid the soft flannel up over my underwear.

He brought the beaker over with a straw. "You're sure? It's not too late to change your mind."

I gulped it down, feeling like I was drowning in sadness. I wanted Tenzin. But I didn't know where he was.

The magic man's voice, distant, nags. From another world, the world of alive. A stranger's voice, not welcome here. I fly in small circles, calling, feathers bristling. Intruder.

Lord Absalom holds out his arm.

Sit. Here.

I glide to the side of the stone table, gripping the back of a chair. He proffers. I feed.

But not with ease. I look up, at shadows swarming around pillars. It came from there, a white blast of rage.

I am afraid.

As meat sticks in craw, the magic man fills me with his want. Tugging, tugging, making a soft, warm pain in me, like a spreading wound.

His voice, soft, loud, soft. "Call the spirit's name."

I remember how close he stands to my host in that dark space under the house. We abandoned her body. Now I feel threat.

I bend toward my Lord Absalom. I will tell him of the wolf man's wish.

He opens his book. "Tell me the name of the one to call."

I listen. The magic man's voice drowns in unshed tears. He is a lost wind in his own gale. He says a name.

"Susie?" I cannot be sure.

Absalom states, "There is none named Susie who will answer his summons."

A howl of longing from the wolf-man pierces me. His voice is like something on the box called the radio, drifting in and out.

I send out a query, but it trembles, falters.

He shouts at my host, who lies helpless in the underground cage where he works. "Join me." He is mad with need.

He wants to possess my host.

There are other words, but the connection frays. They blow in the winds of time, scatter like sand. Words are fragile.

Only his intention remains, a dark form, a beast lurking in the fog. He must reach me. In any way.

His hands are on my host body. No!

I must keep the girl safe. But when she is not present in her body, I cannot go there.

The wolf's hands grasp her bare legs, fingers stalking up, taking away cloth. A different cloth, smelling of herbs and forest, folded wet with medicine. This he pushes up against her dark, velvet secret place.

She moans, as the liquid soaks into her softness. Her blood rushes down to meet it, red to green. Her heart beats faster.

Fear?

No. I struggle with the newness. Slot the feeling. *Arousal.* Now I am afraid *for* her.

He has caused her to come into heat, made her receptive. I try to warn her, but I cannot explain. Her brain is slow now, sluggish with thick need pumping up.

The girl roars. Savage like me. Raw and penetrant. One last clear thought.

We say, "Bring Dr. Johann Mueller."

Absalom warns, "There will be a price to pay. A blood price."

"We will pay."

Long maggot-white fingers flick on rustling parchment. The gap of his mouth howls. Johann Mueller. Here, a name is all that is left of what you once were.

The owl attacks, pale feathers, diving fury. *Leave. Leave this place. Not for you to know. Not for you.*

He is large and dead and white. We know him.

Fear chokes the girl, our heart full of hurt, for she cannot bear to see him, the attacker, one so dear, so familiar.

Our heart explodes, goes dead. The betrayal.

Dr. Johann Mueller. Still clutching his secret, still hiding his shame.

~

I came up, gasping, clawing for air, screaming.

Ludwig was right there, and swiftly he undid the buckles and lifted me up. I was shaking, tears streaming down my face.

I must have lost control of my bladder too. I felt warmth and dampness, though at least I didn't stink like urine. The room smelled like fresh turf. Humiliated, I cried harder.

He stroked my cheeks, his hands warm and gentle. I let him.

I managed to talk through my sobs. "You met my father. What did you think of him? Why did you and he argue?"

"I don't understand. I tried to call Luci. I was close, but then your falcon broke away. Something happened."

I implored, "Answer me. You met my father in Brazil. Why was he angry at you?"

"We argued about Emil Abderhalden and his defensive ferments reaction test. Even someone like me, without years of biochemistry, could see this blood test for madness was mere conjecture. Unproven."

I'd heard Aberhalden's name before. Da still kept the letters from his first mentor, though he and Da had long ago broken off contact.

Ludwig took my icy hands in his, warming them. "He became insulted when I told him he was like Abderhalden. Abderhalden's experiments were flawed. Your father couldn't admit when he was wrong either."

It was clear now. Father couldn't accept defeat, though it cost him his life. There had been no cancer. Just a failed medication and overweening pride.

Ludwig drew me to him and I let myself fall into the comfort, the smell of his expensive cologne, the smoothness of his slick dark hair against my cheek.

I cried and cried, and he whispered, "My poor girl."

Then at some point the newfound ease between us transformed into something sharper, pungent, edgy,

He knew it too, alert like an animal to the change, as if my hormones were broadcasting a symphony of sensuality. My nipples poked stiff and hard against the restraint of my dress.

Something savage waxed within; I wavered in the moment between emerging friendship and raw need. And fell, into the deep, slippery abyss.

I threw myself on him, wanting to couple till I was senseless, exhausted.

He'd anticipated me. His tongue darted between my lips. I melted into him. His hands tore off my dress as I bit his neck. I threw him on the floor where he wrestled me under as I bucked, my pelvis grinding against his.

I could say it was our two totems that met that night, glistening naked with sweat and saliva, clawing each other, all bunching muscles.

I could say that, but it does not spare me the shame of it.

The next morning, I woke up in Ludwig's bed, under the custom-made forest green sheets. He was sprawled on his back, one hand flung up to shield his eyes against the ray of pale light peeping in.

We must have made it upstairs and continued our demented lovemaking. I remembered parts of it. I was sore. And wretched. The experience with Tenzin had been beautiful, a dance of harmony. This had been sheer, blind lust.

My back hurt when I tried to move. Ludwig's neck and chest were covered with scratches that must have come from me.

From Cora.

I had to get out of that bed and away from him. Too bad I couldn't get away from Cora too.

I looked at his face, peaceful in repose, and thought about smothering him with a pillow. But I couldn't punish him for what I was.

Ludwig's hand reached out toward me, and a murmur of contentment escaped him. I jumped like I'd been burned and flung myself out of bed, barely landing on my feet. My dress was ripped. I had to get out of his room. I tore his silk purple robe down from its hook and threw it on, banging the bedroom door in my haste to leave.

As I raced up the stairs to the landing, Simone padded down the hall toward me, sniffing distrustfully. I sank down on my haunches and buried my head in her shoulder, grateful for something normal and familiar. When I looked up again, I saw Tamara, glaring. She mouthed "slut" at me.

It was too much. I ran to our bathroom, locking the door behind me, and turned on the hot water full force. Once I was in the tub, more tears came. I'd hoped they'd cleanse me, but instead I was filled with dull hopelessness and self-loathing. I scrubbed for longer than I needed to, till I was red and raw. The purple love bites on my neck still stood out, though.

I wrapped a towel around me and went to my room. Simone was nowhere to be seen. Jochen must have removed her so I'd stay cooperative. I threw myself on my cot, my back aching, and my heart empty of hope.

Absalom had given me my answer, and I owed him his due. I'd promised without thinking. What had I done? Once Ludwig had his answer, he'd owe the Guardian of Time as well. Two bodies, to pay for our knowledge. But if I never traveled there again, could he reach us here?

The connections between our two worlds had to be broken. That was the only way we'd all be safe. Otherwise, someone here would die, just as Tenzin predicted.

Tenzin. Just his name caused a stab of pain. He'd warned me I'd fall into Unruh's hands. He could never love me now.

I slipped on my worn cigarette pants and baggy blue sweater. I opted to go barefoot, despite the cold floors. I wanted to punish myself. I opened the door quietly, looking up and down the staircase before I descended the two flights of stairs into the basement.

The scorpion dealer, an unpleasant hirsute man, had told me the scorpions came from the deserts of Africa. A light was kept burning under their cage to keep them warm, and a blanket swaddled the base.

By standing on a stepstool, I was able to reach the cellar window and prop it open. The cold draft refreshed me, even as it raised gooseflesh on the nape of my neck. I picked up one of the clean flannel diapers to protect my hand. Then I moved the cage and blanket to expose the glowing light bulb, which I twisted hard in its socket till the filament popped. I replaced everything.

I stole back up the stairs, reached my bedroom, whistled for Simone, who didn't come, and moved a chair in front of the door, since I had no way to lock it. I was too miserable to even look out at the treetops and glimpses of the river. I pulled the covers over my head, and stared into the dark, wondering if there was a God. Maybe he'd cursed me for not believing. Or maybe I really was a slut.

∽

I stayed in my room past lunchtime. I had no appetite. Finally, around two, Jochen knocked on my door. "The doctor wants to see you in the study. Change clothes. He doesn't like the pants."

No doubt there would be retribution. I hoped at least the scorpions were dead.

I arrived to find Ludwig pacing, neatly attired in a coat and cravat. Tamara slumped in the chair by his writing desk, sullen, staring at the floor.

I sat as far away from her as I could, in the corner chair under his books of astrology and Tarot. A skull leered at me from its stand.

"Someone left the window open. The scorpions died."

I shrugged.

"And the light bulb blew. An accident? I think not."

"I've been in bed all day." I scratched one of my love bites. I wouldn't have minded another hot bath. Or an exorcism.

"You didn't go to the basement?"

What if someone had seen me? But I didn't think they had. What was he going to do, dust for fingerprints?

"Wasn't me," I said, when he wouldn't stop staring.

"The cellar window doesn't open by itself."

We all sat there. I feigned indignation, Unruh glowered, Tamara pouted.

He turned to Tamara. "It wasn't you?"

"Of course not. I told you."

He glared at me. "You killed my pets. I've got a mind to kill yours."

I should have anticipated this. He knew Simone was my weak point. "Tamara must have done it. She's jealous since she's failed you. She's not a strong flyer."

"I'm not lying," she protested.

"Well, if you're so honest, then what happened with my locket?" I didn't have to pretend to be angry about that. I missed Tenzin. It would have been a comfort to at least have the sacred sand, even though I'd failed him.

Ludwig rubbed his chin. "Let's stop this charade. The truth is, the scorpion venom does nothing to facilitate the journeying. Tamara knows that."

I gasped, and caught myself. "But you put one in my bed in Gonten."

"I didn't want you to guess how I'd made Compound T. I call it a compound, but it's only a simple extract. A bit of deceptive advertisement."

When I said nothing, he continued, "You would be the only one with motivation to kill the scorpions."

"Tamara wanted it to look like me."

"I did not. You've ruined everything since you came." Tamara's voice was shrill.

"Girls. Girls." He addressed me. "A pity, Peppa. I thoroughly enjoyed last night."

My cheeks burned with shame. I wished I could eradicate the memories. My body, a traitor to my will, responded to his frank gaze with a shiver of heat. Cora's doing.

"Did you hope to stop the experiments now that you've gotten your answer?"

"I can't let it happen again." I meant all of it. Incurring our blood obligation to Absalom, coupling like animals on the floor. It had to stop.

He pressed his lips together. "You're serious. Now that I'm so close. Your falcon will hear me. I've been inside you. I've touched you deep within."

Tamara gasped and ran from the room.

Ludwig ignored her and spoke to Jochen. "Bring me the whip from the carriage house and Simone."

"As you say, Doctor."

I buried my head in my hands. I was trapped.

Jochen's heavy tread announced his entrance. He'd muzzled Simone. He proffered the whip to Ludwig.

"What are you going to do?"

Ludwig crossed the floor in two strides, bringing the whip down hard on Simone's snout. Her howl of pain penetrated my misery.

"Wait!" I screamed. "You almost blinded her."

"So. My pets are dead."

"I did it. I did it. Hit me. She did nothing to you," I begged.

Jochen averted his face, even as he tightened his hold on the dog. He was a big man, but she was strong, writhing at the end of the short leash, the choke collar deep in her neck.

Ludwig shook his head. "Now you want me to *hit* you?"

"Don't hurt Simone. She's all I have."

Jochen's face was sweaty. He reached out and grasped Simone by the loose skin at the scruff of her neck. "I can't hold her much longer."

"Get her out of here. Lock her in the pantry."

Left alone, we faced each other. "You're going back tonight," he warned.

"Who will you sacrifice for Absalom's blood payment?"

"I must punish you for what you've done. But you and Simone are safe otherwise."

I didn't believe him. Something dark was rising up in me, dangerous and bad. I looked around the room for a weapon.

His wiry body tensed. "Do you think a falcon can overpower a wolf? A waif can overpower a grown man of the lineage of Unruh?"

I dropped my eyes.

"Take off my dress. I won't have it ruined."

It fell in a puddle of soft fabric on the floor. It took an effort to stand straight, clad only in my underwear.

I braced myself, but when the whip sliced into my shoulders, I fell to my knees from the pain. A deep grunt escaped me, like the one my father made as he lay dying.

I looked down, watching the blood bead and trickle its way across the carpet, waiting for the next one. Which never came.

There was no word from Ludwig. Finally, I got up awkwardly, the movement sending out new flares of pain. He was looking out the window.

"May I go?"

"No." He turned around and his eyes were bright and wet, his face twitching as if he could barely control himself.

"First this." He pulled me close to him and buried his muzzle in my neck. Disgusted, I realized he was lapping my wound.

I pushed him away. His eyes shone with blood lust. Would he throw me to the floor and spread my legs?

"Done. Go." His voice was thick.

I yanked on my dress, praying he wouldn't change his mind. I sprang to the door, turning around at the last moment to look at him.

And so I saw the single tear that fell to the floor.

33. The Last Supper

As I staggered down the hallway toward the stairs, I heard talking in the kitchen.

I stopped, wondering if I should draw nearer. Tamara or Jochen might be in danger from the planned blood sacrifice. I didn't like either of them, but I felt responsible for Tamara's misery. Not only had I replaced her in Ludwig's bed, I'd unknowingly caused her liver damage.

I was still barefoot, and my light tread made no noise. I peered through the keyhole. Jochen must have sat down at the small kitchen table after locking Simone in the pantry. I could just glimpse his profile; Tamara sniffled, slumped in her chair, as he handed her a handkerchief.

"You'd have been better off with me," Jochen pointed out. "I always fancied you. I'm only a chauffeur now, but I could have showed you a good time."

"Ludwig loved me. Before *that bitch* came."

He snorted. "It's a class thing. He may pride himself on being a self-made man, but he'll never forget his origins. Or yours. Miss Mueller's a hoyden, but when she swishes around in that brandy silk dress, smelling of Air Du Temps, he sees a match worthy of his house."

The bitterness in her voice was like a slap. "Quite a description. Are you taken by her too?"

"Not at all. She's an odd-looking twig of a girl. Not pretty, like you."

Her chair screeched as she moved away from his roaming hands. "You're not making me feel better. Leave me alone."

"At least give me a treat."

She darted out of sight and came back with something in her hand. "You spoil that dog."

He took the lump of meat from her. "She's a noble creature. Why should she have to suffer for her mistress?"

"Does Ludwig know you play ball with her while you should be polishing the car?"

"Poor creature's locked up half the time," he said gruffly, headed for the pantry door.

If he let Simone out, she might sense me and act excited. I darted for the safety of my room, then paused by the small marble-topped table that held the incoming mail. Ludwig had opened a stack of envelopes and taken them to his study. The sharp letter opener still lay there, forgotten.

Dusk was falling. I'd slept for a while, the letter opener tucked under my pillow. Now I took it out. I felt its sharp edge. I studied the perfume bottle with its potentially lethal contents.

I am the god of wrath and vengeance. I was too heartbroken to summon up much wrath. But Simone and I might need protection. Events were spiraling out of control.

Knife or poison?

Much as Ludwig disconcerted me, he was also familiar. I'd eaten his warm potato salad, discussed Ayn Rand and Nietzsche with him. I'd seen him naked.

With Compound T he would die confused, in agony, not even aware of what was happening to him. If he put me in a position where I had to use the letter opener, he would understand. Predators know and respect each other.

So, the knife.

None of my dresses had pockets. Taping it to my thigh was out; the diaper would push past it and likely dislodge it.

I looked around my spartan room for a solution. Four outfits and a new coat hanging in the closet, a pillow I'd put on the floor for Simone to nap on while I read. A stack of books, and my father's journals.

My eyes were bleary, and I still felt dirty. I would probably feel dirty the rest of my life, however long that would be. I went over to the washstand and poured water into the basin, scrubbing my face and my shoulders.

The rusty smear of blood from my smarting cut gave me an idea.

My sanitary pad holder lay under my small stack of neatly folded underwear. The device looked like stocking garters, belts dangling with snaps where the thick pad could be attached. I wiped my fingerprints off the letter opener, then holding it with a handkerchief, I sewed it into place on the thick pad with a few threads that could be easily snapped.

It wouldn't be pleasant walking with this between my legs. I'd have to walk slowly and carefully, but Ludwig would expect that after last night. He would, however, want me to wear the diaper. I'd tell him I was menstruating and already wearing a pad.

Wolves had a keen sense of smell. Just in case, I pulled the pad across my shoulder, roughing up the wound to make it bleed a bit more. Then I put it on. I felt the metal slide against my skin.

I rolled the contraption back down, took a handkerchief, laid it on top of the blade, and tried again. I felt like an incontinent old lady when I stood up and waddled around.

I would have laughed, but I was too depressed.

Jochen fetched me for dinner. When he knocked, he usually stood stiffly outside the door, like a wooden soldier. This time I invited him in. There were still a few rays of sun sliding in through my window, and I wanted to get a good look at his face.

I got distracted when my hyper-acute eyesight picked up the movement of a vole from the yard. I obviously felt threatened by Jochen.

He must have the potential to be dangerous. But did he deserve death?

"What do you want, Miss?" He breathed his tobacco smell on me.

I picked my words carefully. "You mentioned you'd have trouble getting a job elsewhere."

"Are you planning on firing me? When the doctor marries you?"

Whatever else he might be, Jochen wasn't very smart.

"No, it's not that. Does Ludwig know something about you? Something that might make people judge you harshly?"

He looked at his freshly polished shoes. "He offered to help me. He let me become his driver."

Maybe Jochen hadn't fathered a child with his own sister, the way Hans Wäspi had, but he'd done something. I knew Ludwig planned ahead, like me. If he'd told Absalom he had a sacrifice ready that meant he'd acquired someone disposable.

"You didn't—for instance, work at Dachau or anything?" Dachau was the site of a former concentration camp, only a half an hour away from Munich.

A muscle twitched in his cheek. "Dinner is almost served. The food will be getting cold."

I thought of Hans Wäspi, simple, brutal, and so dead. Ludwig acted as the judge, but I'd carried out the sentence.

"Jochen, do you stay here every single evening? Don't you have things you like to do?"

"I like to smoke my Lassos."

"Don't you ever have friends you meet?"

His brow creased. "I like to go to the beer garden before the cold weather comes."

He'd been kind to Simone. "Go tonight. Stay at a friend's house afterwards," I urged him.

He ran his hand through his hair. "What are you planning?"

"It's not me. You shouldn't trust Ludwig."

He looked at me a long time, his face jowly and his eyes squinting their suspicion. "People like you don't help people like me."

I shifted, and felt the metal of the letter opener hard against my tender, chafed skin. "Believe what you want. I'm going downstairs." Head bowed, I descended.

I sat at the other end of the long table from Ludwig, as far as away as I could get. Tamara served him bisque, then put a quivering lump of something blackish in front of me. Having experienced a full Irish breakfast, I knew what it was.

"Don't you want some of this tasty blood pudding," I taunted Ludwig, hating him, hating his house, his crazy staff.

And hating Cora, who wanted it.

"It's for you." His voice had a new crisp edge to it. I could feel the focus radiating from him; I'd felt it from my father too, when he got close to an answer.

I tasted a small forkful and shook my head. "This tastes strange. Even for blood pudding."

"If you go into a hypoglycemic coma, I may not be able to administer sugar to you quickly enough. Not if you're writhing and screaming."

I looked at the pile on my plate glumly. A hypoglycemic coma might not be such a bad way to die.

What might tempt me to live? I let myself fantasize while I forced down the pudding. I could work with Emil at the lab he'd rented while I reapplied to Radcliffe. They might give me another chance. But though I felt Emil was dependable, he didn't love me. Tenzin had. I was sure of it.

Moisture seeped out of my eyes. He was lost to me now.

"I asked if you wanted more mineral water?" Tamara's voice interrupted my reverie. She'd placed a plate with the usual 200 grams of steak on it in front of me.

"Sorry. Yes." The steak looked good, garnished with pepper. I felt full though. "I wish I'd passed on first course. What was that, dragon's blood? It was disgusting."

"It was Ludwig's blood," Tamara said.

Nausea gripped me. I dropped the fork on the floor, started to pick it up, then didn't. I swallowed as the saliva gathered in my cheeks. Any minute...

Ludwig ran over, closing my jaw with his strong hand. The other hand stroked my throat, forcing the lump back down.

"Get some peppermint drops from the kitchen," he shouted.

When Tamara moved, he gave her an evil look. "Not you. You go get a basin. I want Jochen to do it."

Jochen was back in a flash, holding the open bottle of essence under my nose.

"There, there," Ludwig soothed. "Keep it down. It will link us further. Get me my answers, and we'll make a truce. We'll work out some agreement."

I couldn't answer; his hand was clamped around my jaw hard. I tried to nod. He was bruising me.

Slowly he let go. "My blood won't hurt you. You've just had a bit of a shock." He shot another nasty look at Tamara. "Bite your tongue from now on."

Jochen cleared his throat. "Dr. Unruh, I was talking to a few of the fellows, and they're going to meet for a drink. Will you be needing me tonight?"

Ludwig's eyes widened as he considered. "I might. Please do stay."

Jochen rocked on his heels for a moment. "It's my friend's birthday," he said slowly. "Couldn't whatever it is wait?"

Ludwig stroked his beard. "I don't believe it could."

"Well, what is it that you want?" Jochen's voice was rough now, his cheeks showed a hectic pink.

"Isn't it enough that I asked you to stay?" Ludwig's voice had the quiet command of the upper class.

Jochen stared ahead stonily. "I'll be in my room, Doctor."

Nine o'clock came, and Ludwig couldn't find Jochen to assist him. We looked all over the house, in the carriage house with the parked BMW, even in the little tool shed.

Ludwig's eyes narrowed into slits. "He was acting strangely. Do you know anything about this?"

"Maybe he's angry that Tamara's upset. He has a sweet spot for her."

"If you knew more about this man, you wouldn't have such sentimental ideas," Ludwig snapped. He called for Tamara to come down to the basement.

While he warmed the decoction, Tamara buckled the straps on me, looking like she'd like to spit in my face.

"Would you make her leave, please?"

Ludwig stopped fiddling with the flame of the Bunsen burner, looking troubled.

Tamara pulled the strap on my chest even tighter. "I always help him. I'm not going to leave."

As she moved, the gold chain of my locket peeped out from under her collar.

Need grasped my heart and squeezed. "I want my locket." The photo of my family, before things went bad. The sacred sand Tenzin gave me. The locket was balm for my hurt.

"It's mine now. Finders keepers," Tamara taunted.

Ludwig turned to her. "Tamara, theft does not speak well of you. Give it back, and I'll buy you a nice necklace."

Tamara ignored him, going for the cloth to push up between my legs.

I clamped them together. "I won't be needing that. I'm wearing a pad already."

Ludwig's fine eyebrows drew together in puzzlement. "A pad?"

"She's got her monthly," Tamara snapped. "And next time, don't leave your bloody washrag on the sink."

Ludwig ignored her outburst. "That's a shame. I'd actually hoped a little Ludwig might follow our night of passion."

Tamara looked up stricken, as if he'd slapped her. "You want a baby from that slut?"

"You can have him," I shouted at her, enraged and embarrassed.

Ludwig's face hardened. "Tamara, you must not excite the test subject. She has an ordeal ahead of her."

"But I can't believe you would..." her voice trailed off.

He turned on his chair, facing her full on, looking lordly and cold. "Let me explain some things to you, dear. When I want an heir, I choose a lady to breed with. I've been giving you an herbal contraceptive every day with your tea. Look at Peppa. Her finely chiseled features. Her translucent skin. Her eyes, shining with intelligence. And despite her defiance, she conducts herself like a lady."

"It's just expensive clothes and perfume." Tamara snuffled, tears flowing down her cheeks. I felt sorry for her.

"It is *not* just expensive clothes and perfume. You're a farm girl. Find some beefy bricklayer or field hand, get married, spit out some brats. I saved your life; it doesn't mean you have to spend it with me."

Tamara froze, then bolted up the stairs.

He came over, proffered the drink. "It's just you and me now. Let's finish this."

Death lurked in the shadows. Ludwig didn't seem to know, and I didn't care much. My once-beloved father had died in his selfish pursuit of fame, I'd betrayed the man I loved, and the police thought I was a murderer.

If only Jochen had taken Simone with him when he left. I could hear her howling in the pantry.

34. The Falcon and the Wolf

I burst out, flying high, high, speeding, for I sense?

Wolf. Near. How can it be?

Then memory. The girl and the magic man feasted on each other, tasted each other's blood. I am bonded to him.

As her body accepted him, so must I. My foe is cunning.

I soar, seeking the crossing, my strength bearing him, snuggled in like a tick.

As I coast to the ground, Wolf releases his hold, drops, wailing, wanting to run into the woods. The magic man commands him to stillness. Wolf submits and holds the space, a smeared wavering shadow. He cannot take full form.

I shudder at the wrongness of it. *Your kind does not belong here.*

But the agreement is done. I can still taste the night's meal on our tongue, the magic man's blood sacrifice to us.

Absalom awaits, the record keeper, the Guardian. Wolf asks through me.

A girl called Luci.

The nightingale who sang so sweetly.

My voice or Wolf's? They blend, his words become mine, become my wish.

Absalom speaks. "You must pay for the summoning."

"I will make sacrifice. I will make obeisance."

"Describe the sacrifice."

"The man Jochen will be found. We will put a bullet in his temple, then bring his blood to your altar in the golden cup."

"I accept."

A fullness of twittering birds whirling close now, so many—

Light blocked out. Singing one word. *Luci, Luci, Luci.*

Confusion of desire. He wants Luci. I want...

Swirl inside me. Spark of knowing.

I am not like mangled Wolf, forced into the wrong world. My host gifted me a name. Cora.

I cognate. A name means that I am. If I am, then I am the center of my world. All else is other. Other that is near, and other that is far.

She who is near. Not just host body that I am bound to protect, but sister-kin. *Peppa.* I open to her: the crystalline form of thoughts hiding the soft blooms of feelings, the frame of ideas through which she sees the world.

Fierce pride. Stronger together. *We* are Cora. *We* are Peppa.

⁓

Once I put on my father's glasses over mine, and I saw everything double.

Now I saw the back of my closed eyes, knew I was in the basement, but I also saw Luci, saw the Jade World.

Perhaps because she was called by name, she came as the girl in the photograph, gliding into the courtyard. Her chestnut hair was piled in a bun on her head, stray locks twining around her temple. Her clothes were untidy, grass-stained; she was pale, and in places the moss green air showed through.

"Ludwig. Darling. You shouldn't be here. This is the land of the dead."

"I have to know."

"It's all gone now: the days scattered like daisies from a broken chain; our promises like petals from overblown roses, strewn in the wind of time. All that is left is your loneliness and my memory of love."

"I did love you, Luci. I would never have hurt you. They didn't believe me. My own family. My own mother, my sister, they lost faith in me."

Her voice, mild as milk, sweet as hay. "I know, Ludwig. I loved you too."

"Who killed you?"

"Come with me."

And I came too, had too, because I was the vehicle.

It was a gentle spring day in the woods. The pines were long and tall, their shadows shortening as the sun reached its zenith. Her shoes went around the white anemones; his blundered, crushing them.

We, the watchers, drew back, and we could see it all below—the girl perhaps fifteen, the boy a year or two older, serious and lean already, his hair not pomaded yet but thick and bushy.

He stopped, drew her to him, kissed her, hungry and passionate.

I was an unwilling intruder, but I could not steer this journey.

"Make love to me, little one. Here, on this beautiful day."

He was pressing against her now, panting, his hand fumbling with the clasp of her skirt.

Her voice high. "I can't. You're going to university soon, Ludwig. You'll be gone."

"I said I'd come back and marry you."

"After school. You said. It only takes once to get pregnant."

"Don't worry. I'll be careful."

"That's what my cousin's boyfriend told her. Now they took her baby away and she'll never see it."

He became angry. "I would marry you if. If. But it won't happen. Just let me…" He was back at the buttons, opened them, gave the skirt a yank.

She grabbed, her hand finding the waistband just in time. Her voice sharp now. "No, I said no."

"Then do that other for me."

"I won't. It's wrong."

They faced each other now, her hand still on her hips, clutching her skirt.

"If you loved me like you say you do…"

"Why do you have to ruin everything, Ludwig? Our last day together before you leave?"

"Me ruin everything? You obviously don't love me."

She quailed under his cruel words, shut her eyes, but kept her arms close, hugging herself. She didn't reach out to him.

He turned his back on her and went.

Then it was late afternoon, Luci sitting in the woods, watching clouds race across the sky. The weather was changing. And the man who'd been watching her was ready to make his move.

He was on her, a flash, and her legs, her little legs, kicking up, her voice screaming, frantic, but the woods were big and she was far away from home or friends.

Ludwig was at the riverbank, throwing bits of bark into the water, already sorry he'd hurt her, not knowing how bad it would get. How they would all think he'd done it, eventually.

Even his mother.

Because he'd always been a strange boy.

We were back at the table with Absalom, Ludwig an unseen presence, but his regret palpable.

He spoke through us, the falcon and me. "Mr. Sauer. He murdered you."

"He must have been watching me. I fought. He got scared. Killed me."

"I'd make him pay, Luci. I would. But I heard. He was one of the first to die on the Russian front. I can never prove it."

Her voice was dispassionate. "Prove it to whom?"

There was silence.

Then Absalom laughed, a curdled sound, twisting through the air. His filed teeth glittered. "Who is left to prove it to? Your mother, eaten up by tuberculosis and maggots, stinking in the family crypt. Your brother, shot by the Russians. Your sister, burned outside the bomb shelter in Weimar, the door locked."

"Ah." Ludwig had no lungs here, but I could feel the gasp, the intake of breath as if he'd been stabbed. "All dead?"

Then, tentatively, daring to hope. "But can you be sure? We had none of the Land of Aves in our bloodline."

"All eight lands of the dead are known to the Guardians of Time." There was finality in Absalom's voice. "You both have your answer. It is peril to linger. But do not forget my payment."

Luci faded, green showing through her cheeks, her eyes dimming.

Ludwig reached out desperately. "I'm so sorry. Forgive me. Please say you forgive me."

What would she have said?

If the white owl hadn't crashed down into us, breathing fear, panic.

This time I named him. "Father."

"Why do you come here? What do you seek?"

"I know."

The attack stopped. The owl froze, white and still.

I looked at him, my illusion stripped away. The vision, Absalom's last gift, pierced my heart.

The hungry ghost. Father every night in the lab, tying the strap around his arm, tightening it with his mouth, then picking up the hypodermic needle. Like an addict. But this is not an addict; he's a respected scientist, he'll have the answers soon, he'll have his next book out, he'll have an offer from Sandoz.

Only just a little more data. How does Paxarbital work? Does it have side effects?

Perhaps. The headaches every morning must mean something. The nausea. Elevated liver enzymes. But they might settle down again.

It looked so promising on paper. The rats and monkeys did so well.

Just a little more. To see. Perhaps cutting out all alcohol. Perhaps taking the medication with a meal.

Until the day he woke up with a partial seizure. And his memory started to slip away.

He stopped for a month. It was too late. His blood spoke of the continuing damage, day after day, and his mind stayed blurred.

So he hastened the slow deterioration he'd unloosened. He took more.

⁓

"You killed yourself," I said. "You made me think it was cancer and you lied. You're a suicide."

Then an explosion in my head as he flew at me, trying to make me take back the words, knowing what kind of a father he'd been.

Ready to sacrifice everything for science.

Worse than Ludwig. Ludwig had done it out of love and loneliness.

~

I came to lying on the floor. The falcon was a dim presence, eclipsed by the feel of wolf, grieving. But he wasn't a wolf anymore, he was a man, eyes red-rimmed, chest shaking, nose running.

He cradled me on his lap, his tears watering my face.

I pushed away, half falling on the floor, and righted myself.

"This was the reason you put all of us through this? To find out what happened to Luci?"

He'd turned and pressed his eyes against his other arm. His voice came out muffled. "Yes."

"She said she loved you."

"I left her defenseless for that predator."

I found myself in the odd position of comforting him. "You couldn't know."

The sobs stopped for a moment and then started again.

"So your family blamed you?"

"The body was never found. After a while, someone started a rumor. And it spread." He swallowed. "This is not like me. It's just ... you see. I hadn't corresponded with anyone from my town. I left, went to university here. I tried to go back once, when I heard the Americans were abandoning Thuringia to the Russians. On the way, I found Tamara. I never reached home. I had to take her to Munich, to safety."

"What are you trying to say, Ludwig?"

"I didn't know my entire family died."

There was a long pause.

"I thought that I could confront them. They'd apologize, take me back."

"You really didn't know? What about the will?"

"They cast me out from the house of Von Unruh."

He pulled me closer, and I sat there, exhausted.

In the silence the air was electric with warning. Compound T was wearing off, but it wasn't over; something else was going to happen.

Absalom. I could feel him. I tried to warn Ludwig. "We're in danger."

"It's all over. I've been a fool, a deluded fool. You're the best thing that ever happened to me, and I've ruined it. I am so sorry."

I knew there would be no more experiments. "What should we do? Will you go to the police with me?"

"I've already got a letter written. I'll make it look like it was all Silvia's fault."

"Even with the letter, they'll interrogate me. And..." I trailed off. I didn't want to lie for Ludwig.

"I'll go to prison if I have to. But let's be sure we stop Silvia. I've had disturbing news."

He began to tell me.

But then she came, and the world turned upside-down.

35. Reap What You Sow

Her steps were small and mincing, my pumps too tight for her feet. Her eyes were wild, bonfires of hate.

My hair stood on end.

Tamara wore my best silk dress and my lipstick. She'd coiled her hair in an elegant French twist, now unraveling.

If it hadn't been for the pits of her eyes, and the ropes of saliva hanging from her slack mouth, she might have looked beautiful.

I understood. She'd sprayed on the other bottle of Air du Temps, the one with the poison. We stared at her intently, waiting. "She's soaked in Compound T," I whispered.

Her eyes exhibited nystagmus; her head lolled slowly back and forth between us.

Ludwig's eyebrows drew together. "Tamara," he said authoritatively.

And she launched herself on him, transformed into blurring, flailing limbs.

I scrambled away on all fours, terror coursing through me. Absalom wanted his meat. His raptors needed flesh.

Ludwig could have fought her off. Instead, he moaned and cried.

One eye swelled rapidly, black. She drove her fingers into the soft flesh of his groin, pulling. He screamed with pain, but his arms stayed limp.

"Ludwig?" I implored, my voice small.

He was curled into a ball now, her shod feet battering him everywhere.

"Ludwig, why don't you do something?"

He wouldn't talk. I forced myself up, moved in front of him, so he could see me out of the remaining eye. She'd taken off one shoe and was using the heel as a weapon. She wasn't a trained soldier. Her way would take a long time.

Tamara didn't notice me. I pulled off the pad, using my teeth to break the threads that held the letter opener, and held it by the point, leaving the handle clean of my prints.

She'd made inroads. A large gash on his thorax bled freely; I could see the white glisten of a rib.

Was I going to kill her? I couldn't bring myself to.

But I couldn't let her kill him this way.

He moaned again. He looked so vulnerable, his face racked by guilt.

What had Tenzin said about him? "Any being so out of harmony is suffering. Return him to his source and pray he can be reborn again."

My eyes met his. I steeled myself. "Do you want me to give Tamara this knife?"

He nodded. I'm almost sure he nodded.

Then she started in on his face. *Oh. Oh.* I spit out bile.

I pressed the letter opener into her hand. "Show some mercy." Was I talking to her? To Absalom? To myself?

Then I ran to the corner and retched.

―

I huddled into a ball, trying to sort out my thoughts. Ludwig must be dying. The wet sounds of flesh being hit had stopped. Would she come for me next? I forced myself to get up.

She spun around the room, looking wildly about for unseen foes. Ludwig's bruised body lay slumped on the floor in a lake of blood. He might have been wrong about her being a sparrow. More like a shrike, a butcherbird.

A shimmer of gold caught my attention. The locket, still closed, on the floor. The chain was broken.

Tamara was in the far corner, facing the old stone wall, spinning, crooning.

I crept close to Ludwig, keeping his fallen body between Tamara and me. The letter opener had slid under a stainless steel table with a broken Bunsen burner.

I let it be. In her condition she wouldn't see it, but I could grab it if necessary.

I opened the locket, letting the grains of sacred sand drift onto him. With my falcon's eyes every colored mote shone, indigo blue like twilight, red like poppies, white like clouds. They kissed his face, a prayer for mercy, a hope for redemption.

He blinked under the light trickle, beckoned me close. "Peppa. Burn the lab. Burn everything down here. Don't let anyone see."

"I won't." He was dying. I leaned in close. "Tell the Guardians to keep the falcon away." I'd had enough of Cora and her appetites.

His lips twitched in a smile. "Simple. Don't take any Compound T. One more thing. Please promise."

His voice was so faint, I had to lean close to catch his dying words; a few sentences.

My eyes flew open in shock. "What?"

He moaned a single word, "Please."

"But Ludwig."

He moaned, agitated, trying to form more words.

I thought about what Tenzin had said. If he didn't die in peace, it would affect his reincarnation. I didn't believe in that. But what if it was true?

He groaned in pain. "I beg you. I'm beyond redemption. But I've seen to it that you'll be rewarded. I trust you."

My eyes filled with tears of pity. "I promise."

With a sigh, he went. I thumbed his eyes closed. Dead, he looked just like anyone: a professor, brother, husband.

I looked around carefully. Tamara had collapsed in her corner, her breathing frenetic. I left the letter opener where it was. I didn't want my fingerprints on it.

My locket. I ran over, grabbed for the familiar token. The sacred sand was scattered, revealing the photo. I saw it with new eyes.

My mother looked wistful, her face turned to my father, a hint of desperation in her smile. He regarded something on the horizon, his expression curious, his eyes bright.

As if we weren't there.

Ainslie.

Me.

I shook with anger and flung the locket in a corner.

Time for the fire.

I hesitated. We'd pledged two bodies. Jochen had fled.

Tamara looked close to death, slumped, eyes closed, covered with Ludwig's blood. Liver damage? Neural overload?

I approached her warily. "Tamara?"

She was in a catatonic state, but there was no telling how long that would last. She might attack any minute.

I looked around the room, planning the fire, seeing what needed to be destroyed. My eyes fell on the flask of ether, and I knew what I needed to do.

I moved slowly, so as not to provoke her, slid off my dress, and drenched the bell of the skirt. The fumes rushed to my head, making me stagger as I approached her.

I flung the skirt over her head, and locked my arm around her neck. Her gasps finally stopped, and she slumped to the floor.

Now it was safe to move her.

She'd been a victim already, twice over. She shouldn't have to to pay our debts to Absalom.

I tried to move her, but unconscious, she was a dead weight. I flipped her over onto my dress, using its long sleeves to pull her toward the stairs.

Once there, I quailed. Eight steps. I called up to Jochen, but of course he was gone. Simone's baying from the pantry rang out, frantic.

I gritted my teeth, slung Tamara over my shoulder, and felt something in my back give way.

"I am the falcon. I do not feel pain," I told myself. I dragged her up one step. The searing pain ran down my leg now. Disc prolapse in the lumbar vertebra. I pulled her up another step, gasping.

I needed my totem now.

I am the falcon. I can fly.

I felt Cora's power lift me a bit, not much, just enough so the pressure released on the impinged sciatic nerve. The pain was still bad, but I could move.

I dropped her in the hall, limped back down, set the fire, and slammed the basement door.

∽)

Outside the black BMW was gone and the iron gate yawned open. Had Jochen paid me back in kind for my act of mercy?

I staggered down the driveway, crippled by pain, Simone at my side.

An elderly couple, drawn by the commotion, saw me first.

Shock showed on their faces. I hadn't been able to climb the stairs to my room. I wore Ludwig's purple bathrobe. In one bloodstained hand I clutched a small valise of his papers, in the other, Simone's leash. I reeked of Obstler; I'd had to find some liquor to dull the pain.

I spoke first. "Call an ambulance. There's a girl collapsed by the front door. I couldn't carry her."

The woman's mouth stayed open. The man sniffed the smoky air, his eyes widening.

"There was an accident. The basement's on fire."

The man was still hale and hearty. His voice thundered out, another man joined him, and they ran to fetch Tamara. Another neighbor said she'd telephone.

The elderly man's wife took out her handkerchief, daubing ineffectively at my tear-streaked cheeks.

"We heard terrible screams. Whatever happened?"

"I'm Peppa Mueller. Please call Pensione Kaiserhof and ask for Emil Nussbaum," I said. Then I collapsed.

Basel, 1958

36. Girls on the Ward

I LEANED IN CLOSER TO THE YOUNG WOMAN AND TOUCHED THE hem of her sleeve. The green gown smelled like disinfectant, though it was clean and starched.

"Can I call you Celia instead of Mary?" I kept my eyes lowered. I'd noticed direct eye contact made her start to pull the ends of her hair and bite her fingernails.

"I'm Mary."

I kept my voice soothing, the way Mitchell Aaron did when he conducted sessions with Harvard troublemakers. "The name on your records says Celia Schmidt."

"My name is Mary." This time her voice was tenuous, questioning.

"Because you had baby Jesus?"

"Yes, that's right." Her fingers started picking at the ends of her hair. The matron had brushed it back, but Celia always undid her ponytail.

"Tell me again how that happened?"

"The angel came and announced. Then nine months later the miracle occurred."

It was so sad the way young girls couldn't accept the facts of nature. She'd been studying piano in a music conservatory only the year before. Now she was institutionalized. The baby's father, who I'd heard was a violinist from Frankfurt, was probably still hanging out with his *Kumpels*, drinking beer in a *Kneipe*. His life hadn't changed.

"Tell me what that angel looked like?"

"He was very pretty," she explained.

"Did the baby look like the angel at all?" I asked her.

She froze, her eyes like a startled deer. We were almost there. Her mouth hung open. "Why would the baby look like the angel?" she said slowly.

The nurse scuttled up with her tray. "Celia, it's time for your medication."

I pursed my lips and studied the pill. "This is orange. Yesterday she had two pink ones. Did the doctor switch her to Thorazine?"

"I don't see how this is any of your business."

"She's not schizophrenic. She's just having a hard time accepting what happened."

The nurse shook her head at me.

"I want to talk to her doctor."

"I wouldn't push it, Miss Mueller. You've only been off your own medication for a week."

This was true. I'd had a nervous breakdown.

At first, things had gone relatively well for me, despite two weeks with the German police I'd so feared. They had come knocking at the door of the Swiss Consulate the morning after the fire to interrogate me about the partially burned and mutilated body in the basement.

Emil, who'd brought me to the consulate the night of Ludwig's death and spent the night on their sofa, telephoned our family lawyer, Mr. Baer. He and Uncle Alex arrived the next day. Emil met them at the train station, got the key to my house from Mr. Baer, and took Simone back to Basel for me. The Swiss consulate refused to keep Simone any longer, and the Pensione Kaiserhof could not accept a whining and unsettled large dog.

When Mr. Baer and Alex arrived at the police station they were met by Kommissar Gerhard, a mustachioed stalk of a man with slitted grass-green eyes, and his young and eager assistant Frederick, who I thought of as Flunky. The most pressing problem was proper identification. The forged passport that identified me as Kristina Moser was safely hidden under my mattress at Unruh's home. Mr. Baer produced my birth certificate and my genuine Swiss passport. My spirits rose at the sight of the leather booklet based on the clean design of our flag: the welcoming scarlet color and white cross, the reverse of the Red Cross. I'd had enough of Bavaria, with its roaring lions, tongues lolling out. I wanted to return to my homeland, even if it meant going right back into custody as soon as I crossed the border.

After Mr. Baer's hushed conversation with the detectives ended, he came and sat down across the table from me. "It doesn't look too bad. Well, not too good either. A strange turn of events. Dr. Kaufmann won't tell me what you're doing in Munich?"

"I'm waiting for a good criminal lawyer. Can you arrange that?"

"Of course. I have a list with three names, three of Munich's finest. I'm meeting the first as soon as I leave here, and I was able to get appointments tomorrow with the other two." Apparently, money opened a lot of doors.

Alex had been standing back politely, but now he took out a cardboard box and slid it over to me.

"I must see what's inside," Gerhard instructed.

When I revealed Clara Kaufmann's homemade Spitzbübli, stacked neatly in rows, Flunky actually smiled.

"Please. Take one," I urged.

Flunky made eye contact with Gerhard, who gave a slight nod.

As I'd hoped, they both accepted, and offered us cups of coffee to go with the cookies. While Gerhard made the coffee and Flunky washed out some mugs, I tried to ask Alex about Tenzin. He shook his head. "Not now. Don't mention him at all."

I thought for a moment that he was furious with Tenzin; that he didn't even want to hear his name. Tenzin had deserted us. Tears sprang to my eyes and I blinked.

Alex drew closer. Softly he said, "Your friends are still your friends, Peppa. They *all* stand by you." I understood then that something had happened, something he couldn't tell me about in front of the police. Had Tenzin succumbed to some tropical disease? Was he forced to return to India because of an emergency?

Visiting hours drew to a close, and Mr. Baer made some final remarks about the lawyers under consideration. I barely heard him. What if Tenzin had malaria? What if he was lying in the hospital right now? I remembered how my mother shook with chills before she died.

Mr. Baer sighed. "You seem very distracted, Miss Mueller."

"Just make the best choice. I don't know anything about lawyers."

The next afternoon, the police discovered the sealed envelope addressed to Silvia De Pena. I'd placed it conspicuously on the study table, after removing and reading Ludwig's note of explanation, and the extra copy of his letter to her. He'd attached those to the outside of the envelope, so I could vet the contents.

The letter was sealed because he'd mailed it to her address in Paris. As he'd anticipated, it was returned unopened, with a notation that Mrs. De Pena had left no forwarding address. His missive was elegantly vague, adaptable to the situation at hand. It was also a mixture of truth, deception, and outright lies.

> *Dear Silvia,*
>
> *You forced me into using Compound T on human subjects by threatening to ruin me financially. Though the compound served as a spiritual facilitator in the jungle, where we first discovered it, it is plain that on good, God-fearing Christians, the result is the opposite of what we hoped. We have transgressed, Silvia, and I for one, will spend the rest of my life praying for forgiveness. I hope you understand after the disastrous results in the village of Gonten, we can never resume experimentation again. I'm very concerned about the remaining test subject, the young woman you hired to be your caretaker. I've taken the precaution of seizing her dog. Once she contacts me, or I find her, I'll try to arrange for her to visit me. I've spent many a sleepless night thinking of this poor young orphan, struggling to make sense of the horrifying events. I'll take it upon myself to see she is well cared for, and perhaps eventually, I can explain to her what happened.*

Of course, I never told my lawyer, Mr. Salzmann, that I knew what was in the letter the police had found. I played the part of a confused innocent. I'd tracked down Unruh.

I'd swum across the border to Freiburg, where the scorpion dealer had given me a train ticket and cash. Once I'd arrived at Unruh's, I hadn't found an opportunity to leave together with my dog. I'd also been afraid of the police.

I'd noticed Unruh and the maid went downstairs a lot. I didn't know what went on down there till the very last night, when screaming had started. I'd peered down the stairs but been too frightened to go down. When I smelled the smoke, I'd gathered my courage and investigated. I found the maid unconscious, a bloody letter opener in her hand. Unruh was dead. The struggle must have caused a Bunsen burner to tip over and start a fire. I'd carried the girl upstairs to safety, then escaped.

I was lucky. Tamara didn't contradict my story. She was in the hospital, heavily sedated, and didn't remember much. Mr. Salzmann heard that every time she became lucid, she wept and repeated Ludwig's name in a fugue of grief. She readily admitted killing him. The police found the discarded letter opener, protected from the blaze by the steel table. Her prints were all over it.

I hadn't actually arranged things so that she would be the logical murder suspect, had I? I hadn't done it on purpose. But now she was under psychiatric evaluation, her hands bound to the bed, pills being shoved in her mouth, heart heavy with remorse and loss.

In meantime, I benefited from her evident guilt. Right after lunchtime on Friday, October 11, I was called to the interview room. As Mr. Salzmann smiled, showing yellow horse teeth, Flunky removed my handcuffs. Gerhardt telephoned Alex to come pick me up.

I was free. Another witness had come forward, Ludwig's colleague from his time at medical school, whom I'd met when he examined me. Dr. Schnitzler corroborated my account. Flunky brought my possessions to me; a winter coat, my father's notebooks, my cosmetics, the tourmaline necklace, and the locket. I refused the dresses.

My story was ridiculous, full of holes, but the Swiss police wanted me, and the Germans had a solved case, the murderess safely trussed up in the mental ward.

The first snow of the season came that afternoon, early this year. The flakes drifted down lazily, settling on the gravel courtyard of the jail. Flunky awaited us in an unmarked car and drove us to the station. There he parked, entered the station, and watched while I clambered into the red carriage of the train, followed by Alex. Only once the doors closed and the Deutsche Bahn rumbled into motion did he wave and turn away. I imagined him running back into the office, grabbing the black phone that sat like a giant bug on the police desk.

He'd call the Swiss police. I knew what he'd say, since Kommissar Gerhard had warned us. "Peppa Mueller and Dr. Kaufmann arrive in Basel at 8 o'clock. The Mannheim Station has been notified. If they try to get off on German soil, we'll take them back into custody."

Alex had bought first-class tickets and reserved a private compartment. We had a long ride, six hours before I reached Basel and the welcoming committee in blue.

As he hoisted his overnight case up into the luggage rack, words were already spilling out of my mouth.

"How is Tenzin? He's not sick, is he? Is he in danger?"

"Calm down. Give me a minute." The heat was on and the cabin stuffy. Alex arranged his wool jacket on a hook. "He's not seriously ill. He had a bad rash, that's all."

"Is he hurt?"

"He may have endured a beating or two, and they cut off his hair. But his lawyer sent a telegram to his father in India.

The birth and vaccination documents should be verified soon."

"What lawyer?! Who cut his hair?"

"He's in jail. In Lörrach. Let me tell you..."

Lörrach was in Germany. "So he did come? Like he promised."

"He tried. The lawyer told us the German border police stopped Tenzin. His skin was covered with red weals. He didn't have his vaccination booklet to prove he'd received inoculations. He couldn't explain what the rash was from."

My hand flew up to my mouth as the realization struck me. The Conservatory. The pots of Brugmansia had been behind Euphorbias, whose milky sap was known for causing allergic reactions.

Alex raised his eyebrows at me.

I was too agitated to tell him about the Euphorbias. "So what happened?"

"They confined him to the infirmary to wait for a doctor versed in tropical medicine. Tenzin escaped the following night. Unfortunately, a guard on foot patrol picked him up. There might have been a tussle."

"But they can't hold him. He hasn't done anything wrong," I burst out.

"Well, he hadn't done anything wrong till he tried to escape. Of course, we all thought it was better your name didn't come into it. Things should settle down once his parents bring the vaccination booklet to the Swiss embassy in India and assure them he has no dreaded tropical contagion. The ambassador will send a telegram to the Germans."

The waiter knocked respectfully on our compartment door. "Would you like a menu? I can serve you in here, if you prefer."

I ordered pea soup and two Weisswürstl, a late lunch. Alex decided on the same.

"I've also asked a doctor from the Tropical Medicine Department at the university to visit Tenzin. He's from Germany originally; the police might accept his diagnosis of exclusion. But if you can explain why Tenzin has a rash, it would make his job easier."

A knock on the door and the waiter handed me my hot Ovaltine. No more Amaro liquor. I hadn't felt Cora since I'd carried Tamara up the stairs and I was glad of it.

I blew on the steaming mug to cool it and explained about the Euphorbias.

"I'll pass that on. Since Tenzin's known for helping the Mission with their gardens, he could claim he was just sightseeing in the Conservatory."

I blinked back a tear. I'd been hoping to see Tenzin right away, but now I understood we couldn't risk it. If I were convicted, he'd be in even more trouble.

"Thank you so much for arranging to help him. The doctor from Basel and the lawyer."

Alex shifted uneasily. "Well, I would have arranged for a lawyer. I can see the two of you are taken with each other. But someone else got to it first."

"Who?"

"A lady by the name of Violet Strub. She knows him through Father Kneipp at the Mission."

When I said nothing, Alex took a cautious sip of beer. "The main thing is he's got a lawyer, correct? I suppose I'm not the only one he made a good impression on."

The arrival of the soup spared me from giving an answer.

Over the meal we first talked about Simone. Clara and Alex had agreed to keep her while I was being held in jail. The Basel juvenile prosecutor would decide what charges to bring against me, after he concluded interviewing, which could take months. We discussed how much information I would need to share with him and what I could omit.

I ordered apple strudel with whipped cream to finish and was enjoying the first mouthful when I noticed Alex stirring his coffee over and over. The metal clang of the spoon rattled me.

"Out with it," I said.

"You're just like your father. He never could stand 'pussyfooting around.'"

His words whirled in my head.

Alex continued, still looking at his coffee. "I'm trying to put my thoughts in order. You have so much to hide from the police. You don't want to tell them about Emil and me, but you'll have to. We've talked it over. We're prepared to face the consequences. We'll try to keep Tenzin out of it."

The white owl. The white owl circled in my head, sending up storms with each wing beat.

"Are you all right, dear?"

"You said I was just like my father."

"I meant in that respect. You wanted to know what was on my mind."

My head began to shake. *No. No. No.*

"You must have known what he did, Alex." I spat his name out.

He abandoned the coffee spoon. "You found out?"

"Why did you let Emil bring me a syringe of Paxarbital?"

"He what? How could he bring you a syringe? Your father's lab was at Harvard."

"He made it for me. I gave him the formula. I thought I was doing him a favor."

"Oh my God." Alex buried his forehead in his palms. "When did he find time to do that?"

"He worked every night at a little lab he rented from a pharmacist."

"Emil only said he'd brought you a special message, so you'd know it was him. What happened to the syringe?"

I didn't want to think about Tamara. "Who exactly is Carmen Aldebert? Father mentioned in his journal he bought her martinis. He was in a foul mood that evening."

"She works as a senior secretary at Hoffman-La Roche."

Another big pharmaceutical company in Basel. "What could she have said to upset him? She told him about something coming onto the market."

"Librium. Hoffman-La Roche introduced it this year. It's a new class of sedative, a benzodiazepine. Likely to replace barbiturates in time."

I was breathing heavily now, and my thoughts were like pieces of hail, battering the soft bud of my brain. "So Father's work was useless. Why didn't you stop him?"

"From Switzerland? He was at Harvard."

"That's an excuse?"

"Besides, it was because of *my* work at Sandoz." Alex blinked hard. "He wanted a success like mine. He wanted the world to honor *him* because of his discoveries. He resented me."

"But you talked to him eventually," I guessed.

"Carmen and I spoke when she returned. She'd noticed a track mark when he pushed up his sleeves. When I called and confronted him, he admitted it had gone wrong. I begged him to stop."

His expression became alarmed. "Don't look at me like that. I tried."

"How?"

"I said..." He choked. "I said, what about Peppa? Your child."

"And?"

"That's all I said."

My hands curled into fists. "What was his answer?"

Alex checked his pockets for a handkerchief and blew his nose. "It's not important. I didn't succeed. I'm so sorry."

I hadn't realized I'd gotten up, but there I stood, towering over Alex, hands clenched. "What did he say? What did he say?!"

"You're creating a commotion." I vaguely heard doors of other compartments slide back, as people peered out to see what the shouting was about. I didn't care.

I took Alex's shoulders and gave them a shake. "Tell me."

"He said ... I lost the little boy I wanted when my pregnant wife died."

When I saw the first tear slide down Alex's cheeks, I fell back down in the seat. "I'm sorry I shook you," I whispered, watching the next tear exit, slide down the side of his nose, and plop onto the collar of his white shirt.

Then I couldn't see anymore. My own tears blinded me.

I was still crying four hours later, when two Swiss policemen boarded the train in Basel, checked my passport, and asked me to accompany them. Alex patted me awkwardly on the shoulder, but I couldn't form the words for goodbye.

The next morning Mr. Dähler, the Basel prosecutor for juvenile justice, found me sitting on my bed in the cell, steadily weeping, incapable of speech. My eyes were almost swollen shut.

I don't remember much. At least the pills kept Cora away.

At the mental hospital, they told me I cried for two days.

When I stopped, my first words were to the psychiatrist they'd assigned to me. "Tell my aunt I have a wish. Have her hire a priest to stand by my father's grave and recite prayers for a day."

Dr. Künzli was impressed.

And I? I hoped my father would hear the hated prayer, every word of Latin burning like splattered pitch against his cold dead heart. *Father, this is for you, you bastard.*

37. The Caged Bird

IT WAS LATE AFTERNOON, AN HOUR AFTER THE INCIDENT WITH Celia's medication, when the nurse marched me in to Dr. Künzli's dark office. The drapes were kept shut to protect his fragile female patients from the disruptive, chaotic world outside. It was because of his instructions that we had lights out at 8:30 every evening and mandatory naps after lunch. We even had our defecation scheduled from 8:00 to 8:15 in the morning.

He gestured to the chair. "Please sit. Standing can be exhausting."

I was surprised he didn't have a fainting couch in his office.

He was in his forties, fair-skinned, pale eyes, hair an indeterminate shade between gray and blond. It would have helped matters if I liked him more.

He braced his elbows on the desk and leaned forward. "You're disrupting hospital affairs."

"I'm concerned about Celia Schmidt. She's already muddled, and Thorazine will accelerate her mental deterioration."

He gave me a condescending smile. "You're not a doctor, dear."

I glared at him. "I'm going to Radcliffe College when I get out of here."

"They won't take you with a criminal record."

"I haven't been charged."

"You won't be accepted with a history of mental illness either."

"What diagnosis are you considering for me?"

He shook his head and tut-tutted.

I'd been thinking this over, trying out various dialogues in my head so that I'd sound adult and he'd listen to me. "I'm reacting normally. Dr. Unruh was not a friend of mine, but naturally I was very distressed to find his mutilated body on the laboratory floor and his experimental subject insensate in a corner."

"Tell me again about your relationship with him?"

He was a wolf and I was a falcon and we met in a Jade World of green fog and death.

I sighed.

"Come on, Miss Mueller. I can't release you to the police until I'm sure you're stabilized."

"Dr. Unruh knew I'd be scared and confused after the murders I witnessed. He took my dog, hoping I would come to him so that he could help me. He felt guilty about what happened. At least that's what he said."

"And how did you feel about Ludwig Unruh?"

When I didn't answer, he prompted me. "I'm sure you'd never met a man like him before."

Only one. I couldn't imagine ever forgiving my father.

"It was overwhelming," I said. Inspiration struck me. "I wish I'd had someone to protect me. I felt so alone, so vulnerable."

A muscle in his jaw twitched. He was trying not to smile.

We were on the right track. "You know, it's very hard without a mother's loving hand to offer guidance."

He nodded once, the pen scratching away. I continued. "And my poor father did the best he could. Naturally his death was a great shock."

He regarded me with his rain-colored eyes. "So there was no one..."

"I thought often of my godfather, Dr. Alex Kaufmann. I was so frightened of Unruh, although he acted concerned. He sometimes locked me in my room. When he did let me out, I couldn't help wondering what he was doing in his basement." I was laying it on thick. I had to hope the German police weren't communicating with my psychiatrist. It was too much to expect that Tamara had complete amnesia.

"You've mentioned Dr. Kaufmann before. As a matter of fact, he's telephoned almost daily. When he doesn't, it's your aunt, or Mr. Nussbaum."

"Couldn't I have a visitor?" I pleaded.

"I'll talk to Mr. Dähler and see what he thinks. Perhaps we could start with Dr. Kaufmann. He's that scientist over at Sandoz, isn't he?" Plainly he was curious about his colleague.

They put Alex and me in the visitor's room. In the corner poor Celia stared vacantly at her sister, who was holding her hand. I'd heard they had given her a course of insulin therapy.

A nurse lurked nearby, pretending to fiddle with the tea set.

I spoke in English. "They're treating that girl all wrong. She just needs a nudge to admit what happened."

The nurse jerked, then stirred the teacups.

Alex raised an eyebrow. He replied in precise over-enunciated English. His command of the language was good enough to exchange letters about psychedelia with Aldous Huxley, the famous British novelist. "I'm worried about you, not the girl in the corner."

"That nurse is having sex with Dr. Kramer in the supply closet," I lied. Dr. Kramer was a grossly obese man, universally disliked by the staff for his suggestive remarks.

The nurse slammed down the teacup and almost stormed out, before she remembered her duty.

I switched to Latin, speaking very slowly. I'd never tried Latin with Alex before, but he was an educated man. "Say whatever you have to to get me out of here. I have a defense strategy figured out."

The nurse stood in front of him with the teacup. He turned his head quickly away from her and winked at me.

"Stop showing off, Peppa. Speak normally to me."

I rambled on in Swiss-German about how terrified I'd been at Dr. Unruh's, about the hours he spent in the basement, after which his maid returned pale and shaken, and about how I'd just been praying every day that Alex would come rescue me. We finished two cups of tea before Dr. Künzli drifted in.

"Oh, you must be Dr. Kaufmann?"

"Yes." They shook hands.

"Mind if I have a word with you?" Alex said. "I've been in touch with a psychologist at Harvard about Peppa. A Dr. Aaron. He was a close friend of the family."

"Let's go to my office." Dr. Künzli showed the way without even a backward glance at me, the patient in question.

The next day Dr. Künzli discharged me from the asylum and the Basel police picked me up in their wagon. I'd been allowed to change into some real clothes, though I'd chosen a skirt for appearance's sake, rather than the old cigarette pants I loved, relic of my American days. I stared straight ahead and endured Dr. Künzli's limp handshake, before the handcuffs locked around my wrist. I felt like a doll that adults were playing dress-up with. If I went to trial, my lawyer would send Aunt Madeleine shopping, and then I'd be standing in front of the jurists in a navy blue dress with polka dots and Mary Janes. He'd already chosen the dress with Aunt Madeleine. Luckily my hair was too short to braid.

Of course, I hoped I wouldn't go to trial.

I trudged down the corridor past the five locked rooms. I was on the second floor of the holding jail for juveniles. I would serve my pretrial detention here, and the time would be subtracted from my sentence. If I didn't go to trial because the state filed no charges, they would just be lost months of my life. The judge had granted Mr. Dähler the right to deny me bail, based on the gravity of the crime. I'd likely be here for a while. My new criminal lawyer, Mr. Thomas, referred to it as purgatory.

We reached the last room. Matron Schildknecht unlocked my cuffs with one of the plethora of keys that dangled from her belt, then unlocked the door with yet another one.

The room measured about 2 by 3 meters. There was a bed, a toilet and sink, and a table with only one chair, in case I hadn't understood yet that I would be here quite alone. Mr. Dähler denied me the right to have visitors, other than my attorney.

Matron motioned for me to sit, and I chose the bed. The only light emanated from the small, high-set window.

She had a nose like a potato, slabbed onto a pleasant and fleshy face, with the sagging rosy cheeks of a drinker. Spider veins on the sides of her nose confirmed that impression. Only her alert blue eyes betrayed her intelligence.

"Let's make sure you're clear on the rules. Morning alarm at 7 AM. You have half an hour to get washed up and dressed before the guard brings breakfast. At 11:30, half an hour of exercise in the yard. Conversation's forbidden. If we see you talking, it's straight back to your room. I'll be the one bringing you dinner at 6:30. Your light is to be out at nine. If I see it on later, I take the light bulb. And you don't get it back for a week."

"What am I supposed to do all day?"

"Think on how you can help Mr. Dähler do his job."

"Do you have a library?"

"We do, but I doubt you'll like the selection."

I shrugged. "Would you allow me to have a look?"

"I'll take you this evening, after supper."

"Thank you, Mrs. Schildknecht."

Mr. Dähler let me stew for a week. Then he wanted to visit, but my lawyer, Mr. Thomas, wasn't available. The meeting was delayed for another few days. In the meantime, Mr. Dähler would be talking to everyone who ever knew me.

And they'd all tell him I was an odd girl.

The days passed like pearls on an endless chain, white with snow, heavy with grief, smooth and eventless. I tried to ignore the swirling inside, the desire for something to happen, anything. When I felt like screaming, I tapped my forehead against the wall till I got the distraction of a headache. When the urge for freedom got too strong, I paced, up and down, up and down. At least there was no sign of Cora.

November brought a new cold front, and frost formed on the outside of my small window. I was so chilled I forced down the potatoes and meatloaf that Miss Schildknecht had brought for dinner, hoping the food would warm me. She actually took some pains with our meals, but I'd gone off meat—just couldn't stomach it. In fact, I was often nauseated, but that didn't surprise me.

I knew as well as any girl what it meant when your period didn't come. I just forbade myself to think about it. It was a mere biological process, a forming and fomenting inside. I had to focus on getting out of jail. Had to.

After my dinner I sat on the bed, my scratchy wool blanket tented over me, and tried to read the new magazines I'd gotten from the library. The first one sported a cover of a slightly cross-eyed woman holding a rosy infant. The article within had informed me that my natural duty was to be a loyal mother to my children and a good wife. I definitely wasn't in the mood to read about babies. I picked up the magazine *Gabriele*, which aimed to teach me how to be a perfect secretary. The black and white photo of the smiling woman on the cover encouraged me to learn about my boss's hobbies.

I'd learned enough about Ludwig's, hadn't I? Fencing. Poisoning. Impregnating one young woman at your house, driving another one mad with jealousy.

I hurled the magazines to the floor and jumped up. Once I started pacing, I usually couldn't stop, and I fell into it again this time too, measuring my footsteps, counting out loud in Latin. As I reached the wall, I'd bang my head softly against the cold wall before I made a 180 degree turn and marched the other direction. I was so engrossed in this exercise in futility I failed to notice the outside cover of my door window lifting.

The key turning in the lock got my attention, and I heard Matron's heavy tread. I sat down rigid in my chair, my hands folded in front of me.

Mr. Thomas and I had our defense prepared, just like I'd told Alex. But there were times when the foolishness of my claim was so apparent, I dreaded our upcoming meeting. Every word that was said about me by anyone would be weighed by Mr. Dähler, and I had only a flimsy explanation with which to defend myself.

And every extra month I spent in jail made it harder to hide the changes in my body. Even if I claimed rape, it wouldn't stop people from judging me. Nice girls didn't put themselves in dangerous situations.

"Good evening, Mrs. Schildknecht," I said politely, trying to still my legs. I wanted to pounce on her and snatch her keys.

She looked at the bed longingly. "I've been on my feet all evening. May I sit?"

"Of course, Mrs. Schildknecht."

"You may call me Martha." She amended quickly, "Mrs. Martha."

"Yes." My foot tapped back and forth; I'd stopped pacing, but it didn't seem to have gotten the message.

"I can't help but notice you're very restless."

I shook my head.

She bent over and peered at the floor. "What are those magazines doing there?"

"I'm sorry," I said quickly.

"The hobbies of my boss," she read out loud. "Hmm, I don't think my present one has any." She chuckled. "Do you like this magazine?"

"Yes," I lied.

"I'm surprised. I heard you wanted to study at an American women's college."

I didn't answer. I knew I wasn't supposed to want anything like that. I probably wasn't supposed to want men like Tenzin either. Especially now.

She sighed, exhaling a slight smell of wine. "You've read almost everything in the library. Most of my girls are Italian or Czech or Hungarian. They don't enjoy books in German."

"I see." It was the first time she'd mentioned the others. I'd counted ten of us in the exercise yard—one probably an addict, three with dark eyes and curly black hair who might be Italian or Spanish, and a ruddy blonde girl as tall as most men, who had tried to trip me.

After I'd caught myself from falling I turned to see who'd done it. My gaze must have been bleak. She outweighed me by a good 15 kilos, but she quailed.

Whatever you're in here for, I've done worse.

Mrs. Martha was asking me a question. "Have you heard of Agatha Christie? The crime author?"

"The name sounds familiar."

"I just finished *Murder in Mesopotamia*. I'll bring it tomorrow along with breakfast, if you like."

Her unexpected kindness sent a wave of weakness traveling through me, and my shoulders trembled with the effort of holding back tears. "I need medication," I finally admitted, my voice choked.

Her eyebrows shot up. "For what?"

"I need a tranquilizer. I can't take it. The captivity. The enforced idleness. Please. Please let me see the prison doctor." The falcon was beating her wings faster and faster, and my heart kept her tempo in the cage of my chest.

"Mr. Dähler will interpret this as a sign of your guilt," she said flatly.

"Oh." I wiped the tears off the sides of my nose. The thought of what she might report frightened me; I forced myself to become calm.

"You're like a caged bird," she mused. "Look, I tell you what. Tomorrow it's full moon. After the rest of the staff leaves and I wash up supper, I'll take you out to the yard for a bit. You can bundle up, and you'll be fine. But let's just keep this between the two of us."

─────

I did not request the prison doctor again. Mrs. Martha took me outside in the evenings when she could. She brought me the newest books from her British favorite authors, Ian Fleming and Ngaio Marsh. Along with *Casino Royale* came a letter from Emil, and a blue card with pink snowflakes on it from Aunt Madeleine.

I read the letter from Emil, intent on interpreting one tantalizing paragraph. Mrs. Martha watched me for a moment. "Mr. Dähler reads everything," she said quietly, before leaving with my uneaten lunch.

Emil's letter informed me about the dilemma of his foreign friend from school. "You met her once, Peppa, remember. She has long dark hair in a braid that she wears with a turquoise ornament, and she knows a lot about the plants of her native land. The poor thing has discovered some new problems with her entry papers, but she doesn't want to return to her country in the middle of the semester. All her friends tell her it's better to go and get the bureaucratic mess cleaned up straight away, but she's still hesitating. I told her I'd ask you for a recommendation, since she really was taken with you."

I rocked back and forth in my chair as need stabbed through me. I'd never been so sure that I loved Tenzin till now. But were I set free, I was absolutely sure I couldn't see him. Better he were gone then he see me ... in the condition I was in.

No. Not the *condition*. I forced my mind to accept the horror of it. I was pregnant. Tenzin had taken precautions when we made love. It wasn't his.

I thought I'd escaped Ludwig, but now a part of him was deep in me. When the trembling started, I gritted my teeth until it passed.

I pushed my breakfast away and reached for the fountain pen, slippery in my sweaty hands. I had no appetite. I filled half a page with trivialities, only then telling Emil, "My opinion is that our friend should go home at once." The thought of Tenzin seeing me pregnant made me feel ill. Nausea pushed up, and I stumbled to the toilet and heaved up my morning coffee.

38. Brachial Innervation

GLADYS ONCE PLAYED ME A RECORD BY A GROUP OF NEGROES called The Deep River Boys. The lyrics to a song of theirs pattered round and round in the labyrinth of my head as Mr. Thomas and I waited for Mr. Dähler to arrive.

> *The toe bone's connected to the foot bone,*
> *The foot bone's connected to the ankle bone,*
> *The ankle bone's connected to the leg bone,*
> *Now shake dem skeleton bones!*

Modern anatomy informed us that those appendages were connected to our trunk via muscles and nerves. Sensory nerves led to the spinal cord; motor nerves led away from the spinal cord. Fast as lightening, sensory nerves fed information to the brain and motor nerves carried out the commands.

But not if you broke the connection.

The door squeaked as Mr. Dähler shuffled in, carrying his briefcase. He greeted us, laid his case on the table, and began pulling out papers. Next came the Basler policeman who'd been at Sandoz that Saturday; I recognized him from the nametag, Paul Karrer. He was followed by my old friend Manser.

"I'm so glad we could all arrange a meeting, Miss Mueller. We had many schedules to coordinate. Mr. Manser traveled down this afternoon just to see you."

It's not like I would have missed him.

Everyone was waiting for me to say something. "Well, here I am," I said.

They started out gently. Mr. Karrer wanted to know if I'd ever been in a fight with anyone. Of course, I'd maybe argued, but had I ever hit someone before? Or maybe pushed someone. Or...

I assured them I had not hit, scratched, bitten, pushed, stabbed, or bludgeoned anyone before. Mr. Thomas shot me a warning glance. I was being too clever.

Mr. Dähler thought perhaps I'd had a difficult childhood. Had I?

"My father and I were as close as two peas in a pod," I explained.

They asked the question a few different ways, and I maintained that we'd lived a peaceful, studious existence.

Mr. Manser was interested in my drinking habits. I told him my favorite drink was Ovaltine. He asked me about cigarettes, cocaine, and heroin. When he lit up himself, I asked him to please put it out. I thought I might throw up again.

Of course, they asked several times about Compound Totentanz, only they didn't call it that. Whenever they brought it up the alleged poison, I would manifest a tic I'd perfected in front of my bathroom mirror.

Eyelid twitching, gazing off with what I liked to think was a glazed look, I mumbled, "I think Mrs. De Pena fixed it so there was something in our drinks. That's what Dr. Unruh said, at least. He was worried about me after he saw what happened."

"What did happen?"

"I'm not sure. I got sick and dizzy. I never drink. I thought maybe that was normal, until I saw the way it affected everyone else."

"Are you trying to blame this all on Hans Wäspi?" Manser asked, the vein on his temple pulsing.

Mr. Karrer put a restraining hand on his shoulder.

"No. Maybe his sister was sick, and he ran over to help her?" That was the right answer, wasn't it? People wanted to believe the family was sacrosanct.

"Why did you run from the police?" Mr. Dähler asked.

"If you hadn't done anything wrong," Manser clarified.

"I didn't know about the poison then. I couldn't explain what happened. Then when I hid in Uncle Alex's laboratory, I read the newspaper. I was really frightened after reading all those accusations." I felt guilty about mentioning Alex, but there was no way around it.

We'd been there two hours when we finally got to the crux of the matter. Mr. Dähler leaned in close, like a concerned pediatrician about to palpate a child's lymph glands.

"You've said you were too startled to run away when Mr. Wäspi came at you. You explained that Mr. Sepp 'acted crazy,' and that's why you didn't ask him for help. But what would compel you to break Mr. Wäspi's neck?"

"That's what we really want to know," Manser added, looking like he'd like to break my neck himself.

Mr. Thomas gave me an encouraging smile. Miss Martha had promised me I could help her bake Spitzbübli after the meeting. Not everyone hated me.

I took a deep breath. "It's like this," I started.

I warmed to my topic, because I truly did love anatomy. I sketched the spinal cord, the brain, the reflex arc, and the nerve pathways. Manser's eyes glazed over, but I had Mr. Dähler's attention.

"This is certainly very detailed," Karrer protested.

"But my father and I talked about things like this all the time. You asked me so often about our life—you must know that. I saw patients with him. He had me read his papers before he submitted them."

"That's made you too prideful," Manser said.

Dähler silenced him with a look. "I assume this is leading to an explanation of why you would break Mr. Wäspi's neck."

"Of course. I misjudged. That poison drink I told you about. The one Dr. Unruh wrote about in that letter the German police have. It made me dizzy and confused. I only meant to disable him. The brachial innervation—the nerves to the arms," I corrected myself, "come from the spinal vertebra of the neck. Specifically, C4, C5, and C6."

"You expect us to believe this?" Manser exploded.

I kept on doggedly. "I wanted to paralyze Mr. Wäspi so he wouldn't hurt me. My father read a report about a judo expert once who could do that. He showed me the pressure technique."

"What report was that?"

"I don't remember now. I was little."

"Hmmph," Karrer said.

"I just wanted to paralyze Mr. Wäspi's arms," I repeated stubbornly. And I was to repeat it over and over the next ten weeks, every session we had.

―⁓―

Several weeks later I was helping Mrs. Martha in the jail kitchen. She'd made meat loaf and red cabbage, followed by homemade Linzer Torte. She liked to cook more than to clean up, I noticed.

While I scraped the dishes she sat down and poured herself another glass of wine. "It's a lot to clean up. I'll draw the line at offering you wine, but I'll make you a Negerschweiss if you want."

I wrinkled my nose. Whatever Negro sweat was, I didn't think I wanted any.

"Silly goose," she said cheerfully. My company seemed to amuse her. "It's cocoa and coffee."

"I'll take some then. I've never heard that term before." I started filling the sink with hot water and dish soap, reflecting how nice it would be if someone invented a machine for washing dishes.

"My first boss used to say that. It's an old military term from the First World War. He called cigarettes nosewarmers too."

I thought about Mrs. Martha carefully for the first time. Up till now, I'd just been grateful for her kindness. "How did you learn such excellent English?"

"I worked for Section 5. Nachrichtdienst."

"I'm not following you. You worked for a news bureau?"

She chuckled. The more wine she drank, the funnier I got. "Oh, Peppa. Military Nachrichtdienst. Like MI6, and James Bond."

I paused, turned off the water so I could hear her better. "You were a spy?"

"Not so glamorous. We never had martinis or fast cars. I was one of ten at the official beginning of World War II. My boss and I were procurement and evaluation. I procured, he evaluated. I got to be quite good friends with the British military attaché. They did find room in the tiny budget for me to invite him for champagne at the Du Theatre once. That was the most glamour I ever had. But my boss was a genius. I loved working with him. We must have put in a hundred hours a week once the war started." She stopped and heaved herself up out of the chair. "But you wanted a Negerschweiss. I'll stop rambling and get to it."

"No. I'm fascinated. So you know how to use a gun? All that stuff?"

"Yes. Clean it, maintain it, blow someone's head off. All that." She measured out the scoop of coffee and took down the tin of cocoa.

"How did you ever end up running a glorified home for wayward girls?"

"After the war they cut the staff back down to thirty." Her voice was brisk now. "How much sugar do you want?"

I'd made myself eat her carefully prepared dinner and now, a sudden wave of nausea swept through me. I swooned and fell to my knees, grabbing the edge of the counter to stabilize myself. When I looked up, our eyes met, hers sharp and knowing. Even after a few glasses of wine, she was hard to fool.

"You're not used to a full meal. I told you to eat more last week."

"My plate's clean when you come get it."

"Your breath smells like your stomach's empty. You must scrape the food into the toilet."

I didn't want to lie to her, so I stayed quiet.

"It'll just be six more months. Then it will be behind you. The orphanages are clean and well run. Sometimes the babies even get adopted by families."

I grabbed a chair and slumped down in it, covering my face in shock. I couldn't stand to look at her. I hadn't gained any weight. I'd made sure of that. If I went to trial, the last thing I needed was a protruding belly with my supposed captor's child in it. Of course, if I wanted to totally complete my public humiliation, I could claim rape. Better than telling the courtroom my falcon liked the wolf.

Should I claim it was Tenzin's? That we'd secretly gotten engaged? No, I couldn't drag him into this. Same with Emil; it was bad enough that my father was responsible for his mother's divorce.

I stared at the floor, too ashamed to look at her. "How did you guess?"

"Women who have been through it always recognize the others. My child would be turning thirteen."

Her child? She wore no ring. We called all older women Mrs. Her eyes warned me not to ask her more.

"I don't want the baby."

"It's Ludwig Unruh's?"

"Yes."

"I don't blame you. I wanted to keep mine, but the father couldn't marry me, and I didn't dare."

"Do you know a doctor who could ... you know ... take it away."

Her cheeks sagged. "Don't ask me to do that, Peppa. I'll agree not to disclose your condition. But that's all."

She waited a minute before she added, "You're thin and tall. People won't be able to tell. Not if I let out the waistbands of your skirts."

"You're very kind."

―――

I kept down dinner that night, but the next week I'd actually lost more weight. Mrs. Martha had taken me to her quarters to measure me so she could adjust my two skirts. Instead of pinning the material, she packed me off to her bathroom and put me on the scale. I stood there in my stockings and chemise and glanced into the mirror. My belly seemed even bigger next to my shrunken rump and toothpick legs.

"What are you trying to do?" Mrs. Martha asked, frowning at the number on the scale.

"I'm just not hungry."

"Do you want to starve the baby?"

I got up and stumbled over to the toilet, heaving up the cheese and bread she'd made for me half an hour before. I gargled and wiped with the towel she handed me, before answering.

"I don't know." The word "baby" had set me off. I'd pictured a miniature version of Ludwig, complete with tidy beard, cradled in my arms. Ludwig was still with me in a sense, reminding me of my complicity. If it hadn't been for the hateful falcon, I wouldn't have given in to him.

Cora. But she was part of me, just like the baby. Why couldn't I be free of them?

Another wave of nausea passed through me, and my tongue felt thick in my mouth.

As soon as the baby was born, I'd arrange for him to be taken away.

She cleared her throat. "Did Dr. Unruh hurt you when he forced himself on you?"

My cheeks blazed. "He didn't ... I lost my way. I'm weak." I let my totem take control.

She led me back to the sitting room and patted the sofa. "Sit down. You're just a girl. Don't blame yourself."

"But I should know better. I've been in love."

She smiled a little. 'I see you're a closet romantic after all." She took out the tape measure and picked up the skirt. As she worked, she said, "The doctor who looked after me when I was pregnant is still my doctor. He can get you some medication for the nausea."

39. Bargains

THE MEDICATION WAS CALLED THALIDOMIDE. I STARTED IT two days later. Mrs. Martha told me it was a sedative and would help with the nausea. She was busy with meetings and didn't visit me again till late that Friday night, when the guards had gone.

My room was chilly, and she'd brought an extra wool blanket. She got straight to the point. "Giselle said your macaroni and cheese were untouched yesterday."

"The pills make me feel woozy and sleepy, but I'm still sick every time I think of the baby. I don't have morning sickness. I'm scared and revolted."

"You can't punish him for being Ludwig's."

Tears started in my eyes. "I know. I'm not purposely trying to starve him." It struck me we were both talking about a boy. A wolf cub. "I've even thought about a name. Alex. After my godfather." I wiped at my cheek. "Yesterday I had the most horrible nightmare. A feeling of doom. The baby was surrounded by a flock of black ravens, and they pecked at his limbs till they shriveled. I didn't even take the medication this morning. What use is it to be sedated when I still have bad dreams?"

Mrs. Martha didn't know about Absalom and the blood debt I owed him, so the dream didn't have the same ominous meaning that it did for me. She just shook her head. "I have some more bad news. I think Mr. Dähler's decided to prosecute."

I tried to say something and hiccuped instead. A bitter taste filled my mouth.

"He's going to meet with his superior Wednesday. They'll probably charge you with murder the next day."

I took a cautious sip from the water I kept nearby. The hiccups stopped. "You're taking a big risk telling me these things."

"I wish I could help you more. They'll transfer you to another facility."

She waited, then said, "Can't you tell them more about the poison? Make them understand what it did to you."

"I'm hesitant to explain. It's a weapon. Ludwig confided in me. I don't want word of how it can be made and used to spread. What if the Communists get it?"

"Who would sell it to them?"

I swallowed. I hadn't told anyone what Ludwig had told me. Silvia De Pena was still trying to sell Compound Totentanz. The Nazis in Argentina had turned her down two years ago, but now she had graphic proof of how it could work.

"I wouldn't want the Communists to get it," I said again.

"Do you know how it's made? Is that what you were doing hiding at Dr. Kaufmann's?"

"Yes." I held my breath, tense.

She said what I hoped she'd say. "Then it's a matter for our military intelligence, isn't it?"

Switzerland was a country intent on neutrality. I knew very little about politics, but even I knew that our president only kept the honorary position for a year. He and the other federal counselors took the tram back and forth to work. They didn't need armed protection. The Swiss government was based on peaceful consensus, not intimidation and military reprisals.

I thought hard before I asked her.

"Could you do me one last favor?"

A few nights later I lay awake in the darkness, rigid with tension. They came at five minutes past midnight. First, a man in a dark suit, his steps quiet, followed by Mrs. Martha, wearing a conservative navy blue dress and pumps.

"Are you authorized to deal for him?" she said, keeping her voice just a little above a whisper as she switched on the light.

"I am." The man swiveled his head, taking in the room at a glance. He walked over to my lamp and looked underneath. He strode over to the window and looked out both ways, and then checked underneath the bed.

Mrs. Martha put her hands on her hips. "What do you think you're doing?"

"He trusts you. But it's my job not to." He took out photos and a sheath of papers and studied them. "What's your mother's full maiden name, Miss Mueller?"

"Ainslie Iris Armstrong."

He asked me a few more questions along that line. Then he said, "Wait here. I'll be back." When Mrs. Martha started to move, he held up his hand. "You too."

"What if one of the girls hears you?"

"The first thing I learned how to do was move quietly."

When he returned, he was followed by a broad-shouldered gray-haired man with an imperial nose and thin lips. His brown eyes were large and well-set, softening his face. Mrs. Martha flinched when she saw him.

His attention fastened on her, he ignored me. "I must say I was surprised to hear from you. After all these years." His voice was low, his words crisp. His years in high official positions had eradicated a regional accent, though I thought he'd been from central Switzerland originally.

"Miss Mueller said ... it's very important." It was the first time I'd ever heard Mrs. Martha stutter.

"So now it's important. You transferred to the police service. You didn't answer my letters. Any of them."

"Peter," she implored him. I followed her eyes to the wedding band he still wore. Then she looked at me helplessly. "I worked for Peter. Many years ago."

His colorless adjutant spoke up. "I contacted Dr. Kaufmann as you asked. He confirms he will give up all the samples upon receipt of a note from Miss Mueller."

The brown-eyed man took the chair in the room, his back ramrod straight, his whole attention focused on me now. I felt like a book being skimmed. "I've been briefed on the situation. I must warn you not to lie to me. Does anyone in the German government or police know of this?"

"No."

"You haven't shared information about this process with anyone?"

"Just Dr. Kaufmann. And Emil Nussbaum."

"Yes, we talked to Nussbaum." He made a dismissive gesture. "We can handle him, I think. He's a sensible fellow. All the vials are in Dr. Kaufmann's freezer at Sandoz?"

"Yes." If I'd been speaking English, I would have added "sir." There wasn't an equivalent in Swiss-German.

"How many are there?"

"Thirty."

He turned to his aide. "Mr. Hess?"

"Yes, I confirmed it. They're all there."

"You haven't been in touch with the Irish government either?"

"The Irish government? No." I'd never considered it.

"I want all theoretical papers associated with this work handed over to me, through Mr. Hess. The plants in the Basel Conservatory will be quietly destroyed. The vials will be removed to a secured, secret location."

I was scared, but I still said it. "I want to see them. Every year at the same time." The vials had been sealed with signet wax, and Alex had dated them. I knew that military intelligence would have the capacity to deceive me if they wanted to, but my request would make my position clear.

"You wish to bargain with us?" the aide asked.

I kept my eyes on the brown-eyed man. "I only reached out to you because we haven't been at war for so long. I'm assuming Switzerland has no military ambitions."

His eyes bored into me. "I hadn't expected any resistance from you. You need my help more than I need yours. I can simply have Dr. Kaufmann arrested and the materials confiscated."

"Please. I'm not trying to cause a problem. I'm pleading with you not to let the compound be misused." My hands turned clammy as he looked at me, his eyes calm, his face immobile.

Then he nodded. "It was terrible what happened at Gonten, wasn't it? I read the reports, saw the photographs. Here's my answer about military ambitions. Should an enemy come, we will blow up the passes into the homeland. Then, and only then, will we shed the blood of our countrymen." Had I read the quote in a newspaper, I would have snickered at its tone. Hearing it from the brown-eyed man made it real.

I made myself persist, though I was shaking. "You promise me the poison will not be used?"

He thought it over. "We would never open the vials unless we suspected it was being used elsewhere. Then I would order the vials unsealed and examined by our military scientists, so we could determine if it was the same compound."

Still I hesitated.

"Peter does not make promises he cannot keep," Mrs. Martha said.

"Very well. I'll write the note. Will you help me?"

"I will speak to Mr. Dähler's supervisor. I don't think you're a murderess. I've always trusted Martha's judgment." He slid the notepad out to me.

The scratch of the fountain pen made it almost irreversible. I paused, unwilling to sign my name yet. "What if someone overrides your authority?"

He didn't bother to answer. The adjutant said, "That's not likely. You're speaking to the Brigadier."

When he took the note and left, Mrs. Martha walked them out, her tread heavy and her shoulders trembling. She switched off the light before she went, leaving me in the dark.

※

It was a gray day in February, the kind of day when you expect to get only bad news. The sky was the color of an old bed sheet, and the cold bit through the walls. I'd been summoned to the office by one of the other guards—Giselle Gessler, a skinny tall woman with freckles. Mrs. Martha had let my skirt out, and I was able to sit down comfortably in front of the desk Mr. Dähler used.

Mr. Baer stood close by. His brushy mustache couldn't hide a big smile. "Good morning, Miss Mueller. Mr. Thomas is trying a case, so I've come in his place. The court has reached a decision."

I tried to act calm while Mr. Dähler flicked an imaginary spot off his lapel and opened a folder, taking out a document he didn't need to refer to. He frowned at it for a moment, then slid it to me facedown. "I'll get to the point. This is the oddest story I've ever heard. I don't believe all of it for a minute, despite the fact that your aunt claims to have seen you try out the paralytic grip on another child once. But what is clear is that you were faced with imminent danger and acted to protect yourself. The Canton of Basel has decided not to press any charges." He looked at me gravely. "I hope you commend yourself to God's care, Miss Mueller. Death has a way of following you around."

40. An Unexpected Guest

IT WAS THE MORNING OF FEBRUARY 15. THE SKY WAS STILL THE same remorseless gray, but I had a sense of peace. Soon I would be able to see more of it than the little patch over the small courtyard. Even the cold didn't bother me today.

Mrs. Martha escorted me to the front door of the jail. "Miss Mueller, best of luck to you."

"Thank you for all your help, Mrs. Schildknecht." I dared not embrace her in front of the others. I squeezed her hand as the other guard watched Alex's Ford pull up.

Alex's smile lit up his whole face. "Welcome, dear."

Emil waved from the back seat. "Let's take you home, and get you out of that dreadful outfit."

Aunt Madeleine would be waiting back at the house on Rheinweg. It was actually my house, now, wasn't it?

But I wasn't Dr. Mueller's adoring daughter anymore.

I settled in next to Alex and gave him a peck on the cheek. "Where's Simone?"

"At your house."

I frowned. "With Aunt Madeleine?"

"She's apologized. Several times," Alex reminded me. Of course, Mr. Dähler had asked me why I'd run away, and I'd told him about the conversation I'd overheard between Madeleine and her husband. In a subsequent interview, she admitted to Dähler that she'd discussed sending me to a girl's finishing school and disposing of Simone. Afterwards, she sent me a gift of embroidered handkerchiefs and a note of apology. Another time it was a box of Lindt pralines. But her greatest gift had been to tell Mr. Dähler I'd tried out a paralytic grip on another child. She'd perjured herself.

I craned my neck as the car glided down my street, the linden trees now bare black against the slate sky, the river a broad ribbon of silver. Alex found a parking place and I scrambled out, the taste of freedom flooding my veins like wine.

Then I saw a movement behind our neighbor's curtain. The Basler newspaper hadn't published my name, but they didn't need to.

I ducked into the shelter of my house.

Aunt Madeleine was in one of her color-coordinated outfits, a powder blue sweater set and a powder blue skirt

I saw that she was embarrassed, uneasy. Alex had told me in the car that she might divorce Pierre for portraying me as mentally unstable to the press. I walked toward her, taking her hands in mine. Strange, I hadn't remembered her being so short.

Unbidden came the phrase *I am the god of war and vengeance.*

That was the past. Wasn't it? I took a deep breath. "Thank you for coming and getting the house ready." Emil told me the furniture had been covered with cloths, the rooms dank and cold, before her arrival yesterday. The maid she'd brought had dusted and polished; the furniture gleamed and the parquet shone. A vase of dried flowers stood on the entrance table. I heard the clink of glasses in the kitchen.

I cringed. Oh no. There was going to be a party for me.

She smiled and reached out to take my hat and coat. "We planned a little celebration for you, darling."

I hoped Pierre wasn't there.

"Come to the living room. Just two other people. We didn't want to overwhelm you."

Alex took my hand. "It's all right," he whispered, and together we walked in.

I'd spent so many days in this house, but now I felt disconnected from it. The familiar room was like a stage set. I spoke, an actress mouthing banal lines. "Wonderful to see you all. I'm so glad to be home."

I took the proffered glass of champagne from Elena Nussbaum, Emil's mother. "Nice to see you again."

She answered, but I didn't hear her.

The other guest, tallish and well built, still wearing his suit jacket, had his back to me, studying a photograph. It could have been Tenzin, except for the short hair.

Tenzin's in India, I reminded myself.

The man turned around.

The glass fell from my hand.

~

He looked better than ever. His eyes glowed with intelligence and affection. The newly short hair set off his high, broad cheekbones. Madeleine and Emil looked anemic next to the welcoming copper glow of his skin.

When he opened his arms, I flew to him, registering Madeleine's startled expression out of the corner of my eye.

"I'm so sorry I couldn't reach you," he said once, twice, till I laid my finger on his lips.

"We'll talk later. So you've met my family."

"Alex picked me up yesterday and took me to meet your aunt. She invited me today."

"I thought you were in Asia?"

"Not yet. I finally got the telegram from New Delhi. The officials inspected my vaccination book and other papers. I postponed my flight home for the chance to see you. I'm returning to India in a week."

My heart sank to hear he'd be gone so soon, though I wanted to keep my secret safe.

Emil had left to get Simone, and she darted to me, barking and wagging her tail. I sat on the sofa and invited her up, ignoring Madeleine's disapproving glance.

I was pinned down with her big head on my lap. Tenzin brought me my glass of champagne, taking the opportunity to sit down next to me. His thigh felt like it burned through my dress.

Sandwiched between him and Simone, listening to Elena chat away just as if she'd been part of my life all along, watching Alex lean back in the armchair and quaff his beer, I at last felt at home.

The party was over. Emil left first, stating he had work to do. Of course, I'd told him about the danger Paxarbital presented, so now he was trying different molecular arrangements of the sedative.

Emil's mother ambled off next, flushed from drink, her comments increasingly maudlin. Alex sat for a while longer, studying me, sipping his beer. He took his glass to the kitchen, where my aunt was tidying. The sound of running water drowned out their conversation, though I could hear their voices, his reassuring, hers agitated. When he emerged and got his coat, he addressed Tenzin. "I'm glad you got to see Peppa's home. We should go now; give her a chance to rest."

Tenzin started to speak, then swung himself off the couch. "Of course," he said, his tone distant.

Alex kissed me on the cheek. "Telephone me if you'd like to talk." Tenzin slipped out the door after him, a short "Goodbye" his farewell. His eyes were regretful. I watched him walk away till he disappeared into the gloom of dusk.

My aunt flitted about the kitchen while I dried the glasses. I sipped the rest of the champagne in my glass while I studied her, her face so different from my father's square one, his curling ginger hair and hawk-like nose. Only the brown eyes were exactly the same, cool despite their warm teak color. Whoever coined the term "doe eyes" had never met my relatives.

She gave a small, tremulous smile. "I fixed up your bedroom. Come look."

The newly laundered sheets crackled with starch, the duvet had been aired and fluffed. She opened the closet to show the outfits she'd brought from Zurich. "I know you were never fond of clothes. But you're a young lady now. That Emil certainly has turned out handsome. You'd never guess he's Jewish."

I shut the closet door and turned around to face her. "I won't be going out with Emil. It's strictly a friendship."

She cleared her throat. She was going to say something I didn't like. "I know you find me overbearing, but I'm just concerned. This Tenzin fellow. He's nice-looking for a Chinaman, and polite. But really—to sit so close to you on the sofa."

"Did you tell Alex to take him home?"

"I telephoned Emil yesterday after Alex brought Tenzin by for introductions. Emil says you're romantically involved with him. And then Alex let it slip he has a son back home! You can imagine what people are saying about you."

"Frankly, I'm more worried about being called a murderess than a slut."

She sat down heavily on my bed. "It's all gone so wrong, hasn't it?"

I shut my eyes. She didn't know the half of it. Last night I'd had a nightmare about a molting wolf, haggard, pawing over a pile of decaying sparrows. When he gulped one, bones crunching, the rest arose, flying at my eyes. My screams woke me.

When I opened them again, I saw only concern on her face. "Look, I'm grateful to you for organizing the party today and for getting my house ready. But I'm very tired. The last time I was here was when Father died. I need to get my bearings now."

"You used to call him Da?"

I glowered at her, silent.

She compressed her lips. "Sorry. I'm being insensitive. I'll go run my bath." She had her suitcase in my father's room, still mostly packed. "Tomorrow, we can make a list of what to keep in the house and what to replace. It could use a bit of redecorating."

Anger coursed through me. I didn't want her here. I didn't want to smell her sweet expensive perfume, hear her restless straightening of books and glassware, end tables and rugs.

I got up, stalked down the stairs, and to the phone. She trotted after me.

"Who are you calling?"

"The Schweizerhof. I'm booking you a room for tonight and tomorrow. After that, you can decide."

She stared at me. "You can't think I'd leave you here alone. After all you've been through."

"I won't be alone. I have Simone." I closed my eyes for a moment, lost in the sense memory of Tenzin, his arms around me, his urgent mouth on mine. It was just as well he was gone, but all the same I was angry that she'd dismissed him from my house, the unsuitable Asian lover.

I dialed the number, made a reservation for her with instructions to mail me the bill, and hung up. Then I ordered a cab. She stood by my side the entire time, mouth set tight, as if inwardly rehearsing a speech.

I didn't give her a chance. "Can I make this any clearer? I want you to leave. I'm twenty now. I say who comes and goes in this house."

She stomped up the stairs, and after a little while I heard the thumping as she dragged the suitcase down the stairs. I saw her to the door and shook her hand, the way I'd seen Mitchell Aaron and Da shake. "You'll probably sleep better there. This house is full of ghosts."

She looked at me, uncomprehending, and sighed. "Promise me you'll at least call Alex if there's any trouble. He could be here in fifteen minutes."

"I'll call him if I need anything. But I'll be fine. Goodnight."

I whistled Simone to me. We went and sat in the kitchen, at the little breakfast table, as if I were going to prepare a small supper. Which I wasn't, though I had no doubt my aunt had stocked the refrigerator and pantry as well. I was sorry I couldn't be nicer to her.

Truth was, I had no appetite, and I couldn't bear to go to our study. It was too early to go to bed, and the sitting room seemed deserted and too quiet now that my company was gone.

Maybe I should have stayed in jail with Mrs. Martha.

I put my head on my arms, wondering what I'd say to my father if he walked in the door right now.

I heard someone knock.

41. Gentleman Caller

Tenzin filled the doorframe. He didn't come in. The fumes on his breath indicated he'd gone to a bar instead of the tram stop. I couldn't read his mood.

Emotions whirled inside, a complex mixture of dread and hope, wrapped in the hot sheen of desire. I decided to feign ignorance. "Did you forget something?"

He shook his head, gave me his hat, and stamped the snow off his shoes. "No. Did you?"

I looked around, puzzled. "What?"

"Peppa, I thought we had feelings for each other. You even let me..." He shook his head, looking hurt. "We spoke about getting engaged. Was I supposed to buy you a ring? I'm sorry if I disappointed you."

"Those were never definite plans." Cold air slipped into the house, like the breath from a crypt, and the weight of Ludwig's baby dragged at me like a stone. "Come in."

He crossed the threshold, stood warily inside. "We've barely talked. I've been worried sick about you. And I would think you might have been concerned for me."

"We just saw each other," I pointed out, feeling defensive.

He looked at me incredulously, then took two steps and pulled me to him. He kissed me, his hands sliding around my waist.

I froze. The dress covered my belly, but he would feel it. As soon as he realized I wasn't responding, he let me go.

"Just explain your customs. I'm an honorable man. And I care for you ... very much."

I wrung my hands and turned my head to hide the tears brimming in my eyes. "It's not that. My time in Germany changed things."

"Oh." He thought for a minute. "I don't care what happened with that bastard Unruh. All that matters is that you're all right."

I didn't think that quite covered a pregnancy.

His voice turned impatient. "Look at me, Peppa."

I raised my head, a challenging glance to hide my shame.

"You can't be angry I didn't come to your aid. Alex told you, right? My lawyer talked to him right away."

"The lawyer that Violet Strub hired."

A crease formed on his forehead. "Yes, that's right. Violet helped me, just like she helped you. But we're talking about my failure to reach you in Munich. I wouldn't just have dropped off a syringe of Paxarbital and then vanished."

I refrained from pointing out that Violet hadn't known she was helping me. "At least Emil came."

"I tried. Oh, I tried. I was arrested. When I escaped the infirmary and the guard found me in the forest, I fought back. He beat me for it once he got the cuffs on. They cut my hair too. They weren't gentle about it."

"I'm sorry." I made sure my voice didn't sound sorry, though of course I was.

Better Tenzin thought he failed me. I couldn't bear for him to guess the truth and to despise me.

He looked defeated. "I couldn't get to you."

I made my voice cold. "You broke your promise."

His eyes flashed. I'd never had that furious look directed at me before. I took a step back. "There are some things beyond my power to control," he said, voice tight. "But I can control my comings and goings. I won't bother you anymore."

His anger was too much, and my knees trembled. "I'm sorry. I know you tried. With everything that happened, I just have trouble trusting people. But I don't blame you."

He stood irresolute in the hallway.

"Please don't leave angry."

"But you want me to leave?"

"No. Stay. Just talk to me as a friend."

He sighed. "I don't understand you. Can we at least get out of the hallway?"

I motioned him into the kitchen, where Simone sniffed his trousers before she wagged her tail.

He made himself at home, taking a chair and a glass, which he filled with tap water. He petted Simone absentmindedly. "So. How did Unruh really die? You told the German police his maid killed him."

"He died in front of my eyes—quite horribly."

"Tell me. You need to tell someone."

I sat back down, then got up, pacing. "I've gone to great pains not to tell anyone. Why should I tell you?"

"I helped you. Told you to kill him if you must. You had a hand in his death. I feel it."

Tenzin waited and, when nothing more came, finished his water. He got up and rummaged through my kitchen until he found half a bottle of wine from the party. I made no move to help him, and he ignored me, opening cabinets until he found the wine glasses. Then he poured himself a healthy serving, sat back down, and stretched his legs out.

"It's an ugly story."

"I expect so. I'm listening."

So slowly I started talking about Ludwig, Tamara, and Jochen, until the words poured out faster and faster. I left out an account of the night Ludwig and I spent together and the blood sacrifice Absalom demanded from us.

When I looked up at last, it was an hour later. The bottle was empty.

"Are you going to say anything?"

"I'm thinking," he replied. "Do you want me to make you an Ovaltine?"

"I was considering having some wine." My teeth were chattering and my head ached.

He rummaged through the cabinets again. "Don't see any. There's an unlabeled bottle up here. Smells like schnapps."

"Don't drink anything unlabeled." I realized I'd shouted. I hadn't told him about my father and his self-experimentation either, just that I'd encountered an inimical force that drove me back from the Jade World.

He gave me a puzzled look, found a bottle of Beaujolais pushed into a corner, and expertly uncorked it, pouring me a small serving and himself some as well. "Do you feel responsible for Unruh's death?"

"In a way. I was the catalyst. Tamara was just a simple farm girl. She envied me."

"She had reason to be jealous of you?"

"I was the stronger test subject," I explained lamely.

"Hmm." He played with the rim of his glass, decided to let that go. "It was time for Ludwig to die."

"That's easy for you to say. You're good. You're a good person. It's harder for some of us."

"I know what it is to be a good person. Like the Dalai Lama. So I have an example before me, and I try. But of course I'm not a good person. I killed a man. I left a son behind. And now I let you down."

I was sick of my own lies. I wanted to change the subject. "You'll see your son soon."

"Not till May. But when the thaws come, I'll go up with the transport trucks, and then make my way on a mule."

"You'll be leaving so soon," I said, despite myself.

"I can't stay with Violet Strub forever. People will talk."

"I can imagine. I wonder myself."

He stared at me. "No one saw me come in. I hoped I could spend the night. I'm not involved with Violet."

I felt a drift in my gut, like a trail of bubbles. Was the baby quickening already?

It was time for him to go.

"I feel so … I'm questioning everything about myself." I was still trying to sort out my needs from the raptor's. I drank the wine in one gulp. "I need to be alone."

He got up. "I'll telephone you if I may, before I leave. I would like to see you again."

I forced myself to smile. "Please call me later this week."

Tenzin was a candle flame in the terrible darkness that had beset me. I was no longer sure of my place in the world; the myth I'd created about my safe, happy life here had been shattered.

42. A List of Names

I SLEPT TWO HOURS, IF THAT. SIMONE'S PEACEFUL PRESENCE ON my bed made my twisting and turning more bearable. At least she was safe, and wouldn't be hurt. But I couldn't take her with me where I was going.

In the morning I stumbled into the kitchen, bleary eyed, and drank two cups of coffee followed by an Ovaltine. Aunt Madeleine had thoughtfully bought some bread, and I forced down a slice of that. By nine I was dressed and waiting in the sitting room for our lawyer.

Mr. Baer came, punctual at 9:30. His stuffed briefcase disgorged a great sheaf of papers.

I rubbed my eyes. "What's all this?"

"Legal bills. I assume you were pleased with Mr. Thomas."

"Yes, very." I'd noted Mr. Dähler's frequent flinches at Mr. Thomas's remarks. The tone was gentle and deferential, yet they insinuated the police were incompetent and their reports misinformed.

I picked up a piece of paper at random. "Lunch at the Baur Du Lac in Zurich. A bottle of wine, smoked trout as an appetizer. One steak, one perch. What's the next thing on here? I can't read it."

"Coffee with schnapps. Mr. Thomas had lunch with a psychologist close to Dr. Jung to get some expert advice. It's how these things are done." He waited for a moment, and when I didn't respond said, "Don't be upset about the expense. Your net worth is well over half a million francs, not counting the real estate holdings."

I'd been thinking about my prison meals. Mrs. Martha served me extra potatoes and a portion of cheese once she realized I couldn't get down any meat. She probably bought the cheese herself.

I actually missed her.

Then what he'd said penetrated my thoughts. "That can't be right. I helped Father with the stock market portfolio sometimes. It was big, but not that big."

"But you're forgetting about the trust fund from your grandmother."

"Grandma Mueller?" My grandfather had sold his pharmacies to Amavita at a very nice profit.

"No. Your father didn't tell you?"

"There's a lot my father didn't tell me." My voice sounded bitter, and I swallowed, trying to modulate my emotions.

"But you were so close."

"That's what I thought too." That's why I didn't bother to try to make any friends or go out and see something myself. It had been enough.

Except when I realized what that tiny world had been about. Secrets. Denial.

I tried again. "Grandma Armstrong then?"

"Yes. There's three hundred thousand to be used for your education. You haven't heard from her in a while then?"

I'd have to ask Alex about that. Or maybe I'd just ask her myself. If I could.

"Is she still alive?"

He looked at me, surprised. "She must be. Your father told me you'd inherit Brandford Castle and the surrounding lands, and no one's contacted me."

Brandford Castle. I remembered it. The last time I'd seen it was in 1951. Endless rooms filled with marble-topped fireplaces and exquisite furniture, tended to by an army of maids, footmen, and a self-important butler. I'd always been afraid I'd damage something. I liked the outdoors better, the kilometers of wild forest and the river.

Mr. Baer prompted me. "I have some bank papers awaiting your signature."

I dipped the fountain pen into the well and started signing, skimming the papers as I went. When I was done, he sat, squirming as if his tie was too tight.

"There's one more thing I must tell you."

"Yes?"

"This is the third letter I've gotten from Munich. It's from a law office."

I must have gone pale, because he said, "It's not bad news. But you own a house there too now. And an apartment. The house is damaged. They need to know if you'd like to approve renovations."

"How can I own a house there?"

"Ludwig Unruh changed his will shortly before he died. He gave the letter to an associate, a Dr. Schnitzler, who must have forgotten to forward it to the law office. Otherwise, surely the German police would have thought you had a motive for murder." He waited for the implication to sink in. It was too late now. They couldn't interrogate me again after I'd been set free and the death attributed to Tamara.

Beads of sweat sprang out on my forehead. Ludwig everywhere. His baby in me, his house waiting for me, an unknown associate protecting me. Even after death, I was still caught up in his designs.

"The details of the will can wait until ... you're more comfortable with the situation. But the house is partially burned down. It's still salvageable. Prime property. You're now the signatory on his bank account, and the lawyer would like a bank draft of twenty thousand Marks to begin renovations."

I signed the necessary paperwork, trying to keep my bread down in my stomach.

"There's also a bequest of fifty thousand Marks for Tamara Schüssler. His murderess. It has not been paid out. The lawyer needs instructions from you."

Poor mad Tamara. "Pay it out then. It was an accidental death."

"I'm afraid I can't. Tamara Schüssler has disappeared."

"What!"

"A tall blond man claiming to be her uncle came to the hospital. He must have carried her out; she was too ill to walk, according to staff. German police are searching for her." Mr. Baer waited for a moment before inquiring tactfully "Is there anything you'd like me to tell the German police?"

She was with Jochen. I didn't trust Jochen, but he might be preferable to what awaited her in prison or the mental ward. Or perhaps not.

"There's nothing I'd like to say about that for now."

"Also, a minor odd thing. The lawyer was instructed to wire fifty thousand Marks to Brazil, to a certain bank account. He doesn't even know who the recipient is. He's uneasy doing so."

I thought about Ludwig's remark when I'd asked him what he'd done with Miss Eugster, the proprietress of the Bäsebeiz. He'd said she was on a beach in Brazil.

"Ludwig believed in paying his debts. *Alles in Ordnung*. I don't want to discuss him or his will anymore."

"Are you ready to go to the bank now, Miss Mueller?"

"Yes."

He looked at my baggy sweater and the loose wrinkled skirt that draped my shins. Here I thought I'd done well to wear a skirt.

A click of irritation escaped me. "Fine, I'll go change. Make yourself a coffee if you want. But I have an assignment for you as well."

"What's that?"

I looked down at my pencil-thin thighs, hidden under the voluminous fabric. "Contact the Indian Embassy and tell them I want a vegetarian cook." Though Cora seemed to be gone, I wanted to avoid the things I associated with her: meat and Amaro.

His face showed doubt, which only increased when I said the next thing: "I also need a discreet private investigator. Someone who gets results quickly."

～

That day and the next passed quickly. The evening of Mr. Baer's visit, Tuesday, Tenzin called and invited me to a fundraising gala at Violet Strub's house that coming Saturday. I could tell he was disappointed when I declined, but I couldn't see wearing a form-fitting evening dress. We settled on a dinner date for Thursday night.

Wednesday morning the Indian Embassy called with the name of a Raja Singh. He was having problems finding work because he spoke only English and Hindi. He loved to cook. I phoned his boarding house in Bern, and he promised he'd take the train to Basel Thursday evening. That afternoon, Mr. Schär, the detective, came to my house. I received him wearing a pair of boy's trousers I'd just bought and a bulky wool sweater. I'd been cold a lot lately. To his credit he didn't blink, and quietly declined my offer of a coffee.

"I'm at your disposal, Miss Mueller."

"Are you good at finding people? Digging up things?"

"Yes."

"And I can count on your discretion?"

He smiled, the crow's feet wrinkling around his eyes. I liked him. He exuded a quiet competence. "Yes."

"How good are you?"

He looked to the right, as if recalling things, and then closed his eyes. "Your dog is in the bedroom above us. You drank Ovaltine this morning. You didn't eat breakfast. You're keeping all the doors locked and the curtains drawn in every room on the ground floor."

"That's right."

He looked at me sympathetically. "Feel like everyone knows too much about you?"

I nodded.

"No one will be finding out more from me."

"Good." Here's what I want you to do." I handed him the piece of paper, folded once, with the list of six names. "I need addresses for all of them; supplemental information on the starred ones."

I felt the nausea rise up again and ran down the hall to vomit. When I came back, he eyed me cautiously. "Are you not well?"

"It will pass," I said. I'd have him check into orphanages in Ireland after he was done with his other work.

Then I thought of something else. I'd telephone Mrs. Martha, see how she responded.

He shook my hand. "I'll see myself out."

43. Blood Sacrifice

By 5:30 I'd caught up with the last of the estate work and written some polite notes to my father's concerned acquaintances at Harvard. I stared at the telephone, deliberating.

Finally, I picked it up and dialed.

She answered after three rings. "Mrs. Schildknecht here."

"It's Peppa. Can you talk?"

"For a moment. Miss Gessler is serving meals." Her voice was carefully neutral.

"I wanted to do something for you. I have a very good detective."

"Yes?"

"But I don't know. Maybe you don't want me to."

"You'll have to tell me what you've got in mind."

When she hesitantly agreed to my plan, I noted down her private mailbox information.

Her voice got quieter. "Miss Gessler is coming back with the cart." The food trolley had a rickety wheel; it made a racket down the long corridor. "I'm glad to hear from you. Anything you send to my mailbox is safe."

"I'll write. Have a good evening."

"Sleep well, dear."

Simone, seeing me set down the telephone, found her leash and dragged it over to me, the metal clinking on the parquet floor. It was a ploy I could never resist.

The sky was smudged with charcoal clouds, the clear blue of summer just a distant memory. Another snowstorm threatened; the air was dense and heavy, the light a dim dirty yellow. Wisps of fog curled up from the river, and the streets were still and deserted. The houses seemed to shrink back from the icy streets, protecting their families, ensconced in bubbles of warmth and light.

My house was dark. There was no reason to hurry home.

I walked for a long time. It was pitch black except for streetlights, but I knew my way around. I stood for a few minutes on the bridge, looking at the odd jumble of houses on the far bank, before I turned back to my street.

A passel of ravens had collected on the bare branches of the tree in front of my house, and they cawed loudly as I came closer. The light from the street lamp shimmered on the snow, a shining pool. The three steps to my house though, were in shadow.

The ravens cawed louder, and inside me the falcon shook her wings in warning. Simone whined, low, a line of fur rising on neck.

Time to get inside.

I'd taken the first two steps when I slid on a patch of ice and came tumbling down, slamming into the pavement.

I pulled myself up and staggered into the house. The last image I had before I blacked out was Absalom's filed teeth.

───

The emergency room doctor pulled aside my bedside curtain, checked his notes, and started speaking, his tone curt. "You didn't give your husband's name. The form is blank."

His cold blue eyes challenged me to speak.

He wasn't going to make me say it, was he?

"My friend and I have the wedding planned for summer," I explained, face burning.

"Even so. Your fiancé should be here."

I swallowed. My life with Da at Harvard had sheltered me from the condemnation society could visit on single women. "He ... my fiancé lives in Dublin. In Ireland."

His eyes narrowed, and he flipped the chart closed. "You've lost the child. It was a boy. The bleeding seems to have stopped, but you need to stay overnight."

I sighed, a mix of relief and sadness. It was done with. I wouldn't need to find an orphanage, give over my baby to the care of strangers. "I can't stay. My dog's alone."

"The nurse called Dr. Kaufmann, as you asked, but there's no answer. Perhaps someone else, since your fiancé seems to be unavailable"

Tenzin had given me his number at Mrs. Strub's. I wrote it down for the doctor. "There's a Mr. Engel staying there. My dog trusts him." Simone would be patrolling the corridor, distressed and vigilant. My front door was still unlocked. The ambulance crew had retrieved me from the living room floor, lying in a puddle of blood, the hallway phone next to me.

"I'll have the nurse call." He paused. "I'm curious. Were you hoping to miscarry, starving yourself like this?"

I clutched the bed sheet closer, silent. He must despise me.

"In any case, you need to eat more," he said brusquely before he strode out.

I'd forbidden Tenzin to come to the hospital. He must have been watching the street from the front window; he opened the front door as soon as the cab pulled up the next morning. He ran down the freshly shoveled steps, Simone at his heels. His strong shoulder supported me as I hobbled to the front door.

"Did you hit your head?" He inspected me anxiously.

"The head's all right. I just had a nasty fall. The doctor said I was dehydrated and underweight. The anxiety's been making me throw up."

He stopped in the hallway, stricken. "I can postpone my trip again. I can't see my son till late spring anyway. Just as long as I get there before the May monsoon starts."

"No. But I do have something I want to talk to you about."

"What is it?"

"I need some information verified first. Your plane leaves when?"

"Next Tuesday morning, from Zurich. Where I planned to go to school."

"Don't you wish you could still study? Sometimes they have internships with Jung himself, though he's quite old now."

He became quite still. "I'm afraid that wouldn't be possible," he said shortly.

Tenzin had no money. But I could change that. If I were to be the dispenser of vengeance, I could balance the scales by rewarding the worthy.

I changed the topic. "I'm less nauseous today, but weak. Any chance you'd scramble up some eggs for us and make me some strong coffee?" I'd gotten hooked on diner breakfasts in the States.

"Just show me where your skillet is."

⁓

Tenzin left midmorning. I'd canceled our dinner date that night but promised him I'd go to the ball after all. He'd mentioned

Violet Strub so many times, he'd whetted my curiosity. Or so I told myself, ignoring the stab of pain in my heart.

After he left, I checked to make sure the doors were locked and the curtains drawn. I didn't want to be disturbed. Then I called Mr. Schär with my new request, marveling at the irony of it. I'd asked him to find Mrs. Martha's daughter and discreetly take some photographs of her.

I had no photographs of my child. I hadn't wanted him. So why were my eyes wet?

I went to the drawer where I kept my father's journals, removed the one containing the account of his Brazil trip, and took it to the kitchen table. The kitchen shears removed Ludwig's head from the charcoal portrait my mother had made. I gathered some fresh candles from the napkin drawer, put them in a bag with the drawing, and went to the study. On a silver platter I arranged three candlesticks with candles. I placed the drawing of Ludwig in the middle.

I didn't have a butter lamp or words of prayer, except those of the Catholic Church, and those didn't suit me. Some of my mother's poetry books were quarantined on one library shelf, and I leafed through one till I found a poem I liked.

> *Oh! breathe not his name, let it sleep in the shade,*
> *Where cold and unhonoured his relics are laid;*
> *Sad, silent, and dark, be the tears that we shed,*
> *As the night-dew that falls on the grass o'er his head*
>
> *But the night-dew that falls, tho' in silence it weeps,*
> *Shall brighten with verdure the grave where he sleeps,*
> *And the tear that we shed, though in secret it rolls,*
> *Shall long keep his memory green in our souls.*

I read out loud as I burned the portrait, Ludwig's image the closest I could come to picturing my unborn son.

44. Violet Strub

IT WAS SATURDAY, AND THE CLOCK HAD JUST STRUCK SIX WHEN Tenzin knocked. He looked so handsome in his tuxedo. The short hair accented the exotic cast of his features. He moved in a loose, sure way that was different from the men here. A sensual way.

I felt the heat of arousal sweep through me and bit my lip. Tenzin deserved better. I'd ravished Ludwig like a starved beast, feeding off his lust. I gave Tenzin a chaste peck on the cheek before joining him in the taxi.

This time I was able to appreciate the winding drive, bordered with cypresses. I noted the curving balcony upstairs, already occupied by a few smoking guests, despite the cold. We were greeted by a butler, impeccably attired, who took our coats. Savory smells drifted down the hall. The ballroom was on the second floor, and we walked up the stairs past a blur of faces, until I saw the director of admissions from the university on the second-story landing. I introduced Tenzin and tried to make small talk for a minute before excusing myself. I felt his eyes, curious, on my back.

Others had recognized my face too. Figures turned and discreet glances were thrown my way. Perhaps the old Peppa, the one lost in her thoughts, wouldn't have noticed. Despite Cora's absence, my new eyes didn't miss anything—a drop of wax sliding from the tottering candle at the end of the massive sideboard. I walked quickly, heels clicking, and righted it, just before it fell on the wedge of Brie.

Tenzin followed me. "Oh, that's what you were doing. How could you see that from where you stood?"

When I refused to answer, he said, "Sorry, that's a silly question. I almost forgot."

He almost forgot what a freakish thing I am. I consoled myself that the falcon couldn't manifest without Compound T. No one need know. Why, I was a confident woman of means now. Thanks to a shopping trip with Aunt Madeleine I was even dressed appropriately, in a sky blue backless evening dress with a white mink stole. I wore red lipstick and black eyeliner, though I'd decided against my mother's pearl choker.

Then our hostess approached Tenzin, the happy smile on her face that most women had around him. She was beautiful. Her chestnut hair was thick, bobbed around her heart-shaped face. Her eyes, big and shining, really were violet. Her clinging dark pink, satiny dress showed off her hourglass figure.

I wanted to leave, but instead I took a glass of champagne from one of the circulating waiters. Maybe I could go talk to the administrator again? He was the only other person I knew.

It was too late. She wore a light perfume, slightly sweet with a woodsy note in it. "Thank you so much for coming." To my surprise she spoke English.

"You don't mind, do you? Tenzin said you'd lived in Massachusetts."

"No, that's fine. We can speak English. But perhaps you know a bit more about me than I do about you, Mrs. Strub. You sound British?"

"Call me Violet. I'm from Devon. This is my husband's house. I came to Basel because of him."

The family name niggled at my memory. Hadn't I read something about him once? "My thanks to both of you for inviting me."

Tenzin had drifted alongside us, and his expression was odd. Where was her husband? Conveniently away?

An awkward silence ensued, after which Violet shrugged. "I'll need to greet some more guests and get ready for my fundraising speech, but afterwards, let's talk." She leaned closer, right next to my ear. "Thank you for not telling anyone about hiding in my greenhouse."

I nodded, still perplexed about Tenzin's expression. Then she saw a sour-faced old crone, and her smile lit up. "Excuse me. That's one of our most generous donors."

"Why did you look at me like that?" I asked Tenzin.

"I should have told you. Her husband's dead."

So she was conveniently widowed and available. "She looks young. Was her husband young as well?"

"Yes. He died on a climbing expedition in the Himalayas. His family invested heavily in the cogwheel trains that made the Alps accessible. In his free time, he liked to mountaineer. She went with him sometimes."

"Was she there when he died?"

"No. She stayed at base camp, I think. They didn't ever find his body, so she couldn't even give him a decent burial. She doesn't like to talk about it."

I watched her move around the room, bright and smiling. Now that I knew, I could see grief sagged her cheeks and tears made her eyelids heavy. The wound had still not healed. But to most of the other observers, she'd be a gay hostess, concerned for their comfort.

The evening was just beginning. If she could stand her grief, I could bear mine. I let the bubbles of champagne tickle my throat, thinking of the last time I'd had some. It had been the night I'd seen *Swan Lake* with Ludwig. I'd forgotten I hated him that night.

I was just heading to get my coat when she caught up with me again. "May I convince you to have a night cap with me? The other guests are amusing themselves quite well." I heard the raucous laughter from the ballroom; copious amounts of alcohol had made inroads into the Swiss reserve.

I was curious about her low, intimate tone, so I followed her into the darkened study and sipped at the cordial she'd poured for me. If she had a disclosure to make about Tenzin, it might affect my plans. He was a cornerstone; I trusted no one else as much.

She took a sip of her drink. "Excuse me for meddling, but I've gotten to be quite fond of Tenzin."

Suspicion stiffened my voice. "What's this about then?"

"I see, like me, you prefer coming to the point. He's leaving Tuesday, perhaps never coming back. Part of this is because of you."

I waited, tense, noting an unraveling thread on the rose dress. She continued. "Bhutanese take the breaking of a promise very seriously. If you don't want him anymore, can't you at least forgive him? He feels so dishonored."

"He's been talking to you about me?"

"Not in so many words. More his questions about how things are viewed here. He's asked me if going back on one's word is unforgivable."

She was a beautiful woman, at ease in society in a way that I wasn't, untainted by men like Ludwig. "Do you want him? Is that why you paid his lawyer, put him up here?"

The answer was a long time in coming. "He's not yours to give. Tenzin will go where his heart leads him. Right now his heart is set on winning you back."

I couldn't hold back my gasp. "It doesn't seem that way."

She looked ill at ease. "Perhaps I shouldn't have spoken of it. I know he doesn't want to press you after your terrible experience."

I swayed slightly, feeling ill. I could not involve Tenzin in my life right now.

"Of course, there is the question of Sherub."

"Who is Sherub?"

Now her voice was distinctly cool. "His son's name. Didn't you know it?"

The cloying sweetness of the liquor became bitter in my mouth. I was so self-absorbed, I'd forgotten.

I put the glass down. I certainly wasn't going to explain myself to her. "You've given me a lot to think about. I'll need to be going now. Thank you for the invitation."

Monday morning Raja made idli, Indian rice cakes, for breakfast, and I feasted on those, washed down with the tea he called chai. He'd found ground cardamom powder at some little store only Asians knew about, and the air was redolent with it. I took Simone for a walk, my boots making fresh prints in the snow, then waited for Mr. Schär to arrive.

When he rang, I led him into the sitting room and offered him some coffee, which he declined. He took out my folded sheet of paper and pages of additional notes.

"Here's the first one: Lupe Gonzales of St. Gallen. She lives at 66 Teufener Strasse. You only wanted her address."

"Yes." Lupe had hidden me in the abbey for nine days when I'd been out of work. The postman would be delivering an envelope with nine hundred francs in it to her now that I'd confirmed she still lived there.

"And this next name: Antonio Simonetti of St. Gallen. I've confirmed he still lives at 25 Felsen Strasse."

"Good, good." Antonio Simonetti was the young man who'd loaned me the money for the train fare. He would receive three hundred francs.

I looked over the next paper as he spoke. "Mrs. Maud Armstrong, born Maud Martin, will turn seventy this May. She still lives in Brandford Castle, on the outskirts of the village of Cong, on the West Coast of Ireland. Her health is good. She's reputed to have strong views on politics, religion, and most other matters."

I wondered if Mr. Schär knew she was my grandmother. A quick check of his face, the corners of his lips tightened, told me he did. "Let's go to the next name."

"Gladys Rumpole still attends Radcliffe College. She graduates next year with a major in art history and a minor in German."

I nodded. Gladys didn't need money. She needed to believe my father had given a damn about her. Mr. Baer would be mailing her the tourmaline necklace that Ludwig gifted me with. I hoped she'd assume the necklace was a sentimental remembrance from Father.

"The child you asked me about. I did locate her. She was adopted by a family in Lausanne. I have a few open cases right now and won't be able to go till next month."

I pushed Mrs. Martha's mailbox address to him. "Please write a note when you send the photographs. Some kind of report about the girl. Don't make anything up, but write about something that would make Mrs. Schildknecht feel better."

"What do you want? Some details about her pony?"

"That could be nice."

His eyes narrowed. "You don't want to write yourself?"

"I won't be here. Let's finish with our list."

"The last two." He drummed his fingers. "Now we come to the meat of the matter, yes."

My stomach tightened.

"This Jochen Dietz. I made discreet inquiries. The German police do not suspect he left with Miss Schüssler. I can't turn up any sign of them in this short a time. My apologies."

"Keep looking. I'll make sure Mr. Baer pays your fees. What about the records from Dachau?"

"Those are sealed."

"Weren't you able to find anyone ... anyone who'd been there?"

"One woman. I've written down her account."

"Well, what was it? Tell me."

"You'd better just read it."

I read slowly and carefully, trying to contain my rising anger. Jochen had been a dog handler for the SS. The witness had once seen him set a German Shepherd on a prisoner. The man had died.

Deep inside, I could feel the dark wings beating, fanning the rage. I breathed in sharply, stuffing Cora down. "Ah. I see."

"Shall I put in a word to the German police? About him and Miss Schüssler?"

"You're better at finding people than the police, aren't you?"

"I could use ways that would not strictly hold up in court. But might I ask what you will do with the information?"

"It's better you don't know."

He looked at me, eyes hooded.

I shrugged, irritated. "I don't know myself yet. We've got a promise to keep first."

"We? May I ask who's working with you?"

Why had I said that? Cora was gone, wasn't she? The wings beat, feathering my memory, sending a frisson up my spine. Birds of prey were hunters. "No one you would have met."

It was his turn to shrug. "Very well. It's good you have help, as long as he's reliable. You're a bit young to be taking this all upon yourself."

"It's my responsibility. Tell me about the final name."

"Here's the last known address. She and her husband have vanished since then, but they haven't left the country by boat or plane. They must still be there."

As soon as Mr. Schär left, I telephoned Tenzin.

Violet answered, her voice neutral. "Peppa. Good morning to you. He's helping Jakob. I'll have to fetch him from the greenhouse. May he call you right back?"

"I'll wait here."

She switched to English. "We're on the same side, you know." When I didn't respond, she said, "I believe you do care for him."

"I do."

"After he leaves, I thought you might come for tea and scones some time."

"That would be nice. Thank you." I'd be many kilometers away.

When Tenzin called me back, I invited him over for an early dinner before he took the train to Zurich. If he already had plans with Violet on his last night in Switzerland, he chose not to mention them.

When the doorbell rang, my heart skipped a beat. I peered in the mirror by the door and pinched my cheeks, putting some color in them. I'd dressed in a soft cashmere outfit of oyster gray, a dress and matching jacket. With Raja's meals of lentils, rice, and vegetables, rounded off with ghee and homemade yogurt, I no longer looked like I'd just risen from the grave.

When I saw Tenzin's genuine smile, I felt the stiffness leaving my body. He was my friend, after all. Even if he didn't know everything about me.

We sat at the dining room, and I rang the bell. Raja came in with a pitcher of the yogurt and rosewater flavored drink he called lassi. I enjoyed Tenzin's look of surprise when he saw the small, dark-skinned man with the wire spectacles and turban.

"This is Raja Singh, my new cook. He cooks vegetarian food. I've already tried his dhal and a cauliflower curry. Delicious."

"I hope tonight's dinner is tasty as well," Raja said with a small bow, setting down the pitcher of thick creamy liquid.

After he left, Tenzin raised his glass dutifully when I toasted him, before he asked, "What about some wine?"

"I have a serious matter to discuss. We can drink afterwards." I leaned toward him, intent. "This was going to wait till dinner, but I have a proposition for you."

He put down the glass with a thud. "That sounds very businesslike."

"Well, it can be, because I need something from you, and I could give you something in return."

"So that's how it is?"

"The other thing between us. We need to forget about that. It's not your fault. It's not because I don't trust you."

"Then why?"

"I can't say."

We sat for a few moments, quietly. He suspected I'd slept with Ludwig, of course. But he didn't know all of it. He didn't know about the kind of father that raised me. He didn't know about the consequences of Cora's night of blood lust.

At last, he wearily said, "Let me hear your proposition."

"Come back from India within a month. I need someone reliable to live here while I'm gone." Now that I'd dared this much, the rest spilled out. "You can live here and be the caretaker. I hired Raja so you'd have food you like. Set up the butter lamp. Make yourself at home."

"What would I be doing here?"

"Just watch Simone, walk her and keep her company. Perhaps you could volunteer at Jung's clinic at Küsnacht. Uncle Alex has some connections."

"What would be the purpose of that? I'm no longer pursuing a degree."

"I know your grandmother won't pay for your studies. I'll pay for your schooling if you want to go. And Sherub. I haven't forgotten about him. You could bring him."

"His mother would never let him go. And even if she did, everyone stares at Asians here."

"Please come back," I said. "There's enough money. Money's not the problem. I have no one else I trust as much."

His mouth quirked down. "If I did this for you? Then we'd be even? For my previous failure?"

"I don't want you to think of it like that. But I'd be very grateful."

"If you trusted me again, would your affection return?" He looked at me challengingly.

This was a precarious question. "My affection for you has never been in question," I said. "But I can't let anyone close."

He thought it over, frowning. The aroma of curry drifted from the kitchen, along with the clatter of pan lids and the clink of Raja's wooden spoons.

"If you ask this of me, I'd rather cancel my flight and go to India on the first of May. I can travel to Bhutan and see Sherub straight away, before the rains start."

Relief shot through me. "Yes. Yes. Even better. Then I can leave next week."

He reached across and took my hand. "Where are you going?"

"Just a vacation. Where no one knows the story of Dr. Mueller's daughter."

"Don't lie to me, Peppa. Don't do that."

He wouldn't let the matter drop if I didn't tell him something. "I'd like to visit my grandmother. Maud Armstrong. She lives near Galway."

"You're just going to visit your grandmother?"

"There are some Egyptian scrolls in Dublin I'd like to look at. Perhaps do some other sightseeing there as well."

He looked skeptical. "Let's talk about it some more over dinner."

I convinced him. When he left, I pressed myself against him as much as I dared, and gave him a chaste kiss on the cheek. I wished I could pull him upstairs and to my bed.

But I'd decided on a different course of action for my life. Cora had showed me my true nature. I was a hunter, a bird of prey. I would only damage people like Tenzin, just as Da had damaged Ainslie and Gladys. That's what people like us did.

Alone in the study, I took out the packet of letters I'd removed from Ludwig's office in accordance with his dying wish. I'd passed them onto Emil that first night at the Swiss Consulate, along with the key to the locked room on the second floor of Ludwig's house. He'd mailed them to Mr. Baer's law office, where I picked the package up after my release.

I fanned out the envelopes with the big, bold writing in purple ink. The faint scent of her spicy perfume still rose from them.

I'd seen them before, but I wanted her scent to stay with me.

The last letter Ludwig received from Silvia De Pena was postmarked Dublin.

I kissed Simone on her cool nose and stroked her soft fur, but my mind was far away, on the phrase I'd seen in Silvia's occult book.

I am a god of War and of Vengeance.

Author's Note on Psychedelics

WRITING SUSPENSEFUL FICTION INVOLVES A DEGREE OF artistic license. Brugmansia is an actual plant genus, closely related to Datura, which includes the noxious Jimsonweed. Both plants are members of the Solanacea or Nightshade family, notorious for causing disturbing hallucinations and severe physical symptoms. I would never recommend that someone use these plants to take a trip.

However, there have been many dedicated and responsible scientists whose research with psychoactive plants fascinates me. Swiss scientist Dr. Albert Hofmann accidentally discovered the effects of LSD in 1943, spilling some onto his skin and then, famously, riding his bicycle home under the influence. The fictional character of Dr. Alex Kaufmann was inspired by his life and work. Among many, I also salute ayahuasca researcher Dr. Dennis McKenna, ethnobotanist Wade Davis, and Dr. David E. Nichols, consultant on a chapter in my book.

For the record, I believe that responsible experimentation under controlled circumstances could open new doors of perception and expand consciousness. The addictive potential of hallucinogens is low. Access to pure ingredients, a quiet natural setting, and an informed positive intention naturally provide a better experience than randomly trying out weird stuff in a club full of strangers. However, ingesting psychedelics can still be disturbing, or even downright dangerous, in any setting. I don't personally advocate amateur tripping, but if you must sample, then please educate yourself using a resource such as Erowid (www.erowid.org).

Know your plant allies. Respect them.

Acknowledgments

THANKS GO TO THE EXPERT TEAM AND NEW FRIENDS AT FIVE Directions Press: especially developmental editor Ariadne Apostolou, cover designer Courtney J. Hall, and book designer and editor C. P. Lesley. My gratitude to web designer Stefano Massa for making my author website rock.

My Swiss advisers provided valuable help. My mother, Viraja Mathieu, shared her recollections of Switzerland in the 1950s, as well as being one of my first readers. Her words of praise meant a lot to me. My cool cousin, Ulrike Fischer, suggested the concept of the Bäsebeiz, the mountain inn where the massacre takes place. Lawyer Peter Morach and retired detective Max Blum provided information about Swiss jails and trials.

A visit to The Falconry School near Galway, Ireland, provided firsthand experience with raptors, as well as inspiring a location for the second book, *The Falcon Strikes*. My gratitude to Dr. David E. Nichols, who has researched psychoactive drugs since 1969, for gently making me realize just how little about pharmacological analysis I really knew, when he corrected two chapters.

Thanks to the many beta readers in various writing groups, especially Kelly Jarosz and Ted Moorman. I appreciated the thoughtful analysis from one of my youngest readers, Ella Kollstad. Joan McArthur went above and beyond the call of duty by copyediting. Writer Marisa Lankester and JJ Marsh, author of the Beatrice Stubbs series, provided insightful advice and valuable support, as did editor John Hudspith. I appreciate Adriano Vigano's candid conversations about publishing and the marketplace. Sarah Fuhrmann caught a few discrepancies when she translated the first three chapters into German. Thanks also to Hilarie Burke, whose positive attitude is contagious, and Cindy Heppelmann, who believed in this book. And to my best animal friend, Ellie, an affectionate pit bull mix: the snuggles helped when I was down.

To my husband, Jerry Mahoney—I couldn't have done it without you.

About the Author

GABRIELLE MATHIEU LIVED ON THREE CONTINENTS BY THE AGE of eight. She'd experienced the bustling bazaars of Pakistan, the serenity of Swiss mountain lakes, and the chaos of the immigration desk at the JFK airport. Perhaps that's why she developed an appetite for the unusual and disorienting. Her fantasy books are grounded in her experience of different cultures and interest in altered states of consciousness (mostly white wine and yoga these days). *The Falcon Flies Alone* is her debut novel.

Visit gabriellemathieu.com for the inside scoop on Peppa's world and sign up for the occasional Totem Tribe newsletter.

Follow her on Twitter: @GabrielleAuthor

Like her on Facebook: gabriellemathieuauthor

Reviews are appreciated.

Also from Five Directions Press

The Last Wife of Attila the Hun

Joan Schweighardt

I FELL TO MY KNEES AT THE STREAM, SO EAGER TO DRINK THAT I did not think to offer a prayer until afterward, when I was satisfied and my flask was full. I was exhausted. My skin was parched and I was filthy; but according to the map my brothers had given me, I was very near my destination. I continued on foot, pulling my tired horse behind me.

I had not had a full night's rest since the terrain had changed. The land was flat here. There were no caves or rocky ledges where I could shelter myself. The forests, so sacred to my people, had long since been replaced by endless grasslands. As I trudged through them, I felt that I had left more than my loved ones behind.

When the sky darkened, I used the single live coal I carried from the previous night's fire to light my torch. I was sure that the light could be seen from some distance. I expected at every moment to hear the thunder of hooves beating on the arid earth. But on and on I walked, seeing no sight other than my own shadow in the gleam of the torch light and hearing no sound but that of my horse plodding along beside me.

When the sun began to rise, I saw that there was a sandy hill ahead, and hoping to see the City of Attila from its summit, I dragged myself on. But the hill was much farther away than it had seemed, and it took most of the day to reach it. And then it was much higher too, the highest ground that I had seen in days. My horse, who was content to graze on grassy clumps and to watch the marmots who dared to peek out of their holes, made it clear that he had no desire to climb. I had to coax him along, and myself as well, for now I was afraid that I would reach the summit and see nothing but more grass stretching out to the far horizon. I imagined myself wandering endlessly, seeing no one, coughing and sneezing in response to the invisible blowing dust, until my food ran out and my horse gave way.

I crawled to the top of the hill and looked down in amazement at the camp of make-shift tents below. In front of one of them a fire burned, and the carcass of an antelope was roasting over it. There were many men about, perhaps two hundred, all on horseback except for the few tending the fire.

It was not until I heard the war cry that I knew for certain that the scene was real and not some trick of my mind. I had been sighted. The entire company was suddenly galloping in my direction, a cloud of dust rising up around them. I forced myself to my feet and spread my arms to show that I carried no weapon. When I saw that the men were making their bows ready, I dropped my head and lifted my arms higher yet, to the heavens, where, I hoped, the gods were watching carefully.

Part of the company surrounded me. The others rode past, over the summit. When they were satisfied that no one was riding behind me, they joined the first group. Upon the command of one of them, they all lowered their bows. I began to breathe again. A murmur went up, and while I waited for it to subside, I studied their horses. Of the two that I could see without moving my head, one looked like the ones the Romans rode—a fine, tall, light-colored steed. The other looked like no animal I had ever seen before. Its legs were short and its head was large and somehow misshapen. Its matted mane hung down over its stout body. Its nose was snubbed and its eyes bulged like a fish's. Its back was curved, as if by the weight of its rider. Yet its thick neck and large chest suggested great strength.

The murmur abated, and the Hun on the horse I'd been scrutinizing cried out a command in his harsh, foreign tongue. I looked up and noted that he resembled his horse. He was short and stout, large-chested, his head overly large, his neck short and thick, his nose snubbed. The only difference was that while the horse had a long mane and a bushy tail, the Hun's hair was thin, and his beard, if one could call it that, was thinner yet. He seemed to be waiting for me to speak. I stared at the identical scars that ran down the sides of his face, wide, deep mutations that began beneath his deeply set eyes and ended at his mouth. "I've come to seek Attila," I said.

The Hun, who appeared slightly amused, looked to his companions. A murmur went up again. While they debated, I took the opportunity to scan the other Hun faces, all hideous replicas of the one who had spoken to me. Of course, I had known the Huns were strange to look upon. Although I'd been hidden away during the siege, I'd had a description from those who had seen the Huns and survived to tell about them. In fact, there were some among my people who mutilated their own faces after the siege, believing this would make them as fierce as their attackers. Still, none of this had prepared me sufficiently to look upon them with my own eyes. Some wore tunics and breeches, not unlike the ones my own people wore. Others wore garments made entirely of marmot skins. With some on Roman horses and others on Hunnish ones, some dressed like Thuets and others in skins, they looked like no army I had ever seen before. Their confusion over how to respond to me only heightened the impression of disorder.

"Attila!" I cried. My brothers were sure I was mad, and when I heard my shout I thought they must be right.

The startled Huns stared for a moment, then they took up their debate again, their voices louder and more urgent than before. Finally the leader nodded, and the man whose argument he had come to agree with rode to my side and took my horse's reins from my hand. While he started down the hill with the horse, another Hun poked me from behind with his riding whip to indicate that I should follow. Half of the men began the descent with me. The other half stayed on the summit, looking off in the direction from which I had come.

I was brought to the fire, where I reiterated my desire to see Attila. One of the Huns pointed beyond the tents. I followed his finger. There were a few dark clouds converging on the eastern horizon. "Can we ride?" I asked, pointing to my horse. The Hun gestured for me to sit. The meat had been removed from the fire and torn into pieces. The horseless Huns were distributing it among the riders. One of them brought a piece to me, and another brought me a flask of what smelled like Roman wine. I ate the meat—which was tough and bland— and kept my eyes fastened on my horse and the sack that hung from his side. I tasted the wine and, to the amusement of the Huns who were watching, quickly spat it out—for this is what I imagined a woman who had grown up alone in the forest would do.

After the meal, I stood and pointed east. "Take me to the City of Attila," I demanded.

The Falcon Strikes
Falcon Trilogy 2

Although still battle-scarred from her last encounter, Peppa Mueller cannot rest. Her determination to keep a dangerous formula out of untrustworthy hands takes her to Ireland. Yet even as she seeks solace in the arms of a handsome Irishman, her inner falcon senses the presence of a known and deadly enemy, one with a totem as powerful as her own.

The conflict endangers Peppa's grandmother. The enemy will stop at nothing to succeed. The Irishman turns out to have designs of his own. But the demands of Peppa's heart may pose the greatest challenge of all.

FORTHCOMING IN 2017

This book was typeset using Athelas, a body font inspired by British literary classics, with headings in Imperator Bronze, a display font designed by Paul Lloyd—here used to indicate the epic nature of Peppa's battle. The leaf type ornaments come from Type Embellishments One LET Plain.

PRAISE FOR GABRIELLE MATHIEU

"Unpredictable, intelligent and imaginative, this story soars into the unknown. Climb on and enjoy the flight of your life."
—JJ Marsh, author of the Beatrice Stubbs series

"Quirkier than hell on a hot day. It has that unsettling and surreal *Twin Peaks* feel to it."
—Editor John Hudspith

"An intriguing blend of science and the occult—it will keep you reading."
—David E. Nichols, PhD, Distinguished Professor Emeritus, Purdue University College of Pharmacy

Five Directions Press publishes contemporary women's fiction, historical fiction, science fiction, fantasy, and memoirs.

For more information, see www.fivedirectionspress.com.

FIVE DIRECTIONS PRESS

Printed in Poland
by Amazon Fulfillment
Poland Sp. z o.o., Wrocław